# Blackbir

## Harbingers, Book I: Child of Earth

# Jane M. Wiseman

Shrike Publications

Albuquerque, New Mexico

Shrike Publications
Albuquerque, New Mexico

Publisher's Note: This is a work of fiction. Names, characters, places, and incidents are a product of the author's imagination. Locales and public names are sometimes used for atmospheric purposes. Any resemblance to actual people, living or dead, or to businesses, companies, events, institutions, or locales is completely coincidental.

Book Layout © 2017 BookDesignTemplates.com

Blackbird Rising/ Jane M Wiseman . -- 1st ed.
ISBN 978-1-7328141-1-0

For Will and Wallace

*Green Grow the Rushes, Oh*, an old folk song with many mysterious verses, could have acted as a secret communication.

# MAP OF THE KNOWN WORLD

UNKNOWN LANDS

**The Sceptered Isle**
1. The Western Isle (Girldom of The Sceptered Isle)
2. The Eastern Baronies
3. The Southern Primary
4. The Fire Isle
5. The Ice Realm
6. The Lyre Lands
7. The Burnt Lands
8. The Mountain Fastnesses
9. The Realm of the Asp
10. The Trade Road Fortifications
11. The Silk Lands
12. The Forgotten Realm
13. The Unknown Lands
14.

# MIRIN'S WORLD

# Contents

# CHAPTER ONE

# Blackbird's Eye

D o you remember the day Johnny the Traveler said black-birds are my friends? You may have been too young to remember it, and too much has happened since then. But I want you to try.

I had given Johnny a skeptical look when he said it, the thing about the blackbirds. "The Child of Earth is not my Child," I reminded him.

"I told the blackbirds about you," Johnny replied. "Now they're friends of yours."

Or are they foe?

I hope you do remember the day Johnny came to visit us, Jillie. That was a good day. Then there's the day I hope you don't

remember. The terrible day when everything we knew fell burning into ruins. I hope the Children, in Their mercy, have blocked
it from your memory. I wish They had blocked it from mine.

The blackbirds flap over the little rise in the meadow to settle
and flutter and fuss.

*Foe*, I scream inside myself when I see them.

Not friend.

Foe.

I hear their shrieking. I stand stunned at the edge of the
meadow. Past the flurry of wings and beaks I see our gutted
cabin, a thin trail of smoke rising from its roof. I see the soldiers
of the king poking around it, the dark form of a man on horseback directing them. Strewn down the furlong of meadow
between me and the ruins of our house, I see crumpled piles,
maybe cloth, distorted and lumpy. I tell myself I don't know what
they are, but in a different part of myself, I do. They are bodies.

Blackbirds perch on them. Five or six. They step delicately on
and over the lumpy forms of our father and mother, cut down as
they tried to run for the safety of the brushy forest verge.

And there's a smaller bundle, too. *Jillie*, I whisper, and my
heart wrenches loose from me. I see, tossed out beside you, a
splash of bright yellow. My mother had made you a poppet out of
leftover cloth from her new yellow holiday kirtle.

You loved that doll.

From somewhere, I hear a drum pounding. I can feel the
pulse beating in my ears, and I realize the sound is my own heart.

The drumbeat is so loud I think the soldiers must be able to hear it, even though they're at the other end of the meadow. Though I know in some sensible part of me that the sound is enclosed inside my body, I still find myself backing into the underbrush and crouching down.

These men patrolling the ruins of our home, they're soldiers of the king. They wear his scarlet livery. They are slashes of scarlet in and about the gray of the smoldering, stove-in cabin, almost gone back to the earth our father hacked it out of. Slashes of scarlet roaming the vivid meadow.

Down the meadow, the hovering birds bob and toss and jerk their heads. *Are they feeding?* I have a powerful urge to rush these birds, scream at them, chase them off the bodies. Something holds me back. That something keeps me alive.

The scene that is spread out before me makes no sense. The pounding drum. The ringing in my ears. Aren't we all loyal subjects of the king, all in our family? We have never done any wrong, not to the king, not to our neighbors. I want to scream at the soldiers and tell them so.

Instead, all words are driven out of me as if some massive dangerous animal has slammed me to the dirt.

From over the meadow I can see the shingles our father had split himself, still glowing on what is left of our roof. In flashes, I have a chilling notion of how the whole thing happened. I feel as if I'm rising, hovering like one of the birds, and I think I see it—the soldiers throwing burning brands on the low roof to force all of you out through the only door.

A blackness comes across me, there in the meadow, and then a flash, and in that flash I see it.

The burning shingles don't collapse at once. Our parents grab at you. You're crying in panic, Jillie. They burst to the door, help you crawl out, and try to run. They don't get far.

The soldiers ride all of you down.

Evil stalks beside these soldiers of the king. Their leader is not dressed in scarlet. He's dressed in black. The way he holds himself is wolf-like. Sinister. Like one of the Dark Ones.

I shake my head to clear it. Now my body is back crouching low to the earth, where it belongs, in its hiding place at the verge of the meadow. I'm in my leather tunic, the one our mother made for me of rabbit skins from my own trapping expeditions, and I'm wearing my brown woolen trousers. Boys' clothes, forbidden but practical for hunting. The tunic, buff and brown and mottled, blends in with the dapples and overlapping shadows at the meadow's edge. And the trousers are the same color as the forest behind me.

If I had been wearing my regular clothes, my kirtle, my white headcloth and apron, I would have stood out against the forest backdrop. I would have been dead by the third step I took into the meadow.

Though I don't understand what I'm sensing or even exactly what I'm seeing, I find myself edging backward into the brush. From there, hidden, I stare and stare at this thing I can barely fathom, something so out of the realm of possibility that I don't and can't believe it.

From where I hide, I see the soldiers moving down into the meadow toward the bodies. As they near, the blackbirds explode upward in a raucous storm of feathers and beaks and claws. I shrink down even lower, flattening myself on the ground as the blackbirds fly over, back into the woods beyond me. One stares at me, as it strafes me, one eye dark, foreboding, the other filmy white with blindness.

From wanting to rush at the blackbirds and flail at them with my hands, I become one of them. I'm rising again, soaring far overhead. I scream and scream.

The soldiers stop, look over their shoulders in my direction. They come down the meadow toward me, and as they do, one final blackbird rises shrieking from the meadow's verge, going at them with talon and beak. They duck back and hasten toward the cabin, where their leader sits his horse.

They mount up, too, and they all ride off.

I watch myself soaring on wide black wings. My eye scans the landscape for the dark leader. My beak opens wide to accuse him, and my talons spread, ready to fasten deep into his flesh.

But the bodies distract me. In a dive that bolts from the zenith of the sky, I arrow down to those bodies, desperate to reach them.

Instead, I slam back into my own body where it's standing stunned now at the ragged edge of the meadow. I'm a girl again. I turn and run. As I zigzag terror-stricken through the trees, something bangs and thwacks against me. It is my rebec, hanging from its shoulder strap. Everything I've known and loved has just been destroyed. My rebec is the one good thing still with me in a world gone gray and horror-filled.

If only I could let you hold my rebec right now, Jillie. Somehow the feel of it might help you recall the good memories. I used to take it with me everywhere, even into the woods while I hunted. You remember this, Jillie. I know you do. When I rested under the shade of the tall trees, I played it. If I hadn't had it with me that day, that terrible day, I would have lost not only my family but the one way I know to get to the buried place inside me where my second sense dwells, the one Johnny the Traveler helped me find.

Whenever I play my instrument, I feel connected to myself. I play it to feel connected to all of you, my family, now that you're gone.

See, my rebec has four strings. Remember running your fingers across them? Hold that memory. Please hold it. Think about the sound the strings make. Pretty, isn't it? Think about how I used to make the strings from the guts of the rabbits I brought home. And think about how I played upon the strings for you. With this small bow. Shall I play you a tune now? You're not here to listen to it, but in my mind, you are.

> *I'll sing you one, oh.*
> *Green grow the rushes, oh.*
> *What is your one, oh.*
> *One is one and all alone and evermore shall be so.*
>
> *Blackbirds rising, blackbird's eye,*
> *Green grow the rushes, oh,*
> *One lone blackbird in the sky,*
> *Green grow the rushes, oh.*
> *One is one and all alone and evermore shall be so.*

It's a good song, the first Johnny the Traveler ever taught me. During that winter before the soldiers came, he taught me to play other songs, but this song about the blackbirds was the first one and—I could sense, even then—the most important. The song changed everything—everything in my life, everything in yours. Everything in the Rising, too.

# CHAPTER TWO

# One is One and All Alone

This is how I, Mirin Far-meadow, was thrown willy-nilly into the events of the past four years. Why did the soldiers kill all of you? That was the question that haunted me as I hid in the woods. Poaching a little, that's not wrong, not really. The most it would have earned me or any of us would have been a sound scolding and a fine levied by the beadle, especially in our village, where everyone knows each other and nobody bothers to enforce the harsher laws. So what were the king's men and their dark leader doing that day, standing over my dead family members and my ruined home?

I had no answers, just a thirst that burned me all the way through. I wanted justice. Justice is the way the Children make the crooked things of the world straight. It's a way to understand what happened to all of you, and to me, too. That was the good, bright feeling that rose in me.

But another feeling rose up beside it on dark wings. The thirst for vengeance. Justice, vengeance. They're not the same.

For the first few days after the slaughter and the burning, these twin thirsts were hidden from me. I crouched in the woods, trembling for fear the soldiers would come back and take me. I found berries to eat, but my traps and fishing lines were useless. I had no fire starter to cook anything I caught. So I knew I needed to get back to the cabin and try to find a way to stay alive.

As the days went by and I grew weaker with hunger, I decided I had to make myself try. There came a day I crept out and picked my way cautiously across the meadow toward the cabin. I'd been watching. No one had come about the cabin's burnt-out timbers. The others in the village must have been too frightened to approach it. Now a light breeze was bending the grasses and rustling the trees at the verge of the meadow. Birds were singing, and none of them were blackbirds. It was a bright early harvest-tide day to make a person feel glad to be alive, a strange contrast to the dark and somber weight I carried with me.

As I neared the place where I'd seen all of your bodies, panic rose in me. My breath came fast and hard, and my heart thumped painfully in my chest. I needed to see, but I didn't want to see.

I crept to the body of our father. Then our mother. "No," I heard myself saying. *This is not my father. Not my mother. These are nightmare creatures someone has fashioned in their shapes, then savaged and distorted and bludgeoned.* The odor of death assailed me and drove me back.

With dragging feet, I forced myself to go to the spot farther away, where I'd seen your body, Jillie. I thought I remembered where, but I didn't spot your little broken self in the grasses of the meadow. I spent many moments casting this way and that, just in case my memory played me false. In several places, the meadow grasses had been crushed down. There were some brown stains I took for blood.

But you were gone.

"Jillie," I screamed out. Then I clamped a hand over my mouth and choked back my voice. On unsteady legs I rushed up the hill toward our cabin and cowered there.

This may sound unlikely, but it's true. Until that point, I hadn't cried. I had existed in some kind of frozen place where I couldn't think and couldn't feel, just lurked about like some wary creature. Now, kneeling under the wide sky beside our cabin, I cried.

I cried for the sight of our parents, their fineness and beauty and goodness trampled and destroyed and gone forever. And I cried for you, Jillie. Where were you? What had happened to you? Were you dead, too? Had someone taken your body away? These questions assailed me like an army of attackers.

As I knelt in the dirt, I spotted your yellow doll. I'd seen it the day of the slaughter. I'd seen it beside your body, and now here it was in a different place entirely. I picked it up, feeling a deep sorrow, and held it to my nose, trying to breathe in your scent, some small essence of you, anything. The doll was stained with blood.

And then my hidden place inside opened its doors. Out of it stepped a certainty. It told me you weren't dead. Yet I thought I had seen you lying sprawled in the meadow beside our parents. How this could be, I had no idea. I had seen our parents' bodies now, and there was no doubt they were dead. Even on the day of the slaughter, I had known it. But you had been a vague smaller shape further away in the grasses, and now, getting to my feet beside the cabin, I looked down at your doll and I knew you were alive.

You gave me hope, Jillie. Otherwise, with the odor and horror of blood on me, I think I might have given up. But I felt despair, too, because I didn't know how to go about finding you, and the doors to my second sense were tight shut when I looked there for some hint.

You have to understand. I know things I'm not supposed to know. Our father called it my second sense, a knowing underneath knowing. Some might call it witchcraft, but it isn't that. I hope you don't think of it that way, wherever you are now.

But it isn't perfect. It tells me some things and withholds others.

As I steadied myself against the wall of the cabin and clambered to my feet, fear made me practical. I needed to go in, but I needed caution, too. The soldiers had ransacked the ruins for valuables, but I needed to find anything they'd left that I could use.

A quick glance around the yard told me the soldiers had driven our pig off. His pen stood empty. By now, they'd probably sold him or eaten him.

We were going to eat him ourselves as soon as it got a little colder. He fattened himself on acorns all summer long and into harvest-tide, but we couldn't afford to feed him through the winter. Instead, he would feed us. Our father would butcher him while you and I ran into the house and held our ears and hugged each other and cried. I don't know why. I'm not that tender-hearted about the rabbits I trap. Our mother would dry and salt the meat of our pig, and we'd all hope he lasted us until spring, or near to. That's what happened, year after year, to all our pigs. But this year's pig was food for the soldiers.

They wouldn't have gotten much else. We didn't have much. They probably took our father's gold brooch, the only really valuable thing any of us owned. Remember how he used to polish it in the firelight, and show it to us, and tell us stories about it? You might have been too young to understand or remember. That brooch alone might have paid the soldiers for their trouble, if they'd come marauding.

But my second sense told me they hadn't attacked our family because they thought they'd find anything valuable. In fact, they were probably amazed when they did. I thought of the dark leader on horseback, directing his men. They had killed our parents for some other reason, and I didn't know what that reason could possibly be. And they'd taken you. Why?

Rather than torture myself with that question, I shoved the ruined door to the cabin open and peered around the main room. I could reach almost everything with a piece of half-burned timber I'd picked up in the yard. If you remember our cabin at all, you'll remember how small it was. Crouching in the doorway, I began poking around into the wall niches closest to me. The soldiers must have taken our father's fire steel and tinder box. My hope that I'd be able to feed myself died alongside the other, bigger deaths.

I stepped down from the sunken doorway over the sill into the cabin. I stepped over the fallen-in scorched planks of the door. I crept in, hoping a roofbeam wouldn't come down on me, and poked around with my stick.

When I was so little I barely remembered it, our father had dug the cabin into the ground, planed the dirt smooth for a floor, and erected walls of wattle and daub against the spaded-out rectangle of the cabin's single room. You weren't even born then, but I have a dim recollection of neighbors gathered around to help, and our mother ladling out stew into bowls as the neighbors stood around in our dooryard. I have a dim recollection of our mother singing.

As if I were some ghost, I stood up now in the middle of the burnt-out cabin and watched our father, long ago, making the room and the walls. I watched him make beautiful carvings along the rooftree. Through some ghostly scrim, I watched him add a steep-sided peaked roof of shingles to make sure the rain would shear off into a trench he had dug, and not straight down into our dwelling. I watched as my mother looked at him fondly while he puttered around doing the things he loved best to do, figuring things out, making things better.

With a shudder, I came back to myself. The vivid picture of our parents talking it over, the building of our cabin, faded back into a time before memory. There was a time before we lived in the cabin. Maybe a time of dream, a mysterious time I saw only in flashes, when the three of us lived somewhere else, before you were born, Jillie.

But here, in reality, I realized the whole damaged structure of our cabin could come crashing down on top of me. I needed to move carefully.

The back of our cabin, where we slept, was less dangerous than the front. The beams holding the roof up were scorched but not burnt through.

Moving into the acrid scent of burnt-out wood and cloth and books—yes, books—we had a few of those—I found one of my two woolen kirtles not too badly charred to wear. I was still carrying your doll, and now I set it aside. Working fast, I shed my tunic and trousers and pulled the kirtle down over my head. I ripped undamaged material from the other kirtle to give myself a makeshift headcloth, crinkling my nose against the singed smell. I knew that if I were caught in boys' things, it would go even worse for me, now that I was a fugitive. As for the tunic, I bundled it up under my arm. I would need the warmth. The nights were getting chilly.

I tucked the rest of it, my trousers and my snares and fishing line, into a niche in the wall where I used to keep all my hunting things. Last, I brought your doll to my lips and kissed it. I laid it gently in the niche as well. I turned away and didn't look back. If I had, I might never have left the broken shelter of the cabin.

As I headed back outside, I nearly tripped over one of our books. Its cover was burned off. Most of the pages were burned away, and the rest were badly scorched. A beam of sunlight through the gaping holes in the roof showed me one of its wood-cuts: a fierce dog or maybe wolf with lolling tongue stood upright, like a man, wielding sword and shield. My eyes filled with tears. It was the book our mother had used when she taught me to read. The story of Man-Dog Rough-Gray.

You probably know it. Everyone grows up with that story. Even if no one where you are has taught you to read, I'm sure your minders, whoever they are, have told it to you. The treacherous dog-man, and the valiant ones who oppose his evil-doing. It is a thrilling tale.

I squatted down now and reached out a hand to the ruined book. I think I had the idea I'd take at least this one page off with me into the unfriendly world. But when I touched the page, it crumbled away to ash.

Dashing the tears from my cheeks and dragging my sleeve across my nose, I put myself to rights. I crawled out of the cabin. I'd decided now. I'd leave the woods and take my chances in the village. I might be able to scavenge for food, and it might be someone there could advise me what to do. We had friends there. Maybe not exactly friends. People who were friendly to us.

I made my way to the village, keeping to the brush, not daring to walk the path. Our cabin was on the outskirts. The townland where all of us villagers planted our crops stood between our cabin and the village, and past our cabin, on the far side, the meadow and the woods stretched beyond.

I hid at the edge of the village for a few days, not sure what to do next. Now that I was there, I was afraid to trust anyone. One woman spotted me lurking in the alley behind the granaries and lured me out with a piece of bread. I was starving by then, with only a few handfuls of berries in my belly, so I snatched it, and she ran back to her house as if the Dark Ones were after her.

But the next day, thank the Lady Goddess, or the Children, or maybe luck, it was Fair Day. Everyone was at the fair set up by the far end of the village. It wasn't much of a fair. You probably don't remember our village very well, but trust me, it was small. Our village fair was too unimportant to attract the traveling mountebanks from the Lyre Lands. In bigger towns, they set up their marvelous boxes where puppets dance on strings to the wails of their tsambouna. I'd heard about those. Grendan had been to one of these performances and had told us other village children all about them. But I had never seen them.

Still, even in our small hamlet, Fair Day was a rare treat. We villagers had our footraces and games of strength and chance, our sweetmeats, our peddlars' carts of ribbons and pins and new pans, our singing contests. Our mother won the singing contest once, but then she never entered it again.

Near about every person in the village was at the fair.

There in the deserted end of the village, I stepped boldly out of my hiding place. I'd have to find something to eat, or risk returning to the ruins of the cabin to get my snares and head back into the woods again.

I was just starting to think that might not be such a bad idea. Maybe I could find fire-making materials here in the village. The word *steal* drifted across my mind but I quickly shoved it away. I was no thief. So I didn't think about how I'd get these materials. But somehow I'd get them, or so I told myself, and then I'd live in the woods like one of the wild imps of the stories.

My imagination was leading me down these hopeful paths when a door banged open with a clatter against the wall of the house just opposite where I stood. I couldn't keep myself from yelling, the fright was so sudden. But it was Goodwife Cailin, a friend, or at least acquaintance, of our mother's. Our mother didn't really have friends. She was friendly, but she never did make friends with the other women of the village, not really. I remember thinking it was because our house was so isolated from the rest of the village. Now I know it was because our mother was afraid. And because she was different. She stood out, and she didn't want that.

Yet our mother was no coward. I learned this, later. Her fear was not for herself. Her fear was for our father, and for us, her children.

Right then, I was afraid myself. I knew Goodwife Cailin for a kindly woman, though. She rushed upon me and smothered me up in her cloak, hugging me to her. "It's true, then, what they've told me, Mirin—you're alive," she said. I leaned against her. Her comfort was solid. I could have stood that way forever. Then she held me out from her. "Alive but only just, I'm thinking. You look so thin. How are you keeping?" She thrust a piece of gingerbread into my hand, and I greedily ate it, inhaling its spicy aroma, paying no attention to proper manners or thank-yous. That's how hungry I was.

"I don't know what to do, Goodwife Cailin," I told her between big famished bites. "I try to stay back in the alleys and look out for soldiers. If I see them coming, or if I see the watchman, I hide." I licked the crumbs from my fingers.

"But where do you sleep? How do you eat?" I know my dirty face and torn clothes told her all she needed to know, so I didn't answer her. "What must you do, girl? You can't live like this."

I began to cry.

She comforted me.

"Goodwife," I wailed. "They've taken Jillie. They've taken her, and I don't know where."

Goodwife Cailin smoothed my hair off my face and looked into my eyes. "They're all dead back there, Mirin," she said, pity in her gaze. "You alone are left." Before I could argue with her, her voice turned brisk and practical. "You must go to the priests. That's the only way you'll stay alive."

"There are no priests," I said, snuffling my nose on the sleeve of my already filthy kirtle.

"No, not here," she said. "But in the market town, there's a temple to our good Lady Goddess, and you can throw yourself on the Goddess's mercy there. The priests will have to take you in. They won't have a choice. You don't need to tell them much. Don't tell them anything about how you came to be orphaned. No one will recognize you there and be tempted to turn you in. You're old enough to walk there. It's dangerous on the road for a young girl, so take care. You're as slight as a child, though. No one will bother you." She stood for a few moments, her lips compressed, her eyes worried, as if she weren't really believing her own words. "But if you stay here, someone will be tempted to tell the beadle. There's a bounty on your head, girl."

Looking over her shoulder to make sure no one was watching us, she picked up a stick. Then she bent down and quickly drew a map for me in the dirt: the path out of our village, the meandering way it took up-river to the point where it branched off toward the market town, the largest town in our Hundred. Then she drew a round enclosure. I knew this must represent the palisades of the market town. Within the circle of the town, she drew the street leading to the temple from the market square.

A burst of hoofbeats warned us that soldiers were riding through the fair. No one in the village could afford a horse. It had to be soldiers. Goodwife Cailin grabbed me in her strong washerwoman's arms and thrust me behind a tangle of barrels. "Stay there," she hissed at me, then whirled to face the commotion, curtseyed as the soldiers rode past, and made off in the opposite direction as soon as they'd gone.

I lay trembling behind the barrels for a long time. Then I began to cry, because she had flung me down so hard I had fallen on my rebec. I was sure it was smashed. It wasn't, though. I pulled open the drawstrings of its oiled bag and drew it out. I hugged my knees to my body and cradled the rebec in my arms, inspecting it from the beautifully carved neck to the graceful curve of its belly and its tailpiece. It was fine. My bow was broken, though. When I pulled it out of the bag, I saw it had snapped in two. I knew I could repair it. Just then, I suppose because I needed comfort, I longed to play my instrument. I could have used my fingers to pluck the strings. But of course I didn't dare.

*I'm fine. Not hurt, not taken,* I whispered to myself. I would go to the market town. Along the way, I'd look for some tough vines to bind the broken parts of the bow together. One of the rebec's strings had also flopped loose from its peg, but that was easily fixed. In the shadow of the barrels, I set about threading the string back into the hole our father had made with his awl in one of the hitch-pins he had set into the bowl of the instrument. Then I tied the string off in the tight, neat knot our father had taught me to make. I couldn't help myself then; I strummed a few notes, softly in case anyone might be within hearing, but no one opened a door or window or called out.

The soldiers were gone. Even from where I was hiding, I could tell a frightened hush had fallen over the village after they had thundered through. But now the villagers were flocking back to the booths and carts of the fair. I could hear shouts and laughter, and through the hot, still air of a warm day at mid-harvest tide, I could hear the big chunk when one of the strong lads of the village tossed the log. Probably Grendan or Ware. Ware was bigger and stronger, but I hoped Grendan was winning that contest.

I felt a small smile beginning to curve my lips. Grendan had clapped a raw-knuckled friendly hand on my shoulder last Lady-Day, and the other girls had looked over at me and giggled.

I ducked my head now, startled at myself for having such an ordinary thought, a thought from an ordinary world as remote from me now as the stars hanging on their golden chains above. I chased this ordinary thought away. Already, I think I knew that old life of mine had ended.

Around my hiding place, everything was still. I was alone behind the barrels.

After a while, I sidled out into the street and stood up, holding my rebec carefully by its neck. I eased it back into its oiled bag and slung it by its strap over my shoulder. Then, when I was sure I wasn't observed, I bent down over the map Goodwife Cailin had drawn me in the patch of dirt off the edge of the path. After I had memorized the map, I rubbed it out with the toe of one of my turn-shoes.

I noticed then with dismay that the shoe was nearly worn to tatters. Both shoes were. Our mother had made them from rabbit skins I had trapped myself, and they were warm with the fur side inward. She'd made a small pair for you, too, Jillie. Do you remember those shoes? But now, several seasons later, my shoes were near worn out. I didn't know how they'd hold up during the many leagues' walk to the market town. I thought maybe I'd be able to get a ride on the back of a farm wagon. Someone I didn't know, who didn't know me and my dismal, dangerous history, might stop his wagon and let me hop on. Someone heading to the market town to sell the produce of his steading, as our father had often done himself.

It was too late in the day to start walking, so I hung around the village until dark. I spent a restless night curled up on the back step of the village hall, making sure to keep an eye out for the watch and slip into the shadows whenever the watchman passed by. But at the tail end of night, I was so tired out, I slept right through his approaching footsteps. I woke with a start. He was standing over me, holding his rushlight high so that the shadows wouldn't obscure my face.

"Is that you, Mirin Far-meadow?" His voice sent me into a panic, and I rose to run. But his hand shot out and he pressed me back down on the hard stones of the step.

"Yes," I quavered.

"The Lady Goddess keep you in Her care, girl," he said. He unpinned his cloak, slung it off his shoulders, and tucked it around me. "In the morning, just leave the cloak there on the step. I'll get it then. But mind, be off before the beadle comes to open the shutters."

I nodded.

He put his hand down briefly on my shoulder. "Poor child," he said. Then he hoisted his rushlight back up onto its pole and strode away.

I knew I might not be so lucky the next time I got careless. The next watchman might not be this one, Hungry Geb, but instead Kenelm One-eye, who hated the world and everyone in it. I was sure that included me. These two men shared the job of night watchman. I doubt you remember them. I keep trying to jog your memory, Jillie. I keep hoping something will come back to you, something that may help you.

But that night I knew for certain I would follow Goodwife Cailin's advice. I would leave our village and head for the market town as soon as it got light.

And I knew another thing, knew it for a certainty. I'd look for you, Jillie. Whatever Mistress Cailin thought, something inside me told me you were alive. I didn't know how I would do it, but I would search for you, and I wouldn't stop until I'd found you.

The next morning, I did the only thing I could do. I headed out for the market town.

I walked along the roadway, overtaken by cart after cart, and none of them stopped for a ragged girl holding out her hands in the weeds, a beggar, somebody misfortunate, dirty, perhaps dangerous. I walked, and then I trudged, and then I limped.

Along the way, just as I thought I would, I found some vines I could use to repair my rebec's bow. That made the walk easier. I fitted my rebec against me and began to play and sing as I walked along.

> *I'll sing you one, oh.*
> *What is your one, oh?*
> *One is one, and all alone, and evermore shall be so,*

I sang.

> *Blackbirds rising, blackbird's eye,*
> *Green grow the rushes, oh,*
> *One lone blackbird in the sky,*
> *Green grow the rushes, oh.*

I played all of the verses of Johnny the Traveler's song straight through. Once I finished, I began playing and singing them all over again. As I sang, I saw that a cart pulling past me had slowed to a stop. A farmer sat on the wagon seat, looking back over his shoulder at me. As I came abreast of him, he gave me a cautious smile. "That was right pretty, young mistress."

"Thank you, good sir," I said, and dropped him my very best curtsey.

"If you're headed to market, do you need a ride?"

I nodded and smiled.

"Come up here on the wagon seat beside me and play and sing to me as we ride. The way won't seem so long then."

I looked up into his homely honest face and thought how our parents had cautioned us not to go with people who were strangers to us. *It's not safe!* they'd tell us. *Never do this!* they'd say. But I had no choice, not really, and the man looked kind.

So that's what I did. I hiked my skirts, climbed up over the big front wheel of the wagon, and sat down on the wagon seat at his side. He never hurt me or gave me the least reason to worry, thank the Lady. Or luck.

I played and sang as we rode along. After I'd played all the way through the blackbird song, I stopped, lowering the rebec and the bow to my lap.

"Good sir?" I said shyly, after a moment.

"Yes, child?"

"I'm looking for my sister. My little sister. Have you seen a little lost girl along the road?"

He shot me a curious look. It was so intense I nearly shrank from him. Suppose he had heard. Suppose I had just confirmed his suspicions. Suppose he took me straight to the beadle's men. But he said only, "No, young mistress, I've not seen such a girl. You must be worried about her."

"I am," I said.

We clumped along in silence for a while behind the man's plodding ox, and then I took up my rebec again and played another tune, a light-hearted tune I'd heard around the village.

The man took me all the way to the market town gates, and there he dropped me off. He questioned me, and when I told him I had no parchment allowing me to enter the town, he said he'd have to drop me off beforehand.

"Stay right here, young mistress," he told me, letting me off beside a little copse of trees outside the town. "In the morning, it may be you can get into the town." Then he guided his wagon into line at the portal gate. "Stay there, mind," he called after me. "Right there."

I waved my thanks, wondering at his insistence. I didn't think he'd inform on me. Maybe he would have if he had known there was a bounty to be paid for turning me in. Times were hard. People were poor. But how was he to know about the bounty? I wasn't important enough to have my criminal status posted all over the Hundred. Only in our village.

*I'm a criminal*, I thought. *Wanted by the authorities.* It was not right. I'd done nothing wrong, and great wrong had been done to me and the ones I loved.

I waved again to the man until he had driven forward and was obscured by another wagon, and then another, and then another. I sat down at the side of the road with my rebec, a ragged girl unnoticed by the wagoneers and too far away to attract the attention of the guards.

I decided to sit there until dark. I knew the farmer was wrong. There was no more likelihood of getting into the town in the morning than there was right now. Not in the regular way.

I had already decided not to follow the farmer's advice. As soon as it got dark, I'd figure out how I would sneak into the town.

I didn't tell the farmer that, though. He might have gotten suspicious. So I had just nodded and smiled at his advice.

# CHAPTER THREE

# Like a Fish

As the afternoon drew on, the wagoneers grew more urgent and loud, yelling abuse at each other, trying to cut each other off. I realized that if a wagon hadn't reached the head of the line by dark, the wagon-portal guards would close the big doors of the palisades, leaving that unfortunate wagon outside. The wagoneer would lose the early evening time of setting up and also lose the pick of the best places for his wagon. So he'd be at a disadvantage the next day, when the doors would reopen and crowds of people would be admitted through the small wicket gate to buy the wares of those ready to do business.

I moved into the grassy triangle between this wagon-portal and the much smaller wicket gate for foot travelers, and sat down to watch. Other ragged beggarly-looking people had the same idea. Several spindly trees gave us all a bit of shelter from the sun, which was beating down on us in spite of the cooler air this time of year. From there we could watch where the road divided into an uneven Y, a broad road for the wagons and a narrow path for the foot travelers. While the wagoneers waited for the inspectors, many of the wagons disgorged passengers who then bustled over to the wicket gate.

As I watched, I recalled the many times our father had taken the village wagon off to this same market town. When it was his turn to drive his wares to market, he always invited other villagers along, the ones who were going there to to buy, not sell. Or people who had small items for sale, not enough to warrant taking the town ox. These foot passengers were people like that.

Our father was always coming and going. You may remember that, Jillie, how restless he was. He usually waited to go to market when it was our turn to use the village wagon and ox. But not always. Sometimes he slung a sack over his shoulder and headed off on foot, or got a ride. He never left with very much, because we didn't grow very much, and what we grew, we needed. And he never came back with much, either, maybe a few coins he trickled into our mother's hands. I sometimes wondered why he bothered at all. He had a wandering heart. That's how I explained it to myself. I thought maybe I had a wandering heart, too. Our father had promised to take me with him to the market some day, and I longed to go. He never had taken me. Now he never would.

On the broader arm of the road's Y, the wagon-portal guards stopped each wagon and demanded each driver's bit of parchment authorizing the wagon's entry. I watched the guards rove around the wagons, peeking under the canvas coverings and prodding into boxes and barrels with their staves. They made sure no wagoneer was bringing contraband through the palisades, including unauthorized passengers.

But the foot-travelers flowed briskly down the narrow arm of the Y and through the wicket gate. They showed their parchments and were let through almost immediately, although one or two were stopped and searched.

As I watched, I decided that the wicket gate might be a better bet for sneaking in than the wagon gate. I thought so until I saw one of the other ragged beggars try to wheedle his way in. When he could produce no parchment, the guards began shouting at him. Then they hit him with the flats of their swords, and one of them cut him a great gash across one cheek. He fled howling past me down the roadway, holding his hand to his bloody face, the guards trotting in pursuit, although not very fast. They were laughing. When they had run him off, they returned to their post. Many of the wagoneers had turned to watch this little show. They were laughing too, and so were the people lined up at the wicket gate waiting their turn.

As the guards strolled past me to their posts, sheathing their swords back into the baldrics that hung from their shoulders, I shrank against the little tree where I was sitting, making myself as small and inconspicuous as I could. One of the guards stared in my direction, but then his attention was drawn instead to a beggar woman not very far away from me, trying to clamber to her feet. He motioned to her, but she began clumsily to run. She must have known what was coming. I saw she was pregnant. She couldn't move very fast. The guard caught up with her and seized her by the arm. Though she cried out for help, he hustled her roughly to the wicket gate's guard house and shoved her inside. When she came out again, it was dusk, but I could see her clothing was torn, her headcloth was gone, and she was crying.

The world can be an ugly place, Jillie. I know you know that, you more than most.

After witnessing these things outside the town, I decided I wouldn't try to sneak in by the wicket gate after all.

Darkness fell. I couldn't help it. Tears rolled down my cheeks. I shoved a fist into my mouth to keep from sobbing. Even when I was hiding out in the woods or on the outskirts of our village, I hadn't felt this alone. Part of my distress was this: I saw how unlikely it was I'd ever find you in a world so wide and harsh.

By now, the guards were gone. I knew they wouldn't hear me. Still, the people around me might hear. I knew there were bad people in the world who were drawn to weak people. As young as I was, I'd learned that much. I couldn't seem weak. I couldn't invite unwanted attention. I didn't know these other dirty-looking people around me, fewer now. I didn't know their intentions. They were probably just poor unfortunates, as I was myself. But I couldn't know. I was afraid. And underneath the fear, I missed my family. My family I'd never see again.

I wondered again what had happened to your body, if Mistress Cailin was right that you were dead. But I didn't believe it. The message from my second sense had been too strong, and besides, your body had disappeared, and your doll had shown up in a completely different place. Someone had taken you. If you were dead, why hadn't these someones taken all the bodies? Why just yours?

You know how, in the dark, all our fears and worries become magnified? I began to worry then. I remembered the way the kindly farmer had fixed me with his intense look, when I had mentioned my lost sister. I remembered how he insisted I stay by the gates of the town. Suppose, I worried, he had gone to the beadle as soon as he'd entered the gates. Suppose, in the morning, someone rushed from the gates to seize me. I knew then that whatever the risks, I had to get to the sanctuary of the priests of the Lady Goddess. I had to get inside the town.

Side by side with these fears and worries, I mourned. I mourned our parents' lives so brutally ended. Their mutilated bodies insisted on rising before my inner eye, no matter how hard I tried to replace these sights with the way I remembered them in life. I mourned their absent love and care. I mourned you, Jillie. I knew that even if you were alive, you must be hurt and terrified.

I called each of your three loved faces up in memory and yearned after it. I forced myself to think of our parents as they were, not as I'd last seen them. Our father, strong and broad-shouldered. His serious mild brown eyes, his hair just beginning to be streaked with the first hints of gray. Our mother with her lovely fall of honey-colored hair and her soaring voice. You, Jillie, the little sister who tagged along after me everywhere and tried to imitate everything I did. Your arms reaching up to me. Now that I couldn't, I ached to hold you.

As I lay on the lumpy ground with my boy's tunic pulled around me for warmth, a cold moon rose on the little copse outside the palisade walls. By its light I saw a huddle here, a huddle there, not very many. People trying to sleep.

I dithered. I needed to go. I needed to find a way in. But still I waited. A silvery sound pealed out faintly over the landscape, sending a chill up my spine. Then I realized— the bells, the temple bells of the Lady Goddess. The evening went by, the moon climbed higher, and still I hesitated. I had no plan.

A second tolling of the bells decided me. By then, it must have been a full candle-measure later. If I were ever going to move, I needed to do it now. Very quietly, I stood, shifting the bag containing my rebec to a more comfortable fit against my shoulder. None of the huddles of people around me stirred. From my days of hunting, I knew how to move silently. I made my way step by step out of the thicket, pausing often to make sure no one was following me.

When I was well clear of the population of beggars in the thicket, I began prowling the perimeter of the palisade. No guards were out patrolling. They probably all thought the tall pointed stakes and the sturdy gates were protection enough. Once the guards slid the gates' big timber beams into their bolt holes, their day's work was done. After the gates had closed, night guards probably patrolled the town inside. After all, even our small village had its night watchmen.

The moonlight glowed over my surroundings. By its light, I could see what I was up against. The palisades were high and slanted outward. Their pointed tops looked sharp. There would be no easy way over. So I made my way around the perimeter, looking carefully for any loose boards or rotten spots where I might slip through. It took me many furlongs of walking to get around to the far side. The market town backed up to the forest there. Now I saw where the people of the town got their water. A little river transected the back corner of the town. It ran out of the forest, under the palisade. It must exit under the palisade again on the other side of town. This river, I thought, probably fed into the big river parallel to the road that led past the town.

*Here's my way in*, I said to myself. Our father had taught me to swim.

Most of the people from around here would never think of swimming. They'd all been told the stories of the water naiads, how they twine their tendrils of blue hair around you and pull you under and hold you there til all your breath bubbles up out of you, and you drown. I know. I had a few village friends, and they all thought so. But our father had taught me these were only stories. "And besides," he'd said, one of the rare times he talked about his beliefs. "Your Child is the Sea Child. Water is your friend. The fisher-bird watches over you—a good water spirit, not a demon." His Child was the Earth Child, but he told me about growing up along the sea and learning to swim in the company of many boys whose Child was the Sea Child. They weren't afraid. Neither was he.

Jillie, your Child is the Earth Child, like his. I never remember you swimming. You may have been too little. You may have been afraid. I can't remember. That bothers me. I want to remember everything about you. Everything.

But I could swim. You must remember how I used to come home dripping and happy from some stream I'd found in the woods.

I knew I could swim under the palisade wall and into the market town.

Before I could tell myself how foolish this idea was and talk myself out of doing it, I kicked off my ragged shoes and tested the water with a toe. Making sure the oiled bag with my rebec was securely tied, I eased myself shivering into the water. By the bank, it came up to my waist, bunching my clothing up into an unwieldy mass about me. Inching forward, I could tell the waters of the deeper channel in the middle might not come over my head. Close, though. That was fine. There was plenty of room for me to sink beneath the surface of the water and swim under, with nothing to show that I was there. Oh, in the day, probably. But not at night, not even in moonlight as bright as this.

I was worried for my rebec, but I had no choice. I took a breath, propelled myself to the bottom, and drew myself by my hands along the channel, root filled, rock filled, and sandy, to the palisade. Feeling my way blindly, I had a moment of panic when I encountered the bottom of the palisade with, it seemed, no way under. I thrashed to the surface, enduring another moment of panic when my sodden kirtle caught on some projection under the water. But I wrestled my tunic and kirtle free and threw myself gasping on the bank.

I waited a long time, afraid my thrashing about had alerted someone on the other side of the palisade. No one came to see what the commotion was about. My shivering was like to rattle the teeth out of my skull. I stripped out of my wet and heavy clothing and wrung it out as best I could. With or without my clothes, I was freezing cold, but there was no other way. My clothes would only hold me back. Perhaps the strap of my rebec bag as well. I wrapped my wet clothes around the rebec in its bag and laid the bundle carefully underneath a little bank where the river had hollowed it out into a muddy alcove. Maybe I'd be able to come back for everything later. In the meantime, I tried to make sure it was all well-hidden. Trying hard to be quiet, I beat my arms with my hands to warm myself and stepped to the water's edge. I hesitated.

I went back to my bundle and extracted the bag with my rebec. I could not leave it behind.

I held my breath. I drove down again to the sandy floor of the channel, pulling through the water with my hands and kicking with my feet. I felt my way to the place where the bottom edge of the palisade extended below the river's surface but not all the way to the bottom.

I felt a surge of optimism as I pulled my way underneath. Halfway through, the strap on my rebec caught on the jagged edge of one of the palisades. I was trapped there. From the pressure of holding my breath so long, I was starting to see spots on the inside of my eyelids. For long, precious moments I worked to free the strap, my fingers clumsy and swollen. *Foolish girl, thinking you could bring it with you!* That was the thought that flashed into my mind as I struggled with the strap. I found myself flailing and kicking out in panic.

Without knowing exactly how I had freed myself, I suddenly shot to the surface on the other side, my breath coming in great noisy wheezing. I tried to quiet myself, but I gasped again at the sting of the cold and the scrapes on my legs and ribcage where the rough timbers had rasped me cruelly as I wriggled under.

My legs and arms were numb, and my hands were, too. I managed to pull myself out of the water and lay limply on the bank. The night around me was quiet. My struggles hadn't attracted any unwelcome attention, Lady be thanked. Now I hauled myself trembling further up onto the bank of the river against the inside of the palisade and hugged my knees to my chest, trying to get warmer and gingerly touching the parts of me that had been scoured raw.

After a moment, I eased the rebec's bag open and felt inside. Damp but not soaked. My rebec might be ruined, but maybe it was not. I wouldn't be able to tell until morning when I could dry it out and try it, but I pulled it from its bag and hung it around my neck. I took out the mended bow, which had miraculously not broken again, and tucked the bag into some weeds at the edge of the palisade. At least this way the soaking-wet inside of the bag could not damage the instrument further.

*Now what?* I asked myself. And you're right. I know you want to ask it. Go ahead. Yes, I was as naked as the Lady made me. If any guard had caught me, I don't know what would have happened.

I looked around in the moonlight. I needed some clothing. Indeed, for modesty's sake, but more because I feared I'd die of cold. In this fortnight of my troubles, the days were warm but the nights were cold, signaling the winter to come. I'll assure you of this: if you were as cold as I was, you wouldn't have worried very much about modesty, either.

If you are actually listening, and not just a figure wandering through my imagination, you probably find my words shocking. A well-brought-up maiden should not find herself in such a situation. I wonder if that's your situation now, Jillie. A well brought-up young maiden cared for, even loved. I hope so. I pray to the Lady so.

Was I a well-brought-up maiden? Not by town standards. But our parents had taught us honesty and modesty. They'd also taught me to take care of myself. Our mother had taught us this prayer: *Lady Goddess, help me, for I am weak. Teach me to keep myself neatly. Teach me to be clean. Keep my hands busy with honest work. Let not my hands go to picking and thieving. Help me always toward the right thing. And Lady Goddess save me when no help is near.* The Lady Goddess knows, there was no help near.

I was whispering this prayer to the Lady, just on the off chance it might work, when something caught my eye. Was it the power of prayer or the power of luck? I saw I was sitting close behind a set of small buildings, houses, probably, each with its neat dooryard. Flapping at the edge of one, a thing.

My heart started beating faster. Ghost? No. A clothesline, and on it a cloak that someone had forgotten to bring in. I edged to the fence, reached, and snatched at the cloak. I pulled it over the low fence to myself. I wrapped myself in that cloak and began to cry again. *Let not my hands go to picking and thieving.*

But I made myself stop. No time to sit around wailing. Time instead to get far away from that yard. I began creeping away down the line of palisades, keeping as much to the shadows as I could. After a while, I heard voices calling out. *It is the Watch*, I told myself.

And here the Lady saved me a second time that night. Or luck.

The moon, which was going down, slid behind a low bank of clouds. I pressed myself against the palisade wall as the men of the Watch stamped by. They didn't see me there. They appeared to be heading for a dimly lit door, and went in. As I stood back scarcely daring to breathe, I heard the faint sounds of singing. The Watch were wetting their whistles. The building must be a tavern.

I was safe, at least for now.

# CHAPTER FOUR

# Friends of Mine

I must have slept huddled up against the wall. Bright morning roused me. I came to myself with a jolt and scrambled to my feet, looking wildly around. Nearby I spotted a cluster of buildings, maybe the town granaries. I hurried behind them, looking around to make sure no one was watching me. In the shadow of these buildings I tried to smooth out my hair, which was still damp, and I pulled the cloak more tightly around myself, feeling to make sure the rebec and bow were not damaged.

To my horror, the cloak revealed itself in the light of day to be dyed a bright festival yellow. Its owner would come looking for it, and she'd spot me in an instant. So I tried to slink along the wall of the palisade. I knew I had to work my way around the perimeter until I got close to the wagon and wicket gates. Those led directly into the market square. And I knew from Goodwife Cailin's map that the temple of the Lady Goddess was directly behind the square.

I had to get there. Otherwise, I was as unsafe here as I was in our own village. More unsafe. In our village, there were people who knew me and our family, people who thought kindly of me. They might stand up for me if I were taken by the soldiers. Here, I was a stranger. No one cared. I'd actually committed a crime here. At home, perhaps I could have thrown myself upon the king's justice, bounty or no bounty. Here, I had illegally gained entry to the town and had stolen a cloak. Two crimes, Lady help me. In these dangerous times, when everyone was on edge, even petty crimes were taken very seriously. But if I could reach sanctuary, I'd be safe. Then the priests could help me decide how to go about searching for you, Jillie.

I felt a surge of optimism when I began hearing the rumble of wagon wheels, the shouts of soldiers, and the cries of vendors setting up for business and calling out their wares to customers. I was getting close to the market square. From the time I realized how hard it might be to enter the town, to the unfortunate discovery of my stolen cloak's bright color, I was feeling mostly fear and despair. But now—

My joy was cut short. A heavy hand clamped down on my shoulder and a bellowing in my ear nearly blew my brains out the other side.

"Thief! Thief!" screeched the person holding me, a large woman. I knew that already, for her cloak was ample, draping me like a tent and reaching to the tops of my bare feet. Clearly, she was the owner of the yellow cloak.

A few passers-by turned to look at our little drama at the edge of the footpath. Instead of rushing to the woman's aid or running for the authorities, they quickened their pace down the path away from the two of us. It was a market day. They had no time for petty theft. They needed to get to their places in the square or risk losing sales to their competitors. Let this woman take care of her problems by herself.

She seemed well able to do that.

"Thief!" she yelled again. Grabbing me hard by the arm, she started shoving me ahead of her down the path. *Probably taking me to the beadle*, I thought with despair. We must have made a strange-looking couple, a large woman pushing and dragging a thin girl stumbling along in a bright yellow cloak much too big for her. As we came closer to the center of town, a woman passing in the other direction stopped and stared at us.

"Now, Aina, what's this?"

"This beggar stole my cloak."

"Taking her to the beadle?"

"By the Lady Goddess, yes, I am, and what are you interfering for, Old Cwen? Always interfering. Let me by. It's going to take all morning, doing this."

"I'm guessing you were headed to the market to sell your eggs." The other woman, the woman called Old Cwen, was round and fat and old. She was peering into the large woman's basket. It did hold eggs, a good dozen. My mouth watered.

"I'm going to miss the best part of the day," the woman called Aina said. Her voice started rising again.

"Aina, hand her to me. I'll get her to the beadle. You go on to the market."

Aina regarded her skeptically. "And you, I suppose, have nothing better to do but interfere, Old Cwen."

"I was just returning from a difficult birth, and then I had to stop by the gate to meet with some folks on a matter of urgent business. I'm wore out. I'll not do anything else but rest this day. I can take her."

"Take her, and may the Dark Ones take her too," said Aina and shoved me to Old Cwen so hard that I tripped over the cloak and tumbled at Old Cwen's feet.

I picked myself up and faced Aina. I shrugged out of the cloak and held it toward her. "I'm sorry! I didn't mean to take it."

Aina's eyes widened and she took a step backward. I realized I was stark naked without the concealment of her cloak. I realized she was shocked to the bottoms of her feet.

Old Cwen exclaimed as Aina snatched up the cloak. "Child! We can't have you like this, not like this." Old Cwen pulled her own cloak off and wrapped it around me.

"Nine Spheres, I'm late for the market. Take her, then, and see the beadle marks her down for a sneaking thief." Aina strode off fast toward the square. "An immodest thief!" she screamed back over her shoulder.

Old Cwen looked down at me, then looked harder. "You're a poor misfortunate young one, I'm guessing," she said slowly, picking her words. She reached out to touch my tangled hair. "No thief, except out of necessity. Best come with me." She didn't lay hands on me. I was free to run away. I didn't, though. When I looked at Old Cwen, I saw compassion. I saw safety. I followed her back the way I had come, and then down a long lane over a footbridge that crossed the little river to a different part of the town.

We reached her house, a thatched stone longhouse. Compared to my own house back in my village, it was grand. She led me inside and steered me to a settle before the banked fire in the center of the main room. She took a poker and stirred the fire up, adding a few turves from the stack by the door. The smoke rose to the smoke-hole in the roof.

I was shivering. I stretched out my arms to the fire, and I think I may have moaned.

"Soon you'll be warm. Wait here," she said. "You won't run away?"

I shook my head no.

She must have believed me, because she disappeared for a moment. When she returned, she held a roughspun brown woolen kirtle. She unwrapped me from the cloak and exclaimed in dismay.

"Good sweet Lady," she said. "This won't do." She left the room again. When she came back, she held a ragged coverlet, which she draped about me. "Now sit there," she told me. She bustled to the back of the house and returned trundling a wooden tub before her. She situated it before the fire. Then, with an iron hook, she swung an enormous black spouted kettle from the fire, where it was hanging over the flames, and she tilted it over the tub, pouring in steaming water. Another disappearance and reappearance, this time with a large wooden bucket of cold water, which she poured in with the hot.

"There," she said. She bent down and stirred the water with a finger. "Get in that."

I think she thought I'd run for it, because she moved to position herself between me and the door. I think she thought I wanted to stay filthy. But I didn't. I got up from the bench, discarding the coverlet, and stepped up and over, into the tub. And sank down. The relief was such a joy that I didn't think about my predicament at all, just how good the water felt on my body—the warmth, the feeling that the filth of a sen'night and more was being soaked off me.

Suddenly I gasped in fright. My rebec! I rose from the water and looked wildly around.

The woman had moved over to the settle and had seated herself there with a weary sigh. "Are you looking for this?" she said, holding the rebec up to me by the strap.

"Yes," I said.

"Well, here it is. Now get back in that water until you're clean enough for me to get a good look at you." She bent down with difficulty and plucked a small wooden firkin of soap from under the settle and handed it to me. It was harsh yellow soap. Its astringent odor made my eyes water and stung the scrapes and scratches the palisade had made on me as I'd swum under, but I didn't care. I lathered the soap all over me, even my hair. Then I plunged under the water to rinse myself off.

"Good," she said. "Get out now, girl. You don't want to stay in that tub until the water cools and you get more of a chill than you've already taken."

I climbed out of the tub. She had a fresh coverlet waiting, and with this she toweled me off. Roughly, but I didn't protest. I let her do her worst on me. At last she stepped back and stared at me. Stared at me hard. "Better," she said at last. She picked up a small pot of salve beside her on the bench and daubed it on my cuts and scrapes, then handed me the kirtle.

I thanked her prettily, as our mother had taught us, and put the kirtle on. It was shapeless and brown and ugly, but I didn't care. The stinging of my scraped body was eased. I was warm and dry and modest. But I was hungry.

She saw that right away. She had gotten a good look at my skinny ribcage and sunken belly.

"Come here," she said. She led me to a table underneath a window at the front of the house and sat me down there in a real chair. I hadn't sat in a real chair very often. Benches, low platforms piled with bedding, tree stumps, rocks, yes. Chairs, hardly ever.

Then she brought a bowl of steaming porridge and set it in front of me and handed me a wooden spoon.

I ate and ate and ate.

She took the bowl away. "You'll make yourself sick," she said. "You can have more later."

I began to cry.

"There, my girl. There," she said, and her expression, which had started to grow exasperated, softened. "You'll tell me all your sorrows later. For now, go on up to the loft so you can have a good sleep. You're as limp as the fag end of an old rope." She led me by the hand like a little child to the ladder leading up into the loft under the thatch at the other end of the longhouse from the fire, far enough away so the smoke rising to the smokehole in the roof wouldn't suffocate anyone up there. I climbed up and sank into the soft furs spread out on the lashed slats of the loft. Sleep took me. I knew nothing more until dark, when the rich smells of a savory stew woke me and caused me to look over the ledge into the main hall of the house.

The woman was down there, stirring the stew over the fire in an iron pot. She must have heard the boards creak, because she looked up into the rafters and saw me peering down.

"Hungry?"

I nodded.

"Come down, then."

So I did, and after a trip to the jakes behind the house, I ate more, this time more slowly. When I had eaten my fill, she motioned me over to the settle before the fire, and we sat there side by side.

"I'll never be able to fill you up, starveling girl. Now then," she said. "Tell me everything. Start with why you stole Aina's cloak. No, start before that."

I did. What did I have to hide? I was completely in her power. She could turn me over to the beadle any time she wanted to. She listened to the whole story in silence. When I stopped talking, after I got to the part where she grabbed me away from Aina and took me to her house, we simply sat together for a long time, staring into the fire. Every so often she rose to give it a stir with the poker. Her face was thoughtful.

"And this?" she said.

"What?"

"This." She indicated my rebec. "What is this."

"It's my rebec. It may have gotten ruined when it got wet." The thought made tears rise into my eyes again, but she handed it over to me, and I calmed down, holding it and stroking it.

"It plays music?

"It used to. I don't know about now," I said.

"Try it and see."

So I did. I made a little trill on it, but only using my fingers. The rebec was the worse for its wetting, but it still played.

"Pretty," she said. "Can you play tunes on it? And sing?"

"Yes."

"Play me a tune, then," she said. "And sing."

And so I did. I went back to the loft for the mended bow, and I played my favorite song. *I'll sing you one, oh*, I sang. After the first verse, I moved to the second. *I'll sing you two, oh. Two, two, the long-lost boys, clothed all in green, oh*. And I sang my favorite part, the blackbird refrain.

She held up her hand, stopping me. "Who taught you this song?"

"Johnny the Traveler," I said. "He's famous."

"When did you meet this man?"

"A while back, last winter. He stopped at our farmstead and stayed the whole winter season and a bit longer than that."

"Your parents knew him?"

"My father and Johnny were friends from boyhood. They went to the wars together."

"And then he moved on? Johnny? Before all this happened to your family?"

I nodded yes. But something in her voice made me turn and stare into her face. She knew something. Something important. She was looking back at me through different eyes.

She must have seen the question in my face. "We'll talk about it tomorrow," she promised. "But now, go back into the loft and sleep. After what you've been through, it's a wonder you're not ill. In the morning we'll talk about Johnny the Traveler."

"You know him too?"

"Yes," said the woman. "A little." She coughed and ducked her head.

As I put my foot on the bottom rung of the ladder, I turned to her, suddenly feeling shy. "What shall I call you, Goodwife?"

"Everyone calls me Old Cwen," she said. Her voice sounded strange, kind of strangled.

I nodded. Then I looked over at her, stricken. "Old Cwen, my sister is missing. They took her. I have to find her. I have to."

"Go on up to the loft, child. We can't do a thing about that now. In the morning we'll think about it," said Old Cwen. She had turned brisk again. She put a firm hand on my back and guided me to the ladder. "I promise," she said.

I climbed back to the loft. I lay looking up at the starlight as it filtered through the thatch, running my hands over my rebec bow. The mending hadn't held. The vines were too flimsy, and they'd been through too much. The bow came apart in my hands. In the morning, I thought, I'd try for a better repair.

I lay in Old Cwen's loft trying to will myself to sleep, but sleep wouldn't come. I kept thinking about you, Jillie, about where you were, how badly you might be hurt, how I'd ever find you. I kept rehearsing what I'd say to the priests of the Lady Goddess to convince them to help me look.

But finally, I began to drift. My thoughts drifted toward Johnny, and I began thinking about my rebec. Our father made my rebec. You may remember watching him figure it out, with Johnny. They spent days bent over Johnny's own rebec while our father studied how it was made. Then, after Johnny left, our father made diagram after diagram on the back of our shovel with a lump of charcoal. Finally, maybe you remember this, our father made a rebec for me, this one.

But Johnny the Traveler is the one who taught me to play. One bright morning at the beginning of the winter before our parents were slaughtered, do you remember Johnny appearing in our dooryard? How he brought his own instrument with him to our house? As he played it beside our hearth stones, he saw how much I longed to touch it and bring thrilling tones from its strings, just as he did. And he saw something more.

He'd come planning to stay with us only a few days, but he talked to our parents. "I've said what I came to say, Dru," he told my father. My parents' eyes strayed uneasily in my direction, where I stood listening. "But now I've seen something unexpected," Johnny continued, tilting his head toward me and putting a hand on my shoulder. "Let me train her," he said to our parents. At first our mother demurred. I didn't understand why.

I was angry with her. "He's going to teach me how to play the rebec, just the way you taught me to sing," I said, shrugging off Johnny's hand and stepping to her. "Why is that wrong?" Our father stayed silent, and so did Johnny. "Please let him teach me,

Mother. Please?" I begged, turning my back on the two men. Somehow I knew she was the decider.

Over my head, she exchanged a troubled look with our father. "She's still young. Still just a child. And there are so many dangers," she murmured. I remember how she drew you to her, Jillie, and comforted you. You hadn't understood fully what we were saying, or why, but you had felt our parents' deep unease, and you'd started to cry. You have always been like that. The sensitive one of the family.

Think about how young you were, only around six. And how much older I was, still a girl but almost out of girlhood, in that strange time betwixt and between. I was already helping to support us with my hunting, already doing some of the hard work of adulthood. I resented being spoken about as if I were a child. By now, you must be around that age yourself. By now, you must know what I mean.

Our mother's frightened reaction gave me some vague notion she thought it was not fitting for a young girl to play music. I couldn't see how. It seemed to me then that our mother was constantly deciding something we did or didn't do was somehow unbefitting. She was constantly urging caution. I had begun resenting what I judged to be her timorous behavior.

Almost past childhood, I'd taken my place as family provider alongside our parents. Our mother had fashioned boys' clothes for me so I could hunt more easily, because she knew the practical value of the food I'd bring in would outweigh the risk of someone catching me in forbidden clothing. Compared to the other dangers we all faced—the danger of starvation, of sickness, even the danger of hunting in boy's clothes—the danger of playing music had to be less than nothing. *Dangers?* I thought, at the time. *What is so dangerous about playing music?*

Besides, those adults were discussing me as if I weren't standing right there in front of them. You probably remember how much that used to infuriate me.

"Elsebet, I understand your fears," Johnny said to our mother on that day, the most important of my life next to the day of our parents' slaughter—in a way, more important. "But Mirin's gifts don't come along every day," Johnny said to our mother, "and we know I might not be around to—"

*To what?* I thought. Something in our parents' faces alarmed me. Something deep inside me scared me more.

Johnny looked over at me. He smiled at me. "I may not be able to come by here again for a long time." His voice was reassuring. Our parents' expressions less so.

Finally our mother nodded. "If it's to be, it's to be," she said, and turned away, blinking back tears. "I know there's a justice," she said. "I know it." She sounded as if she were trying to convince herself. I didn't know what she meant. Our father went to her and put his arm around her. They both ducked through the low door of our tiny cabin, and they stood outside talking. I remember you going to crouch by the fire, your small face miserable and uncomprehending.

As for me, I couldn't hear what our parents were saying, but really, I wasn't listening. The bad feelings sank back down underneath, hidden away, and the good ones bobbed to the surface. I was going to be allowed to play! To learn! Now I was too excited to pay attention to the bad feelings. I was going to learn to play this marvelous instrument which had awakened beneath my fingers. It was a sort of magic, and it would be my magic.

"Let me teach you, Mirin," said Johnny. We sat down together at the hearth stones, and he gave me my first lesson, helping me place my hands on the strings. After that, he showed me how the bow worked upon the strings. He pulled you to his side so you could watch, too, Jillie. He saw how left out you felt.

That winter changed me. Johnny's lessons opened a new world that shimmered with the notes from his instrument, and at first that's all it was, although that was enough, and plenty. But gradually I became aware something else was happening inside me as Johnny helped me master his instrument. Neither of us talked about what this something else might be. Johnny had mentioned my gifts. I began to think he wasn't just talking about music. Sometimes I doubted I was truly feeling it, this strange idea about what Johnny knew, but when I looked into Johnny's beautiful scarred face, I saw my feeling was telling me true.

He stayed with us the entire winter. When spring came, he told us he had to leave.

"I've taught her what I could," he told our parents. "She has learned faster than anyone I've ever seen take up the instrument. What I glimpse in her is real. You've heard it for yourselves, some of it, and you know we need it. The rest is up to her."

I wasn't sure what he meant by that. I was so overwhelmed with sadness that I wasn't paying a lot of attention to that statement of his, although I've thought about it many times since.

"Mirin, listen to me," he said on the day he walked away from us. He had slung his rebec over his shoulder and taken leave of my parents, embracing them with affection. He had reached down to place his hand lightly on your head in blessing, Jillie. Now I was keeping him company down the path as far as our village, just a few furlongs away. You probably don't remember much about our house and village, but the path met the road toward the market town there at the edge of the village, and there Johnny would walk away from us.

I lagged along numbly beside him, not wanting to look at him. I knew he would read in my face the mixture of sadness and resentment I felt. Johnny put his hand on my shoulder, turning me toward him so he could look into my eyes. "Your father has promised to get a rebec for you so you can keep playing. I know you will. I want you to think about that, what it means to you." He spoke slowly and carefully, searching my eyes with his.

"Why can't you stay?" I asked him, blinking back tears and pretending to be brave. There was something I knew. Johnny's admonition triggered it. Something underneath knowing, and it was a heavy and sad thing I knew.

"I have work to do, Mirin, and it can't wait." Johnny looked away from me now. "We both do, you and I." He put his hand on my head and murmured a few words. I knew he was praying to my Child.

Our mother worshipped the Lady Goddess instead of the Children. I wonder how well you remember our mother teaching us about Her. I wonder if you still worship Her. You and I grew up knowing about the Lady, although our mother never made the trip to the market town to go to Her temple. Our father left our religious training, such as it was, up to our mother.

But as Johnny prepared to leave, I knew he was praying to the Children, and I knew he was praying for me.

He waved farewell to our parents now, as they stood together arm in arm in our dooryard, and he waved to you as well. All of you stood watching him go.

I looked up into Johnny's face again and saw a sorrow so deep it frightened me. I felt the breath knocked out of me.

Now he put his hand on my arm, but he didn't look at me. He looked far off down the path as it wound under the trees. One by one, blackbirds flew out of the bracken to light on the branches of the big tree standing at the bend. Their eyes glittered under the trees. He looked around him at the shafts of sunlight coming through the trees, and he raised one hand to the birds.

He turned and smiled at me, speaking matter-of-factly now. "You and I have explored this gift the Children have given you. Now I must leave, but you'll keep playing. In days to come, I know you'll find out more and more about your gift. A gift like yours is powerful, Mirin. You can use it for good. But you can use it for ill. The choice is yours, and the choice will always be there for you to make. I know you'll use your gift for good."

He gave me a smile and a wave, as if he were just taking a walk down the path and would be back soon. I watched after him until he rounded the bend toward the village. As he walked away, the secret doors inside me opened up, what our father used to call my second sense, and I knew that I would never see Johnny again.

As I thought about all these things from the past, turning them over and over in my mind up there in Old Cwen's loft as if these thoughts were mysterious stones smooth from handling, smooth from tumbling end over end in the sea, I knew I wouldn't be able to sleep. Everything that had happened was too terrible, and how it connected with Johnny was too confusing. My fears and worries for you were too overwhelming. I needed to find you. I had to.

I was wrong about the sleeping. I slept instantly. For the first time in many days, I had no bad dreams.

# CHAPTER FIVE

# Green Grow the Rushes, Oh

I slept much too long, halfway through the morning. Low voices below me in the main room of the house wakened me at last. I lay there balling my fists up in frustration. Sometime the day before, I had concocted a plan. I'd hire myself out to this woman, Old Cwen, as her servant. Not even hire myself! I'd agree to work for free, I'd go before the beadle and let myself be bound to her, even that. I'd be brave and do it, and she'd keep me. I wouldn't even ask to be her apprentice, someday to be set up in a business of my own. I'd just stay with her and work for her, and in return, she'd keep me. And then, once I had a stable life and wasn't running away from anything, I'd get the priests of the Lady Goddess to help me search for you, Jillie.

What Old Cwen's business was, I didn't know. I didn't care. Whatever it was, I'd help her with it. All thoughts of vengeance had faded away. Safety, hunger, sleep. These all seemed more important. I hadn't forgotten about finding you. Finding you was a big part of this imaginary plan of mine.

But why would Old Cwen agree to such a thing? Agree to keep a lazy girl who slept half the morning away? She'd want me gone. "Starveling girl," she'd called me, and she had said, "I can't fill you up."

"Girl," Old Cwen called down the longhouse to me. "You're awake?"

"Yes, Goodwife."

"Come down, then. There are folks here wanting to meet you."

*Folks*, I thought. What folks? Soldiers? Watchmen?

I leaned cautiously over the edge of the loft and peered down. Two men and a woman, ordinary-dressed.

They stared up at me.

"Come down, girl. They mean you no harm," said Old Cwen.

I slipped from between the furs and pulled my borrowed kirtle over my head. I climbed down the ladder and turned to look at them. They were standing now, and looking back at me.

"Go on out to use the jakes, and then to the well and wash," said Old Cwen. "Then come back in here. These ones have something to talk over with you." As I went out the back door, she called after me, "Mind, jakes first and then the wash. Not wash and then the jakes."

"Yes, Goodwife," I replied. I didn't argue with her. Of course I knew that the jakes came first and then the wash. Every small child learns this from its mother. She might not realize I had been brought up with a mindful mother, though. This is what I said to myself, so I wouldn't take offense, because my first impulse was scorn. *Old Cwen must think I am stupid.*

As I dragged up a bucket of clean water from the well and washed, I realized that, no, she didn't think that. She knew only that I was a vagrant and a thief. I wiped my hands dry on my kirtle and started to go back toward the house. But then I stopped and stood still, looking up at the trees around me to keep the tears from rolling down. I was a girl with no mother at all.

As I turned to go back in, I thought about running for it. Old Cwen had seemed kind, the day before. She hadn't taken me to the beadle, as she had told Aina she would. But in the night, perhaps she had had second thoughts. Perhaps these people were here to arrest me, even though they didn't look like beadle's men. And one was a woman. Beadles didn't take on women.

I saw them all crowded around the lone back slit of a window, watching to see what I would do. No point in running. They'd be on me in an instant. I held my head high and went inside.

The older of the two men summoned me to a place beside him on the settle. The woman and the other man just stood looking at me. Now I had a good view of him, I saw the other man, the younger one, was not very long past boyhood. He stood a little apart. His cloak was blue, his eyes as blue as his cloak, and hair the color of the ripe barley standing in the field was ruffled up into a cowlick that made him look even younger than he probably was. He wore it short, like a peasant, and of course that wasn't remarkable. Every man we knew wore his hair hacked off like that. Our father did, of course. I noticed this young man's hair especially because the older man wore his own hair long, like a lord's.

But as I stared up at this tall young man, something I saw in his face made me look away, and be afraid. I made my way over to the older man, a neatly-bearded man in a green cloak. He looked to be around my father's age. I sat down, trying not to tremble.

Old Cwen stayed in her sleeping cubicle overlooking the little back garden, leaving me alone with the strangers. Slowly others came into the room and sat or crouched around the fire, or leaned against the wall. There were six of them now. Three men, three women.

"Now, girl," said the man beside me, the older man. "There's nothing to fear. Old Cwen is taking care of you. You can rest easy."

I nodded. I wasn't sure I believed him, but his voice was low and soothing.

"My friends and I do need to hear your story, though. Will you tell us about your family, what happened to them, and how you were driven out of your village?"

"I wasn't driven out. I left on my own."

"If you had stayed, what then?"

"I would have been caught and something bad would have happened to me."

"I'd say that means you were driven from your village."

He was right. I nodded again.

"But start at the beginning, when you found your family murdered."

I had to get a hard grip on myself. When he asked the question like that, so matter-of-factly, I wanted to scream at him. I wanted to hit him. Or somebody. I wanted to cry. I wanted my mother and father. But also. I hesitated, thinking about what he had just said. *Murdered*. I had been thinking of our family as executed, even though I didn't know why. But murder was a crime. The authorities did this terrible thing to them. Was this man saying the authorities were criminals?

He waited.

"I know this is hard for you, child," said one of the women.

I looked over at her. Her kind eyes gave me the courage to square my shoulders and tell them what I had seen, and how I had left my village, and why I had come to the market town, and how I had sneaked in.

They all nodded and smiled at this part. I stared back at them, puzzled.

Then I said, "There's one other thing. My sister Jillian. They've taken her. She's alive somewhere, and I need to find her. The priests in the temple—" I hesitated at their expressions. "They're holy people. Surely they'll help me find her."

They all stared at me, their faces full of pity. One of the women, the kindly one, had tears in her eyes.

"Now, girl, I'd advise against going to the temple," said the bearded older man beside me on the settle after a moment. "That was a good plan, the best I'm sure the goodwife could come up with. But she doesn't know how it is, at the temple here. How could she? We do. I'm not at all sure the priests will give you sanctuary. Even if they do, where are you then? You won't be able to leave the temple, and they won't want your keep on their hands. They'll find a way to rid themselves of you, and you'll be worse off than before. As for your sister—"

Here the woman with the tears in her eyes turned away and wiped them with the back of her sleeve.

"—I doubt they can help you find your sister," the man said gently.

"But they are holy people," I said, dumbfounded.

"Are they?" After a moment, he went on, "No, you're much better off here with Old Cwen. No one is looking for you here. You won't have to explain yourself to anyone. We'll say you are a young cousin, that your parents sent you to Old Cwen to apprentice with her." He made a sign to the woman who had cried, and the others stepped to the door in a little knot, conferring with each other.

The woman sat down on the settle now and took my hand. "Dear child," she said. "We've heard some things. Your sister—" she hesitated.

"No," I said. I saw what she was about to say. "No. No."

"We've heard they killed her," she told me simply.

I collapsed against her, and she held me. It was too much, Jillie. The hope, and now this. Old Cwen brought a cool cloth, and she and the woman bathed my face and comforted me. After a while, I realized the whole group of them were standing around me.

The man I thought of as their leader spoke to me again now. "This is hard news to hear. Will you stay with Old Cwen? It will be much safer for you if you do. You see how harsh the world can be. Let us help you."

"Why are you helping me?" I wanted to lash out at him. "You don't even know me. Others think I'm a criminal and a thief." I was feeling reckless. "Did you know that back in my village, there's a bounty to be paid to anyone finding me and turning me in?" I grew more and more angry. Why were these people smiling at me?

This man, the leader, didn't answer my question. "Now then," he said. "We'd like to know one thing more. We'd like to know about the visit of Johnny the Traveler to your home last winter. Are you able to tell us about that?"

"You've had a blow, child. We'll come back if you want to talk about it later," said the woman. I really looked at her now. She was thin and rangy. But I saw that cords of muscle stood out on her arms. I looked from one of these people to the other. They were all like that, all somehow honed for action. I wasn't sure I'd ever met people quite like them. But as I thought about it, I realized that no, I had met such people. Had known such people. Johnny had had that same sense about him. A kind of tension. I realized something then, something that amazed me. Our father. He had it, too, Jillie, that same rangy look.

"We can come back, if you like," the leader said now, echoing the kindly woman's words.

I shrugged. "I'll tell you now." I made my voice hard, my eyes hard. I threw up a wall around myself, and so I was able to tell them. Again, they listened intently as I talked.

"And you say that Johnny was a friend of your father's?" said the leader, after I had finished.

"Yes, he and my father called each other childhood friends. That's what they said."

"And he taught you a little about how to play the rebec? Johnny?"

"Yes."

"May we see it?"

I got up, climbed the ladder to the loft, and came down with it in my hands.

"Can you play on it?" the leader asked.

"Yes, a little bit."

"She can, sir," said Old Cwen, from the back. "I heard her play it, and sing, too."

"It's damaged, sir," I said. He reached out and I handed it to him. He turned it over in his hands and examined it carefully.

"Yes, I see," he said.

"But it still plays," said Old Cwen. "I heard her play it."

The leader handed my rebec back to me. "Play something on it."

"Play the song you played for me," said Old Cwen. "I told these ones about that song. That's why they're here."

Everyone was staring at me, so I raised my rebec and began to pluck at it uncertainly. "My bow was broken. I mended it, but—"

"Here," said another in the group, the younger man, the one with the cold eyes. From under his cloak, he pulled another bow.

Without stopping to wonder why he would have extra rebec bows stashed under his clothing, I took it with gratitude, and I began to play. I played and sang the first verse of the song I knew. *I'll sing you one oh.* At first my voice was uncertain and trembling.

But as I sang, it strengthened. My voice is a creature of its own, Jillie. That's how I think of it sometime. A noble creature. And this brave creature sang out now.

As I sang, I saw the leader make a warning motion at Old Cwen. Old Cwen stepped to the window and drew the shutters closed.

When I ended the verse, the leader sat back against the settle and breathed deeply. The others, too, all seemed to have been holding their breaths. They all looked at each other and stirred, as if they were coming out of a trance. "There are other verses to that song," said the man. "Do you know them?"

I played him the second verse, and I sang along. *I'll sing you two oh. What is your two oh? Two, two, the long-lost boys, clothed all in green oh. One is one and all alone and ever more shall be so.*

"There are more verses. Do you know them?" said the man.

So I sang and played the whole song straight through, and the blackbird refrain.

> *Blackbirds rising,*
> *Blackbird's eye.*
> *One lone blackbird in the sky.*
> *One is one and all alone and ever more shall be so.*

At the end, the six of them sat and stared at me, and they exchanged glances with each other, too. Behind them, Old Cwen shifted from one foot to the other, twisting her hands in her overdress.

"Johnny the Traveler taught you this song." The leader stated this rather than questioning.

"Yes."

"With your father's permission."

"Oh, yes."

"May I take a look at your instrument again?"

I handed my rebec to him, and he exhibited it to the others. "See there?"

My father had carved designs all over my rebec, intricate vines and flowers intertwined. On the neck he had carved a fisher bird, its own long neck stretched out along the neck of the rebec, its beak pointing upward. "It's a fisher bird because the Sea Child protects you," my father had told me. "And the fisher bird is Her harbinger."

"See there?" the leader said again. He showed the others my father's fine carving on the tailpiece. My father had fashioned the tailpiece into a clever little blackbird.

The others all looked at each other and then over at me. I felt bewildered by them. But their leader was asking me a question. "So then, when Johnny the Traveler left your cabin, you continued your practice?"

I looked at him, uncertain.

"You continued to play the rebec?" he prompted.

"Yes. That's when my father made my rebec for me. Johnny the Traveler taught me to play on his own rebec, but when he left, of course he took it with him."

"Can you describe it for us?"

"Yes, sir. It is bigger than mine and made of a different type of wood. Cherry, I think. My father made mine from one of our pear trees, when a storm brought it down. And Johnny the Traveler's rebec has a weasel carved on the peg-board."

"Is this the instrument?" The young man who had handed me the rebec bow now unslung a cloth bag from his shoulder and pulled it out—Johnny the Traveler's rebec.

"Oh, yes!" I said. It was Johnny's. I would recognize it anywhere. But as I took it and ran my hands over it, I saw it had been badly broken. Then repaired. Someone had shattered it. I felt a deep sorrow, looking at it in my lap. Everything was broken. My family. Johnny's beautiful instrument. Maybe I myself was broken. Then I looked up at the young man in surprise. "Why do you have Johnny the Traveler's rebec? And what happened to it? Why is it broken?"

He didn't answer me, just took my own rebec from the leader and sat turning it over in his hands and running his fingers along the water-damaged bowl and peg board. "This is a nice piece of work," he told me. "I can fix it for you."

"Thank you," I said. I had wanted our father to carve a weasel like Johnny's on my own rebec, but he didn't. Instead, he'd carved the fisher bird. But then he'd also carved the blackbird. I remember looking at my father and wondering. *Blackbirds are your friends*, Johnny had told me. Did my father know this, too?

The young man rubbed his thumb over the rebec's blackbird tailpiece, looking at it intently, as if something bad would happen to him if he were to look away. As if somehow the blackbird were a lifeline someone had thrown to him in the sea, and he had to hold onto it or drown. "Your father was a fine maker," said the young man slowly. His voice had dropped low.

I loved him then for saying so. Our father had carved the rebec bowl out of a single piece of wood. I was afraid I would never play the rebec again, after Johnny left, because our father said he'd make me one and then could never find the right piece of wood. But one day, just as spring was turning all the trees to delicate green furred things, he brought back a blackened piece from the pear tree blasted by lightning at the beginning of the forest. Under his clever hands, the grain of the wood appeared, the blackened ruined part was pared away, and the instrument shaped. The last work he did on my rebec was the carving of the blackbird.

Old Cwen was bending over the young man's shoulder for a better look. She shuddered and stepped back. "A bird of ill omen," she said.

"No, goodwife," he told her. "The blackbird is a good bird."

I looked at them both doubtfully. Johnny had said so, but then I remembered the blackbirds in the meadow, and the bodies of my family.

"They keep holding up these new gods for us to worship, but many of us remember the true gods and their ministers and minions. The blackbird is a good creature, the harbinger of the Child of Earth," the young man told Old Cwen.

Old Cwen was backing away and shaking her head no. "They are dangerous. Birds of death."

What she said made me shudder. But something else the young man said left me puzzled. I glanced over at him. My father had carved my own Child's bird on my rebec, but he'd also carved the Earth Child's. As I thought about this, I had one of those experiences that come on me, the moment my second sense opens to me. How can I explain it to you, Jillie, especially if this kind of thing doesn't happen to you? It's as if a deep well gapes suddenly at my feet and I'm staring an eternity into it. It feels like falling. *Something about the blackbirds...*

"So you'll follow our advice?" The leader was speaking again and leaning toward me. Then he stopped and looked at me, his forehead furrowed in concern. They all stared at me.

I shook myself, coming back to the here and now.

"You'll stay with Old Cwen and become her apprentice? You'll not try to run to the temple and claim sanctuary?" he said to me after a moment.

I thought hard. I wasn't sure how or why, but something was telling me these people did not mean me harm. They wanted to help me. "Yes, if Old Cwen will let me," I said finally, looking to her for confirmation or rejection. She beamed back at me.

"That's best. That's a bargain, then." The leader held out his hand, and I took it. His big hand enfolded my own. Tears pricked the insides of my eyelids as I thought of our father's hands.

One of the others, the woman who had given me comfort earlier, came to stand beside me. She put her hand on my head and intoned something in a low voice. I couldn't quite make out the words. Something about the Children. While she was doing this, the others dropped their gaze. I knew she was praying, probably to the Child of Earth, since the young man had mentioned Her. But whoever she was praying to, the woman was clearly praying for and about me. It was clear she meant me well.

They all got up to leave. Before they did, the leader turned to me. "You have a gift. I'd like to see you cultivate it." Those were Johnny's words, I realized. Almost the same words. I looked up into the leader's face. Almost the same eyes.

The young man spoke then, turning my attention away from their leader. "I will take your rebec to mend it. I'll bring it back to you in three days, maybe sooner. Do you trust me to do that?"

I handed it to him wordlessly, even while something twisted inside me.

He saw that. "I'll keep it safe. I promise. I promise you will see it again, and soon."

I couldn't trust myself to speak, so I just nodded. It was my last link to all of you, my lost family. My only link. But this young man was a person you didn't say no to. I could see that right away.

He looked around at the others. "Hear my promise to this child. If I fail to bring it back to her, all of you have heard and will hold me accountable." He turned back to me. "What do they call you?"

"Mirin. Mirin Far-meadow."

There was a pause. All of them exchanged looks. The young man was speaking again. "I promise Mirin Far-meadow this: I will mend her rebec and bring it back to her. All of you have heard this promise."

The six of them all nodded at me, as if this were the most solemn vow in the Sceptered Isle, and not just an offhand way to placate a young girl.

I wasn't sure how to respond, so I simply dropped them a curtsey.

Then they filed out of the house into the bright afternoon light of early harvest-tide.

But the leader stepped back into the house again.

"Mirin Far-meadow, I have one more request."

"Yes, sir?"

"Don't sing your song to anyone but us and Old Cwen. This is confusing to hear, I know. But if you sing your song and the wrong person hears it, you will put yourself in danger."

I could tell my mouth was gaping open.

"You will put us in danger, too, and Old Cwen. Do you understand?"

"No, sir, I don't. But I promise not to sing it."

He smiled at me then, and that smile showed me why he was the leader of these people, whoever they were. It was a smile to inspire love and loyalty.

"But you can sing it to me, child," said Old Cwen, when they had gone.

After our supper that night, and before I climbed up to the loft to sleep, I did.

*Two, two, the long-lost boys, clothed all in green oh*, I sang.

"And now go to sleep. I doubt you'll ever get enough sleep, worn out as you are."

In time, though, under the care of Old Cwen, I grew well-fed and well-rested. And I had my rebec back.

As promised, three days later the young man returned to the house and handed me the mended rebec and the bow he had let me use. Then he whisked away before I could even thank him.

*I'll sing you one oh*, I played and sang. *One is one and all alone and evermore shall be so.*

But I didn't feel all alone any longer.

# Chapter Six

# Wicked Little Charm

I was content. Content in the everyday things, anyhow. The group of people who had visited me were right. The longer I lived in the market town, the more I realized how foolish it would be to go to the temple of the Lady Goddess for sanctuary or for help finding you, Jillie. I knew Goodwife Cailin meant well, but she was wrong about those priests. They wouldn't have cared about some beggarly orphan with a lost sister. They would have sent me packing, and the Lady knows what would have become of me.

But Old Cwen actually cared about me, and I cared about her.

Under the contentment, though, there were things that were not so easy for me to forget and shake off. My lost family. The new and unfamiliar surroundings. The feeling that, although I was a stranger here, a danger waited for me, even deeper than the danger someone would recognize me. And the rage underlying it all, especially the rage about you, Jillie. About what had happened to you. Some of my rage transferred itself to the mysterious group that had visited me. These people were sure you were dead.

It's hard to explain to you how this made me feel. I was sad, of course. But I was angry, too. I had known deep inside that I was to look for you, and now those feelings had no place to go. They were stuck inside me.

I know the people who had visited me meant me well. But they also made me uneasy, especially the younger man. He had done a kindly act for me, mending my rebec, and it seemed as though taking on the task was somehow deeply moving to him. Yet whenever I met his eye, his gaze was hostile, even suspicious. I didn't know what that meant.

Mostly, though, as the year wheeled into winter and then spring, if I glimpsed one of them about town, any of them, not just this one young man, they didn't acknowledge they even knew me. I had a strong feeling they were keeping out of my way. Who were they? I tried not to think about it. The few questions I had asked Old Cwen about them met with evasion and silence, so I stopped asking them.

But they knew something about the deaths of my family. And they knew something about me that I didn't know myself. These feelings unsettled me.

Old Cwen kept me too busy to worry about these matters much. I had promised to be her apprentice with no idea what her business was. I discovered soon enough that she was a healer, and very well-respected. My tasks were easy. I went out every day through the market town's wicket gate with my collection bag. I made myself new snares, too. I scoured the nearby woods and streams for the herbs and plants and sometimes animals Old Cwen needed to concoct her cures. Our mother had already taught me about many of the herbs Old Cwen wanted. This was easy work, if a bit awkward, since I had to wear the shapeless brown kirtle as well as an overdress and headcloth, and a hooded cloak in cold weather.

As I wandered the woods, I looked out for blackbirds. I'd see them here and there, but they never paid me any mind. They just acted like ordinary birds. After a while, I stopped trying to spot them. If they were my friends, they were keeping quiet about it.

Every day, when my collections were done, I would go back in through the wicket. I would proudly show my bit of parchment. It identified me, in the beadle's own hand, as Lynet 'Prentice, Kinswoman to Old Cwen the Healer. The leader of the group of people who had visited me suggested that to Old Cwen. "It would be a good idea to call her something else. Just in case anyone here has heard about her flight from her village."

Old Cwen picked out the name Lynet. It seemed to mean something to her. She went to the beadle to get the parchment for me that would allow me to come and go at will.

I tried to become Lynet. I tried to forget I was really Mirin. Old Cwen and I agreed it would be far safer for me (and, I suspected, for her as well) if she called me only Lynet.

One matter worried me. I finally gathered the courage to ask Old Cwen about it. "What if I see Aina?" At her blank look, I prompted, "The woman whose cloak I took?" The words came out of me slowly. I said "took," not "stole." I didn't want to remind Old Cwen that I was only a dirty sneak-thief.

"Oh, child," Old Cwen said, taking my hand. Her eyes were kind. "Has this been worrying at you and troubling you?"

I nodded yes.

"Don't be afraid, not a bit," she told me. "It's getting on to summer now, and she hasn't seen you for many seasons. You look healthy and strong. Not like that draggle-tail waif Mistress Aina caught by the ear and screamed at. She'll never recognize you."

I felt more and more like Lynet, less and less like Mirin. Sometimes that gnawed at me. It seemed as if I were leaving my family far behind me. It seemed as if I, too, were somehow complicit in your deaths. I know that doesn't sound reasonable, but that's how I began feeling. Sometimes, when I was alone in the woods and knew no one was by to hear, I screamed until my throat was raw, and I vowed revenge, vowed it aloud. Sometimes I made this vow to the Lady Goddess, and sometimes, hesitantly, to the Children. Sometimes I made the vow to no god at all, just to myself.

I went further. There are certain herbs in the forest that are evil to their roots. Everyone knows of these; no one talks about them. But only a few know how to use them. I'd never thought of them at all. Something inside me said, cold and vicious, *You know how.*

These herbs are hard to find. Whenever I was out and about in the forest, I had my eye out for them. After a few turnings of the moon, I had collected enough of these herbs to concoct a rough charm with them. I knew that on certain nights when the moon was in a certain place in the sky, I could go into the forest and burn this charm. I could say a name, and ill would befall that person. Somehow I knew these things.

One late summer day when Old Cwen was out attending to a dying woman, I took the herbs from the place in the loft where I'd hidden them. I stole to her workbench and put hands on her potion-making implements, an act strictly forbidden me unless she herself was there.

I had enough herbs for one charm, and I made it. As if the Dark Ones were after me, I cleaned up the mess I'd made. I opened the window and swatted at the fumes with my apron, clearing them out of the longhouse, and I burned thyme to mask the vile smell. Then I whisked up to the loft with my charm. When Old Cwen came back that evening, I kept sneaking anxious looks at her, but I saw she was none the wiser.

Now it was only a matter of waiting for the moon, and I'd use the charm. The person I fixed on was that dark leader of the soldiers. I really didn't know how responsible he was for my family's deaths. But my second sense told me he was.

This was witchery for sure.

In the end, I couldn't do it.

There's a price to be paid, for witchery. I'm not talking about stoning, which is what you're probably thinking. That only happens if you get caught. I'm talking about how, every time you do something like this, you lose a piece of yourself, something you really value about yourself. It might be I'd have to trade away kindness. Maybe love. Before you think of me as some virtuous person unwilling to make such a trade, I'll confess to you what stopped me, and then you won't think me so very virtuous. My second sense told me what I'd have to trade away. After all that effort, I lay in the furs in my loft, night after night, and my second sense taunted me. *You'll have to trade away your music.* So I felt trapped, paying the price for my dark temptations.

That alone filled me with guilt and fury.

Still, every time I looked at my wicked little bundle of herbs, the unbidden sight of Johnny rose before my inward eye. *You can use your gifts for good or ill,* he had told me. He had told me he knew I'd use my gifts for good.

I had to be content with that. You'd think, if I had well and truly learned my lesson, I would have destroyed that charm. But I didn't. If you were to go to Old Cwen's house right now, this very day, and search in the place in the loft where I'd tell you to look, you'd find the charm. Anyone can find it. Anyone can use it. This is a black mark against me, and the Children know, I'll have to come to account for it some day. But I could never bring myself to destroy the charm, even though I knew I should.

In spite of these dark thoughts, I was content in the everyday matters. I'd rise early. Each day in late morning, I'd bring the contents of my bag back to Old Cwen. She and I would pound and mix and simmer and decant the potions she made into small leathern bottles and wooden boxes she took down to the square on market day to sell to the townspeople and others who came from all around to get her cures. These were good potions, not wicked. I was proud. I served a famous healer. In the early afternoons, she went about visiting and comforting the sick. Then, after my collecting the next morning, feverfew, comfrey, buckthorn and burdock, as well as many others, we'd go back again to our compounding table. Our round of activity rarely varied, broken only when she was called out to minister to some suffering woman in the throes of labor.

Old Cwen was not a midwife, so our waking and sleeping were not disturbed at all times of the day and night by distraught husbands roaring outside our windows to come quick.

But in bad cases, the midwives of the town would call Old Cwen to come to them and consult with them. She had potions for the soothing of pain, potions to hasten labor, potions for ailing infants who would not breathe or feed, potions to help the mother make more milk, potions for the fevers of mother and child that sometimes followed even successful births, and potions for desperate cases when the mother was dying. These potions would ease her out of this world across the border into the Land of the Dead.

I was proud of Old Cwen, proud to be known as her apprentice.

"You have a gift for this work," she told me. Short-handed, she had allowed me to assist her in a difficult case, a man whose skull was stove in by falling masonry. Old Cwen and I, using tools she had devised, prised the skull pieces up so his brain could breathe. That's what Old Cwen said. It needed to breathe. Indeed, we could spy it in there, throbbing away. He got better, and we became known as miracle workers. Then he sickened and died, but Old Cwen said we had done what we could. His relatives thought so, too. They paid our fee, and they praised us to their neighbors. His death was only, they said, the will of the Lady Goddess. No mere humans could thwart that, but they saw how hard we tried and how successful we were, if only She had not decreed otherwise. Our reputation spread.

Occasionally the leader of the group of people who had visited me came by to talk to Old Cwen. He happened by one early morning shortly after this incident. I was eagerly describing it to him when I saw Old Cwen frowning at me.

"You should be getting your bag and implements and out into the forest by now, girl," she said.

Crestfallen, I did as I was told. As I was heading out the door, I was also listening. The leader was speaking to Old Cwen in an undertone. I fumbled with my bag at the doorsill so I could hear more.

"You shouldn't be drawing so much attention to yourself," he told her.

"I know it, sir. I'm proud of my skills and all, that's the thing."

"And you should be. But you know what could happen if—" He looked up, looked over at me and smiled. "Headed out to gather herbs, are you?" he said to me. There was a chill underneath his smile. I nodded and hurried about my business.

Not many days afterward, I returned from the morning's gathering to find the entire group of them huddled about Old Cwen's fire. She turned her face to me as I entered. She looked stricken.

The leader rose as I came through the door with my morning's gleanings. "Put down your bag, Lynet," he said, calling me by my false name. "Come here to us. We have something to tell you."

My heart dropped into my shoes.

It was something I had done. I knew it. I must have done something bad. They all looked very grave.

I approached them. I had no choice. I really wanted to turn and run.

"Don't be afraid. You've done nothing wrong."

The leader could read my mind. That frightened me even more.

"Lynet, where is your rebec?"

"In the loft, sir."

"Get it, please."

Never thinking once of disobeying him, I climbed up and took it down from its peg, and the bow with it. I would have liked to carry it as I went about my herb gathering, but too many things could happen to it. Now that I had it back, I was very protective of it. I could trip over a thick root and smash it. It could fall in the river and get wet again. So I usually left it on its peg during the day.

I came slowly down the ladder with it slung by its strap around my neck.

"Come here to us and play for us."

I played and sang. I can't remember what. Some innocuous tune I had heard about town.

"That's a good repair job, Wat," said the leader to the younger man, the one who had fixed my rebec. "Sounds very good."

The young man, whose name I now knew as Wat, nodded his thanks. He looked amused. The smile lit up his face. They were all trying to hide their smiles.

"Nine Spheres," said the leader. They all laughed a little, the leader too, shaking his head and making a grimace. I didn't know then what they were laughing about. Later I figured it out. They were laughing at their leader for making a mistake, for violating one of his own strictest rules: no names in the presence of outsiders. He had just revealed Wat's name to me, and I was an outsider to their circle. He held up his hand and the others stifled their laughter behind their hands. "Never mind," he said. "It won't matter." Then he turned back to me. "Lynet," he began. Then he looked over at Old Cwen. They exchanged a look full of meaning, a look I didn't know how to interpret.

The leader looked down at his feet and then back up at me. He started again. "Mirin, you have done everything we asked. You've helped Old Cwen faithfully. She tells me you're a good worker, and that you even have the talent to make a good healer some-day. So you're no sham apprentice. You're the real thing."

I glowed under this praise.

"But you are wasted here."

Now my face fell. What did he mean, wasted.

"Don't take her from me, sir," Old Cwen burst out. "She's be-come like a daughter to me."

"We all have to make sacrifices," he said, and she sat down heavily on a stool at the long shelf where she compounded her potions. She bent over her work, but I saw her brush away a tear. Now I was becoming seriously frightened. They were going to take me away from Old Cwen. How could I bear it, another sep-aration?

The leader left the fire and went to Old Cwen. He put a hand on her shoulder. "I know how much you are missing your Keelie." His voice was kind. I saw another tear drop from her face onto her apron. "And I know you're missing—" He stopped abruptly.

Then he turned to the rest of us and repeated what he had said: "We all have to make sacrifices. And now, under these new circumstances—"

*Why?* I was thinking. *Why do I have to make sacrifices? Haven't I sacrificed?* My home, my family. *What new circumstances?*

Now he approached me directly. "You have the talents for a healer, Old Cwen tells me. But you have another talent. This." He pointed to the rebec. "We need this talent of yours right now."

"For what?" I was baffled. "And besides," I said, surprising myself with my vehemence. "I am not that good at playing the rebec. I'm not as good as Johnny the Traveler."

"No. But no one is as good as he was."

I froze. *As he was.* That's what the leader said. As if Johnny the Traveler were dead and gone. As if he were in the past.

"You're his best apprentice, though. The best we've heard."

One of the others, a man who hadn't said much, a man standing always beside the leader, nodded at me. "Even when your instrument was cracked and damaged by the water, we could hear it," he said in his grave, gravelly voice. His dark intense eyes under his straight brows were encouraging and kind.

They all looked at me, and at my rebec.

I stared down at it. I concentrated on it hard, to keep from crying. I looked and looked at the blackbird my father had carved there. The Earth Child's harbinger, not the bird of ill-omen and death.

"You must be very confused," the leader said to me.

"Yes," I said.

"We do things the authorities don't like. And we need to exchange messages among ourselves about these things. That's what Johnny the Traveler did for us."

*These people are smugglers,* I thought. I'd heard about people like this. A strange fury rose inside me. "Johnny the Traveler was a bad man? No, he wasn't. He was my teacher. He was my father's friend." I saw then that I too was speaking of Johnny the Traveler as someone who had faded away into the past.

"Johnny the Traveler was a very good man," said the leader. "And so was your father. Both of them collected information for us. That's why your family was killed."

"No. No," I said. I ran to Old Cwen and threw myself into her arms. She hugged me to her hard. I was horrified at what the leader had just said, that our father really was a criminal and maybe deserved being hunted down, but I also knew I was about to be taken away from Old Cwen. I'm ashamed to tell you now, Jillie. That was my overriding fear, in the moment. I looked up into Old Cwen's face. "Don't let them take me away from you."

She smoothed my hair. "Now, Mirin," she said to me. "These people are your friends. They are your father's friends. They're here to protect you, and they've done that. But now. Now they need you." I could see in her eyes how much she didn't want to be saying those words.

"Why should I do what they need?" I twisted from Old Cwen's arms and turned to the others. "Why should I do what you tell me to do?"

The leader had gone back to the fire now. He sat with his hand on his chin, his eyes brooding. "Too many times," he said.

The other older man nodded. "Somehow, they know."

I looked from one of them to the other, confused. Then something strange stirred inside me, some voice spoke. My second sense. *Someone is betraying them.*

One of the others, a woman whom I had barely noticed, a woman who always seemed set apart from the others, stepped forward. Her words jarred me out of my thoughts. "You see?" she said to the leader, jutting her chin at me. "This is not going to work. She's too young, and now. Now she knows things she shouldn't know." Her darkly beautiful face was ruthless in the flickering firelight. Her hand moved to her belt, and when she did that, I saw the gleam of metal underneath her cloak. I don't know how I knew, but I knew she had a knife there. I knew then I was in danger. She went on, her eyes hard. "What do we really know about her, after all?"

I could see the leader was considering this young woman's words, but I could see he too had noticed what she was doing with her hand. He gave her a small shake of the head no.

"She's right to ask that question," the younger man said to the leader quietly. The exotic young woman went over to stand beside him and put a hand on his arm.

Old Cwen clutched at me and looked up at the leader. "No. Don't do this," she said to him. "I won't let you."

"You don't have anything to do with it," he said, and his voice was ice. "Be still, woman. This is a matter for us to decide."

The younger man, the one called Wat, moved over to the fire and stood staring into it, as if he were trying to work something out. Trying to decide about something. Now he turned to face the young woman who had spoken so passionately about me. "I hear what you're saying," he told her. "But this girl has a talent that doesn't come along very often. I have to think about that. We all should." Her whole demeanor toward him changed at these words. Ignoring the hard glint in her eyes, he stepped over to the leader and nodded toward me. "I agree to it. I'll take the responsibility for her. Leave her to me."

He and the leader exchanged a long look.

"You're sure?" the leader asked him. "After what happened last time? Everything will fall to you, after all. I won't force you to do this."

"I'll see that she knows what to do." The younger man glanced over at me. "And does it."

After a moment, the older man, the leader, nodded.

"And if she doesn't?" This was the ruthless woman.

"Leave that to me," said the younger man, the one called Wat.

The ruthless woman started forward, as if she were about to grab him by the cloak, when the leader held up his hand. She stopped.

"Leave that to Wat," said the leader.

"And if she doesn't?" repeated the woman.

"Then you'll let me deal with the consequences."

"Very well, then." She compressed her mouth into a thin line.

"I know you don't like it, Eris. But it's my decision." At her outraged look, he said to her, "Listen, Eris, it's decided now. She's one of us. She'll know all our names."

"And betray us." Eris practically spat this out.

Betray them? They were thinking I was the betrayer. I had been standing a little apart from them, watching as they decided my fate. I felt a rush of fear and anger.

"I'm no betrayer," I said, maybe a bit too loud, for they all looked around at the window and the door, and Old Cwen hastened to pull them shut. I was thinking then of the eighth verse of Johnny's song. It rang in my head and told me *danger*.

*I'll sing you eight, oh.*
*What is your eight, oh?*
*Eight for the foul betrayers.*
*Eight for the foul betrayers.*

The leader's eyes were serious. "I don't think you are a betrayer, Mirin. And now you will meet us all. I am Avery." He considered me carefully as he told me this.

I looked back at him, uncertain, confused. I was supposed to say something, to know something, but what?

He smiled and looked around at the others. "You see?" he said. I had no idea what he meant. "Just a young girl from a small village," he said to the others. "It's quiet in that village of hers. Protected. No one knows anything of the wider world there. Dru knew what he was doing, when he brought them there."

With a jolt, Jillie, I realized he was talking about our father, Drustan.

He turned back to me. "I knew your father well. You remind me quite a bit of him."

"Doesn't she, though?" That was Wat. But he looked troubled.

"I am Torrin," said the woman who was so kind to me at our first meeting. She smiled. "Oh, and I can see a lot of her mother in her, too. And hear her mother's beautiful voice."

"You knew my parents?" I was bewildered.

"Conal," said the other man in the group, the older quiet one. He extended a calloused hand and I took it.

"Lorel." This was the woman who hadn't spoken yet. As I found out later, she never said much. Only acted.

"Eris. You know that already." This was the woman, younger than any of the others except, or so it seemed to me, for Wat. Eris, the woman who opposed me joining them. I stared back at her, fascinated. She looked like no one I had ever seen before— high-planed cheekbones, honey skin, almond dark eyes. The hostile gaze she returned to me told me plainly: *if it were up to me, I'd have you killed, betrayer. I'd kill you myself.*

"And I am Wat, your new master," said Wat, throwing the woman Eris a warning look. "You're bound to me," he told me.

I looked at him skeptically. I saw what I'd seen before. He was not much older than a boy himself. "Do we go to the beadle and seal it?" *I'll have to be brave,* I thought to myself, *if that's what I have to do.*

"No, that's not our way, but you are, just the same."

*Bound,* I thought. *I'm just a poor bound girl now.*

"Gather your things together and say good-bye to Old Cwen," he told me. "We'll be traveling." I had been thinking of him kindly, because he was the one who had repaired my rebec, but now he gave me that cold look of his, so cold I shuddered. I ran to Old Cwen and put my arms as far around her ample figure as I could reach them.

"What am I supposed to say happened to Lynet, then?" she said over my head to them. Now she didn't sound tearful any longer. She sounded angry.

"You'll think of something," the leader, the man named Avery, told her.

"Will she be all right?" It was Eris again, turning to the others. She meant Old Cwen.

"Yes, Mistress Eris, I'll be fine, and you know that. But I don't have to like it," said Old Cwen.

"It's settled, then. Do your master's bidding now, Mirin," said Avery.

"Eris—" Wat began, reaching out to her.

Eris spurned him angrily, but Avery cut in before either of them could say anything.

"Eris," Avery said, "I'll see you outside for a moment. Wat has work to do here." He waved the others away. They quietly left Old Cwen's house. Through the front window, I saw the rest of them heading off in different directions. Avery took Eris by the elbow and steered her outside. Only Old Cwen, Wat, and I remained. Wat stood looking after Eris, his eyes bleak.

"You heard your master, Lynet. Get your things. I mean Mirin," said Old Cwen. Then she threw her apron over her head and ran into the back cubby where she slept, and slammed the flimsy door after her.

Wat and I stood and listened to her sobbing for a moment.

"It's a testimony to you, Mirin, that Old Cwen thinks of you so fondly," said Wat. "I'm sure you won't disappoint me in the performance of your duties." He gave me a stiff smile that didn't reach his eyes.

I curtsied to him, silently. And, I know, sullenly. Surely he could see that. But he said nothing, merely waited. *What duties?* I wanted to ask him, but I saw the iron in him, so I scurried to the other end of the longhouse and up the ladder. I gathered to-gether the very few things I owned. There was a basket I had woven myself, and a wash cloth Old Cwen had given me, and a yellow festival day scarf she had embroidered for me with her own hands. There was the new bag Old Cwen had helped me make for my rebec and bow, and she had shown me how to em-broider daisies around the mouth. I had wanted to embroider a blackbird on it, with a bright, knowing eye, but that was beyond my skills. She was going to teach me, despite her misgivings about the bird, and now she never would.

I looked around at the dim loft that, for close on a year, had become so dear to me, and I rubbed my face against the furs. I glanced over at the place where extra leather thongs bound the slats of the platform to the poles of the loft and reinforced it, the place where I had tucked my charm. I could take the charm with me. I could use it, if these people put me in danger. But some-thing inside me said, *Leave it.* So I turned toward the ladder. It was time to go.

I hesitated. *We'll be traveling,* this new master of mine said. *Maybe this will be an opportunity,* I thought now. *Maybe I'll be able to search for you, Jillie.*

But I came down the ladder more slowly than I had gone up. Leaving Old Cwen meant leaving my new-found feelings of se-curity, leaving a kind of family.

Wat stood at the door, holding my rebec out to me by its strap. He was beginning to look annoyed.

I took the rebec from him, tucked it and the bow into their bag, and slung that over my shoulder. I put the other things in the basket.

The door to Old Cwen's cubby burst open again and she herself burst out. We hugged again, tightly. "Take care of yourself, Lynet, my little kinswoman, my best apprentice," she whispered to me. She stood back as Wat opened the door, motioning to me. "And you," she said to him. "You, young Master Wat. Treat my Lynet well. If she does ill, don't beat her. Promise me you won't."

Wat just smiled at her, a tight little smile I was soon to know all too well. "Until next time, Old Cwen."

"Here, child," she said, and thrust a small bundle at me. "Put that in your basket. A few potions you may need."

I took them from her and leaned down to kiss her whiskery cheek. I'm not very tall, and I've grown since then, but Old Cwen was as round and short and stout as an apple. Over her shoulder, I noticed Wat's impatience growing with every moment. I hurried to follow him out the door.

It was a long time before I saw Old Cwen again, and I never returned to her house. I never searched for my charm tucked into the thongs in her loft. But there was a part of her I carried with me always.

# About a Boy

I was in the box bed in the wagon, and we were jolting down the rough roads to wherever Wat had decided we must go next. I huddled into the furs. It was stifling and airless inside that box, and the jolting and jostling made me feel a little sick. Up on the wagon seat, Wat was whistling a flat kind of tune. Every so often, he'd call out to our ox, Millicent.

I thought of Millicent not as Wat's ox now, but as our ox. Wat was my master, and I was bound to serve him, even though I didn't have the mark. He told me we were traveling so far away from my village that I didn't need a false name. So I was Mirin again. "No one will recognize you, and no one will connect you to that Mirin wanted by the crown in some far-away hamlet," he said. "But just to be safe, we won't use your last name. If anyone asks, tell them you are an orphan and have no surname. The fewer names and identities to remember, the safer," he added.

This emphasis of theirs on being safe, and on having many identities. It had gradually become clear to me. These people weren't the smugglers I'd taken them for at first. It was worse, Jillie. They were rebels against the king.

I'd heard all my life about this sort of folk. In childhood games the villains were always the rebels, and they hid, and we chased them and beat them with willow switches when we found them. Then the chasers became the chased. I had taken my turn at playing a rebel all my childhood. But to be one? That was hard.

Even harder was to realize that our parents had been among these rebels—our father for certain. Our mother I wasn't so sure about, but she must have gone along with it. My most vivid memory of them both was the way their faces looked in the flickering firelight, how they gazed with love at each other. They couldn't have been at odds over a matter so important.

And Johnny the Traveler was one of the most famous rebels of all. His music allowed him entry to places none of the other rebels could get to. Palaces. Forts. Walled towns. Johnny, my teacher. I called up the deep compassion in his face. Not a man for killing and sneaking. Nor our father or mother. As I lay in the wagon box bed and thought over these matters, my eyes burned with anguish and rage. My entire family were dead because they had rebelled against the king, and Johnny the Traveler was dead, too.

Then I thought about you. You were no rebel. Nor I. We were just children. How could we know about such things? But now I did, and now I believed you were dead. *You must be*, I told myself. Avery and the others had been sure, and later, when I asked Wat about it, he'd confirmed it. "They took your sister away, but she was too badly injured. She died," he said. He didn't sugar-coat it the way rich people sugar their almonds and confits. I didn't ask him any more after that.

As I lay in the wagon box bed, thinking these things over, I realized we were slowing.

"We're coming into Withiel," Wat called down to me. "Start getting ready."

Wat and I were performers. He juggled and did acrobatics to announce our presence. Then I sang and played my rebec. That's why these rebels needed me. Wat needed a partner. Something had happened to his previous partner, so I was the musical part of the act now, the one people came to hear play and sing.

Withiel, as I knew by now, was the biggest town in the Hundred, situated at the fork where two big rivers joined. They were called the Dourdin and the Dourkam. Withiel was one of our best places to perform. It attracted many travelers and many who came to do business at its big markets. That meant more coin for us.

Inside the box, I began burrowing among my things for my costume. It was pretty. It was the only pretty thing I had in a life that had turned ugly again. My costume was a long yellow close-fitting kirtle. The hem was a red band with yellow and green flowers and birds embroidered on it. I loved it. I wore a white hood that framed my face as if I were a picture in a rich man's house. I didn't wear a headcloth, as the Lady Goddess bids women to do, so my long wavy hair curled free of the hood. And

I had red leathern slippers with pointed toes that curled up. All of these articles of clothing had seen a lot of wear, but they were lovely. Someone had once paid a lot of coin for them. I knew that whatever we took in from our performances went to Avery, but he let Wat have some of the take to buy supplies for us. Wat must have used a fair bit of it for this costume, although, knowing what I now knew, I found this hard to believe. We barely had enough to eat.

"Are you decent?" Wat called down.

"Yes," I said, stepping out of the wagon box bed and up onto the wagon seat, being careful not to rip my kirtle. The skirt was narrow.

"Take the lines, then."

I did. Our ox, Millicent, was a mild and lovely animal. She sensed the change in the tension on the lines threaded through the ring in her nose, and tossed her big head, but she stepped on as before. She never gave me any trouble when it was my turn to steer her down the lanes.

Wat jumped down into the box bed and closed the door. Soon he was back on the seat beside me, dressed all in green, his juggling balls in a cloth bag at his side. I offered him the lines again but he shook his head no.

"You're doing well. Keep going. See the spot down there, past that little stand of trees? Turn in there."

So I did. Millicent knew her way. She stopped under the trees even before I pulled back on the lines. Wat swung off the seat and reached up a hand to help me down.

From the trees I could see the palisade wall of the town.

"Will they let us enter?" I asked. Some towns would; others made us perform outside. This was the biggest town we played to. Depending on the insecurities of the moment, sometimes we were waved right in, and other times we had to perform outside.

Wat was a performer, all right. While he pretended to be a vagabond juggler, he collected information and brought it back to Avery.

And I? I was the bait.

"Looks like we'll have to set up right here," said Wat, squinting at the gates. "I'll give our favors to the post-guards, and they'll see them distributed. Then we just wait. The people will start to gather soon after." He was right. He handed over a small leather bag of gilded acorns to the guards, and they handed them out to those coming and going through the gates. People in Withiel, and in a number of our regular venues, knew that was the signal that we were in the area, and then they'd hurry to our performances.

As soon as they realized we were outside Withiel, that's what they did. As word spread, the people of the town began milling around our wagon, laughing and clapping. By then Wat had handed me up on top of the wagon, right on top of the box bed built into the wagon's body. That was our stage. Wat did a few backflips and vaulted up onto the stage with me. He built up excitement with his acrobatics and his juggling tricks. He was very good at them. The members of the audience gazed up in awe.

"And now," he announced, "the lady will play and sing for you." He boomed this out in a commanding voice, nothing like his actual voice at all, which is deceptively quiet.

That was my cue. He stepped back, and I stepped forward to the edge of the stage. I already had my rebec ready. I tucked it against me, took up the bow, and began by playing a jolly tune that had the audience clapping along. Then I began to sing. By now I knew all the most popular songs. "Three Sparrows Flew Over Hill and Dale." "Lord Roger and Lowly Alison." That one was bawdy. My mother would have forbidden me to sing it. "O Come to Me and Tell Me All Your Love." That one made the maidens swoon and inch their hands closer to the young men they favored.

I won't deny it. I loved these performances. In life, I might be a poor bound girl or maybe even a stolen girl, an orphan, thin and not very pretty. But on the stage, I was larger than life. I was radiant, and so these people of the town loved me. On stage, something happened to me. The gods caught me up and sang through me. I know you think I'm a little crazy for saying so, but that's how it felt.

Here's a confession I'll make to you. Wat made me stuff wads of cloth into the top of my kirtle so it would look like I had breasts. I had none, none anyone would have noticed. And he made me rouge my cheeks and lips with a special cream. I looked older. I looked (if you didn't look closely) beautiful, and somehow, the aura about me shone.

By now I knew he and the others in their group were right about one thing. My voice was enticing. And so was my playing. Beyond enticing. I know you think I'm immodest for saying so. But it's the truth. "You're a natural," Wat told me. "Put those gifts to use." Only Johnny had known the real truth of it, though, where my gifts had come from. They came from the Children and flowed directly back to Them. I knew it was so, though not, just then, what that meant.

You might be wondering what Wat had done before I came along. At first I supposed he roamed the countryside juggling and somersaulting by himself. Later I found out he had had another partner, a musician like me, but a man. Then this partner had died. Had been taken by the soldiers and killed. I found this out in a roundabout way. Wat wouldn't talk about it. He kept acquiring partners, and they never turned out. After the first one died, he'd very briefly had one more partner, the woman whose clothing I now wore. Their partnership hadn't worked out, either. The longer Wat and I worked together, the more I didn't want to know what had happened to her, that unknown woman, and how she'd gotten such beautiful clothes.

The longer Wat and I worked together, the more I wondered what would happen to me if he decided our own partnership wasn't working out.

This day, the townspeople were restless for more. "Play us a tune to dance to, lass!" one called up to me. Another joined in, and another. I looked over at Wat.

He hopped off the wagon stage and upended his fanciful hat with the little bells on it, passing it around. He had done that at the beginning of our performance, and had poured the coin into a special strongbox built into the wagon. Now he passed his hat again. Again, it came back filled with coppers, and even a silver penny or two. He grinned up at me. "These good people want to dance!" he cried out.

Wat never grins like that, and his voice is never this jolly loud voice he uses for the performances. But he turned into a different person when he became Kenning the Juggler ("Kenning the Juggler and His Merry Musicians" read the sign on the side of our wagon, wreathed in painted oak leaves and acorns). I turned into a different person too. I didn't have a stage name like his, and I was only one musician, not the many advertised by our sign, but no one ever complained. ("You're just that good," Wat told me once, and that made me glow with pride).

Now I struck up a lively tune, and another, and another, as the townspeople danced about the wagon, kicking their heels high and swaying, and twirling their partners around and around until they were dizzy and lay laughing in the grass.

The horn blew; last call for anyone wanting to go through Withiel's wicket-gate into the town before it grew dark. Still laughing, calling up to us and to each other, many arm-in-arm, the people drifted away and back into the town.

"A good take," Wat was telling me when we realized a man was standing at the foot of the wagon stage and looking up at me.

"Mirin? Could that be little Mirin?"

"No," Wat called down at him. "You're mistaken."

"That's little Mirin, from back home in my village," the man insisted. The horn blew again, and he turned to go before he was shut out of town for the night. Pointing at me, he yelled back, "That's Mirin. You sing as well as your mother did."

I was frozen with fear. "I don't know him," I told Wat.

"He knows you, though." Wat looked grim. "You're sure he's not from your village?"

"My village is small. I know everyone there," I insisted. "I don't know this man."

Wat bit his lip, considering. "Take off your costume. We're going to leave."

With a chill, I realized what Wat thought. The man was an agent of the king. If we didn't act fast, we'd be taken.

I rushed to put on my ordinary kirtle, the same one Old Cwen had given me. Before I was out of the box, Wat was there beside me, stripping off his green leggings and jerkin and pulling on his long trousers and tunic. I turned my back so I wouldn't see.

"Why, what a modest maid you are, Mirin," he said. "Stay in the box." He vaulted onto the wagon seat and backed Millicent into the turn-off, then headed her out toward the road away from town.

I disobeyed Wat and climbed back onto the wagon seat beside him. A thought had struck me. "Wat," I said.

"What is it?" he asked, but I saw he wasn't paying me any attention. His mind was on what might be happening behind us.

I risked angering him. "Wat, suppose that man knows something."

"I'm guessing he does," said Wat, glancing over his shoulder.

"No, but Wat— Suppose he knows something about Jillie."

Wat turned to stare at me. He didn't mince words. "Jillie is dead. You know that."

Before I could make Wat really angry, a confused shouting came to us from back at the Withiel gates. Wat urged Millicent on. But Millicent wasn't built to go fast. Wat's face had gone tense.

"Wat—"

"We'll talk about it later," he said. Then he looked over at me again, and he saw I realized the danger we were in. His expression softened. "Don't worry," he said, "I know this land around here."

I sat silently, but I did worry. All my thoughts about you had fled, Jillie, and now I knew the king's men were coming for us. They were about to take us, maybe kill us, maybe something worse. I could feel myself going pale and shaky. I could see Wat was worried, whatever he was telling me.

"If things get bad, I want you to get back into the box," he said. "I mean it, Mirin." Then, glancing behind him, he said, "Do that now."

I rose to my feet and held on, preparing to clamber over the wagon seat and drop down to the platform behind us.

The wagon swayed and swerved.

"No, hold on. Just hold on," he called out sharply to me over his shoulder. We went jouncing off the road and down a narrow path leading into the woods. But the trees were sparse. If horsemen were coming up behind us, they'd be able to see us easily. They'd be able to catch us.

Brush scraped against the sides of the wagon. Wat steered Millicent off the road over a stony place and straight for a bank of thorn bushes hidden back off the path.

"Protect your face," Wat yelled at me. I threw up my hands just in time. We crashed through the thorn and then I thought for a moment we'd tip over for sure. The wagon angled up and then abruptly down. We bottomed out with a sickening thud, and then we were through the thorns and going down a steep incline. The waning day's last rays of sunshine had caught us in a golden glitter on the roadway. Now suddenly we were heading down a dim tunnel. On both sides, steep banks rose around us. In moments, they were higher than the wagon. Overarching low trees and shrubbery blotted out the twilight. We rode deeper down a submerged darkening green path.

Wat pulled up on the lines, and Millicent obediently plodded to a stop.

He raised his hand. We sat listening. A clatter of hooves sounded from the road above. We heard the sound of men calling out to each other. The hoofbeats stopped. They'd seen where we entered the wood on the narrow track. Now the hoofbeats resumed. A party of horsemen were on us in less time than it took us to draw in breath. But then the hoofbeats faded as the horsemen swept on past us. They had headed down the little path where we'd turned off the main road. And now they were passing right over our heads as we sat silent in the tunnel below them.

"There now," said Wat quietly after the hoofbeats had faded away. "They don't know about this place."

"What is this place?" I said, looking around me in the faint light.

"We'll stay right here," said Wat. "They'll realize they've lost us, and they'll be back past in a while, so no talking." We sat quietly, and just as he'd said, they came pounding back. At the turning onto the main roadway, we could hear them speaking urgently to each other. For one frightening moment, I heard them above us, stirring and poking pike staves into the dense shrubbery over our heads. But now full dark was coming on. After a while, we heard them leaving.

"We'll stay here for the night. In the morning, we'll move on," said Wat, after we could no longer hear the horses. "I don't trust this place in the dark. We could lose a wagon wheel down here if I steer us wrong."

"What is this place?" I asked again.

"This? It's a holloway."

"A holloway."

"That's right. We used to hide down here, me and—we used to hide down here, before, whenever we were in this part of the Hundred," said Wat. "Lucky I remembered where the entrance is."

"What's a holloway?"

"This," said Wat. He gestured around us. I could just make him out in the dark. "Let's get into the box bed. We may as well sleep. That's about all we can do, right now," he said. "Even if the moon comes up, no light gets down here."

So we felt our way into the box bed in the dark. I lay on my back in the furs, looking up into nothing. I couldn't sleep. My heart was thumping in my chest. Wat couldn't either, it seemed. After a while, he said, "A holloway is an old, overgrown trail made long ago, so long ago it has etched itself down into the earth."

"The Old Ones?" I guessed.

"Before the Old Ones."

That silenced me for a moment. People before even the Old Ones had lived here and had made this trail. I could scarcely imagine it. I thought about the steep pathway cut down into the bank, and the overarching foliage. "It's sort of a tunnel," I said.

"Something like that." Wat's voice came out of the dark, and I could tell he was easy now. "The path has worn down so far below the fields that it's a deep gouge in the earth, and the undergrowth and trees have made a kind of roof for it. So yes, you're right. Sort of a tunnel."

"Wat—"

"What is it? Mirin, you need to sleep. We need to sleep," said Wat.

"They know about me," I said.

"Yes, they do," said Wat.

"What will we do?" I was afraid to ask him, because I was afraid of the answer.

"I have a plan," said Wat. I could hear him shifting over on his side, and soon his regular breathing told me he was asleep. He could do that. Under any circumstances at all, he could roll himself into his cloak and fall asleep.

I didn't have that knack. I lay in the dark wondering what Wat's plan might be. I was a liability now. We were hidden deep in the earth where no one could see. What would he do about me?

Or to me?

With that thought to keep me company, I didn't think I'd sleep at all, but somehow eventually I did. When I woke, a twilit green was filtering into the wagon box bed through its slats. Birds were whistling all around. Dawn, then. I struggled to sit up.

Wat was already awake, propped against the side of the box, his knees drawn up.

I stumbled out of the box and down off the wagon to find a place to take care of myself.

When I returned, he was on the wagon seat. He leaned down and gave me a hand up. "We don't want to make a fire down here," he said. "Everything is dry this time of year. It would all go up like a pile of tinder if we did." He reached down into the pouch dangling from his belt and pulled out a hard lump of bread. He handed it to me. I gnawed on it. Then I realized. "What will you eat?"

"I don't need anything right now," he said. "We'd better get on our way." He chirruped to Millicent, and she pulled us through the long cool green tunnel, starred with field flowers, bursting with birdsong. The sun rose higher and filtered down to us in a luminous green haze as we crept down the gouge in the earth, the banks still so high they towered far above us.

"It's beautiful here," I said.

Wat glanced at me sidelong, but he said nothing.

His silence made me even more nervous than before. I stopped talking then. I wasn't sure I could talk. My mouth was dry. I wanted to talk about you, Jillie, but I didn't dare. I wanted to ask Wat how he and the others in the group—the Rising, they called themselves—were so sure you were dead. Could they all just be telling me this so I'd stop hoping and stop looking? Could they be telling me this so I'd be easier to handle and do their bidding? But then I thought of the woman named Torrin, the kind one, and how her eyes had filled with tears when she told me what had happened to you.

We were in that tunnel—the holloway, Wat had called it—for most of the day, and for all that time, I was alone with my thoughts. Thoughts about you, and fears about the intentions of the Rising toward me.

Wat was silent except for an occasional soft call of encouragement to Millicent. When I glanced sidelong at him from time to time, I could see he was preoccupied with some difficult thoughts of his own.

I didn't brood all day long. Sometimes the strange beauty of the holloway distracted me, and I was content simply to gaze around me. I marveled at how far it was taking us, a long gash in the surface of the earth, a subterranean roadway. As the afternoon drew on toward twilight again, I realized Millicent was climbing. Our ascent was gentle, unlike our abrupt descent an entire day ago into the depths of the earth. The last furlong was steep again, but Millicent was strong. She pulled us out under the first stars at a big river.

"The Dourdin," said Wat. "We're down-river a way." When he spoke, I nearly jumped. He'd been silent so long. "We'll camp here for a while," he said. "They won't find our traces, those men back there." He gestured east and north, where the river bent under the trees. It was the way we'd come, but instead of using the roundabout way of the roads, we'd cut across the land using our own hidden highway.

Wat pulled the wagon up near a cleared place where a stone bridge arched over the water.

"The Old Ones built that," Wat told me.

We let ourselves down off the wagon seat and made our way over to the bridge-pier nearest us on the eastern bank of the river. When I put my hand on the stones, they were still warm from the day's heat. So old. Not as old as the holloway, though. I marveled at that.

Steadying ourselves against the abutment of the bridge, we leaned over the river in the gathering dark to drink from the rushing water. I was completely parched. The cold water felt good splashing down the neck of my kirtle as I bent for a drink. I realized then how hungry I was, too. We hadn't eaten, not really, for well over a day.

Without being told, I moved up the riverbank scrounging for twigs and small branches and brought them back to the wagon. Wat made a neat pile of these and lit them with his fire-steel and striking stone, carefully nursing a spark in the char cloth into a flame.

I got my snare from the wagon box bed and pushed into the brushy area beside the river, coming back not too much later with a rabbit for our dinner. I dropped the rabbit by the fire.

The air was getting chill now, even though it was summer. The fire felt good. I reached out my hands to it.

Wat moved away from me to the wagon, and when he returned, he was coming at me with our sharpest knife.

I gasped. I'd been thinking about this in the night, and through most of the day. How he'd handle it. The liability I'd become to him.

Wat smiled, although the smile didn't reach his eyes. "Silly goose. I'm not going to hurt you. Come here." He pulled me into the circle of firelight and turned me around.

In spite of what he had said, I felt the fear rising through my body. He gathered my hair into one hand behind my head and raised the knife.

I flinched away from him and looked around wildly, but he clamped a hand on my shoulder and made me stand still. For a slender man, he was strong.

"You're a goose, you know that, Mirin. Listen, I'm going to cut off your hair."

"No!"

"Yes, so hold still and don't squirm so. I don't want to cut you by mistake." He hacked and hacked and hacked at my hair. It fell about my feet in wisps and waves. I could tell I was about to cry, but I tried to hold it back. Wat didn't like it when I cried. "You must be strong, not weak," he would tell me, exasperated, when I did.

At last he let me go and held me out from him, examining me in the firelight. "Yes, that will do," he told me.

I wasn't beautiful any longer. My hair was the only really pretty thing about me, I thought, and now there it lay. Everything else was just an illusion. How could I convince the audience I was beautiful if I didn't have my long wavy hair?

"You're a boy now," Wat said to me. He smiled a little at my expression. "You're as thin and flat as a boy," he said. "Now we don't have to stuff your costume with rags. Or, well, we do, but not in the same place."

I blushed at this, but in the dark he wasn't able to see it. At least, I hope he wasn't. I stooped down to pick up the rabbit and began skinning it with my own knife.

"We'll have to find you another name, though." He thought for a moment. "You'll be Gimot. Or. . .or Ioco."

"Those are ugly names," I said, looking up at his profile against the banked firelight. "How about Young Johnny?"

I couldn't make out his expression, but he bent down to grip me warmly by the shoulder, the first affection I'd ever had from him, although I had experienced friendliness from him sometimes, when he was in a genial mood, and respect always. "That would be perfect," he said, his voice husky. He turned away. "But no. It might draw the wrong kind of attention," he said after a moment. His voice sounded normal now.

"Very well, then. Gimot or Ioco." I was resigned. I used to be beautiful. Now I was ugly. An ugly, skinny boy with an ugly name. It didn't matter. I was just an object this man—all of them, really—shaped to do their bidding, some cog in the machine of their hidden purpose, like the wooden teeth of the great gear I'd seen back in Withiel or some of the other towns, helping to winch up the town gate. Big wooden machines made up of many small parts.

I began skewering pieces of rabbit on the sharpened twigs I'd piled at my feet. I poked up the fire.

"Let's call you Aedan," Wat said after a moment, hesitant and low, his back to me.

"That's better," I said, surprised.

"It was my brother's name," he said, turning to look at me. A shadow crossed his face, or maybe it was the firelight.

There was that word again, *was*.

"But what will I wear?" I said, breaking into the moment.

"You'll wear the green Kenning the Juggler costume." Now Wat's voice was brisk and practical. He squatted down beside me and began roasting the pieces of rabbit. "For tomorrow's performance, we'll garter the leggings and lap them over at the waist. They'll fit you well enough. The jerkin can just hang loose on you." It was tight on Wat, showing off his muscles to the women in the crowd. It would look silly on me. I'd look like I was wearing my older brother's cast-off clothing.

"And what will you wear?" I asked, thinking, *tomorrow's performance*. We were going to continue to perform. Wat had already worked out where.

"I'll find something," he said. "Or just juggle without a costume. I'm not the main act, not the draw that people pay good coin to hear and see. You are."

"They won't pay good coin to see me now."

"I think you're going to be surprised. Yes, they will."

As we ate our rabbit, the juices dripping down our chins, Wat reached out and took one of my hands. He turned it over and stared at it in the firelight. "Dark Ones take those thorns," he said. "Does it sting?"

The thorns in the brush during our wild descent into the holloway had scratched us both badly.

"I'll make a salve for us in the morning," I told him, trying not to yank my hand out of his. But Jillie, it was strange. I feared his touch. After all, I'd just decided he was about to kill me. Yet in an unsettling way, part of me wanted him to touch me. The place where his hand had clamped down on my shoulder tingled. His hand on mine now was warm. I think I must have been hungry for human connection. Starved for it.

We slept well-fed that night, and I felt closer to Wat than I ever had. He wasn't going to kill me. His plan was all about how to use me. As long as I was useful to him, I felt safe.

Before dawn, Wat unshipped the long pole he kept underneath the wagon. It was tipped with iron. With it, he pried the "Kenning the Juggler and His Merry Musicians" sign off the wagon and fed it to the fire. He fed our gilded acorns to the fire, too. They popped and leaped in the flames as he threw them in by the handfuls. And—what hurt me most—he threw in my beautiful costume. First we ripped off some long strips of yellow cloth. But we put the rest of it in the fire. After all the evidence of our former act had burned to ashes, we stamped the fire out and got back in the wagon.

"When we get to the next town, I'll find some paint. We'll paint this wagon a different color," he said. "I'll change the seat. Or something. Give ourselves a different look." Wat was clever with his hands. He had built the wagon box-bed himself. And then, I recalled how he had repaired my rebec. I brushed the thought away.

When I thought about things like that, I thought about our father, Jillie. I thought about our father and how clever his hands were, too, but I tried to keep the memory of him far away from me. It was too painful otherwise.

We set off. Wat appeared to know where he was going. I sat on the wagon seat beside him while he guided Millicent with the lines. He sat the wagon easily. Silly, I know, but I want to say he sat it royally. As if he were a king and this were his throne. But when I looked at his hands holding the lines so loosely and con- fidently, I had to suppress a shudder. They were the hands of a killer.

You'll think I'm a bit off in the head, saying that. Was it my second sense? Only morbid fantasy, I supposed. I tried not to dwell on it. He hadn't hurt me, had he? Only cut off my hair.

The next day, we pulled into a modest-sized hill town.

"Here we try it out," said Wat. "Our new act. Listen," he con- tinued. "When we reach our stopping place, we'll set up as before. I'll just start juggling. People will see us, spread the news to their friends. We'll get our crowd, you'll see."

We were nearing the town gates. My heart was pounding. I had never sung as a boy before.

"Will they think I'm a boy? Will they really?"

"Yes, they really will," Wat said. "You have that lower, smoky voice that could be a girl's or a boy's, either one, and you look very young, so your voice can be much higher than a man's. Than mine."

I couldn't help giggling. It was a nervous giggle, and it startled me, so unused I was to any silly childish act like giggling, but it felt good. Wat gave me a sidelong smile. I knew he was trying to relax me. We both knew that Wat himself had a dreadful voice. He croaked like a raven. No one would have paid Wat to sing. They would have paid him not to sing.

"Now listen," he said. "You'll sing your usual things. Just pretend you're a boy while you're singing them. Don't flirt with the men the way you usually do."

"I do not!" I was outraged.

"Yes, you do, and it has worked out well for us. But don't do it from now on. You can wink at the girls, though. That is going to work." He sounded satisfied and confident.

I was glad. When he had pulled out his knife the night before, I was sure he had decided, now I'd been recognized, that I was too big a liability to use.

That was the thing about these people. However much they might like you personally, they only thought of one thing, how they could use you. If they couldn't use you, you were no good to them. Worse than no good. You were a burden. And they traveled light.

I had a case of nerves worse than any I'd ever had, that afternoon. I was waiting in the wagon's box bed for Wat to finish juggling for the crowd that had assembled around the wagon, just as he had planned.

Through the cracks between the slats of the thin walls of the wagon box bed, I could hear them. You get to be a good judge of crowds, in this business. I could tell the crowd was lackluster. They oohed and ahhed at the moment when Wat must have been performing his final dramatic trick with all the balls in the air at once while doing that little kick-back, kick-up move he does, and when they applauded, I knew he must be passing the circling balls under one upraised leg. That always got a big reaction. Or he could be going for his other big trick, the six-ball shower.

But I could tell, even from inside the wagon box bed, that this was not going to be one of those performances when we filled his cap with copper pennies.

I knew why. Without his Kenning the Juggler costume, Wat just looked ordinary. He had stripped off his tunic and was performing only in his trousers. Peeking through the slats of the box bed, I could see some of the women in the crowd were enjoying that. But he looked exactly like what they thought he was, a poor vagabond juggling for his supper. Or even a ruffian. A long, livid scar reached from his shoulder down his left arm almost to the elbow. His costume had concealed it, but not now.

My heart sank when I thought of the lackluster part I'd soon be playing myself. No glamorous beauty in lovely clothing (if you didn't look very closely). Just a skinny little boy. But it was too late to worry about that now.

Wat was announcing my act in big Kenning the Juggler tones. "And now," he said, with a dramatic pause, "I give you Aedan Silvertongue, the boy with the wondrous voice."

My heart pounded. This was my cue. I threw open the doors of the wagon box bed and sprang onto the wagon seat, just as we'd practiced, hoping all the while I wouldn't trip over the long leggings we had carefully gartered up in strips of yellow cloth (and stuffed with rags in a strategic spot).

I didn't trip. My confidence rose. I struck a pose and stood staring out over the sparse crowd, who were now gaping up at me.

I don't know how to tell you about what happened next, if you've never performed. Something happens on that stage, wherever it is and however rough and cobbled together. You transform into someone else. The Children transformed me, or maybe just some natural quality in the nature of performers. Not luck, though. My voice had nothing to do with luck. It came from a place much deeper than luck.

I made another spring, from the wagon seat to the top of the box-bed, our stage, and twirled around, unslinging my rebec as I did. I was Aedan Silvertongue now, not plain Mirin with her hair all chopped off.

I struck up a lively tune and began to sing. That's when the magic usually happened. The people's eyes started sparkling, and they started beating time with their hands and then their feet. I didn't expect it to happen this time. But it did.

It really did. Wat was right. Don't ask me how, but they loved me.

In fact, they loved me more, especially the girls. As Wat had suggested, I winked at them and flirted. They screamed. They actually screamed.

I sang all my favorites, but as I sang, I swaggered around. Even the older women were looking at me with melting eyes. The men, not so much. But they were still enjoying the show.

Wat was passing his cap around, and it was filling with coin. That cap was our one concession to a costume for him. He had decided the Kenning the Juggler hat would look too silly on me. "You need to break their hearts. This hat won't do," he had told me. So he had been wearing it, and now he was passing it around. I could see it was bulging with coppers.

The end of the performance was a bit difficult. We had started early, because we thought we might have to spend a long time drumming up business. But the people had flocked to us, and now they wouldn't let us stop. From the audience, they called out songs for me to sing, and usually I knew them. I had picked up a lot during our time on the road, especially when we sang at street fairs and I could listen to the other performers.

But at last the horns at the gates began blowing.

Wat called out, "Sending us off with the ever-popular 'My Beloved Has Gone Away.' Aedan Silvertongue, good people!" I took them out with the closing number, to cheers and applause, and our audience reluctantly filed into the town again.

"Will you be here tomorrow, lad?" one woman called out to me as she left. A knot of them, mostly girls and women, turned hopeful eyes in our direction.

"Yes, we'll be here tomorrow," Wat boomed out. "Come back to see us. Bring your friends. Bring your pennies!"

As dusk settled around us, I shed my costume and threw on my kirtle. Our usual routine settled me down. I headed out with my snare to find us a rabbit while Wat got the fire going, and this night I was lucky and caught two. We feasted that evening. Wat was in high good humor. I was a success. Our ruse had succeeded and then some.

He paused mid-bite to stare at me. "This isn't going to work," he muttered.

"What? I thought it worked wonderfully. They really thought I was a boy. They really loved it."

"They did think you were a boy," said Wat. "And they did love it. We got a lot of attention, and I'm thinking it was the right kind of attention, attention that will divert any suspicion away from us. The authorities are looking for a man and girl. But no, I mean—well, look at you."

I looked down at myself. "What?

"You're in girl's things."

"It's getting dark. They've all gone in. They won't see."

"Sooner or later, someone will see. We have to find you boys' things to wear. Stay here."

Wat slipped away into the evening, only now just darkening as the days grew longer toward high summer. When he returned, he threw trousers and a roughspun tunic similar to his own into my lap. They were still damp.

"You stole these off someone's washing line."

He laughed. "The goodwife was taking all the washing down to bring it into the house. When she turned her back—" He made a swishing motion with his hands. "So then. Spread them out by the fire. They'll dry soon enough."

I smiled to myself, remembering the yellow cloak I myself had nabbed in the same way. And Wat's laughter made me feel good. He never laughed. There was always something dark underneath, even when he smiled. But now a thought struck me. "You could have been caught. You could have been taken."

"I wasn't, though," he said.

I soon had reason to be glad of Wat's thievery. Otherwise, I would have had to stay cooped up in the wagon box bed every day until performance time. As late summer made the turning into harvest-tide, I could be out in the fresh air, fragrant with apples and hazy with the drifting chaff from the yelms of thatching-straw the country folk were bundling up in the fields we passed. Mornings dawned softly green, the sun rising on cloudless days, gleaming from the rain on the grassy land. Evenings were mild. I felt glad to be alive. I was pleasing Wat, I was pleasing the people who came to see us, and the weather was fine.

During the fortnights we spent roving back and forth across the countryside, I lived as a boy every day. I moved the way a boy moves, and whenever I saw a boy, I studied him to see just how.

In no time at all, or so it seemed, I became a boy.

Early in those boy days, I found out something else about myself. I found out how much I loved to move and how much I missed not being able to. Since early childhood, I had always been moving. I was running through the forest. Or I was swimming in the stream below our farmstead. Especially that.

"Mirin the fish," our father would say when I came home dripping wet. He'd smile over my head to our mother. She'd take me to the fire to towel me off. I tried not to call those memories up now. They were too painful.

But while my days on the road with Wat were satisfying in one sense—because I loved to play and sing—they were torture in another. I sat from sunup to sundown on top of the wagon seat beside Wat or, even worse, cooped up in the box bed as we jolted over the ruts of the back roads. I wanted to run and leap and twirl around instead.

One morning I had just come back to our fire with a rabbit I had snared, and was sitting on a flat stone, using Wat's knife to skin and gut my catch. I had a peeled green stick at the ready; I'd skewer the meat and roast it for us.

Wat was practicing his most popular moves. Some of the things he did with his body caused our audiences to clap and laugh and cheer. He'd spring straight up, then perform three or four dizzying cartwheels in a row, ending with a handstand, then a forward roll. And when he leaped to his feet, he had all six of his balls spinning in the air.

"How did you learn to do that?" I asked him now

He sat down, wiping the sweat off his face, and took the piece of roasted rabbit I held out to him. "A man taught me. When I was just a boy."

*You're not much older than a boy now*, I thought, studying him.

"A little boy," he said, as if reading my mind. "He was part of this entourage of servants at. . .well, at a place near where I lived. When he wasn't entertaining the nobles, I'd follow him around. All the time. I was probably a huge pest. So then he taught me."

"Teach me!" I burst out.

"You don't need to know those things. You've got your voice and your instrument."

"But Wat—you know how they scream, when I jump up on the wagon seat, and then onto the top? They love that. Suppose I could do more?"

Wat looked at me, considering. "I could teach you a few simple things," he said at last.

That day he showed me some of his moves. I think he was surprised to see how quickly I picked them up. After that, every time we stopped, I practiced. The days on the road didn't seem so long then.

As we traveled, I could tell we were going higher. Millicent really had to work to get us up the steeper roads. We were heading further into hill country. We were heading into the heart of royal might. Late one day, we came around a bend to find a castle and fort looming on a crag above us. "We're going up there," said Wat, pointing the lines in the castle's direction.

Even I knew enough to understand this was dangerous. "Why are we going up there?" I asked him. "They could do something bad to us."

When we'd come to the more heavily fortified towns, sometimes the guards would run us off. Once a guard had started to beat Wat with the staff of his pike. But Wat was too quick for him, doing a series of backflips away from him that ended with the man standing there scratching his head. As our wagon careened away from him, we could see a slow grin start to spread across his face.

"Always leave them laughing," Wat had said to me then. "Old saying among us vagabond ragged scum-of-the-earth players."

Now I was looking with apprehension up the steep road leading to the castle, and the castle itself, perched high on its motte. "Why there?" I asked again.

"We were always going to go up there," he told me. "Now we're just doing it a little sooner than I planned, and in a little different way. We're going to set up outside, gauge the mood of the guards, attract the crowds. I'm thinking we won't have any trouble. Your reputation precedes you, Aedan Silvertongue. Here's the other thing." I could tell by his voice that something serious was coming. "Probably not during this first performance, but sometime during our run up here." He pulled up on the lines and Millicent halted. He stared up at the forbidding ramparts beginning to loom over the road. "When I give you a sign like this—" He demonstrated by tugging at his left ear "—that's your cue to sing that song Johnny taught you."

I sat up straighter. "Huh," I said. He never let me sing that one.

"Try it now," he said. "Let me hear it."

"With my rebec?"

"No, just sing me a few verses."

*I'll sing you one, oh,* I began. I went all the way to the third verse, *I'll sing you three, oh. What is your three, oh? Three, three the rivals...*

"Good," he said. "And you remember how to play it on your rebec?"

"Of course," I said.

"Remember—when I give you the sign, play that."

"All the verses?"

"I'll give you the sign again when I want you to stop. Understand?"

"Yes," I said.

I couldn't suppress a shiver. So far, I had been pretty well insulated from the spying Wat had clearly been sent out to do. Now I'd be part of it. A hanging offense. If we were taken, there'd be no chance I could pretend I didn't know what Wat was up to. And we were approaching one of the most heavily fortified places in the realm.

By now the shadow of the castle was falling across the wagon, and the circling blackbirds above the great towers were calling out their rough and warning cries.

# Chapter 8

# Trickster

Wat was right. People came flocking out of the castle gates to hear and see us. I even saw some of the castle's guards hanging around the fringes of the audience, there just to enjoy the show. Oh, I'm being falsely modest. They came flocking to hear and see me. Somehow, I had become a celebrity. And we were putting my simple acrobatics into the show, too. That really wowed them.

By then, Wat had found me needle and thread, so I was able to shorten the long green leggings so they wouldn't trip me up. I made a row of tuckings so they'd be tighter, and the waist also. We were using the yellow linen strips torn from my girl's kirtle for gartering, and now we wrapped some of the strips around my torso, too, so Wat's big loose tunic didn't look so ridiculous on me. Wat made me turn around so he could admire the effect. "That looks good," he said. "The more they love you, the better for us."

"Wat?"

"What?"

"Where did we get those other clothes, my girl clothes we tore the yellow strips from? Did Avery let you buy those?"

"Oh, those," he said. "Someone gave those to us."

*Someone rich*, I thought. This was the first moment I realized his group might have connections important enough that I could only begin to imagine them. Maybe they weren't some ragtag bunch of criminals. It might have been the first moment I wondered why they were rebels, what they were rebelling against. Because I didn't know. I had no idea.

We played before the castle for three days, and our audience just kept growing. Wat never tugged at his ear, so I knew I was not supposed to sing Johnny the Traveler's song.

But Wat was getting more and more tense. He snapped at me. Once he dropped one of his balls as he was juggling, and he never does that. At our midday meal on the third day, which we were taking on the wagon seat, just bread and cheese we'd bought at the nearby village, Wat stopped. He appeared to be thinking something over, something difficult.

"What?" I said.

"Listen," he said. His voice was hoarse. He coughed to clear it. He pointed his knife down the hill. "See that rooftop? Stone building? You can just barely glimpse it through the trees."

I stood on the wagon seat, steadying myself with a hand on his arm, to peer the way he was pointing. "Yes, I see it." I snatched my hand away from him and settled back down beside him. Touching him. That felt somehow disturbing, maybe too close. This man was not my friend. I had to keep reminding myself of that. I remembered the day he took me away from Old Cwen. I remembered the look he had exchanged with Eris, the dangerous young woman with the knife, as if he were relying on her for guidance about what to do with me.

We sat together quietly. Millicent started casting her big head back and forth, browsing for tender grass.

"That's a small temple to the Lady Goddess," said Wat, after a few moments. "Very charming. I've been in it." Then he surprised me. He took me lightly by the shoulders and turned me to him and looked me in the eye. "You can take the morning and go down there, if you like. Worship at her shrine. She's the goddess you worship, right?"

I was wary. I squirmed out of his grasp. This was some kind of test. I already knew Wat and his group seemed to hold strange beliefs I didn't understand. Beliefs about the Children. Was he trying to tease me out as an apostate to their religion? But he already knew I didn't know much about it.

Then I realized what he was really offering. He was offering to let me go down there by myself. If I did, I could claim sanctuary of the priests. He'd never be able to get me back. He was offering me a chance to leave him, to escape the group.

I glanced back over at him, where he was watching me intently. I shook my head no.

"You can if you want to," he said. His voice was quiet. "From this point, things are going to get dangerous." He looked far away down the road, then up at the trees above us. "You can step away from this. I won't stop you."

"No," I said.

He nodded at me. The moment passed. We pretended it had never happened. I thought about it, though. If he had lost me, what would he have had to tell Avery? What price would he have had to pay? So then—and here I was truly puzzled—why give me that chance?

And I was puzzled about myself, too. Why wouldn't I walk away? I'd had other chances, and I hadn't taken them. If I'd escaped from Wat, no one would have known. They wouldn't have been alerted that I was a bound girl, because I didn't have the brand to warn others of my status. And the priests, maybe they'd help me look for you, Jillie. In spite of everything Wat and the others said to me, I didn't believe you were dead. Not deep inside.

*So why?* I asked myself.

I'd become a boy. Now it appears I had become a rebel boy.

I think I had figured some things out by now. The priests of the Lady Goddess really weren't going to help me. They'd probably just turn me over to the authorities. During our days on the road together, I was surrounded by people, and Wat was always right there beside me. But in a deeper way, I was alone. Our parents were dead. You might be dead too, but even if you were alive, the chances I'd ever find you were small. The world was wide, and I was one lone girl in it.

Now I'd become a boy.

I was good enough at the boy business that I didn't turn to ice with fright when something happened on that third day outside the castle. Something important.

A servant in the full scarlet livery of the castle came striding out of the gates and down to our wagon as we were setting up for the afternoon's performance. He gave us a measured look and drew himself up so we'd know how important he was.

We both rose to our feet. I was so flustered I almost curtsied but remembered just in time and made an awkward little bow. Wat gave a tug at his forelock like the good peasant he was pretending to be. By now I knew he was no peasant, but he was as good an actor as I had become.

"The ladies of the castle command that you attend them this evening," said the servant.

"How flattering. As you see, we are only poor strolling singers and acrobats. How may we serve the ladies?" Wat asked.

"The ladies command that the boy sing before them after the evening's supper."

"And my juggling? Would they wish to see that?"

"No juggling," said the servant. Wat looked crestfallen. "Bring the boy tonight," said the man. "Wait in the kitchen. The wenches will bring you both something to eat. Then the boy will sing."

Wat and I both bowed low.

"Don't be late," the servant said over his shoulder as he threaded his way through our gathering audience, looking around him disdainfully until he reached the castle gates and disappeared through them.

"They don't want my juggling," said Wat. He made a sad face that got me laughing harder than I had laughed since—well, maybe since before, since I was at home with my family.

"I'm glad I amuse you, Aedan Silvertongue."

"We'll be rich," I said, getting a grip on myself. My laughter was beginning to edge into the hysterical.

"Yes. And even better, we'll get inside the castle."

"And we want to do that?" I asked cautiously.

"Yes, we do. And here's the place where you'll sing Johnny the Traveler's song."

By that point, I had almost forgotten about the song, and the secret sign. "Suppose they don't let you come before the ladies with me? How will I see the sign?"

"In that case, sing the song straight through, all of the verses. But I'll find a way to be with you. Don't worry."

I did worry. I worried about going before the ladies alone, and not just because I wouldn't see the secret sign. I worried they'd discover I was not a boy. I worried about what they'd do to me once they found out. And I worried about what the secret sign could mean. I knew it would put us in some kind of danger, especially since I could see Wat was worried, too, in spite of his reassuring words.

As we set up for the afternoon performance, he kept stopping and thinking, then coming to himself with a jolt and starting in again with the positioning of the wagon just so and the tethering of Millicent far enough away so her lowing wouldn't disturb the singing but close enough so he could keep an eye on her. Meanwhile I swept the area around the wagon clear of debris and searched out any of Millicent's droppings to dispose of them down in the ravine behind the wagon.

These worries couldn't last long, because we had a show to put on. It was as successful as the others. More people came, some from the surrounding villages, and we also noticed repeat customers in the audience. Afterward Wat had to shoo away a gaggle of girls who waited to try to speak to me.

After the horn had sounded and the people had left for the castle, we got ourselves ready to go in too. Time was getting short. I examined the Kenning the Juggler costume with despair. It was looking pretty shabby. In spite of the work I had done to make it a better fit, it still sagged in places, and there were places where I had actually had to patch it.

"This is going to be a disaster," I told Wat as we trudged up the hill. "They're going to take one look at us and turn us out."

"They may. We can try, though."

"But what if they do?" I persisted.

"Then I'll just have to find another way in."

"That would be really dangerous," I said.

"Yes. So I want this plan to work."

"I'll do my best," I told him.

"I know you will. I knew you would." He stopped and bent down, taking my face in both his hands and tilting it up to his. "I told them that, back at Old Cwen's house, remember? I told them I was sure you would become a faithful servant, and you have."

"They were ready to kill me back there, weren't they? You've thought of doing it. Killing me," I persisted.

Wat didn't answer. We resumed walking.

I stopped again. "But I don't even know what this is about!" I burst out.

He turned to look at me. "It's better that way. Safer."

"Safer for you."

"Yes. Safer for you, too."

"No, it's not. If they take us and torture us, they won't stop just because I don't know anything. They'll think I do, and they'll keep on."

He stared at me, the first time I'd seen him shaken. "Yes, you're probably right. Yes. But you'll do what I say, and you won't betray me—us. Now stop talking, because we're getting close to those guards. We don't want to rouse any suspicions."

He was right, I thought. I would do what he told me to do. And I didn't understand why.

I'm still not sure why. I suppose it had to do with our parents, and with you, Jillie. I believed Wat and the leader and the others when they told me our father had been part of their movement, or whatever it was. It added up—the visit of Johnny the Traveler, and other small things I had hardly noticed at the time. The nights our father went missing, with only a vague excuse when he returned. The frightening time our mother found him bleeding and barely alive outside our door one morning, and nursed him herself, and wouldn't call a healer. I was pretty young then, maybe too young to wonder much at their behavior, but I wondered at it now. And the season before he and our mother were killed, he'd been gone an entire fortnight and more with no explanation. He'd left, taking his knives with him, the sharp ones you and I were never allowed to touch, Jillie.

Our father had believed in these people and had given his life for them. I suppose, when I served them, I felt I was honoring our father's life, and our mother's. Making sense of their senseless deaths. That's the only way I can explain it.

Well, and maybe one other thing. Maybe it meant a chance to do something, to find something out, to punish those responsible for our family's deaths. I had only a vague idea of how I'd do that, and no means or methods at all. When I thought of this simmering wish of mine, part of me felt like a foolish child.

The guards admitted us to the castle, not without scornful glances at our poor and patched clothing. Just inside, the same fancy servant waited to escort us to the kitchen. We trekked through the castle's outer bailey and then up the steep path into the inner bailey of the castle's motte, around to the back of the cook house. There the servant left us, telling us someone would come to get us when the time came for me to sing.

"You'll stay here in the kitchen shed and wait," he said to Wat. "We'll bring the boy back to you afterward."

Wat made him a slight bow.

"You see?" I hissed at him as the servant went back out into the bailey.

"No. I see nothing. Just follow my lead," said Wat calmly.

The cooks' helpers bustled around us, casting annoyed looks at us when we got in their way. Course after majestic course left the cook house for the great hall of the castle's keep—large roasted fowls and beeves and pigs on platters. Big bowls of sweets and fruit. Handcarts piled with bread.

I could feel my mouth watering.

"Here," said someone, a big rude girl in a stained apron. She thrust a trencher of meat scraps at me, and one at Wat. We signaled our thanks and silently devoured the meat, then the bread of the trencher, soaked with the rich juices. Even I know it's rude to eat the trencher. But that's how hungry we were. So we did it.

Wat casually backed up to a table loaded with fruit. When he stepped away, he held two apples. I was about to smile when the same girl popped up out of nowhere.

"Thief!"

Wat glanced over at her. As casually as he had stolen the apples, he began juggling them. The girl's mouth gaped open. "No thief," he told her. "I just need to keep in practice."

After performing some of his best bits for her, he placed the apples back on the table.

She rushed to them, grabbed them up, and a third, and turned back to Wat.

"Can you do three?"

Wat gave her his winningest smile. "I surely can, young mistress," he said, and put on another show, first with three apples, then four, then five. Finally six. He did his famous six-ball shower for them. By now, kitchen wenches from all across the cook house were coming down to us to watch.

They scattered back to their places when the cook arrived with a bellow. Wat replaced the apples, or seemed to, but when he turned back to me, as I stood there trying to suppress my laughter, he still had two of the apples. He handed one to me and coolly bit into his.

In spite of my deep misgivings about him, Wat always knew how to relax me when I was as tense as one of my rebec strings about to fray and snap.

After a long wait, a servant came to fetch me. Not the same servant, another one. This one was dressed in blue, and more simply than the scarlet-clad fancy servant we had first encountered. "This way, young sir," he told me. As Wat moved to walk beside me, the servant pointed at him. "Not you. You're to wait in the kitchen."

"I think there's been some mistake," said Wat politely. "As I told the other man, my young brother here has severe stage fright. He can't sing at all when he's rattled. And you see—" Here Wat pointed at our poor patched selves.—"We're not used to lords and ladies, not us."

I was nodding along earnestly as he told the servant these things.

"The other servant and I agreed it would be best for me to accompany Aedan to the hall. We agreed I could stand by the door, out of sight of their ladyships, but I could stand where young Aedan could see me, and give him encouragement."

I gave the servant my best helpless puppy look.

"Oh," said the servant, nonplussed. "I see. No one told me that."

"It would be best," said Wat. "Otherwise, I'll wait here." Then to me he said, "You won't be long, Aedan. They'll send you back to me in a few moments, never fear. This is not the usual place we perform," he told the servant. "We don't mind. We were flattered to get their ladyships' invitation, but I told young Aedan, I did, don't worry, boy, they won't hold it against you when you can't sing. They'll just send you back."

The blue servant gave us both perplexed frowns. "Oh, very well," he told Wat. "Come along. But wait where I tell you, and don't let their ladyships see you." He gave us both a look of distaste. "I can't imagine why they'd want to hear this boy, but they do."

"That's fine, then, good sir," said Wat. "We'll do their ladyships any service within our powers, feeble as they are and poor though we be. Just make sure young Aedan can see me while he sings."

"Oh, very well," said the servant again and stumped away. I had the feeling he'd had a long career with "oh, very well" as his boon companion. We marched along behind him. We crossed the castle's bailey again and up a broad sweep of stone steps to the large brass-bound doors of the keep. We entered. I looked around, overawed. The servant steered us through a warren of small rooms to the rear entrance onto the grand hall, and led us in.

We stood beside a fire at one end of the hall. It was backed by massive stones. Far at the other end, the banquet guests had gotten to their feet and were milling about, conversing and slapping backs and laughing. A silent fleet of brown-clad servants cleared away the remains of the meal from rows of long tables.

"Wait here. Right here. Do not move," said our blue servant to Wat. He pointed to a spot at one side of the fire, beside a tall chest. Wat obediently moved to the spot he had indicated. "Your brother will perform there." He pointed now to a small raised dais in front of the fire.

"I will be able to see him from here," said Wat. "You have my thanks, good sir."

The servant only sighed. To me he said, "The ladies will be seated in chairs on the other side of the fire. Sing to them from the dais. Do not think to approach them. Unless they ask you to, of course. Do whatever they ask you to do."

I nodded.

"Don't sing much. Just a few songs. Unless they ask you to, of course."

I nodded.

"Sing your best songs. Songs appropriate for the high station of their ladyships."

I nodded.

He looked at both of us skeptically. "Nothing bawdy."

I shook my head no.

"Master Charlo will motion to you when it's time for you to come to the dais," he said to me. At our confused looks, he amended, "Master Charlo, the personal servant of our good earl's lady, the one who came to you to command your performance."

We nodded. Now we understood.

"Good," he said. "Now wait here until Master Charlo summons you," he said to me. "And you," he said to Wat. "You stand here where I've put you. Do not move from this spot. Is that clear?"

"Yes, good sir. And, good sir?"

"What is it?" I could see the blue-clad servant was at the end of his tether.

"About our payment?"

"Oh, that. You'll be paid after I escort you back to the kitchen. I'll get you both afterwards. Don't head out on your own. Wait for me here." He was speaking slowly, as if we were too stupid to follow directions. Now he looked at me. "Master Charlo will signal to you when their ladyships have had enough of you. Then just leave the dais and come to stand here with your brother until I have time to get you. Thank the Lady Goddess they'll be far enough away that your patches won't seem so obvious. Or your stench."

We both bowed.

"Fine, then." He rushed away with a harried expression. We could see him at the far end of the hall now, conferring with the scarlet-clad Master Charlo. Master Charlo looked over at us with an annoyed expression, and I wondered if he would rush down the hall and eject Wat from it. But at that moment, a grand lady summoned him to her side. He assisted with her skirts and voluminous veil, bound at her temples by a fillet of gold, as she rose from her chair at the head of the head table.

"That will be the lady of the earl," Wat said to me. He was scanning the crowd around her.

"What's wrong?" I asked him. He was staring hard at someone, and every part of his body had tensed up.

"See that man? The one dressed in black, with the fur cloak? Count about three people left of her ladyship. See him?"

"Yes," I whispered.

"That man—" Wat swallowed hard. "He's one of the most dangerous men in the realm, one of those six or seven always around Audemar."

Audemar was our king. I stared at the man with interest. This castle must be full of important people.

"If you see him around anywhere, get away from him. I mean it."

I didn't have time to question Wat, because now Master Charlo was edging down the hall by the side of the earl's lady as she made her way toward us. She was followed by five younger women.

"Her daughters," said Wat. He glanced at me with a worried look. "I really am going to have to give you encouragement so you don't choke."

"Suppose I sing the wrong thing."

"Don't worry about what Master Blue said to you. Just sing some good songs. These are women like any others. Those girls are going to love you."

"And Johnny the Traveler's song?"

"Sing it second. It won't be a good one to lead off with, but just in case Master Blue is right and they actually don't want you singing very long, we can't risk missing our chance."

I didn't think to ask, *What chance? Chance for what?* I was too worried. "Some of my songs are bawdy."

"Don't worry, young Aedan. Just sing. They'll like it if the songs are bawdy. Trust me on that."

"And Wat—"

"Yes?"

"Do we smell?"

"Oh, that. No, he was just insulting us, Master Blue was, so we'll know our place. We do not smell."

That was all the time we had to talk through my case of the jitters, because Master Charlo was seating all the ladies and seeing that they were all supplied with reticules and napkins and scarves.

Master Blue came forward bearing a small table loaded with fruit and cheeses. With a flourish, he made to set it down before the lady of the castle, but she waved him off. He slunk to the back of the group with it, put it down, and tiptoed away.

Wat nodded to me. "Steady," he whispered. He gave my hand a squeeze. I looked into his eyes then. He looked back at me. I thought to myself, *I'm really seeing you, Wat, and you're seeing me.* That felt strange.

I didn't have time to dwell on this novel feeling, though, because Master Charlo glanced in our direction, bent down again to her ladyship, stood up, motioned to me and pointed at the dais.

I walked over to it on feet I couldn't feel. I felt cold all over. I went up the three small steps to the top and waited, but the thought of Wat standing just behind me was almost a physical feeling. As if he had a hand on my shoulder, and all his trust resting on me. This feeling sent a chill up me. *I'm doing this thing for a purpose I don't really understand, but I'm playing a part in something our parents believed in so strongly they were ready to die for it.* That was my thinking, along with the other jumbled thoughts and fears, and that one steadying thought gave me the courage I needed.

After casting a poisonous look in Wat's direction, Master Charlo turned to the group of ladies and said, "Honored Lady of the castle! My dear young ladies! May I present the sensation making its rounds about the Hundred, Aedan Silvertongue?"

I unslung my rebec and bowed deeply to the ladies, wondering nervously if I was supposed to start singing right away, but Master Charlo continued talking, in lower tones, in a different voice, directly to her ladyship.

"These are poor strolling players, my lady. Country entertainment."

The young ones tittered, but their mother just sighed. "Master Charlo, never fear. We know this is some poverty-stricken patched youth from the countryside. Stop apologizing and let's hear him. It's what my daughters want. I trust this will shut up your continual begging and pleading," she said, looking around at the girls. They exchanged smiles and looked down demurely. "So let him sing," she said, and sank back into her chair with a grumpy expression on her face. "These modern ways," she muttered. She roused again. "In my day—" she began. Then stopped herself and made a weary wave of her beringed fingers in Master Charlo's direction.

He gave me a significant look.

I gathered it was time to begin. I made sure to position myself on the dais so I could see Wat and my audience, too. I played the most enchanting of all my songs, "The Maiden Looks Out From Her High Tower, A'la, A'la."

By the end of the song, I knew I had them, even the grumpy lady of the castle. They were perched on the edges of their gilded chairs, all of them. Their eyes sparkled. Their hands beat time. Their feet had begun tapping. I was so thrilled with myself that I almost headed straight into the second-most enchanting of all my songs, "Three Sparrows Flew Over Hill and Dale," but I remembered in time.

I began to sing Johnny the Traveler's Song.

*I'll sing you one oh,* I sang to them, drawing out the line into yearning and romance.

> *What is your one oh?* I sang.
> *One is one and all alone and evermore shall be so.*

The oldest daughter wiped her eye with a corner of her veil. I sang the refrain, and she sat up straighter.

> *Blackbirds rising, blackbird's eye,*
> *Green grow the rushes, oh,*
> *One lone blackbird in the sky,*
> *Green grow the rushes, oh.*
> *One is one and all alone and evermore shall be so.*

After that verse, I moved into the second.

> *I'll sing you two, oh.*
> *What is your two, oh?*
> *Two, two, the long-lost boys,*
> *Clothed all in green, oh.*
> *One is one and all alone*
> *And evermore shall be so. . .*

I had been glancing in Wat's direction through this performance, and I was surprised now to see him tugging on his left ear. *That's it, then,* I thought. The song was now so short as to sound odd, so I hesitated.

But I regained my composure, continued into "Three Sparrows," and kept on going.

After five or six songs, I could see Master Charlo trying to get her ladyship's attention. She saw too and gave him an annoyed look. He shrank back.

"Splendid, young Master Aedan. Please continue," she called out to me. "Refreshing," she said over her shoulder to her daughters. "Not the usual thing."

The daughters were sighing.

I gave them my full set, and then some.

Finally I played a surefire closing number, "Good night to Stars and Moon and Every Golden Thing," and gave a flourishing bow.

The earl's lady rose to her feet. Following her cue, so did her daughters. They all applauded, and so did many of the servants and laggard guests, who had been heading for the doors to the outside but had stopped and had all started congregating at the end of the hall, listening too.

I stepped down from the dais, bowed to them all again, and walked with unsteady legs back to Wat, who grabbed me by both arms and whispered in my ear, "Excellent, Mirin. You have done everything I've hoped for."

Then his head snapped up. He stared at someone across the room, a man dressed in brown, maybe one of the servants.

Master Blue appeared behind us then, so we couldn't talk further. His eyes were shining. "Oh, my young master, what a voice you have!" he gushed at me. I smiled at him with what I hoped was a look of shyness and pleasure.

And Master Charlo too made his appearance, although he looked less pleased. "Very fine. Very fine," he muttered at us. "Our great earl's daughters would like to meet you, young sir."

"But I am dressed in rags," I told him. "Little more than rags. I'm not fit for their presence."

As I said this, I suddenly worried that Wat might have wanted me to accept. But Master Charlo was already nodding.

"So I told them," he said.

"Suppose we arrange a meeting tomorrow," said Wat. "I can try to find my brother something more appropriate to wear."

Master Charlo conferred with her ladyship and came back to us. "The young ladies are disappointed, but their mother agrees with you. And with me, I might add. Our kind lady of the castle will arrange for you to come here early tomorrow," he said to me. "Her ladyship will appoint a waiting man to dress you in better clothing and to—and to see that you are bathed and deloused before that. Wait for my message."

He turned away from us, looking annoyed, and headed toward a group of brown clad servants to scold them and make them re-do something they'd been doing wrong.

Wat and I went in a daze away from the castle and back to our wagon. Wat had a small but nicely heavy bag in his hand, and when we poured it out on the wagon seat, its contents glistened in the moonlight. Silver dirhams from the far-off Realm of the Asp, and odd-looking coins from the Burnt Lands, and even some gold.

"As successful as we'd hoped," I said. I was happy, and I was sleepy in that way I always get after the stresses of performance.

"More successful. Too successful. We're going to have to figure out what to do about that bath."

"I want a bath." I had decided that in spite of Wat's reassuring words, we did smell.

"Have you thought about how you'll look, in that bath, to the waiting-man?"

I froze.

"I'm too tired to think about it now," said Wat. "We'll fasten on a plan tomorrow. But really," he said. "Very, very successful."

I realized he was talking about more than my fine singing and its enthusiastic reception by the lady of the castle and her daughters. He was talking about something else.

As I drifted to sleep in the wagon box bed, fragments of the evening floated into my mind. The delighted faces of their ladyships. My rubbery legs. Master Blue and Master Charlo. Wat juggling apples before the astonished kitchen wenches.

And one other thing.

As we walked back across the outer bailey toward the castle gates, we'd passed a plainly-dressed man. He and Wat had exchanged a look, an intent look, and I realized something. The man was the same young man Wat had stared at after my performance. Was there some sort of signal sent between the two of them? And what? And why?

But in spite of the excitement of the day, and in spite of the anxiety of the coming bath, sleep rose up to claim me. Not til morning did I think about these matters again.

# Chapter Nine

# Playing for Time

By morning, I had a bad case of jitters. I could see Wat did, too. After we breakfasted on some of the scraps we had managed to snag during our march the night before back through the kitchen shed, Wat sat thinking a long time. I tried not to interrupt.

Finally, he looked up at me. "We'll go in together." He sounded certain, but his eyes betrayed him. I could tell he was far from certain. Wat's eyes were a clear azure, like a cloudless noontide sky. But when he was angry or worried, they turned. They became somehow duller and sharper at the same time, as if you were to stare into a pond reflecting a clear noontide sky at the moment a cloud passes over. Or as if you were to sight down the blade of a sword made of fine-tempered steel. As you see, I'd had a long time to study Wat, and at close quarters, too. I knew how to read him, and I read that he was sick with worry.

"How? How will we manage that? Master Charlo is on to you now. He won't allow it," I said.

"Probably thinking I'm looking the place over to see what I can steal," said Wat. "Yes, you're right. But I'll manage it." He summoned up a smile. "You're modest. You know that? You're too modest to bathe in front of strangers. I need to be there. That's what I'll tell them."

"Will it work?"

"Maybe," he said.

"What if it doesn't."

"I'll create a diversion."

"How in the Nine Spheres will you do that?"

The corner of Wat's mouth quirked up in what passed for one of his enigmatic smiles.

But people were starting to drift down the road in our direction. They wanted to be entertained. Wat didn't answer me. He headed over to our wagon and disappointed them by slapping a large NO PERFORMANCE TODAY sign on the outside of the wagon, and shaking his head firmly at the many who couldn't read. I wanted him to tell me about his plans, but he wouldn't talk about it. Instead, he made me go back into the wagon box bed.

"Otherwise every young girl in the Hundred is going to come crowding around to see if she can catch your eye," said Wat as he shuttered me in.

"I look like a girl," I shouted through the slats.

"I think that may be the point," he said in a reasonable tone of voice that sent me into a suppressed fury. "You're not threatening. The mothers don't fear you'll run off with the daughters. You're like a pet. But they can pretend to dream about you. Girls that age. That's what they do." He was sitting on the wagon seat, leaning back against the box bed, so we could have a conversation just as if we were face to face.

"No, not today. Sorry," I heard him call out to someone.

"I'm a girl that age. I don't have thoughts like that."

"You haven't had time to. If you were home with your mother, you'd be having them about now."

"That's a lie," I said between gritted teeth. Why was I getting so angry? Maybe so I wouldn't think about what it would have been like, if I were home with my mother. Maybe because Wat hadn't bothered to answer my question.

"Not a lie. It's just the truth," said Wat. "And keep your voice down. Sorry, no performance today," I heard him call.

"How would you know what girls think?" I muttered.

"Oh, I know," he said.

He was infuriating, Wat was. I think he enjoyed it. But he was my master, so I knew not to push him too far. He had never beaten me, not yet. Once he was about to.

"Remember your promise to Old Cwen!" I had screamed at him.

"I made her no such promise," he told me as he circled around to get behind me with the strap he used to hobble Millicent.

But in the end, he didn't beat me. I don't even remember what I had done to get him so worked up. Probably something dangerous. Every now and again I noticed it. He feared for me. Yet he wasn't allowed to. That frustrated him, almost beyond bearing.

The time of our summoning drew closer, and the people had all wandered off, so he let me out of the box bed. He still hadn't told me how he planned to create a diversion. I pulled the Kenning the Juggler costume on again. It was all I could do. The people in the castle would see the boy they expected to see.

"We won't stuff the rags in," Wat decided, looking me up and down. "They may fall out at the wrong moment, and we don't want any extra attention. You'll be fine. You look fine. The servants are not going to be looking too close, down there."

I turned away to hide my blushing. This part of my costume always made me feel uneasy and wrong. "But when I step into the bath, they'll notice," I said, pressing the point.

"They would indeed, but we won't let them see."

"How do you plan to keep them from it?" *Answer me, Wat.*

Before he could explain, we noticed Master Charlo shouldering past the guards. He came down the hill toward us.

"Follow my lead," said Wat to me. I suppressed an annoyed grimace. Wat was always figuring out some plan, I'd have no idea what it was, and I just had to follow along, the instrument the master played upon. "Don't forget your rebec," said Wat.

When Master Charlo was near enough to speak but not so close that we could give him any vermin or diseases, he addressed Wat. "None of your tricks, young man. Just the boy. I want just the boy."

Wat bowed to him.

Master Charlo reached out his hand to me, then snatched it back. "Come with me," he said. He turned on his heel and started marching up the hill.

With a helpless glance at Wat, I followed the elegantly clothed Master Charlo. But I quickly realized Wat was right behind me.

At the gate, Master Charlo turned to me again. When he saw Wat, he frowned. "Fellow, I told you—just the boy. Not you."

"Good Master Charlo," said Wat, with another low bow. "My brother is very modest. He is frightened near to death. He'll not be able to sing."

It was true. I was frightened, frightened near to death. I didn't have to act it.

"I need to come with him," said Wat. "At least for the bath and the dressing of him. He hasn't been parted from me since he was a baby, when we were orphaned."

If Wat thought that heart-tugging story would affect Master Charlo, he was wrong. "Nonsense," Master Charlo snorted. "The boy is to come with me. You are to stay." He looked over at the guards. "See that this fellow remains outside." Both of them stepped forward. They were very large armored creatures with solid, inscrutable faces under the cones of their helmets. They both carried menacing steel-tipped pikes.

Wat simply made another of those obsequious bows. "As you wish, Master Charlo. Aedan," he said to me. "I'll be waiting here for you, never fear. They'll send you out to me soon."

"He'll sing, or he'll wish he had," said Master Charlo. "No one goes against a direct command of her ladyship."

I began to cry. It wasn't hard to make myself do it.

"What a pathetic excuse of a boy you are," Master Charlo said to me. "What those girls see in you—"

"Their ladyships?" asked Wat, his voice innocent.

Master Charlo gave him a sharp look. "Yes," he said slowly, with a kind of menace. "Their ladyships."

"Well, go then, and do your best, brother," Wat said to me in kind, unctuous tones. "They won't hurt you. They won't hurt him, will they? When he can't? Sing?" he said to Master Charlo.

Over Master Charlo's shoulder, I arched an eyebrow at Wat. He gave me the smallest of shrugs back. We hardly had to speak to each other, Wat and I. That's how well we knew each other by then, at least where giving a performance was concerned.

*Really? You're going for that again?* I was saying to him.

*Might as well* was his reply. *Might work. Worth a try.*

Master Charlo's face clouded up the way the day was clouding up, big thunderheads boiling from behind the castle keep.

*It's not going to work this time*, I thought. *You could fool Master Blue, but not this man.*

"Come with me," Master Charlo snapped. I stepped in behind him and the guards stepped aside. "Both of them," he said tight-lipped to the guards.

Wat gave me a small sidelong smile as we came through the gates together at Master Charlo's heels, but when the man turned to make sure we were following him, and probably to make sure Wat was not scouring the place for items to thieve, Wat had made his face as open and sincere and concerned as it was supposed to be.

Wat's ruse had worked again. It really had. Now I did have to act. Act to suppress an admiring exclamation, one actor to another. The fright I felt was too overwhelming, though.

We threaded our way through the castle outbuildings, as before. A patter of rain was starting to fall. I lifted my face to the sky. The rain felt good, comforting somehow, but I knew there was nothing comforting about our situation. Only Wat's quick thinking saved us this time, as last time, but I knew our luck had to be running out.

Finally we came to an obscure shed with steam rising from its smoke-hole. A woodsy aroma wafted from the shed into the damp air. It reminded me suddenly of home.

Master Charlo knocked. A man stuck his head out and glanced at us. "Which one is the boy?"

"Which one do you think?" Master Charlo's voice was full of exasperation.

"Come in, then," he said to me, and opened the door wide. As Wat made to follow me, he put a hard calloused hand out. "Not you." To Master Charlo he said, "I'm supposed to bathe one stinking fellow. Not two."

"This man is his brother, and he says—" Master Charlo began, then clamped his lips together. He turned to the two of us. "The boy is to go in. You may stand outside," he said to Wat. "I'll send someone to make sure you don't wander around. I have things to do." He stalked off, stopping to talk to another servant, pointing back at us. The other servant, one of the lower-order brownclad ones, began making his way over to us.

Wat looked at the man who was about to bathe me. "My brother is very modest and very frightened. It would be better if I bathe him. You can stand outside."

"No," said the tub man.

That was it. There was no arguing with the man. I could see that, and so could Wat. Wat shrugged and turned to lounge against the side of the shed. The servant Master Charlo had sent to watch Wat was nearing. The tub man motioned me inside. I had no choice. Our luck had indeed run out. I went in with him.

There was a large cask steaming with hot water before a roaring fire. I saw stone crocks filled with fragrant soaps and lotions. I saw a suit of clothes, bright and lovely, laid over a bench. I saw large soft towels at the ready. I wanted to get into the cask.

"Put that fiddle down on the bench." I did so. "Strip," said the man, "and don't give me any nonsense about it or I'll see you beaten. I don't want to hear about your damned modesty. Just do it. Get in that tub."

"Will you look away?" I said in a timid voice.

He just stood there with his arms folded over his leather apron. "What are you, a little girl? Strip and get in the tub. Don't think I'm going to touch you. I don't want your vermin. Leave those silly-looking clothes in a pile over there where I can pole them into the cistern." When I hesitated, wondering why he was going to dump my Kenning the Juggler costume into a cistern, he barked at me. "Do it. Do it now."

Playing for time, I bent down and unwound the yellow cloth from around my tunic and then the cross-gartering from each leg. I dropped the long strips of yellow cloth beside me on the floor.

I turned away from the tub man and began to pull the green tunic over my head.

With an impatient grunt, the tub man snatched it from me and threw it to the floor. And then he had the drooping leggings off me.

He let out a bellow of surprise. He came at me, and I dodged around the cask of steaming water, trying to knee him in the groin as I darted past him. I missed. That made him angry. He caught up with me. His pig eyes, too small for his lump of a face, were narrowed and glinting. He drew back a meaty fist.

There was a scuffle from outside the shed. The tub man and I both whirled around in time to see Wat and the brown-clad servant hurtling through the door and into the shed, falling on the floor and fighting.

"Nine Spheres," said the tub man. He moved around the cask to pick up his long pole and stood over the two as they rolled and fought, looking for a chance to rap Wat on the head with it.

I bent down and lifted one of the stone crocks of soap. I heaved it high and brought it down on the tub man's skull as hard as I could as he was leaning over the fighters. It barely staggered him, but just enough so that Wat had time to knock the servant to the ground, spring up, and get the tub man by the throat, twisting the man's leather apron straps tight about his neck. Wat shoved me aside as he hoisted the tub man up by this improvised garrote. "The door," he said to me over his shoulder. I kicked it shut. When I turned around, Wat had thrust the tub man into the cask, pushing him under the water, holding him down. "Now hand me that pole," he said.

I stood frozen. I grabbed up the tatters of my clothing and held them to myself.

"The pole," said Wat. His voice was tense. He bore down on the man in the cask with both hands. Cords of muscle stood out on his arms. Water flew everywhere as the tub man struggled for his life.

I reached down with one hand to get the pole, still trying to keep myself covered up with the other. I handed the pole to Wat. He shoved it straight down into the water and leaned on the tub man's chest with it, keeping the man under. The man thrashed and kicked, but soon weaker. Soon not at all. A stream of bubbles erupted from the water. Then the water was still.

"You did well, Mirin," said Wat, stepping back and casting the pole aside with a clatter. "You bought me a bit of time."

Still trying to cover myself with my ripped jerkin and leggings, I stood staring in horror at the man in the cask. Wat and I were both soaked, and Wat was breathing hard.

The tub man's clothes were billowing up to the surface now. "You killed him," I said.

I looked down at the brown-clad servant, who lay sprawled at my feet, his eyes open, his mouth gaped wide. "And him."

"Yes," said Wat, not noticing my half-naked state. "Singing is your talent. This is one of mine."

# Chapter Ten

# Unmasked

We had to move fast then. First, I made sure my rebec hadn't been damaged during the struggle. It hadn't. *Fiddle indeed*, I fumed to myself. *Little girl indeed.*

I drew on the ripped leggings and tunic as Wat was poling the tub man's corpse out of the cask. Without the yellow strips of cloth, which lay in a heap at one side of the cask, the leggings puddled around my ankles, and the tunic drooped to my knees.

I helped Wat hoist the dead weight of the man over the lip of the cask. Even more water sloshed over us. We were soaked. With a mighty heaving, we dragged the tub man out of the cask and pulled him to the cistern in the back corner of the shed. We shoved him in headfirst and had a lot of work to get his legs bent down in there with him. They wanted to stick straight out. Next we stripped the dead servant of his brown livery, dragged his body to the cistern too, and crammed him in likewise. It was a tight fit, but after we had finished, no one looking in through the door would have been able to see that a couple of dead bodies were stuffed in the cistern. Even if they entered the shed, they'd have to go over to the cistern and look in.

"Now we've got to get you dressed," said Wat, really noticing me for the first time. "You look like a wharf rat out in the rain."

"I can't put on those clothes. I'm wet. I'm dirty and sweaty. I stink."

"I'm going to put this servant's clothes on, and I'm wetter and dirtier and stinkier than you," said Wat. Then he stopped, hands on his hips. "Well, then," he said, shrugging. "There's the tub. Hop in."

"Where you just killed a man? Where a dead man's corpse has been bubbling out his last—" I was aghast. "No."

"What do you suggest?" His tone was dangerous.

I suppose it was the shock. I just stood there shaking my head as he pointed me to the clothes. Instead of forcing me into them, he bent down and smoothed the sopping fringes of my hair back out of my face. "Listen, Mirin. We have to be fast. I'll see what I can do."

In the back of the shed, he found a bucket filled with more steaming water. It must have been there so the tub man could use it to pour water over my hair while I was sitting in the cask. After a moment, Wat got the hint and turned his back while I climbed out of my ripped and filthy clothes and dropped them into the cistern over the bodies. I used the towel to dip into the bucket. The towel, the soaps, the lotions. It wasn't as good as immersing myself full into a lovely tub, but it was good. I used the remainder of the water to pour over my dirty hair and rinse off.

Only then did I step into the clothes laid out for me on the bench. Miraculously, they had escaped soaking. Mostly, anyhow. There were small clothes! I had never owned any. On top of those, I pulled on finely-woven pale cerise linen trousers, smooth as butter against my clean skin. A linen tunic with billowing sleeves and real silk banding on the placket. A buff leather jerkin, tanned to exquisite softness. A cerise cap with a jaunty little blue feather.

"Look at me!" I twirled around Wat, showing myself off.

"Fine. Now let's get out of this shed before Master Charlo sends someone after us."

"No, but really look. Aren't I gorgeous?"

"Yes," he said impatiently, pushing me toward the door. Then he sighed. He slowed and took me by the arm, turned me around. "Yes," he said. He gave me a smile, and it was genuine, in spite of the worry in his eyes. "You look wonderful. You'll be a big hit with their ladyships. Get your rebec. Ready?"

He led me out of the shed and around the inner bailey, as before, to the castle keep. The rain had stopped. The sun's rays poured down gloriously on us from behind a cloud. But the fear had gripped me again, and that kept me from noticing much.

Wat paused to look around. "I'm not sure where this servant was supposed to take you."

Before he could puzzle further, Master Charlo's voice snapped us to. "There you are! Hurry, lad, you don't want to keep their ladyships waiting." He hustled up, seized me by the arm, and marched me off without a look at Wat. Wat had been careful to pull the servant's hood far up over his face, but he was so brown and anonymous in the servant's clothes, and Master Charlo was in such a hurry, that he hadn't needed to. Master Charlo didn't even notice the damp patches blooming over Wat's shoulders, where the servant's tunic, too small on him, strained across.

"Back to your duties," Master Charlo called over his shoulder at Wat. "And get that fellow out of the castle any way you can. The other fellow, the older one." He didn't wait for a reply. That was the first moment I wondered what the intentions of their ladyships toward me really were. I soon found out they had no thought of giving me back to Wat. As far as they were concerned, they had commandeered me into their service. I was theirs now.

Master Charlo paused at a big door that led, as I found out, to the private apartments of the earl, his wife, and their daughters. There was a son, too, but he was off fighting on the northern frontier.

"Here's our beautiful young man," Master Charlo said to her ladyship when we were admitted into her chamber. He was practically purring, like a satisfied big cat. The chamber was enormous. Not as large as the dining hall but very large, a bed as big as my whole house back home, piled with furs; a fire as large as the one in the castle's dining hall, or close to; and, as before, the lady of the castle and her daughters seated on gilded chairs before it.

"Bring him here," said her ladyship.

Master Charlo gave me a little shove with the tips of his fingers. I came to the great lady of the earl. She reached out her hand to me and ran the back of it down my cheek while I worked hard not to jerk away from her.

"Smooth as a girl's," she said. Behind her, her daughters tittered, holding their veils up to their mouths and cutting their eyes at each other.

"We want a private performance," she said. Behind her came a chorus of yesses from the young ladies. "Where should he start, girls?"

"The sparrow song," called out one.

"The one about the maiden in the tower, the one who's waiting for her handsome champion to rescue her," said another, all in a rush.

The oldest sister stood up and came to me. "But I want the one about the very lonely person, the one who finds herself all alone," she told me. The rustle of her silk-trimmed clothing, the heady scent of her perfume, her perfect complexion over-awed me. I couldn't think what song she wanted. "One is one and all alone," she said. "The blackbird song." She bent closer to me, giving me a look so charged with meaning that I nearly turned and ran.

She knew something. Was she a friend, or was she about to reveal my part in a grand act of treason?

But she simply returned to her seat and sat looking at me expectantly.

"I'll sing your song for you, lady," I told her. I began Johnny the Traveler's song, singing it all the way through to the third stanza. I began on the third. *I'll sing you three, oh,* I sang.

> *What is your three, oh?*
> *Three, three the rivals. . .*
> *Two, two, the long-lost boys*

*Clothed all in green, oh.*
*One is one and all alone*
*And evermore shall be so.*

*Blackbirds rising, blackbird's eye,*
*Green grow the rushes, oh,*
*One lone blackbird in the sky,*
*Green grow the rushes, oh.*
*One is one and all alone and evermore shall be so.*

Before I could launch into the fourth verse, the oldest daughter stood up and made a frantic gesture. Then she fell back in her seat.

"Diera!" cried one of the others. "Mamma, Diera has fainted again!"

There was a great flurry, the earl's lady, the sisters, Master Charlo, all hovering about the slumped over figure of the sister named Diera. Master Charlo shoved me out of the way into a corner as a healer came scurrying into the room, ushered by another man. Part of me registered who this other man was. The inconspicuous man from the night before, the one who had exchanged a glance with Wat.

I was ignored now as the healer helped the others lay the oldest of the sisters down on the sweet flags and rushes that thickly layered the floor. He bent over her. Diera. That's what the others had called her. He chafed her wrists, took potions from a bag he was carrying, selected one, and forced the little leathern bottle's contents past her lips.

The other man, the one Wat had looked at, turned on his heel and practically ran from the room, but no one noticed him. They were all clustered around Diera.

I moved quietly nearer, then stepped back, thoughtful. Old Cwen and I had attended several cases like this, young girls who became emotionally overwrought. The best thing to do for them was to take them off to a private place and let them rest.

The earl's lady returned slowly to her chair and lowered herself into it, holding onto the arms as if she were too weak to sit down under her own power. "It's the fits again, isn't it, Master Charlo?" I heard her say in a low voice to the servant as he hovered around her solicitously and brought her a cloak. "How will we find a husband for her if she is prone to fits?"

I'd bet everything I had that Diera's episode was no fit. I'd bet everything it was a well-practiced performance. And I wondered about that man, the one who had run from the room. These things were connected. Somehow, they were connected with Wat and why he had wanted so badly to get into the castle.

I started playing very softly. I chose some comforting tunes you might play in a sickroom, or to get a fractious child to sleep. I didn't sing, just seated myself on one of the big stones ringing the fire and bowed the rebec to produce the most soothing tones I could.

The Lady Diera sat up and looked around in apparent confusion. "Did I—was it another one of those—"

A sister of hers, another of the older ones, stroked her forehead and helped her back into her chair. "It will be fine, my darling. Just a temporary thing." A pensive little group, they all turned their faces toward me where I played.

"Another time, young Master Aedan Silvertongue," her ladyship called to me. "Master Charlo will show you to your quarters." That's when I realized I had been appropriated into the noble household and away from the custody of Wat.

"No, Mother," cried the youngest daughter. "Let him sing! Oh, please do!" The others clamored as well. Her ladyship put her hands up to her temples. But then Diera joined them. "No, Your Ladyship, do let him sing." I noticed Diera called the lady of the castle "Your Ladyship," not "Mother."

"He sings so beautifully. It will soothe me," Diera persisted. "Haven't you heard the music he has been playing all this time? I feel much better now. His music makes me feel better." The younger girls petted her and smiled at her. Their mother relented, so I played and sang for a long time. Finally Master Charlo summoned a servant to lead me away.

As we progressed back through the inner bailey, I looked for Wat, but he was gone. My tension rose. From the ramparts, a cloud of blackbirds flapped up, circled, settled back down.

"Nasty birds," the servant muttered. "Kar," he shouted at another passing servant. He gestured at the ramparts. "Tell that boy—you know, what's-his-name, the one who works in the stables—to get his bow and shoot those birds." Under his breath, he said, "They make a mess everywhere." He looked at me. "Want a bow? Want some target practice?"

I shook my head no. "I'm not good at that," I said.

The servant took me down into the lower levels of the castle, although not the lowest. That was where the dungeons were, I discovered. With a distracted nod toward the door of one of the rooms, he left me there.

At least my room had a window, although it was barred, cut high into the wall at the top near the ceiling. Through it I could see the feet of passersby. It let cold drafts in. The room was bare. There was a shelf for a bed, and a thin blanket spread on it. There was a chest where I could store my beautiful new clothes. There was a chamber pot. My room, in other words, was a kind of cell. But the door was not locked. I could come and go. Probably not outside the castle walls, though—not without permission.

I took off my clothes and hung them up. I wrapped myself in the blanket, crawled onto the shelf, and tried to sleep. Our plan had worked, Wat's and mine, at least to the point where no one had unmasked me. Not yet.

But where was Wat now? I worried about how he would know what had happened to me, and how he'd be able to come into the castle and get me and take me away with him. Or suppose he decided it was too risky to do that. Suppose he just rode away in the night, as we had done before when conditions got dangerous. These thoughts haunted me. It was a long time before I could get to sleep.

It didn't matter. I slept through the early morning with no one to see about me. I woke finally when the sun poured more directly through my little window and onto my face. What was I to do? I couldn't put on my festive clothing every day, but I had nothing else to wear.

I pulled the linen trousers and tunic back on and left the cap and jerkin, and my rebec, in the chest. Then I went looking for something to eat. No one paid me any attention as I wandered the castle grounds. It was as if they all knew who I was and knew that I belonged here, when only a day ago I would have been stared after with suspicion, followed around to make sure I was not up to some bad deed, and probably thrown out of the castle with a warning not to come back.

I found my way to the kitchen shed at last. With no ado, a kitchen wench handed me a piece of bread and a pear. She drew me a mug of small ale.

I ate the food as if I were a starveling. Then I went back to wandering the grounds. I tried hard not to go near the bathing shed. If anyone had discovered the bodies in the cistern yet, or wondered about a few missing servants, no one had raised any alarm. When they did, though, I knew the guards would march straight to me. The next day, although I tried to stop myself, I still couldn't keep from walking past the bathing shed from time to time.

I felt a gnawing anxiety in the pit of my stomach. Trying to avoid undue attention, I made my way down to the outer bailey and prowled restlessly back and forth before the main gate, but I forced a casual air that wouldn't arouse suspicion. Maybe I could find how to slip out of the castle. There didn't seem to be any easy way. The walls were high fortified stone. They weren't some rustic palisades I could outwit.

Finally I worked my way back to the staircase down to my room. A serving maid passed me in the hall. "Oh, there you are, Master Silvertongue. Here. These are for you." She thrust a folded set of everyday brown woolen trousers and tunic at me and hurried away.

*Good*, I thought. I was looking much too conspicuous in my singing clothes. Now I could blend in better with the rest of the servants. Maybe I could find a way out.

As I was sitting on the bed shelf in my room, scuffing a disconsolate toe against the stones of the floor and wondering what to do with myself, the same serving maid thrust her head into the door. "They'll be wanting you to entertain at dinner, Master Silvertongue."

I nodded to her. She disappeared. So then I took my rebec out of the chest and spent some time tuning it and practicing on it. When suppertime came, I had gotten myself back into my fine things. Hanging my rebec from my shoulder, I appeared at the dining hall doors. The same servant in blue—Master Blue, Wat had dubbed him—motioned me over to him.

"So," he said. "I see your performance before her ladyship was a success. Now you are one of us. During dinner, you will sit there—" he pointed to a stool in the corner— "and you will play pleasing music. Do not sing. If her ladyship desires singing after dinner, she will let Master Charlo know, he will let me know, and I will let you know. Otherwise, play right through until I tell you that you may leave for the kitchen to get something to eat. Understood?"

I nodded yes.

"Good lad," he said. He looked me up and down approvingly. "You are much cleaner now." Then he hustled away.

That's the way it happened. I played. After dinner, the earl's lady asked for singing, so I went back to the dais beside the hearthstones, and I sang. Four of the young ladies were there, but not the oldest. Diera. The one who had pretended to faint. I didn't sing Johnny the Traveler's song. Then, afterward, I was given some food in the kitchen.

For the next two days, I lived in a state of perpetual fear. Each night, I played at dinner. Afterward, each night, I entertained the daughters and the lady of the earl. Diera did not reappear.

On the third day, after my entertaining was over, I went to the kitchen shed as usual and then, as usual, gulped down my food while I hurried to my room. Silly, I know, to think of that room as a refuge. Somehow it calmed me to be there. This particular evening, I was licking the last of the grease from my fingers, trying to make sure it didn't end up staining my finery, when I saw, down the shadowy corridor, that the door to my room was ajar. Light poured out of it.

My heart began to pound. I needed to run, but where? Before I could think it through, one of the castle's guards stepped out of my room and pointed at me. "You," he said. "In here."

It was useless to try to run now. With dragging feet I approached my door. He grabbed me by the shoulder and shoved me inside. *Here's where they finally arrest me*, I thought numbly.

A man was in my room, and two guards. The man's face was in shadow.

"Sit there," this man told me, pointing to the bed shelf. I did, rubbing my shoulder where the guard had wrenched it. "You know why we're here," said the man. His voice had an odd lilt to it, as if he normally spoke a different language than ours.

"No, sir." Those were the words that came out of my mouth, although in another part of myself, I was wondering why I was bothering to lie.

"Surely you do know."

I made myself look as wide-eyed and innocent as possible. "No, sir. Have I done wrong?"

As the guard lifted his rushlight torch higher, I felt the kind of paralysis you experience when you suddenly notice a serpent before you, ready to strike. It was the man Wat had warned me about. What had Wat called him? *The most dangerous man in the realm.*

The man stared at me hard through narrowed eyes. "The one who came here with you a few days ago. That was your brother?"

"Yes, sir."

"And his name is—?

"Kenning, sir. He is a juggler. He is the best juggler." I felt all the breath had left my body. I worked to get the words out.

"Kenning. Your brother."

"Yes, sir."

"I take it Silvertongue is not your actual surname."

"Oh, no, sir. Kenning thought it up. He thought it would be a good thing for me."

"What is your real surname?"

I looked up, trying to act surprised. "We don't have one. Maybe we did." I pretended to think about it. "Maybe we had one, when I was a baby. But then our parents got took with the plague, and then—well, if we did have one, I don't know what it was."

"I see," said the man. His face was impossible to read. Maybe it was the rushlight, but his eyes looked deep-set, hooded, reptilian. "Where did Kenning go, after you had your bath on your first evening here, and the servant brought you to Master Charlo?"

"I don't know, sir. They didn't let me see him after that." I let the tears well up in my eyes. "I told them he would be worried, but they haven't given me leave to go to him." Now I was puzzled. No one was confronting me about the men in the bathing shed.

But suppose they had Wat, and this dangerous man was testing me with his questions? Suppose Wat's story and mine didn't jibe?

"See these guards?" the man said, breaking into my worries.

I looked from one of them to the other. Summoning up my confidence again, I nodded.

"They'll be in the guard house at the main gate. If your brother makes any kind of contact with you, go to the guard house and let them know to send for me. They'll know what it is about."

"Who shall I say they should send for? Oh, sir," I burst out. "Is Kenning in trouble? He is a good brother. He'd never do wrong."

*Oh, no,* I thought. I had overplayed my hand. Surely this man knew that Kenning and I, Aedan, were young rogues roaming the countryside, scamming whomever we ran across. My talents as a singer would only made our roguery more successful. I couldn't possibly be naïve enough not to know what my brother was up to.

But the man said only, "If you hear from your brother, tell the guards to send for Sir Caedon."

"Yes, sir." I figured this man was Sir Caedon himself. He looked to be a bit older than Avery, quite a bit older than Wat. He was simply dressed, but as I stared at him, I saw the signs of wealth about him. Soft white hands. Linen cloth of the best quality in his plain dark tunic and cloak. The best leather on his feet. A hint of gold about his wrists and his neck. A jeweled brooch at the shoulder to fasten his sweeping black cloak.

As Caedon turned to the door, he stopped and looked me carefully up and down. To the guards he said, "You may go. Leave one of the torches."

The guards saluted him and clumped down the corridor.

Caedon took the remaining rushlight and lifted it high. He laughed.

"Aedan Silvertongue, is it? You're a girl."

"No, sir, of course not, sir, I—"

"Easy enough to find out the truth of it," said Cadeon. He placed the torch deliberately in its bracket. Then he unsheathed his sword. "Stand up. Strip."

"But sir, I—"

Caedon moved the tip of his sword until it was at my throat. Gently, with the very point, he tilted my head up. I could feel a trickle of blood running down my neck.

"You see my blade is very sharp," he told me.

Trembling, I obeyed his order.

"Yes, indeed. I see," he said. "No, don't move. Stand still and let me look at you."

With the tip of his blade, he touched me there. And there. And there.

He laughed again. "Now why in the Nine Spheres would you do something like this, Master Aedan? And how did you manage it? Why not come into the castle and sing as a girl? I find this quite intriguing."

I was silent. Actually, I doubt if I could have spoken, even if he'd turned his blade on me in earnest. All words had left me.

"Of course I could get the truth out of you easily if I wanted to," he was saying past the red roar in my ears. "There are very simple methods I could use."

He watched me as I shivered, and he laughed again. "But I don't want to," he said. "I can find out your reason without those methods, interesting as they might be to apply." He walked all the way around me, coming back face to face, too close. His eyes traveled up and down my body. His gaze was almost a physical thing.

I flinched, and he smiled, a smile that turned his mouth cynical and crooked. His face was long and pale in the rushlight. His eyes were strangely golden. Like a wolf's, I imagined. A memory intruded itself into the moment, the time I had tumbled down while playing and had come face to muzzle with the beadle's mastiff Bogo, a dog poised to bite. I thought of Man-Dog Rough-Gray in my book at home. A thousand thoughts compressed themselves into a single instant.

"Now let me puzzle this out," said this man, Sir Caedon. He sat down on my bed shelf and looked up at me past steepled fingers, his eyes glittering in the rushlight. "This conundrum you've handed me. You've gotten into the castle using your ruse," he said. "Someone wanted you in here. So they could do what? No, don't answer that. I don't need to hear your lies." He considered me further.

I wasn't sure I could stay standing. I wasn't sure I wouldn't collapse at his feet. The dank air seeping in from the high narrow window of my room was chill against my skin, and the smoke from the rush light was pungent. I wondered if I would be sick. A bitter taste of vomit rose in my throat.

"I'm thinking that same someone is probably in the castle right now. I'm thinking that if I could find him, I'd be able to discover what he wants here."

I felt a glimmer of hope now. Surely Wat was long gone. Or was he? What did he think to get out of our little game? I realized

I didn't know. I had thought he wanted a way to come and go from outside to inside so he could listen in on the conversations of important people and send the information along to Avery. I had thought, when the earl's lady had me detained, that his plan had come to nothing. But maybe that wasn't his plan at all.

"Interesting," said Caedon. "You're the very portrait of conflicting doubts and fears, my dear. I'm beginning to think you really don't know much. I'm beginning to think you're only a pawn. But you've been very helpful. Yes. Very, very helpful. I'm going now." He sheathed his sword. "I suppose it will be useless to tell you to send the guards for me if you see your brother, or whoever he is." He plucked the torch from its bracket and held it high, examining me from head to toe, taking his time about it. "But if you were to do that," he said at last. He stopped for a moment and looked hard at me again. "If you were to do that, you'd find yourself rewarded very handsomely." He reached out his hand as if he were about to touch me, but he didn't.

He turned on his heel and left the room.

I stood frozen, listening to his footsteps echoing away from me down the corridor.

I crept trembling in the dark into my blankets and covered my nakedness.

At first, I couldn't think at all, just lie there horror-struck.

As the first light of dawn turned the cell-like room from full dark to a dim gray, I forced myself to think over what had happened.

Now the bodies would be discovered. Surely Sir Caedon would question Master Charlo next to find out what he knew about Wat, and that would lead the castle authorities straight to the bodies. Master Charlo would see right away that Wat must be the killer. Still, he might not realize I was involved. I had a moment of hope.

Master Charlo already thought Wat was in the castle to prowl around and thieve and rob. When Sir Caedon led the castle's guards to the bodies, Master Charlo would recognize the dead tub man, and he'd see that Wat had killed some other man whose dead-white swollen body got pulled from the cistern too—but Master Charlo really might not realize who this other man could be. The body wasn't wearing servant's livery. It had no marks of identification on it.

Master Charlo didn't know that Wat had taken the servant's clothes. As far as Master Charlo knew, this other murdered man might be any random castle dweller that Wat had come upon and murdered too. The servants looked so interchangeable to Master Charlo that when he had seen Wat escorting me into the castle keep, he had simply accepted Wat as the servant he had assigned to keep an eye on us. Wat had relied on that, and Wat was right. How was Master Charlo to know the real reason Wat had killed the men? Master Charlo thought I was a boy.

My heart sank. Fooling Master Charlo was one thing; fooling Sir Caedon quite another. Sir Caedon would see right away that I was connected to the killings. He knew I wasn't what I seemed.

At least Sir Caedon's questions told me he hadn't found Wat. Not yet.

I could only hope that Wat had hitched up Millicent and had gotten out of there, abandoning me to whatever fate Sir Caedon eventually decided for me.

That was the only thing Wat could do, I argued to myself. He might have tried to inquire after me when I wasn't escorted back to the wagon that night, or he might not have risked it. But I didn't come back, and he could draw his own conclusions about that, including the fear that things had gone very wrong and that I had been unmasked.

My dread magnified as I lay huddled in the dark. Wat must have known—must have known from the outset—that the bodies would be discovered, and that sooner or later they'd be traced back to me.

Whatever he thought or knew, he couldn't possibly have tried to come into the castle after me and spirit me back out. He'd only have to hope I knew so little that if the castle authorities suspected me and tortured me, I wouldn't be able to tell them much. In fact, I realized, thinking back on the words we'd exchanged before getting ourselves into the castle, that's exactly what he hoped.

And that's the way it worked in Wat's world. I saw it now. Cut and run. Never jeopardize the great plan, whatever that was. Not for anyone. People died in the service of the plan. The others kept on, soldiers in a shadow army. In fact, although my mind flinched away from the thought, I knew that if Wat had had the chance to do it, he would have killed me himself to make sure I didn't tell the castle authorities even the little I knew. Or that's what he should have done.

He would have had to. His masters would have made him do it. And he was good at it. Killing.

I realized that Wat was my master, but the leader, Avery, was Wat's. Wat was not his own man.

Coming to that conclusion gave me a strange kind of comfort.

But then I forced myself to think past the shock of what had happened to me. To think about what Sir Caedon had said to me, and why he hadn't had me immediately thrown into the castle's dungeons.

My mind circled back to Wat, then. I started to wonder again about Wat. Why had Wat let me go to the castle at all, once it was clear how easily I could be unmasked by the servants sent to bathe me? Why not kill me before it came to that? Or if not kill me, then get away in the night together, as we had fled from the market town when I was recognized.

Something else must be going on. Something important that needed to be done inside the castle, whatever the risk. Something I didn't understand.

My fear was that while I didn't understand it, this dangerous man, Sir Caedon, did.

Between intense bursts of thinking about my situation, about Wat, about what was going to happen to me, I felt a burning shame. My experience standing before Sir Caedon kept coming back to me in flashes. Caedon's sword. My terrible feeling of exposure. Caedon's avaricious eyes. The rage I felt. The humiliation and fear. Beyond it all, the horror at seeing how much Caedon enjoyed watching my utter helplessness in his power.

# Chapter Eleven

# Ride

The very day after Sir Caedon had unmasked me, the bathing shed was buzzing with people. Sir Caedon had probably told them what to look for. I realized I had forgotten something important. The searchers would find the bodies, but they'd also find our clothes in the cistern. Now I realized I really was lost. The Kenning the Juggler costume which I had been wearing, along with Wat's regular patched trousers and tunic, would show beyond doubt that the murders had occurred while I was in the bathing shed with Wat. I was an accomplice. Surely they'd be coming to take me now.

Later that afternoon, amazed that no one had arrested me yet, I couldn't keep myself from edging near the shed and watching the activity, hoping no one was watching me.

A forlorn-looking man was standing outside the bathing shed, and two servants were rolling a cart out of it toward him. On the cart was a rough cloth covering a lumpy shape. The servants handed the cart over to the man, and he began pulling it toward the steep path down from the castle motte to the outer bailey.

Then a little group stepped forward. A woman and two children. The woman was wailing and twisting her hands in her apron. As before, servants of the castle pulled a cart bearing a lumpy covered shape out of the shed. They paused beside her and pulled back the covering. She let out a harrowing shriek and fell over the body. That's what it was. Even from across the bailey, I could see what it was. It was probably the servant's body. He had had a wife and children. Wat and I had destroyed their lives. Someone stepped up to the woman and helped her as she, too, pulled her cart toward the castle gates. I watched as she struggled down the path with her burden and out into the world beyond, her fatherless children trailing behind her.

*Now they'll come for me, whether Sir Caedon tells them to or not,* I thought then. *Maybe,* I thought, my heart sinking low, *it's only justice that they take me.* I'd helped to murder an innocent man and leave his family destitute and unprotected. I had to wonder whether I was any better than my family's killers.

The next few days were torture. The flashes of shame continued as I kept waiting for the blow to fall on me, incredulous that it hadn't. Day after day, it didn't. I hadn't laid eyes on Sir Caedon again.

Several days later, I made my circuit around the inner bailey once more and saw that the bathing shed was quiet. On that particular day, I returned to my room and sat on the shelf bed, as always, to wait for my summons later to play at the evening meal. I couldn't think. I couldn't even practice on my rebec. A sen'night at least had gone by. How many more days would it take, I kept wondering.

Even though I thought I was prepared, I jumped as if someone had knifed me when the door of the room swung open.

It was only the maid-servant, though. "Are you ill, young master? I hope not, because their ladyships have commanded you to come to them."

"Now?"

"Yes," she said. "Go to the little antechamber." She hustled away, closing the door behind her.

Finally. This was where they'd grab me and haul me off. I struggled into my good clothing and took my rebec. A sick kind of doom descended on me. When I closed the door to my room, I thought it was the last I'd ever see of it. I was right.

By now, I knew the way. In only a few days, my life in the castle had become routine. I was one of its inhabitants, serving the vast needs of one of the Sceptered Isle's great noble families.

By now, I knew what the maid servant meant by "the little antechamber." It was a small room just outside the private chambers of the family. It was the out-of-the-way place servants sat on benches against the stone walls, waiting for their assignments. Master Charlo would thrust his head in and summon someone to empty the chamber pots down the noisome slit that led to the sewers running into the castle moat, or to take their ladyships' dainty personal things down to be washed in the laundry shed with the enormous steaming tubs and the raw-armed laundresses. Or he'd send someone out to the kitchen for fruit and sweets. Or he'd tell someone to go in to their ladyships and play them a tune.

It was mid-afternoon. Unless you were in the kitchen, it was a dead time of day in the castle. No one was in the antechamber but me. I sat on one of the benches and leaned against the wall. The sense of dread I felt was overpowering. I felt a trickle of sweat between my shoulder blades.

The door creaked open a crack. I jumped up, expecting to see Master Charlo's sour face, the face he presented to his fellow servants, not the one he presented to their ladyships. Or Sir Caedon's face. But that was not what I saw.

It was the Lady Diera, the first I'd seen of her since her fainting act many days before. She darted a quick look about the room. Then she stepped in and closed the door behind her.

"Mirin," she said to me. "We're heading out for a drive in the countryside. You're coming with me to entertain me. It will be the driver—we can trust him—and me, and you. We'll drive out as if on a pleasure jaunt. We'll come to a little stand of trees. Wat will get you there."

I nearly fell down. My knees actually buckled.

"Why—" I began. "But you—"

"No questions. Just do as I say. We have very little time to make this work. Follow me."

"My lady, stop," I said.

She turned back to me with a look of irritation.

"Did anyone see you come here?" I asked her.

"No. I made sure of that. Follow me."

"But Sir Caedon—"

She gave me a startled look.

"He found me out, lady. As you have."

"That's something to think on," she said after a pause. "He can't stop us now, though. He left the castle yesterday for his estates. Do you know that man hopes to marry me?" She paused and looked at me, her eyes thoughtful. "What you're telling me makes me think he's used you to set a trap for me, and for Wat. We've played into his hands. He wouldn't have gone away otherwise. But it's too late to do anything about it now. So come with me. At least let's get you out of here." She turned on her heel and strode out of the room, a different person from the fragile girl she had seemed to be.

I trotted after her.

As we made our way through the castle's inner bailey, I saw how she took the long way around to avoid the bathing shed, then down to the outer bailey.

We ended up in a place I had never seen before, the stables and mews. A red-painted open carriage decorated with gilt was waiting for us. A driver with his hood pulled up was seated on the box, his hands on the reins. He stepped down and helped us both in.

"We have to hurry," Diera told the driver. "Really hurry. Something has happened."

He nodded.

Diera made a big show of settling herself grandly on the seat of the carriage, spreading the fine linen of her skirt so every spangle and jewel glittered and shone. How I admired her presence of mind. She motioned me to a bench across from her. I perched on it, holding on in alarm as the carriage jostled over the cobblestones toward the gate, a bit too fast.

The castle residents stopped what they were doing as we drove past, bowing their heads and pulling their forelocks respectfully.

When we reached the castle gates, the guards, too, bowed.

"Driving out into the country, your ladyship?" asked one.

"I am. The weather is so fine," Diera replied, smiling down graciously upon him.

"Your ladyship, be careful. There's reports of bandits, and—"

"Leofric will keep me safe," she told him, nodding at her driver, who pulled his forelock obediently. She motioned to the guard to let us through. He did.

My tension didn't ease as we left the castle behind. I thought that at any moment, soldiers sent by Sir Caedon would intercept us. And I saw, from how white her knuckles were as she gripped the sides of the gaily-painted cart, that Diera was thinking the same. As the cart proceeded down the hill, I saw her face was drained of color. She kept touching the circular brooch clasping her cloak at the neck, a beautiful thing. She saw me looking and managed a smile. She unhooked it and handed it to me. Picked out in enamel-work, a blackbird rose from green rushes. Around the circumference there were letters. I read them. *Diera owns this.*

"You know your letters," she murmured, her brows arched in surprise.

"Yes, lady," I said. I handed it back, and she pinned it to her cloak again. I thought again about my beautiful costume, when I first sang from the wagon box stage. *Someone gave it to us*, Wat had said. Maybe this fine lady was one of the wealthy supporters Avery could count on for help.

And then I felt that strange sensation I get when my second sense rises from the well deep inside, the place it usually stays hidden. I keep trying to describe it to you, Jillie. You know the feeling you get in the summer, when the air gets so sultry it splits the sky apart in a mighty flash? That feeling. And words came to me then.

*Your life and this woman's are connected.*

Before I had a chance to think about the deep message I'd received, we were jouncing past the little spot where Wat and I had set our wagon up and tethered Millicent. I turned to look, but wagon and ox, of course, were no longer there. Those events seemed part of a distant past, when they had actually happened only a sen'night or so earlier. But I was distracted from the strange sensation that had made the hairs on the back of my neck stand up, and the thought about some connection with Diera sank down again into that inaccessible place inside me.

Diera leaned forward. "Take the other way, Rafe. Not the way we planned. I've had news Caedon's men may be following us. Go left at the crossroads. Then a right at the next lane."

*So the driver's name isn't Leofric*, I thought. *It's Rafe.*

This man, Rafe, gazed back over his shoulder at her, and they exchanged a long, intense look. Not like grand lady and lowly manservant. Not like that at all.

Before I could think through what this could mean, she turned to me. "Caedon is hoping to nose me out as part of the Rising, and he's hoping to catch Wat. I'm thinking we got out just in time, but only just. As soon as we find Wat, the two of you must move fast. I won't stop long enough to tell him about this very disturbing development. I'll have to go straight back. I'll leave it to you to tell him."

Rafe, the driver, took the turning at the crossroads, and then the next, down a disused-looking lane overgrown with grass and weeds. We pulled up to a little stand of trees. I looked around for our player's wagon, but it was not there either. Instead, a man came out from under the trees, a hooded man on a large brown rouncey.

"Here's where we part company, Aedan Silvertongue," said Diera. The driver, the one she'd called Rafe, climbed from his box and handed me down to the ground. Before I could even thank them, Rafe was on the box again. He backed the carriage expertly, urged it forward, and it sped away down the road we had come. Diera turned on her carriage seat to watch me. "You make a fine boy, Aedan Silvertongue," she called after me. "And you sing like the eala." At the turning, she and the carriage were gone.

The man on the horse leapt down and pulled me into an embrace so tight I thought I wouldn't be able to breathe.

"Wat! Wat! I thought you had left me." I was sobbing against him, and he was holding onto me fiercely.

"Never, Mirin. I'm your master, and you're my faithful servant, isn't that so?"

"I thought you'd have me killed, once they took me."

"Never."

"But you don't understand. They unmasked me. They know, Wat. I'm not sure why they let me go, unless—"

"Unless they're tracking you back to me. We need to ride," said Wat. He vaulted back into the saddle and reached down his hand to pull me up behind him.

There were so many questions I wanted to ask him. So many puzzles. But I just held on, and we rode as fast as I think I've ever ridden before. I wasn't even frightened. If the horse stumbled and went down, if we were killed, well. We were going to be killed anyway. There were people looking to find us and kill us.

A sudden thought struck me. The driver of Diera's carriage. Not Leofric. Rafe. He had seemed familiar to me. Now I knew why. He was the man who had exchanged a look with Wat, that night at the castle when I had first come there to play and sing. The man who had come in during Diera's fainting act, and had gone speedily away.

I snugged myself against Wat's back and tried to wipe all thoughts out of my head. Tried to move with the pounding rhythm of horse and rider, to hold on tight, my arms about Wat's waist. Wat clasped one hand about my mine, holding it close. He would never let me fall. Wat's body was warm and familiar, although I had never been physically this close to him before. But I knew what I was feeling was a false sense of security. Wheels were moving within wheels. Wat was in terrible danger—maybe all of them were—and it was because of me.

# Chapter Twelve

# Six Proud Walkers

By that evening, after exchanging our exhausted horse for another, Wat and I were far enough away from the castle that we could breathe a little. Wat eased the horse up and slowed it to a walk. We made our way at a respectable gait through a little glade down a path that led to a small stone house tucked under the side of a hill. A light shone from the single window facing the path.

Wat swung out of the saddle and helped me down. I staggered against him.

"Wait," he said to me. "They don't know we're here." He nodded toward the house. He meant the others in the Rising, the ones I had seen at Old Cwen's house. "I need to talk to you about something before we see the rest of them."

I had a hard time concentrating on what he was trying to tell me. The late afternoon sun slanted down on me, hammering me with its bronze gong.

"How much do you know about the man who drove you and Diera away from the castle?" His tone was guarded.

"His name is Rafe. He's called something else in the castle. Leofric. That's all." Then I paused and squinted up at him past the throbbing in my head. "And you saw him, at the castle. You looked at him, after I finished singing. When we were crossing the bailey after my first performance, I saw you look at him again, and he looked back. And then later, when Diera pretended to faint, he was there, too."

"Right," said Wat. He looked at the ground, his eyes thoughtful. "You're very observant, Mirin. That's a good trait to have. Listen to me carefully," he said after a moment. "I want you to say nothing about Rafe when we get in there." He pointed with his reins toward the stone cottage. "Some people know about Rafe, and some don't."

"And I'm not supposed to know about him," I said. I suppressed a shudder. One more way I was a liability to Wat and to the Rising.

"No, you're not supposed to know about him. But now you do. Let me explain something. I may as well. If you know why you shouldn't talk about it, you're less likely to slip up. It's wrong to keep you in the dark the way we've been doing. We've been trying to keep you safe, but I don't think that's the way to do it." He reached into the pouch at his belt and pulled out an object. He showed it to me. It caught the last of the light as it waned over the mountains.

I breathed in sharply.

"Do you recognize this?" Wat asked me.

"My father. Why do you have my father's brooch?" A chill came over me, and a terrible anger boiled from somewhere deep inside me.

Wat saw it. He put a hand on my shoulder. His voice was gentle. "This is my brooch. Your father made it for me. He made one for all of us, the Six."

I had heard Wat use this term before. I knew the Six were the Rising's leadership.

I remembered my father telling me about making his own brooch. Along with all of his other talents as a maker, he even knew some goldsmithing, although of course he rarely practiced it. He said he learned it from an old man he knew, back when he was a boy. I used to wonder why he didn't set himself up as a goldsmith. The strip of field allotted to us in the village townsland barely grew enough to feed us.

My mother had made an exasperated sound when I brought this up to her once. "How would we get the coin for the materials? Who'd have the coin to buy anything he made? We're all poor folk here."

When she said this, in that tone, I thought I hated her. But I didn't. Later I understood. She was afraid for him.

The golden brooch frightened her most of all. It was beautiful. The whole of it was encircled by a golden ring as big around as my fist. The ring enclosed six rough figures of men. That was the backing. My father put his cloak on and pulled the cloth of it across his body to fasten under the ring at his right shoulder. The cloth of his cloak hid the figures that backed the ring. "They're a secret," he told me once, when I wanted to see them. He made the cloth secure with a long pin, as long as my hand. On the head of the pin, he had fashioned a golden blackbird.

"Why a blackbird?" I'd asked him once.

"My Child is the Child of Earth," he had told me, a rare thing, since he hardly ever spoke of his beliefs. "And the harbinger of the Earth Child is the blackbird."

"What's a harbinger?" I had asked him.

"It's a messenger. A signal that the Earth Child is near and will act to right any wrong," he said. His face grew so solemn then that I knew not to ask any more questions. I wanted to, badly. *What wrongs?* I wanted to ask. But I didn't. My mother had come to the fire, then, where he and I stood looking at his brooch, and she gave him a warning look.

But Wat had a brooch just like my father's.

"Do you remember the sixth verse of Johnny's song?" Wat asked me now.

"*Six for the six proud walkers,*" I quoted, looking down at Wat's brooch. I remembered what Johnny had told me earlier. Now it seemed like a long time ago. I'd looked at his own brooch, the twin of my father's, and I'd listened as he had told me there were four more walkers. *Where are the others?* I'd asked him. *Someday you may meet them,* he'd answered. "These. These are the six proud walkers," I said to Wat. "Johnny told me that. Johnny has one of these brooches too. Had."

"Yes," said Wat.

"You're one of the Six."

He nodded.

"And Johnny was one. And Avery is one. And—"

"And Conal," said Wat.

"And my father was one."

"Yes," said Wat, "and there's one more. Rafe is one. But no one knows he's inside the castle—only Diera, of course, and the other members of the Six."

"There aren't Six any more," I said.

"You're right. Your father and John are—" Wat stopped.

I saw how hard it was for him to say it. "My father's brooch was lost," I said quickly. "I think the soldiers must have taken it."

Wat nodded slowly. "And John's brooch was taken. But the rest of us have our brooches. We almost never wear them. It's too dangerous. So now you understand, Mirin. About the Six. About Rafe. No one must know he's in the castle. I mean, the others—"

I saw this was hard for him to talk about, too. He and Avery and Conal, and this man Rafe, were all the leaders. The others were only followers. They must not know. And I was only a follower, the least important of all. But I knew.

"Why can't the others know?" I asked Wat.

Wat looked at me for a long time, so long I was beginning to get uncomfortable. "We think someone is feeding information about us to Audemar," he said finally. "We think it may be someone close to us. Rafe and Diera think so, too. We're not sure. If it became known that Rafe was working for us on the inside, these betrayers would kill Rafe. So you see how important it is to keep Rafe's presence and name to yourself."

Audemar. That was our king. "Wat, the Rising. . . you're all rebels against King Audemar. But why."

"You don't need to know that," Wat said. His voice was terse and flat. When Wat talked to me like that, I knew he meant, *Shut up. Do as you're told. No questions.*

But I persisted. "Yes, I do need to know. I was nearly killed back there. And. . ." I faltered. "And other things happened there," I continued, forcing my voice to stay calm. "I'm guessing you were nearly killed, too. You have to tell me. It's not fair."

When he didn't answer, I stood on tiptoe and looked him in the eye. "It's not fair," I said again. "You are asking me to risk everything, and I don't know why."

Wat leaned wearily against his horse. "It's hard to know how to tell you. I'll talk to you about it later."

"No, now."

He looked off toward the hills down the valley beyond us. Without looking back at me, he said, his voice halting, "You know the Sceptered Isle was not like it is now. The king at that time, King Ranulf, was powerful, just as powerful as Audemar is now. More powerful, I'd say. But he was also merciful and wise. He knew how much people struggled, just to find bread to eat. You must have seen that, in your village. But you may not know he had plans for a different kind of kingdom. A farwydd had visited him, that's what they say, and this had changed his heart, turning him from the new gods back to the old, the gods of our ancestors. From the Lady Goddess to the Children."

"What's a farwydd?"

"A. . .oh, a person who comes from far. A person who sees far. A far-speaker. Far-seer."

"Huh," I said. It sounded like gibberish. It sounded like Wat might not know what a farwydd was, either. But I wanted to keep him talking. I had to know. "These things you're telling me about happened long ago," I said.

"Not so long ago," said Wat, shifting uneasily. "When you were a baby. Some of them when you were older. When I was a young boy. I remember many of these things. You would have been too little."

"So Ranulf was our king, not Audemar."

"Ranulf was Audemar's father. Ranulf the Good," said Wat. "Ranulf the Fourth in the chronicles, but many people had taken to calling him Ranulf the Good. You don't hear that now. It's forbidden. Audemar doesn't want anyone remembering. When people were starving, King Ranulf sent food out in wagons to all the villages. When plague came, he sent out healers. But he realized that this wasn't enough. People needed to be able to take care of themselves. They couldn't always rely on some big powerful ruler to help them out."

"Yes," I said. "I see. He does sound good. So then we began worshipping the Children instead of the Lady Goddess."

"No, that's not the way of it. King Ranulf never forbade anyone worshipping the Lady. My mother worshipped her."

"So did mine," I said. "And Old Cwen does."

"But Ranulf saw a different way, and he made his son and heir promise to continue the teachings of the Children."

"I see. So why would you oppose King Audemar, his heir?"

"So many questions," said Wat, looking at me at last, exasperated. "King Audemar is a usurper. He killed the rightful heir to Ranulf and undid all the good Ranulf had done. Audemar decrees that everyone must worship the Lady on point of death."

"Oh," I said. "And all of you worship the Children. And Rafe does. So he's in danger."

"It's more complicated than that. All you need to know is this. If you reveal that Rafe is the inside man, you'll endanger his life, and you'll endanger the Rising."

"I promise I won't say anything about him, then. But don't the others suspect Rafe is the inside man?"

"Everyone thinks Rafe is in the Baronies arranging to get us some coin there. We're about out of funds. Rafe's from the Baronies, and he knows people there. You know about the Baronies, right?"

"Not very much," I admitted. And there my curiosity came to an abrupt end. A wave of dizziness washed over me. Wat jumped to me in alarm. He put out a hand to steady me. "Let's get you inside."

Black and green spots were appearing and disappearing in front of my eyes. I felt strange. Wat half-led, half-carried me to the door. He didn't need to knock. It opened immediately. In the doorway stood Avery, the leader, and the other people I remembered from Old Cwen's house.

"She needs a place to be quiet for a while," Wat said. The woman called Torrin took me by the arm and led me inside. She spread a cloak out before the fire and made me lie down.

One of the others, the woman named Lorel, stepped outside, exclaiming when she saw Wat's horse, its head drooping, the reins dangling.

"Lorel, forgive me," said Wat. His tone was contrite. "I have abused this horse."

But Avery warmly clasped Wat by the arms. "Wat!" He looked down at me. Torrin had brought me a mug of ale and was helping me sit up so I could drink some. "And young Aedan." Avery laughed. He bent down to lay a cool hand on my head. He murmured a few of those words they used. "It's good to see you again, Mirin," he said, after. "Wat has told me many fine things about your service to him."

*When has he been able to do that?* I wondered. But Wat was speaking urgently. "Avery, something has gone wrong."

"Were you followed?" Avery's voice was quiet and controlled.

"I don't think so. But something strange is going on."

"Tell me," Avery said. "We'll talk outside." To me he said, "Don't worry, Mirin. Stay by the fire and get warm."

It was a bit past midsummer, but the nights were crisp. The fire felt good. I held out my hands to it. I tried not to think. I was bedraggled. My linen trousers were ruined, and somewhere along the way I had lost the little feathered cap.

Wat and Avery didn't come back into the cottage for a long time. When they did, Avery summoned the rest and they began talking earnestly together. I tried to shut them out. I didn't want to know what they were talking about. Our plan had failed. I felt to blame and, underneath, I felt the burning shame of my exposure before Caedon. I stared into the flames of the fire as if I'd find answers there to all the puzzling things that had happened to me.

"No." A loud, vehement voice interrupted my thoughts. I looked up, recognizing the voice as belonging to Eris, the exotic-looking woman who had wanted to keep me out of the group. "No!" she said again, even louder. "You're all a pack of fools." She strode over to me and grabbed me by the arm, dragging me to my feet and pulling me after her. "Come over here."

She stood me in front of the others. I tottered under her hands. I could barely stand. "Look," she said. She grabbed my fine linen tunic at the placket with both hands and ripped it open. "Look," she said again. I felt I was about to faint. I tried to cover myself with the torn cloth. Eris hit my hands away. "Look there, all of you. She's budding. And soon, she'll be bleeding."

Everyone stood around me and stared. I felt tears come to my eyes and track down my cheeks.

"Aedan Silvertongue," she said to them. Her voice was mocking. "What foolery. You can't pass her for a boy, not for long. You've paraded her around as the girl she is. Look how well that turned out. Now this boy thing. It worked. It did work. But now." She took her hands off me and flung away out the door.

"No." I was shaking my head. "No, it didn't work."

As if coming out of a trance, Wat whipped off his cloak and covered me. He drew me to him and stared around at the others, a defiant stare. "She's mine. You gave her to me, Avery. It's my decision what happens to her, not Eris's. Not anyone's. Not yours, Avery. Mine." In my ear, he muttered, "No crying, Mirin. Don't let them see it. Especially not her."

Avery stepped to the fire and picked up a poker. He knelt down to bank the fire so it would not burn out during the night. Finally he stood and turned to the rest of us. "Get some sleep, all of you. We're tired after a long and troubling day. Wat, you are young. I know you didn't mean your words as a challenge to me. You and I will talk these matters over by ourselves. But now, sleep." With that, he made his way to a corner of the room, wrapped himself in his cloak, and lay down. The others followed his lead. The cottage had only the one long room. We all found places on the floor to sleep.

Wat drew me over to another corner, pointed to a spot against the wall, and waited until I had lain down wrapped in his cloak. I tucked my rebec in the corner, positioning it so it would not get crushed if I rolled over in the night. Then Wat lay down beside me. No one could get to me there, not without stepping over Wat first.

"I can't sleep," I whispered to him.

"You have nothing to be ashamed of. She has," he said, indicating with a nod the window where we could see Eris outlined against the starlight. She had come in but stood staring out, her shoulders hunched.

"You don't understand. He did that to me." I was miserable. I felt like a thing, an object someone has used and tossed aside.

"Who did?" Wat propped himself on an elbow, looking down at me. "Did what?"

"Sir Caedon. And now her."

"Nine Spheres. What did he do to you?"

"He looked, just like Eris made you all look."

"And that's all?"

"That's all? That's all?" I felt the hysteria rising in me.

"Shh," Wat said. "Shh now." He soothed me the way I had seen him soothing his horse. "I just want to make sure he didn't do anything worse. Anything else."

I shook my head.

"Thank the Child for that," he said. "I know it was bad, Mirin. It could have been so much worse."

"But what he did—"

"I know," said Wat. Even in the dimness of the banked fire, I could tell his eyes were blazing. He reached out his hand to touch me. I flinched back.

Wat took both my hands in his. In the dark, his voice came to me raw and anguished. "I promise you, Mirin Far-meadow. I promise this to you. I will never hurt you. Never. Never."

Then I was able to lie down and try to sleep. After a while, I sat up again.

"But Wat," I said. "Why did he let me go?"

"I don't know. Sleep now."

"If it wasn't to track you here, then why?"

"I'm asking myself that too."

"I failed," I told him bitterly. "Eris is right."

"Listen to me. You didn't fail." After a moment, he sat up too and put a hand on my shoulder. "Look, Mirin. You got me into the castle. That's all I needed. The results were—not what I hoped or thought. But at least I found that out. And I found out another important thing. So our plan worked."

A sudden thought occurred to me. I looked past Wat to Eris. She was still at the window. "What did she mean about me bleeding?" I whispered to Wat, lying back down and trying to find a more comfortable position on the hard-packed earth of the cottage floor. "Sir Caedon knicked me with his sword, but I didn't really bleed. Or not much." When he was silent, I persisted. I really wanted to know. "She said I would soon be bleeding."

Now Wat raised himself on one elbow and really looked at me. In the dim light from the banked fire, I saw how startled he was. "Oh holy Lady," he said. "You need a mother."

"I do not!"

"Sleep." And he wouldn't say another word to me.

It was clear he couldn't sleep, either, though. After a while, he got up from his place beside me. I wasn't afraid. He just moved to the bench by the fire, still within reach. Through my drowsiness, I saw someone else had joined him there. Avery, their leader.

I lay watching them sleepily in the firelight, thinking over what Wat had told me. Audemar did sound like a bad king, I thought. But was that enough of an excuse for murder and deception and assassination? Then the faces of my dead family members rose up before me in memory, and I realized that Audemar must be responsible. The dark leader who had watched my burning cabin must have been Audemar's man. A red rage began to rise inside me, and sleep fled from me.

Somehow I must have slept at last. I woke early, before the others, stiff and sore from riding all day and sleeping on hard earth all night. Wat was flung out on his back, and he was snoring a little. He barely stirred as I crept over him to go outside and find the jakes. He must have been more exhausted than I was, especially if he had spent half the night talking with Avery.

There was no jakes. I had to make do in the woods behind the cottage. As I came back up the path, she was standing there barring my way. Eris.

I gave her as level a look as I could summon, but I was afraid.

She drew one of her knives. She was always playing with them. Always practicing with them, throwing them, retrieving them, throwing them again. She was good. Actually, now that I know more about it, the best I've ever seen.

"Why do you want to kill me?" I said to her.

"I want to kill you before you kill me. Before you get us all killed. That's what should have happened long since. Someone should have had the spine to do it. To kill you. Stupid brat."

The crunch of stone behind us made her flinch, but only slightly. I wouldn't have seen it if I hadn't been looking straight into her eyes. She eased the knife back into the sheath at her belt.

"Having a talk, the two of you?" It was Avery.

"Yes, I'm letting our little friend know what kind of danger she's putting us in," said Eris.

"As you know very well, Eris, that's for me to decide. We've talked about this."

"Yes. Brother." She bit that last word out and turned on her heel, stalking away into the woods. Now I understood why Avery tolerated, from her, what he didn't appear to tolerate from anyone else.

"Am I?" I looked up at Avery, anguish in my heart. "Am I endangering you?"

"You may be," he said.

"I think I may be too. Did Wat tell you about—about Sir Caedon?"

"Yes," said Avery briefly. "I know the man. I'm thinking whatever he's up to might not be what we think it is. I want you to put it out of mind, what he did to you. I know that's probably hard, maybe too hard. But try." We had begun walking together down the path, away from the house. I realized that once he had gotten me away from Wat, Avery could easily kill me himself, and Wat wouldn't be able to do anything about it, nor blame Eris. I realized it might be a good solution to Avery's problem with all three of us, especially after what had happened with Sir Caedon. But he didn't. After a while, he spoke again. "Tell me something, Mirin," he said. "Why do you stay with us?"

"I have no choice, do I?"

"Certainly you do. I imagine there were a number of occasions when you could have slipped away from Wat, back there on the road. You could have betrayed Wat, and all of us, while you were in the castle. Easily."

I thought guiltily of the moment Wat offered me a chance to escape to the little temple.

"You could have tried to buy favor with Caedon," Avery continued. "But you didn't. Why?" When I didn't answer, he looked thoughtful. "It couldn't be out of loyalty to me. You barely know me." As if to himself, he said, "You don't know who I am."

I had asked myself the same questions he was asking me now. "It's my father," I said at last. "And Johnny the Traveler. And my mother and Jillie. I didn't know why they were killed. Now I know why. Or a bit of it." I stopped and my hands balled into fists, the anger rising in me the way it had the night before. "And I want them all dead, the people who did it."

"Ah," said Avery. "I'm beginning to understand you better. But Mirin, knowing your family were killed because of us, you might think to blame us for their deaths. And hate us, and wish us ill."

"They were going to kill me, too, if they could find me, you know," I told him.

"Why is that, do you think?"

"I don't know," I admitted. "But that's what I think they would have done, if they had caught me. They killed my family. My whole family!"

"Yes, they did do that. I'm going to tell you why. They did it because your father was a very brave man who fought for us, for our side."

"Wat told me," I said. "But what is that—our side. What side? Wat has told me a little, but I know almost nothing about it, just that my father died for it, for these ideas of yours, and that somehow, to the king's men, it meant killing us all."

"Right now I only ask that the two of us come to an understanding. I'll explain everything to you in time, Mirin. Or better, I'll have Wat explain it." At my skeptical look, he amended, "I'll have him help you understand. So is loyalty to Wat one of the reasons you didn't betray us?"

"Wat is my master. I would never betray him." I surprised myself as these words came marching unbidden out of my mouth.

"Then he is right to protect you," said Avery. He seemed to be suppressing a smile. "That is his duty to you. Your faithful service is your duty to him." He turned around and began walking back to the cottage. I followed.

"May I ask you one thing?" I said, struck by a sudden thought. He turned and waited. "Did the king's men kill Johnny the Traveler?"

"Yes, they did," he told me, and a darkness came over his face that frightened me more than anything else I had felt while I walked with him, even while wondering if he might take the knife from his belt and cut me down. "They tortured John," said Avery slowly. "They broke his fingers to let him know he'd never play music again. They cut out his tongue to let him know he'd never sing. They damaged him in every way one man can damage another. Then they killed him. Do you understand?"

"Yes." My heart broke at his words. Looking at Avery, I thought to myself, *Your heart is broken, too.*

"And they shattered his rebec and threw the pieces in the sewer under the dungeon of that castle that you and Wat entered."

"That—" I stammered. "How do you know that?"

"Wat found them there, afterward."

That's when I saw who Wat's former partner on the road must have been. Johnny the Traveler. The roles between Wat and his partner must have been the reverse of what I had thought. Wat hadn't been the master in that partnership. Johnny was Wat's master, and Wat was bound to him to serve him all his days.

# Chapter Thirteen

# Long-Lost Boys

Wat and I were sitting together under a tree by the little stream that ran beside the stone cottage. I had noticed Avery talking to him privately a few days after our arrival at the cottage. They'd both glanced in my direction. Later that day, Wat promised to tell me things that would make sense of what had happened. I knew Avery must have been as good as his word, must have made Wat promise to explain things to me.

Wat wasn't doing it. He was avoiding me. We had gotten close during our flight, and after. But now, confusingly, I felt a distance between us. Today I cornered him. I wasn't going to let him put his explanations off any longer.

"You said you used me to get into the castle so you could find something there, something important."

He nodded.

"What thing?" I wasn't giving up.

Wat had an apple, and now he was studiously paring it. Without looking at me, he said, "I have a hard time talking to you about all this. I know you didn't go to school, so you don't know your letters. Girls don't go to school. But didn't you have friends who were boys? Didn't they learn about these things in school, about Audemar and Ranulf?"

"Nobody in my village went to school. It's clear you weren't raised in a village, Wat."

"That tone of yours. Calling me 'Wat' as if I were some fellow. Be respectful. Who's your master?"

"You are, Wat, and I do know my letters. My mother taught me. But tell me more about this king."

Wat gave me a sharp poke in the ribs with his elbow, but I just poked him back.

"Insubordinate brat." Wat gave me a lazy smile. I hid my amazement. Here, at the cottage, in spite of everything that had happened, Wat was starting to relax. He seemed more like the almost-boy he was. "King Ranulf had three sons," Wat said at last, with a sigh. "Don't you want to sit here under the trees and not talk about these terrible things? Haven't you been through enough?"

"No," I said, feeling my chin set stubbornly. "Avery said he'd tell you to explain it all to me. I want to know. Now."

Wat didn't look up. He threw the apple core away from him into the high grass. I began to wonder whether he'd talk to me at all, but then he took a stick and began drawing diagrams in the dirt. "See, the crown prince, the oldest brother, was to inherit the throne from Ranulf. That's the rightful order of things."

"Why is that the rightful order of things?" I wanted to know.

"It just is. The other sons, princes of the blood, had lands and castles of their own, but they swore fealty to their oldest brother, as was their duty." He tapped with his stick at an x he had drawn in the diagram.

"Why was that their duty?" I asked.

"Nine Spheres, girl. Will you listen?"

I nodded. A perverse desire to torment Wat had come over me. It felt good.

Wat forged doggedly ahead. "A dis-ease attacked the king, or so it was said. Whatever the cause might have been, King Ranulf sickened and died. The crown prince promised at the king his father's sickbed that he would carry out the king's wishes. He would study the words of the farwydd who had come to the king. He promised to change things to make ordinary people's lives better."

"And he's now our king? This crown prince?"

"No. I thought I told you." Wat gave me an exasperated look. "The crown prince—his name was Artur—the night before his coronation, he was overthrown. He was killed. Soon it was clear to everyone, although no one would say so outright, who had hired the assassins. His own brother Audemar. The second brother. Audemar had the rightful heir, Artur, murdered while he slept. Artur's wife Ailys was sleeping beside him, but the assassins did not harm her. Someone had probably slipped Artur and Ailys a potion to make them sleep soundly through any unusual noises, or maybe. . ." Wat trailed off. "You've really never heard about any of this?" he asked me. He started rubbing out his diagrams with the stick.

"No. My parents never talked about such things, and no one in our village did, either—not to me, anyway." When Wat had begun talking, it seemed to me I was in for a dull history lesson. I was beginning to regret pressing him to explain. Now, in spite of myself, I was getting interested.

After a moment, Wat continued. "This betrayer-brother, Audemar, forced Artur's queen, Ailys, to marry him. Some say he didn't have to force her. Audemar imprisoned Artur's two small sons and had himself crowned king. A short time later, he gave Artur's oldest child, a girl just a bit younger than I was, to a faithful retainer of his to raise. Thank the Children he didn't have her imprisoned, too, like the little princes. Maybe he didn't think of her as a threat because she was so young when he killed their father. Around twelve. She went through a lot. But now she's with this underling of Audemar's." Wat's eyes were hooded, his light-hearted mood gone. He looked like he might have some terrible memories of his own to get past. *Maybe that's why he doesn't want to talk about any of this*, I thought.

But then I thought about what he was saying. Audemar had preserved his niece, Artur's daughter, because she was so young. Not that young. Only a few years younger than I was now. But Audemar had had his small nephews locked away.

"That doesn't make sense," I told Wat. "The princes were much younger than their sister. Why lock them up?"

"Yes, but the princess wasn't a threat to Audemar the way her brothers were. The boys might grow up to challenge Audemar for the throne. But the princess is only a girl."

"What do you mean, only a girl?" I bristled at this. All my life I'd been hearing it. *You can't do this because you're only a girl. You can't do that because you're only a girl.*

"He can marry her off to someone loyal to him," Wat said, sailing past my objections. "If she has children, they'll be outside the royal line. Her husband may be some commoner or lesser noble, and she's a girl, so—"

I made a scornful noise.

"Stop that." He grabbed me by the arm. "Show some respect. I'm telling you things here, things you'll need to know."

Wat let my arm go and dug the point of his knife into the earth. I could tell talking about this was difficult for him. He was scowling at his knife, not meeting my eye. I decided I'd stop trying to torment him. I decided maybe I'd better listen.

"It was complicated, with Artur's daughter, though. After the assassination, Audemar tried to implicate her. Can you imagine that?" Wat's voice had turned scathing. "Trying to pin your own horrific deed on a twelve-year-old girl?"

"They thought she was the assassin?" I looked at Wat blankly.

"No, just that she was somehow involved. They soon saw that would lose them sympathy, the real assassins did, and then they backed off. That's when they sent her away. Get her off people's minds. That must have been their thinking."

"What happened to the little boys? Artur's sons?" I asked. "And why didn't their mother, Queen Ailys, help them?"

"No one knows what has happened to the boys. The older was the legitimate heir after his father. Think about it. At his father's death, by law, that boy actually became our king. So he is in terrible danger. He may be dead. Both boys may be. A fortnight ago, though, we got some information that made us think they're alive, or one of them, anyway.

"And that's what Rafe and I were looking for. We thought they'd been taken to the earl's castle. We thought we knew where they were being kept. But—" Wat fell silent for a moment. "We didn't find them."

*Two, two, the long-lost boys, clothed all in green, oh,* I sang softly.

"See? You know more than you think. Did you know green is the color of the royal family? Artur's color?"

"But King Audemar's is scarlet," I said, shying away from the memory of the scarlet-clad soldiers stalking the meadow where my family's bodies lay. Then I thought of something else I wanted to know. "But the queen? Why didn't she stop Audemar from imprisoning her sons?"

"They aren't her sons. Artur's wife died in childbed, giving birth to the second. Queen Ailys is their stepmother. Some think Audemar deliberately planned it so she would catch Artur's eye. Then, after Artur was dead, Audemar married her himself. Some think Audemar even had Artur's first wife murdered."

"They could have used witchcraft," I said, and shuddered.

"That's just in stories," Wat said with a dismissive gesture.

*So,* I thought. *You don't know everything, Wat.* I didn't believe in witchcraft, not exactly. But I did believe in powers. Some used their powers and gifts for good, some for ill. *I know you'll use your gift for good,* Johnny had told me, so long ago. Somehow, I knew

Johnny wasn't just talking about the gift of being able to play music and sing. He was talking about something deep inside.

Wat was still going doggedly ahead with his explanation. I tried to pay attention. After all, I had forced him to explain, and now he was doing it. "Audemar's no king, although he calls himself king. He's not king by law, and he's not king by spirit," Wat was saying. "Audemar undid everything his father had established to help his people. Besides killing his older brother Artur, Audemar took the lands of his younger brother and exiled him. Then Audemar sent assassins after his younger brother."

"He killed his younger brother too?" This man I'd always thought of as our king—now he horrified me.

"No, he failed, thank the Child," said Wat. He was getting heated. "This youngest son of Ranulf swore to avenge the rightful king, Artur, and restore Artur's older son to the throne. Audemar probably knew he would. Audemar claimed the youngest son was the assassin. By exiling his younger brother and sparing his life, Audemar signaled to the people, *See here? I'm a merciful king*. But by sending his men to kill his younger brother in exile, he hoped to carry out his real intentions. And he hoped to do it far away from the eyes of the small landholders, his biggest supporters. He knew the news of this younger brother's death would filter back, but no one would really know how it happened or who did it."

"Audemar did these things to his own brothers," I said, trying to imagine a person capable of such crimes.

"But the youngest brother is in the realm," said Wat. Now he looked at me. His eyes shone with suppressed excitement. I was beginning to understand why Wat was passionate enough about this cause to turn into a killer. It must be out of loyalty to this youngest brother, I thought, studying Wat's expression.

"The youngest brother has come back in secret," Wat was saying. "So there's hope. The youngest brother swore a sacred oath to the Child of Earth to bring Artur's older son to the throne, if the boy is alive, and if not, to bring the second son to the throne. That's why it was very important for me to get into the earl's castle. Or seemed so." Wat looked thoughtful. "We didn't find the princes. I suppose—I suppose if Artur's sons have both been killed, Artur's youngest brother, the one who has returned from exile, will assume the throne himself. That's more complicated, though. It might look to people as if he wanted the throne for himself all along."

*You've thrown in your lot with this youngest brother*, I thought, looking carefully at Wat. *That's what this is all about*. But I said only, "What about the princess? Why won't she be queen? She is Artur's oldest child, isn't she?"

Wat looked at me as if I had grown a second head. "Women can't inherit the throne. I told you that."

"But at least he plans to rescue her too? The brother who has come back from exile?"

"Of course," said Wat. "She is his niece. He loves her very much. But anyhow, the boys may still be alive. Rafe and I may just have been wrong about where they're being kept."

I was beginning to see now, see it all as Wat laid out the pieces for me. "King Audemar is not our real king."

"No. He is a usurper," Wat repeated slowly, as if I were spectacularly stupid.

"When we were little, we all played a game, king's men against rebels. The king's men were all loyal to King Audemar. The bad rebels were against the king. They were traitors, and we chased them and beat them as they deserved. You and your friends, you're the rebels."

"That's right," said Wat. He had begun to relax again. In the telling, he had tensed. I could tell by the set of his shoulders. I had come to know Wat well by now, so I was glad to see his long body loosen up and his smile appear. He grinned at me. "We're the rebels. See, you do know something about all this."

"And I'm a rebel," I said.

"Yes, you are. A very bad rebel. Why, I think you deserve to be beaten." He made to undo his belt.

I ignored him. I was glad he could joke now, but I really wanted to know. "And my father was a rebel. And Johnny the Traveler."

"Yes," said Wat. His teasing mood changed. In an instant, he grew somber again.

"Avery told me what happened to Johnny the Traveler. It made me sad, Wat." I placed my hand on his arm, timidly. I never touched him, not usually.

"Evil men killed him. And now we're fighting them," said Wat, getting to his feet abruptly and shrugging off my hand. He brushed the leaves from his trousers. "We're fighting," he said again. "But we're losing." He strode off down the path, leaving me to trail along after him.

At least he had told me something, I thought. I didn't feel so ignorant now, and I supposed all that information meant I was safer. These people in the Rising trusted me more. I wasn't sure why, after what had happened with Caedon. After Caedon, I didn't feel better. I felt worse. I was even more of a liability to them now. And I felt tainted.

Wat slowed to let me come up beside him. He looked down at me. "King Ranulf the Good was not some saint, you know. He was an ordinary man with an ordinary man's faults. He was just more powerful than most ordinary men. Here's the difference. He had the will to face himself and try to correct his faults. That, not the power, that's what I call good."

"He had faults? What faults? You and your friends, you'd all die to right the wrong done to him and his family, but you say he had faults."

"Of course he did. This is not some fairy story."

"What faults?"

"Oh—" Wat paused. His face took on a strained expression. "You're too young. Sometime later." He waved a dismissive hand.

"No, now," I told him. "I'm not so young. Eris is right. I'm getting too old to pretend to be a boy." By then, the woman named Torrin, the kindly one, had had a chance to take me off to a private place in the glade. We'd had a long talk. At the end of it, I understood a lot that had been troubling me lately. Things that were happening to my body. At first I was angry with my mother for never telling about such important changes. But as we talked, I realized my mother hadn't had the chance.

I also felt very foolish. So many things I knew! I had watched women giving birth. But other things I had never suspected. I felt young and stupid.

Torrin made me feel better about myself. "We've all felt like that, we women," she had told me. I felt close to her then, as if I were already a woman with a woman friend. "A woman's life is full of secrets. Her body is a secret enclosure."

When I thought of Caedon, though, I felt someone had breached that secret enclosure. Someone not allowed. Someone who took what was not his, and without even laying a hand on me. That filled me with a dark rage. I thought of the charm I'd hidden, back in Old Cwen's loft, and I wished I had it with me. I wished I had the makings of another, and I wished I had Old Cwen's potion-making implements.

"A good man, but no saint," Wat was saying. He had stopped along the path, but now he resumed walking.

I had to speed my steps to keep up with him so I could hear him, he was talking so low. I turned my thoughts away from Caedon and tried to concentrate on what Wat was telling me.

"King Ranulf had a whole other family, a woman he kept, and she had children, too. Three sons, half-brothers to the king's children. And he had other children by other women. I know of at least one more. So Ranulf's remaining true-born son, and his grandchildren, are not the only ones Audemar has hurt."

"Wouldn't King Audemar want to make friends of them, these other sons?" I argued. "Not the true-born son, his younger brother. I can see how King Audemar would regard him as an enemy and a danger. But the other ones? After what King Ranulf did to their mother, wouldn't they all swear loyalty to Audemar? And their mother, wouldn't she?"

"It's more complicated than that, Mirin," said Wat. "She really loved him. In his own way, he may have—oh, who knows," he broke off.

*Telling me these things is torture to him*, I thought.

"These boys, the other sons. The bastards." He said the word as though it made a bitter taste in his mouth. "Their mother is dead now." Wat went silent again and strode on ahead of me.

But I persisted. "Did King Audemar kill her?"

"He sends Caedon out to do his dirty work. And yes, Caedon killed her and her youngest son. The other two escaped."

"Caedon will try to kill them, too."

"He kills them whenever he can catch them." Wat's eyes were grim.

# Chapter Fourteen

# Healing

"Oh, he didn't tell her that much," Eris taunted. "You don't know much, do you, Mirin. Wat tells her only enough to keep her tagging along after him like some puppy," she told the others. She and Torrin and Lorel and I were headed to the stream with washing to do. "Women's work," Eris sneered. "What happened to the Good Ranulf's grand plan to treat all with dignity. All to them means men. Not us."

"Then why do you stay with us?" said Lorel to Eris. This surprised me. Lorel hardly ever said anything at all to anyone.

Eris didn't answer. She resumed her barrage of insults. "Wat told her things, sure he did. Told her just enough to keep her like a puppy dog at his side."

"I'm right here walking one step away from you," I told her. "You don't have to talk about me as if I weren't even here, or as if I were some stupid peasant with no understanding. You can say these things to me."

"You are. That's exactly what you are, some stupid peasant. We don't really know where you come from, do we? That story you told, the one about your family all being killed. You made that up, didn't you?"

"Eris." Torrin's tone was warning.

"I can say whatever I like," Eris told her. She went off by herself down the stream, leaving the rest of us with the washing.

"She's so angry," said Lorel, looking after her.

"I know. But then—" Torrin began.

I interrupted. "My story's no lie!" I said hotly. "Why is she angry at me? I've never done anything to her."

The two women turned to me, amused. "It's the way Wat looks at you, Mirin," said Torrin.

"How?" I was outraged. "He's my master. I'm bound to do his bidding."

The other two just smiled at each other over my head. This infuriated me.

It also made me wary around Wat, and that killed any joy I might have found in gaining the group's trust. If I'd even gained it.

I felt stiff and unnatural around Wat now. Maybe he felt the same toward me. It was hard to tell. In the stone cottage, our duties were divided among us. Wat wasn't directing me in any of the work I was doing now. Avery was in charge.

I found myself hoping he'd send me and Wat back on the road again together, but also dreading the time the two of us would be alone again. My feelings were so confusing to me that I shut them down and avoided thinking about them.

The entire group seemed to have gone quiet. No one went off on urgent errands. Everyone stayed close around the cottage. Everyone except Eris. She was away for long periods of time by herself. No one commented on this. When she wasn't there, I felt relieved. When she was, I felt the crackling static of the air before a storm. I tried not to think about her insults. So what if I was some stupid peasant. Our father was one of the Six, and he had made beautiful golden brooches for the others. He was valued for his skills and loyalty. So was our mother. I felt proud to be their daughter.

I thought about Torrin's words, though. Could Eris be in love with Wat? It didn't seem so, not from the way she treated him. But even if it were true, why in the Nine Spheres would she see me as a rival? I was just a young girl. She was dark, smoldering, glamorous. I was mousy. Without my one gift on display, I was no one. Worse than no one. Sir Caedon hadn't touched me. But what he had done to me left me feeling dirty and unacceptable.

My hair was growing long again, though. At least there was that.

I sought solace from my rebec. Often I went off by myself a little way into the wood to tune it and play it. It eased my heart, and my confusion.

During those days, I became a woman. Torrin and Lorel helped me. I found myself hurting and weepy. But then I remembered some things Old Cwen had taught me. We'd sometimes visit women who felt the way I felt now, or seemed to.

Back then, I hadn't realized why they felt that way. They just did. Old Cwen made a concoction of herbs that eased these women. I knew I could find the same herbs. I remembered how to make the potion, and I did. It really helped. Now I knew, finally knew, what these herbs were for.

Everyone else seemed to realize I was growing up. They no longer treated me like a child, not altogether.

I ached, though, to see Wat withdrawing from me. I doubted Avery would let our master-bondservant relationship continue. Wat seemed to be fine with that, while just a fortnight or so earlier he had guarded it fiercely. He seemed to be making a determined effort instead to do small favors for Eris, get into her good graces. Maybe the talk he'd had with Avery, when we'd first arrived at the cottage, had changed things for him. These days, he seemed to find excuses to stay away from me. Could Wat, too, suspect I was some liar?

All of them allowed me more time to myself when I proved I was a good hunter. Wat had praised me to them about that, at least. Soon I was in charge of the whole food gathering aspect of our quiet life together. The days took on a routine. I brought my snares with me into the woods. It helped that I wore trousers and tunic, with no awkward headcloth. All of the women in the group did, now that we didn't have to blend in with any townsfolk. While I waited for my traps to fill, I played my rebec.

Or I searched out useful herbs, as Old Cwen had taught me. That, too, seemed valued by the rest of them. I was able to stanch Torrin's bleeding one day when she cut herself badly while using a sharp-edged spade to chop turves for the hearth fire. The wound not only healed up, it did not fester. I eased other aches and pains.

So I began to relax my guard. I'd worried about my role, now that my singing appeared no longer needed. But I had these other gifts to offer.

After that, Torrin and Lorel were my friends. They'd been friendly before. Now they went out of their way to look out for me. They even got Conal to start drilling me in using a short-sword like Torrin's.

"I trained Avery when he was a boy," Conal told me one day, as he demonstrated how I should hold my sword. It was so heavy I had to fight to keep it upright as I stood on my guard. "Johnny too. And Wat, later on," he said. "Don't worry. We all have to start somewhere. You'll get the hang of it."

No wonder I didn't feel a full member of the group, I thought to myself. *These men, and the women, too, have known each other for a long time. They'd been to war together. And Avery and Eris are even brother and sister. I'm new to their circle.* Those were my thoughts. But I couldn't help sneaking a look from time to time when Avery and Eris talked together. They didn't look like part of the same family. It was a puzzle, and I found myself wondering about it.

Our peaceful days didn't last. If I were allowed to roam the countryside around the cottage, Eris was allowed to roam as far as the road took her. Sometimes she didn't come back for days. No one seemed troubled by this. It was just what Eris did. But there came a time when the others began conferring with each other in worried twos and threes. Eris had left four days earlier.

She still wasn't back. On the fifth day, she wasn't back. She wasn't back when day dawned on the sixth.

On this morning of the sixth day, Avery, Wat, and Conal talked around the fire. As I moved in and out with game to prepare, herbs to wash, and other small tasks, I caught drifts of their talk.

"—gone too far this time. . . where. . . this may be the time. . . we may have to. . ."

They all looked worried. They brought Lorel into the conversation. Then Torrin. Finally, I joined them, the last to know anything or be told anything, as usual.

"We're thinking something has happened to Eris," Avery said to us. "Are we agreed we're all worried about this?" We nodded. "Conal and I are thinking it's something to do with my niece. Wat has investigated her situation and has shared all he knows about it with me." Here Avery clapped Wat on the shoulder and pulled him close. "Wat thinks it may be time to get her out."

I considered Wat carefully. I saw how he looked at Avery. *He loves this man*, I thought. He doesn't just respect him as a leader.

"High time to get her out, if you don't mind my saying so, my lord," said Conal. "Maybe past time."

*My lord*. That's what Conal was calling him. Avery is a lord? From his manner, I knew he must be gently born. But a lord? And what was this about his niece?

"Wat agrees with me that we may have let things go too long," Conal continued. "He's scouted out the conditions."

I wondered when Wat had slipped away to do this scouting.

"Yes. It's a heavily fortified place," Wat told the others. "It's built on the new plan, from over on the eastern coasts and across the Narrows, the way they build them in the Baronies."

"Like Tam Fort," said Avery.

"Yes, very similar. But there's a way in. And of course we have our man on the inside."

"Thank the Child for him," said Avery. When the others looked at him with curiosity, he said only, "For the safety of all of us, we're not saying who this person is. But he's valuable to us. I hope you trust me with this matter."

The others nodded and didn't press him.

*Rafe*, I thought. Rafe, the man who helped Diera get me out of the castle. Avery knew. Wat and Conal both knew, and I knew. But then I realized something else. They were all talking about the castle. That castle. *They're talking about—*

Before my mind could get there, Avery was confirming it. "I'm worried Diera is in danger."

*Diera*, I said to myself. *Diera.*

*That's Avery's niece*, I thought.

"And I'm worried Eris is in danger, too."

*His sister and his niece*, I thought. But Eris runs around in a leather jerkin and kills anything that crosses her path with those throwing knives of hers, while Diera sits in a palace in a silken kirtle and is treated like a daughter by the lady of the earl.

"We know where Eris was supposed to be scouting," said Conal. "I'll find her, my lord." Avery nodded, and just like that, Conal was out the door and had disappeared down the path.

The next few days were tense. Everyone worried about Eris, and now everyone worried about Conal, too. I kept mulling over the strange new things I'd found out about the group. I worried especially about Diera's place in the group. Clearly she was a member of it. Her role in getting me out of the castle before Caedon could do anything to me had already told me that. I thought back to what she had said about Caedon. *That man hopes to marry me*, she'd said. And I thought about the strange sensation I'd had when I held her blackbird pin.

Two days after Conal had gone off to find Eris, I was heading back into the stone house with a string of fish for supper when I saw Lorel and Avery together by the shed where we stabled our horses. Avery had just ridden in from one of his own search attempts. He swung off his horse, and Lorel took it by the bridle. As he gave her shoulder an affectionate squeeze, I saw her bow to him. She actually made a little bow. Loren didn't defer to anyone, unless it was to Torrin. Lorel went her own way. But to Avery, she bowed.

Before I could piece together what that might mean, a distant shouting silenced us all. In the next instant, we went into action. Avery had drilled us in a plan to meet a situation like this, a plan for danger. Now, without needing to think, the rest of us acted on it. Lorel and Torrin drew weapons from places I had no idea weapons were secreted. Pikes. Brought down from the rafters, a longsword, its double edges on the cutting part of the sword wickedly sharp. Somehow Wat materialized with a bow slung over his shoulder. Where it came from, I couldn't tell you. I'd never seen it before. Wat was slender, but he was all muscle. I had no doubt he could pull a big bow like that.

The four of them—Avery, Wat, Torrin, and Lorel—surged to the entrance, peering out to see how best to deploy themselves.

Wat whirled back into the cottage. He came at me and thrust me into the far corner. "Stay there," he said, his voice steel. "Stay down." He wasn't looking at me; he was looking back at the door. Now he joined the others.

They were ready for an attack. Then the tension evaporated as suddenly as it had built. Everyone relaxed. Wat unstrung his bow. The others let down their guards. The hoarse ragged voice we heard calling was Conal's.

I was just about to protest at once again getting treated like a child, when the others rushed from the cottage. It was clear to everyone from the sound of his voice. Conal was in pain, terrible pain.

I hadn't risen from my crouch in the corner where Wat had shoved me. Now I did.

They carried Conal in, trying not to jostle him. Avery swept his cloak off and spread it in front of the fire, and they laid Conal on it. His face stood out whitely in the gloom of the cottage. I could see his jerkin was soaked with blood. As they turned him to settle him into a more comfortable position, I saw the shaft of an arrow broken off in the meat of his shoulder.

"Were you followed, Con?" Avery asked, bending over him.

"I don't think so," he whispered. "Lost them. . ." He put his hand up to Avery and Avery grasped it and looked down at Conal in anguish. He brought Conal's hand to his lips.

"Lorel and I will go out to make sure no one has tracked him here," said Torrin. She and Lorel disappeared silently out the door and down the path.

Without knowing exactly how, I had pushed past Avery and Wat, and found myself kneeling at Conal's side.

"Caedon?" Wat asked Conal over my shoulder.

Conal nodded painfully. "Eris was there," he said, but he could scarcely force the words past his gritted teeth.

"You need to be quiet," I told him. I looked up at Wat and Avery. To Wat, I said, "I need water. Clear, clean, cold water, new dipped from the spring. Bring me a bucketful." To Torrin, who had just come back into the cottage: "I need you to put the kettle on for boiling water." Wat nodded and stepped away to do these things as I had bid him. Torrin began building the fire higher.

Without thinking whom I was ordering about, I said to Avery, "Get me the rabbit-skin pouch on the shelf, the one with the herbs in it." Without a word, he turned, rummaged through my shelf of herbs and potions, and handed it to me. I shook my head impatiently no. "Not that one. The other one." He brought it to me. I laid it down beside me. Taking my skinning knife from my belt, I started slitting the leather of his jerkin away from the bleeding wound in Conal's side. I tried hard to keep the dirty metal of the knife from touching his skin. I knew from Old Cwen that the Dark Ones would try to get into the wound if the knife were to touch him.

The wound was deep. I saw the gleam of bone and gristle. Blood welled up from it and oozed steadily down his rib cage.

As I was probing it gently, Lorel stepped back inside. Eris was with her. Eris moved to her brother, and Avery pulled her to him and kissed her on the cheek. "Thank the Children you're safe," I heard him whisper to her.

Wat arrived with the bucket as tendrils of steam began curling from the kettle over the fire while Torrin tended it, poking the turves up to a high heat.

Wat put the bucket down beside me. "Here?"

I nodded.

"I need strips of cloth, clean cloth."

"We've just brought in the laundered shirts," Torrin said. She stepped away from the kettle and returned with the shirts, ripping them into strips as she moved to crouch beside me, and handing them to me. I recognized the rag of my fine shirt from the castle. I had mended it after Eris had pulled it off me. But now I tore it into long bandages, grateful for the fine weaving of the cloth.

I began dipping the cloth into the bucket and gently cleaning the wound. I handed another wet mess of cloth to Torrin to wipe Conal's face, where beads of sweat were standing out on his forehead. A cry of pain forced itself past his clenched teeth. I knew what it cost him to show this weakness in front of us. He was a stoic man. But the pain must have been immense.

"The potion bottle. The leathern one with the blue design. On the shelf," I told Wat.

He rushed it to me. It was a bottle of Old Cwen's most potent pain killer. I'm not sure how I still had it. She had given it to me the day we parted, and I had kept it in the bag with my rebec ever since. I uncorked it and held it to Conal's lips. Torrin raised Conal's head so he could drink.

After a few moments, his eyes glazed, and Torrin eased him back down to the floor.

"That's better. He'll feel no pain now," I told the others as they hovered over us. Avery drew his hand over his face and stood and walked away. Soon he was back hunched over Conal again.

When the kettle had boiled, I dipped more strips of cloth into the steaming water and kept working over the wound. At last, satisfied, I packed the wound with the herbs from my pouch.

"Needle and thread," I said. Torrin came back with them. I seared the needle in the flames of the fire, nearly dropping it as it burned my fingers, but I barely noticed. I used the last of the fine linen thread I'd pocketed in the castle while no one was looking. I sewed up the wound as tightly as I could. I laid my skinning knife on the flat rocks rimmed around the fire so its blade would be heated to white-hot in the flames.

"I need the wooden porridge bowl," I said. "And the tongs." Wat handed them to me. I used the tongs first to pick up the glowing hot knife by its handle. Protecting my hands with some of the rags, I took the handle and guided the blade to the wound, pressing it down so the flesh hissed. The others flinched away, but I didn't have time to attend to them. I kicked the knife away.

Next, I used the tongs to immerse the porridge bowl fully into the kettle of boiling water. Not touching the bowl with my fingers, I set it down near Conal on the cleanest spot I could find beside him on the floor.

*Clean, clean, clean.* I could hear Old Cwen talking to me over my shoulder. *That's the key to keeping the Dark Ones away, Lynet. The Dark Ones love dirt. Our Gracious Lady Goddess loves cleanliness and purity.*

With the tongs, I lifted strips of cloth into the bowl, added herbs, added boiling water from the kettle, and let the whole thing steep.

I rocked back on my heels.

"How is he?" said Avery. His voice was near breaking. Only now did I realize the depth of the love he bore Conal.

I pressed the back of my hand to Conal's forehead. "No fever," I told Avery. "That's good, but it's early yet." I wondered how far away Conal had been when he was attacked. I wondered how far he'd had to travel, with wounds this severe. I wondered how he'd managed it at all, getting back to us.

"And no pain?" Avery was asking.

"There will be. I must work fast. I've already used the only potion I have that's powerful enough to keep the pain from him. When it wears off. . ." I didn't finish the sentence, because I could see the herb-infused bandages were ready. Torrin and Wat helped me lift Conal while I packed some of the bandages close against the sewn-up cauterized edges of the wound and wrapped the rest around his torso to keep them from falling away.

"Now," I said. The others looked at me expectantly. *They're sure I know what to do,* I thought in despair. *And I'm not sure. I'm just doing what I think Old Cwen would do. And my mother.* But I thrust the despair impatiently away. I had to act. "We must turn him and get that arrow shaft out of his shoulder. Otherwise, the wound will fester and kill him."

Wat, Torrin, Lorel, and I turned him as gently as we could, being as careful as we could not to disturb the wound I had just packed. I didn't want to start it bleeding again.

I touched the broken off arrow shaft gingerly. "He is going to wake soon. I have to work fast, but I don't know how—"

"Let me," said Wat, kneeling down beside me. He moved the shaft in an exploratory way in the wound. "It's buried deep," he said. "And the barbs are holding it in."

"Two ways to go," said Avery, his mouth in a tight, tense line. "Push it through or pull it back out. Either way will tear his flesh."

"Which is better?" said Wat. They both looked at me.

"Old Cwen and I never treated a wound like this," I admitted.

Avery and Wat both leaned over Conal. "Here's how the arrow entered," Wat said, tracing with his finger.

"So," said Avery. "It would naturally exit here, if it had traveled straight through. I think if we push it out, rather than try to pull it back, we will miss the bad spot. If you hit that spot, the blood gushes up red. When you've butchered an animal, you've seen them, the lanes where the blood runs. If you tear one of them, especially the wrong kind—"

"So if we guess wrong," began Wat. "If we hit it, that spot. . ."

"Then he's dead," said Avery. His voice was grim. "Or we could pull the shaft out the way it came in, and do terrible damage to him. He'd likely never use the shoulder again."

They gave each other a long, level look.

"I'll do it," said Avery at last. "It's my decision." At his direction, we held Conal partway up. Avery helped us, cradling Conal tenderly against him. After pulling on one of his heavy leather gauntlets, Avery took the heel of his hand and shoved the arrow through. The wound seeped an angry purple, but there was no spurt of blood. We all sat back on our heels and took deep ragged breaths. Avery had guessed right. "I've seen battle wounds like this," he said, "but I've never treated one. Just seen it done." He drew a hand across his forehead. He'd gone pale. I worried he might lose his composure, but he didn't. As I was to find out, he never did.

Later, Wat told me about a situation where this same action, pushing an arrow lodged in a man's shoulder straight through, killed the man. "The red blood spurted like a fountain," Wat told me. "No one could stop it. His life's blood pooled on the ground, and he died." He had shaken his head then. "I don't know how Avery did that, feeling as he does about Conal."

But in the moment, I didn't have time to marvel at Avery's presence of mind. I was busy cleaning the wound on both sides, heating the knife again and cauterizing both entrance and exit wounds, packing both with herbs and binding up Conal's shoulder. He had begun to moan. His eyelids had begun to flutter.

"All done," I said. Some of us moved him onto his back again and covered him warmly with all the cloaks and extra clothing we had among us.

"I've seen some that were fine at the outset die of the shock," said Avery. "Keep him warm," he told me. To Wat, he said, "See if you can find some milk. There's a farm a pretty far way down the road, but I think I saw a cow."

Without a word, Wat disappeared out the door and down the path. From the door, I watched him go. I wanted to say something to him, but I didn't know what.

Avery stood for a long time watching over Conal. As he came back to himself, Avery knelt at his side, mopping his face with a clean cloth I handed him. Avery bent close to Conal's ear and murmured something.

"Such a beautiful boy you were, Avery," Conal gasped to him. "You've become such a beautiful man."

"Save your strength, Con," said Avery, kissing him and stroking his hair off his forehead, where a sheen of sweat shone.

I stepped outside to give them privacy. I saw Torrin had done the same. She gave me a brief, fierce hug and strode off toward the stream.

Avery came to the door of the cottage after a while. He summoned me to his side. He too embraced me. "You did well, little Mirin. You are a treasure to us."

"You saved Conal. I didn't know what to do about the arrow."

"We both saved him. We saved him with the help of the Children." He made a gesture I had seen them all make before.

*With the help of luck*, I amended silently.

He held me away from him and looked down at me, speaking slowly and seriously, as if he were swearing an oath. "Never doubt that you'll be rewarded richly, Mirin, when I regain the kingdom for my nephews."

I tried not to let my jaw drop. Avery. Now I saw what Wat was trying to tell me and couldn't bring himself to say, amid all the secrecy and the fear of betrayals and treachery, keeping every bit of information away from anyone who didn't have a strict need to know.

Avery was the youngest son of King Ranulf the Fourth. He was the younger brother of the usurper Audemar. He had thwarted the assassination his own brother had planned for him, and he had returned to the kingdom a rebel. *No*, I told myself. *That's not it. He—he himself is the rebellion.*

"You saved the man I love most in this world. I'll not forget it," Avery was saying to me as I stared at him and took in this new understanding.

Before I could respond, Eris flung herself out of the house and knelt at his feet. Avery lifted her up. "Eris?" He looked at her searchingly.

"I tried to stop them. I couldn't," she said. Then she pushed away from him, her eyes narrowed and angry.

"We'll talk about it later," he said to her. "Get some rest now, and then you can tell me what happened back there."

She nodded, shot me a contemptuous look, and went off down the path to stand by herself under the trees.

"My sister is troubled," said Avery, looking after her. "You mustn't blame her, Mirin. She's had a hard life." At my look of confusion, he corrected himself. "Eris is my half-sister. You've met my niece, too. Diera."

I nodded slowly. And then I stumbled to my knees, exhausted. Avery helped me up and moved me to the old log outside the cottage that served us all for a place to sit in good weather. He nodded toward Eris. "As hard as it is, maybe you and Wat can help her somehow. You're all younger than the rest of us. Wat knows how difficult she can be, but she's a valuable member of the Rising." He smiled a bit at my skeptical look. "Wat knows her well. She's his half-sister, too."

I felt too bewildered and overwhelmed to speak, but I tried. "Wat is your brother?"

"Wat is my half-brother. We have a complicated family. Goddess take the boy. I see Wat gave you the outlines but not the details. It's a lot to take in, little Mirin," said Avery. "You're one of us now. You're in the thick of it. But you've done me valuable service this day. All of us, but me especially."

I nodded again. "Let's wait, before we rejoice and promise rewards," I whispered. "He's not out of danger yet, your Conal."

"You can't take away my joy today, Mirin," he told me. "Nor the pride I feel in you, when I see you coming into your power so young. The pride I feel when I see how freely you give your gifts to us. You've given them even though you don't fully understand our cause. You have capable hands, Mirin. You have your voice. You have high intelligence. But even better, you have a generous heart. Your mother and father were my friends. You are their legacy to me. You are who you say you are. I thank the Children for bringing you to us." He made that sign.

As I turned to go back into the cottage, he caught me by the shoulder and turned me back to him. "One more thing, Mirin. The information Wat brought from his exploration of the castle. He thinks maybe—" He stared down at me, a crease of concern marking his forehead. "Don't make too much of this, and don't hate Wat for not telling you. He's afraid to, because of the uncertainty. But he thinks— he thinks your sister Jillian may be alive."

# Chapter Fifteen

# Sea-Born

They had all made ready to ride out, and they weren't taking me. Lorel had found horses for everyone. No telling where she'd found them or how she'd acquired them. Better not to ask. But at the last, Wat had vetoed my going.

"I'm still her master," he kept saying stubbornly to Avery. "I say no."

I had been smoldering with rage all day, and Wat had been avoiding me. I could see he knew Avery had told me about Jillie. Now he was saying I had to stay at the cottage when all the rest of them were making ready for an important action, to rescue the daughter of our murdered king. "You're my master when it suits you," I said now to Wat, defiant, not even caring if he beat me. "And when it doesn't suit you, suddenly you're not."

I could see Avery was trying hard not to laugh. I could see that infuriated Wat. For some reason, it infuriated me. But at last Avery had had enough. "We're wasting time. She's one of us. I'm overruling you, and I say she goes."

"She's too young."

"I remember a boy whom everyone thought too young. Yet he went with us, and he is coming into his force. Mirin is the same age now as that boy was then."

Although Wat colored up, he wouldn't give over. He tried one last ploy. "Yes, but I'm not—" He stopped. Then kept going. "But she's a girl."

I gained a strange ally in that altercation. Eris rounded on Wat. "You want to exclude her because she's a girl?" I thought she was going to stab him on the spot. That settled it. That shut Wat up.

He pressed his lips together and vaulted up into the saddle. Then he sat silently as I struggled to mount my own horse. I had ridden. But I wasn't good at it. Wat and all the rest of them had been in the saddle since birth. Not I. Poor folks don't own horses.

He didn't help me. They all waited until I finally managed to fling myself on top of my mount. I was slipping in the saddle and sawing at my poor horse's mouth. I was a poor horsewoman.

Wat looked over at Avery as if to say, *You see? A liability*. But Avery just turned his own horse and trotted down the lane, and we all swung in after him. Thank the Children my horse knew what to do.

I looked back over my shoulder for a last glimpse of the stone cottage, our sanctuary, as it disappeared behind us into the trees. We'd been almost like a family there. I felt a tug of longing that I shoved out of mind. No time for thoughts like that. As we rode, I scrutinized the landscape. I thought I recognized some places we had maybe passed, Wat and I, the day we took our wild ride away from the castle and toward the safety of the cottage. I couldn't be sure, though. That ride was a blur to me.

Just the same, I was beginning to get a general idea of the sweep of the land, rolling hills gradually rising in one direction, the high country where the castle was situated, and in the other direction, the low towns and lanes where Wat and I had plied our trade as strolling patched performers. The Riverlands. In the west of those lands, I knew, lay my own small village. From there, my father had told me, even drawing me a map once, the land sloped gradually downward again until it came to an abrupt halt overlooking the cliffs at the edge of a vast sea.

Now I was making a mental map of it all. If you were really alive, Jillie, and if you were in that castle, I was already imagining how I could get to you, and get you out. I knew the castle's layout. I'd do it. Somehow I would. A naïve thought, I know.

The group of us were heading away from the sea and the Riverlands, and into the high country.

We kept to obscure lanes, not the broad highways, but though our way was quiet, we were always alert to any noise suggesting some traveler was just ahead, or coming up behind. Once, Avery led us far from the road into a tangle of trees and underbrush, where we pulled up as the shadows under the trees lengthened, waiting as the rumble of rolling wagon wheels told us a large party of unknown people was coming up the roadway. As they drew abreast of our hiding place, Avery silently signaled us to dismount. We patted and soothed our horses in hopes they wouldn't call out to the stranger horses, and tried to muffle their snorts and blowing with our cloaks. The wagons passed where we were concealed and kept on. Avery didn't let us remount. "We'll stay here until they're well ahead of us," he told us quietly.

Glad of the break, we hobbled the horses so they could graze, and we settled our backs against fallen tree trunks and stumps. Avery pulled his hood down, covered his face with his mantle, and appeared to sleep.

I wandered over to where Wat stood leaning against a tree, looking outward toward the road and listening. My rage at him had exhausted itself. I felt timid. "Are you still angry with me?"

"What? No. You're a goose."

"I'm not," I said, but without any heat.

He put out a hand and drew me to him, still looking out over the trees. "I get worried about you. That's all." We found a place where the leaves made a soft pile and stretched out.

Eris ambled over to us. Her charitable mood toward me appeared to be gone. "What a pretty picture the two of you make," she said.

"Oh, go sit down, Eris," said Wat, surprising me. "You need to save your strength for tomorrow, not for insults and petty spats."

Eris squinted down at me. "Stupid peasant," she said.

Wat sighed wearily, shading his eyes with his hand as he looked up at her. "Eris, she's better born than you or I."

"What, because we are bastards?"

"That too."

"That too?" Eris looked at both of us with scorn. "Anyway, you don't know that. Not really." Then she stalked away.

"Know what? But Wat," I said. "Let me think this through. You're Avery's half-brother, but you're a bastard. That makes you the son of the king, but not the true-born son."

"Just figuring that out?"

"And she's one of the other—"

"Bastards. Yes. Her father was also King Ranulf. That makes us half-sister and -brother. My mother was a noblewoman, although her family disowned her. They wanted nothing to do with me and my brothers. Easy to do. My mother's relatives live in that part of the Eastern Baronies on the edge of the coast just across the border from our own realm, the part near Lunds-fort. They considered Ranulf their enemy. And besides, my mother was a concubine, not a wife. My mother's pack of little bastards. A blot on the family's good name."

Wat gave me a wry smile.

"Eris's mother, now she came from somewhere far away, I think from the Lyre-Lands," he said, shading his eyes to look over at her. She was standing by herself, moodily kicking the dirt with her toe. "I'm not sure who her mother was," Wat said. "She died when I was an infant, giving birth to Eris. I don't think Eris knows much about her mother. Just that she was a bondservant. My mother was not. There's a difference. And—" Wat hesitated. He looked over at Eris again where she stood apart from the rest of us. "You see those bracers Eris always wears? The left one covers her brand. When she came of age, our father did that to her. And the rest of us—we knew he was going to brand her as a bondservant, and we did nothing." Wat looked down at his feet and a blush rose to his cheeks. "None of us said a word. It eats at her, eats her up." He stared over at her for a long moment. "It eats me up, too, what I did."

"What did you do? Name of the Lady, what could you do?"

"Something. I could have spoken up, at least." His voice had dropped to a whisper. "Eris and I grew up together. She's a bit older, but in many ways we're like—" He stopped, then corrected himself. "Once we were like twins, almost. We were close. But when that happened, the branding, everything changed between us."

"I didn't have anything to do with that, and she hates me too."

"She probably doesn't. She's just angry. Angry at the whole world. Angry with me because my mother was nobly born. Angry that nobody thought I should be anyone's bondservant, but everyone accepted that she should be."

"I see that," I said. "But still. Even though you're a . . . even though your parents weren't married, you still come of noble birth. You have royal blood."

"Some might argue that. Others might say that's not the case. That the circumstances of my birth negate any nobility my ancestors might claim, or anything the king my father gave me. They certainly believe that of Eris. No one would consider her royal." As he stared over at Eris, standing alone and apart, I saw the pain in his eyes.

"King Ranulf was your father," I marveled.

"We never saw him. I hardly knew what he looked like. My mother went to him from time to time, then he'd send her back. Then. . ." Wat's voice trailed off.

I was thinking about what Eris had said. And I was thinking about my own status. After all, even though I didn't wear the brand, I was a bondservant too. "So how does that make me better born than you? Why did you say that?" I had to crane my neck to see Wat's face, try to gauge its expression. By now he had gotten to his feet and was peering out toward the road again.

I kept on. "Eris doesn't think so, that I'm well-born. That's pretty clear. She thinks I'm a stupid peasant. And I am, you know. Not stupid. But if being born poor and coming from a little village makes me a peasant, I'm a peasant." I thought over what Eris had said. "I suppose if Eris is a bondservant—" I stopped. "But she's not. Avery doesn't treat her that way, and neither do you. None of you do. Nine Spheres, Wat. Eris isn't the bondservant here. I am. And even if I weren't, you're the son of a king, and I'm just a villager. How can that possibly make me better born than you?"

Wat reached down to pull me up beside him. "Mirin, your father was an earl. Your mother's people were gentlefolks. You're their legitimately born daughter. That's how."

I stared at him, shocked. "My parents were poor. They were villagers," I said slowly.

"No. They weren't. They went to the village to live as peasants so that you and your sister would be safe. They were hunted by Audemar. They had no choice."

"I don't believe you." I felt that whuff when all the air in your body goes out of you.

"Don't, then. It's true, though." Then he said, "I'm tired of all this lying."

The thought of my father as an earl was so foreign to me that I brushed it aside. My mother, the smell of her, like fresh bread rising, and her songs, and her snowy apron, and her simple ways, some lady? No.

A thought occurred to me. "If what you say is true, why don't I have any memory of it? Why didn't my parents tell me? Why didn't my mother teach me about King Ranulf and all of those things you've told me about?"

"You were really small, when your parents left for the village. I expect they didn't tell you anything because they were trying to protect you. The way I've been trying to protect you."

"Why should you try to protect me? You're not that much older than I am." But then the burning thought that underlay all my thoughts pushed my arguments and quibbles aside. "You think Jillian may be alive."

"Listen. She may be. Don't get your hopes up. Rafe and I were able to look through the window of a barred room where some children were being kept. I saw three children, not two. Two boys and a little girl. The boys weren't the right ages. They weren't the princes. The little girl could have been someone else. Not Jillian at all."

I thought over Wat's account of his surreptitious invasion of the castle, after I'd been taken to sing before the great lady of the earl. Wat had told this to Avery and the rest of us. After I went in to sing, Wat had managed to evade the people sent to throw him out, and had hidden in a place he and Rafe had used before, the time Wat had found Johnny the Traveler's shattered rebec. Of course Wat hadn't used Rafe's name when he recounted this experience to the others.

My song before the earl's lady and her daughters had been the signal to Diera that we were near and would be coming for her. But more than that, it was the signal to Rafe that Wat was in the castle. Rafe had searched out and found Wat. Rafe wanted Wat to see for himself what he'd discovered. But to that point, Rafe hadn't had a good look at the captive children. Rafe had gotten word to Avery that maybe, just maybe, he'd found the place where the young princes, the sons of Artur, were being imprisoned. That's what we had gotten ourselves into the castle to do, find those boys. The reason we'd traveled to the castle and set up our little performance. That above all.

I overheard Wat talking to Avery about it. "Rafe can't get to us very easily any longer. He's kept on a short leash, these days. But I found a way to get to him." I wasn't sure what that meant. I wondered if I'd ever know.

During that night in the castle when I lay feeling abandoned and sorry for myself, Wat and Rafe were carefully picking their way to a pair of towers in the castle's curtain wall. Rafe led Wat to a stairway in one of the towers where a tall slit of a window let the light in. From this window they could peer down through bars into a room across from them and lower in the neighboring tower.

As they had watched and waited, an attendant led three children into view. He lit a rush torch and glanced, as if casually, up to the window from which Wat and Rafe were watching. Then he nodded down at his charges. Two boys. And this strange little girl, standing there with them. All of them looked to be around seven or eight years old.

"Those boys were much too young to be the princes," Wat said. "The princes must be around your age by now, Mirin. We had used all our wits to get there, and then nothing. But . . ." Wat stopped, and took a deep breath. "There was this young girl."

"Why do you think that girl was Jillian?" I asked Wat. "She could have been any little girl." Underneath, though, I was feeling queasy. Why keep children in barred rooms like that? Why at all?

"Rafe didn't know who she was. But he did know there had been a lot of talk around the castle about the killing of your parents. A lot of talk about the daughters. One, the older, who had gotten away. But the other—Rafe kept hearing different things about the younger. At first we all heard she was dead. But then Rafe began to hear that maybe she wasn't. This little girl was the right age. Around seven, right?"

I nodded, but I was getting angry. "People were talking about that? In the castle? And you all made me think Jillie was dead."

"That's what we all thought," said Wat, reaching out a hand to me.

I shook it off angrily.

Wat hurried on. "Audemar and his people, they like taking children, the children of their enemies, and— and doing things with them."

"What things?"

Wat just shook his head. "Audemar has his tight little group. They decide things, who to go after. What to do to them. Caedon is a part of that group. I'm pretty sure Queen Ailys is another."

"You've known this about me and my family all this time, and you haven't told me until now?"

"Keep your voice down," said Wat.

"And you've suspected this about me all along," I said, fuming. "That I'm this missing daughter."

"Not suspected. We knew. We had to keep you safe. As far as we can tell, you're the last of your line. Your father was one of the Six."

"But how did you know to find me, back in the market town?"

"That was no accident." In spite of our dire circumstances there in the woods, in spite of my anger, I saw Wat was trying to bite back a smile. I could see him trying to hold it back and failing. I could have hit him. "We had people looking for you, scouring the countryside," Wat said. "We knew you'd escaped from the killers. We just weren't sure where you'd gone. The last we knew of you, one of our people had picked you up and had driven you to the market town gates. We knew if we could get you to Old Cwen, you'd be safe. Our man didn't dare try to take you in. But by the time he'd gotten word to us so that we could arrange it, you had disappeared." Wat nudged me. "Under the palisades. Like a fish."

*Like a fish*, I thought. My father, laughing, saying to me, *Mirin, you are half-fish*. "I can swim. My father taught me. He taught me not to be afraid."

"Of course he taught you. You do know what your name means, Mirin?" Now Wat had turned serious.

I looked at him blankly.

"It means sea-born. Born of the waves of the Great Sea."

"Why the sea? I've never seen it."

"Your father's lands lie along the sea. When Audemar took over, he gave your father's lands to one of his minions, one of those other seven, but by rights they are your father's. Were your father's. They're yours now." He looked down at his hands. Then he held them up. "These are hands of the earth," he said. "The Child of Earth watches over me. But your hands are hands of the sea. The Sea Child is your protector." He took my hands in his and held them up, then turned them over and stared at them as if he could read my entire history there. He cupped my face between his hands and looked at me closely. "Even your eyes are the gray of the sea."

I turned away from him uneasily. "The Children. All of you keep talking about them, these Children," I said.

"Yes, the four Children of the Stars. When the Stars first covered all that is, the Children fell to land, fallen Stars, and each of the four took a part of the land to rule. The Sea Child. The Child of Earth. The Child of Fire. The Sky Child."

"That's what all of you believe."

"That's what the farwydd taught King Ranulf."

"And do you believe that?"

"Maybe," said Wat, looking at me cautiously, letting my hands drop from his.

"You maybe believe in luck, the way I do." I laughed. "My mother believed in the Lady Goddess."

"Many did. It's all they had known. I grew up believing in the Lady. King Ranulf never forbade it," said Wat. "Now it's treason to believe anything else."

A sudden thought struck me. "The blackbird carved on my rebec was a sign to you about me," I said. Wat nodded. "And so was Johnny the Traveler's song."

"Yes, especially that. We weren't sure you were the missing daughter. You might have been part of a plot to set us up." Wat held up a hand to forestall my outburst. "But your rebec and the song. That's how we knew for sure who you were."

I was quiet for a moment. I looked over at Wat. "You were the person who found Johnny's rebec and repaired it, after they killed him."

"Yes," said Wat. "Rafe led me to it."

"Johnny was your master."

Wat's eyes went dark with pain. "John was my brother," he said.

# Chapter Sixteen

# The Symbols at Your Door

Our respite didn't last much longer. Wat had walked away from me to stand alone, shading his eyes with his hand as if looking toward the road, keeping watch. But I knew that he was in so much anguish he had to get some kind of grip on himself before he could move on. I had reminded him of something he had to keep shoving into the background, always, or it would devour him.

I recognized that terrible feeling. I had to suppress feelings like that myself, just to be able to walk around in the world without collapsing into a dark place. Especially now. Now that I knew about you, Jillie. Of course I was glad you might be alive. But Wat's news stirred something horrifying in me that I thought I had buried.

I was torn now. The Rising was about to take action to save Diera, while in the back of my mind a voice was urging me, instead, *What about Jillie? What about finding Jillie? How can I convince Avery to help me find you?*

When it was time to ride, Wat seemed almost himself again. He helped me up onto my horse and showed me a better way to hold the reins. Before he left to mount his own horse, he pulled me down closer to him as he stood beside me on the ground.

He said, low, "You must stay safe, Mirin. Promise me you won't do anything rash just to prove how brave you are."

"I'm not brave," I said.

"Yes, you are," he told me.

I'm not sure why, but my eyes filled with tears when he said this.

He reached up and brushed them away. "The bravest I know."

I realized something then. I realized I was no longer a child. My body had already crossed the boundary from childhood to womanhood, and now, in this moment, I realized that deep inside me I had left childhood behind.

Past Wat, Eris was scowling at me. I ignored her.

We headed out. Now we made good time down the lanes, with no more interruptions. The land rose and rose, becoming more rugged with every league we covered. I felt the pit of my stomach drop. I didn't need to be told we were nearing the castle where so many terrible events had taken place.

Early in the evening we came over a steep rise. Avery pointed out a farmhouse far below us as we paused on the crest of the hill. "That's where we stay the night. We'll go over our plans. In the morning, we'll get Diera. It's pretty simple. Now let's move off this ridge. I don't like the idea that anyone can glance up and spot us and wonder who we are." He led us down past the tree line and into the forest. We paused again at the edge of the cleared land before the farmhouse.

"And we know this farmer is with us?" I overheard Wat ask Avery.

Avery nodded. "Conal and Lorel checked him out. He has proven faithful. He's gone now. He took his family to his sister in the next Hundred. We have the place to ourselves." Now Avery looked over at Conal. "What do you think? Everything seem right to you?"

"My lord, I'd like one more chance to walk through the place and the property."

"Go ahead," said Avery, nodding to him. I saw a glance pass between them. I'd seen it before. I envied the two of them their love and regard for each other. Conal always called Avery "my lord," but I knew him well enough by now to see he used this formality to make sure the rest of us knew he wasn't expecting any special favors because of Avery's deep love for him.

Mostly I felt on edge. We all did. Everyone knew treachery had somehow insinuated itself into the Rising.

Conal motioned to Lorel, and the two dismounted. They melted into the landscape. I marveled at how they did it. Avery stared after Conal. His narrowed eyes and the tenseness of his shoulders as he sat his horse told me how worried he was about Conal's strength after so grievous a wound.

After a while, they returned. "Everything fine," said Conal to Avery.

"Let's head over to the farmhouse," Avery told the rest of us. We rode the horses into a stone enclosure that stood open for us beside the house. Torrin and Lorel tended to the horses as the rest of us entered the house itself.

I stepped to the hearth. There were no turves. "We'll need wood. I'll go for it," I said to Avery. He nodded. Wat looked to him for permission to go with me; he didn't need to say anything. Avery motioned him to leave with me. We wandered the woodlot beside the farmstead, picking up downed branches. We brought them in and coaxed a fire on the hearth.

"Wat," I whispered to him while we did this. "The treachery— are we sure this farmer is one of ours?"

Wat nodded. "He's safe."

"But how do you know?" After what had happened to Conal, I was always looking over my shoulder. It had become clear to all of us. Someone had set Conal up. Someone had known he was one of the Six, and when he was alone, away from the group, they'd seized their chance.

"Come here," said Wat. He motioned me to the doorway of the farmhouse. "Look at that," he said, and pointed. The lintel of the door was covered with carvings. I had noticed them coming in. I had thought they were only decorations.

"They're pretty," I said.

"But look closely," said Wat. "These are symbols. See, here is one representing the Earth Child." I peered at it. It was a carving of a sheaf of rushes, a blackbird perched in the center. It reminded me of Diera's brooch. "And this one represents the Sky Child." It was a carving of some soaring bird. Not a blackbird. I took a closer look. An owl. "This one," said Wat. "The Fire Child." A carving of a fierce bird rising from flames. "And here is yours. The Sea Child." With an intake of breath, I examined it. A fisher-bird, the Sea Child's harbinger, skimming the waves, just like the fisher bird my father had carved on the neck of my rebec. "Do you see now?" he asked me.

"Yes. And look at those." My eyes opened wide. I pointed to the row of stars above all four of the Children's symbols. "Do you know, we had a panel like that in our cabin. The stars. My father carved them on the rooftree. And there were other carvings up under the eaves, but they were too small make out."

"He must have carved all five of the symbols," said Wat. "We all have them. Back at the cottage, a row of these carvings runs along one of the roof beams where they are pretty hard to spot. But we know they are up there. They are a sign of our solidarity, whether Children of the Earth, the Sea, the Fire, the Sky, all one underneath the stars."

"I don't think Old Cwen had a carving like that."

"She worshipped the Lady Goddess," said Wat. "But she stood with us anyway. We don't force anyone to worship the same gods we do. Most of us worship the Children, though."

"Our mothers didn't," I said. "They killed my mother. She was part of the Rising. But yours wasn't. Why did they kill her, Wat?"

He didn't answer. "I watched them do it," he said quietly, after a moment. His eyes were haunted. "I tried to stop them, and I couldn't."

I put my hand on Wat's and we sat there together, not talking. But then, as if we'd both decided it, we moved away from each other, moved around the hearth doing the tasks we needed to do. Wat helped me hoist the heavy pot on the swinging arm over the firepit. I sorted out the bags of dried pease and oats I had brought with me, tied to my horse's saddle. Wat got out his fire steel. Everyone needed to eat.

I stirred the pot. Then we sat down together at the hearth to wait for the others.

"We have something in common, you and I," said Wat after a moment.

"I didn't see the soldiers kill my parents. I only saw my family's bodies after. And not up close, not at first," I said. The others were busying themselves about the farmhouse. "I saw the bodies at a distance, and then I ran away. I thought the soldiers would take me and kill me, too. I was frightened. And later, when I saw them there in the weeds—" I stopped and shivered, trying to shove the memory away.

Wat shook his head. "You were right to be frightened. Otherwise you'd be dead."

"But Wat?"

"What?"

"Why did I see Jillie's body?"

"We think now she must have been badly hurt, but still alive. The soldiers must have come back, after the attack, to search the place. They must have found her. Then they took her to—maybe to Audemar. Maybe to Caedon."

"That explains why I didn't see her body when I came back to our cabin to look for the bodies of my parents. Why did they take Jillie?" I asked now.

"They—Caedon likes to—" Wat stopped. He swallowed hard. He wouldn't meet my eye.

"Maybe they wouldn't have killed me." I was struck with a sudden thought. I blinked back hot tears. "Maybe, if I'd let them take me, I could have helped Jillie. Maybe if I had been braver."

"No," he said sharply. "No, that wouldn't have been the way of it. They would have killed you. They take the younger ones. Nobody your age."

"But they killed your little brother."

"If my mother and I hadn't tried to fight them and keep them away from Aedan, maybe—"

I put a hand on his arm. "Wat, we're torturing ourselves. We have to stop. Both of us."

He nodded, his eyes fixed on the flames.

Eris walked up to him then and stood staring down at him. "What?" she said to him. "You look like someone just stabbed your best friend."

He raised his eyes to hers. "You're my best friend, Eris," he said softly.

Eris made a disgusted noise and walked away.

Wat stood and followed her out of the farmhouse. I looked over my shoulder, watching them go. I saw Wat put out a hand to her, and I saw her shove away from him.

I turned back to the fire, feeling hollow inside. At least there were many small tasks to occupy me. I took them on mechanically, trying not to think. When the water boiled, I added the dried pease and stirred it to make a porridge. I fed more wood to the fire. I set out the few bowls we owned.

Behind me, I heard Lorel summon Eris to help her establish a perimeter around the property. Some of the others went down to the stream beyond the farm to draw water.

Wat came back to the fire and sat down again. His movements were hesitant.

But I had made a decision. I couldn't rely on Wat. I couldn't rely on any of them. Only myself. The lives of all of them in the Rising were intertwined. I, the outsider, I would help them. Of course I would. But then I'd do what I, Mirin, needed to do, with or without them.

I confronted Wat. "I need to find Jillie," I said.

He looked at me silently. "I know," he said finally. But I could see what he was thinking just by looking at him. He was thinking there was no time for that, not now. My need was urgent. The Rising needed something else.

When everyone had eaten, Avery gathered us about the fire. We crouched over the embers, warming ourselves. I decided I would bide my time. As soon as we'd gotten Diera out, I would talk to Avery. If he and the Rising thought it was important to rescue me, surely they'd think it was important to rescue you, Jillie. And if they didn't think that, I'd part ways with them, bondservant or not. Avery must realize he owed me that much.

At the fire, I sang Johnny's song for them. I'd do that for them. I'd do whatever I could for them. It was little enough. As I sang, though, I understood the fifth verse for the first time.

> *I'll sing you five, oh.*
> *What is your five, oh?*

*Five for the symbols at your door...*

I understood the importance of the song to them then. It wasn't just a kind of code they could use to pass messages. It was more than that. It was what bound them together.

Their faces shone. The words of the song reinforced something powerful in them all, the sense they were united in a great purpose. I looked from one to the other, envying their solidarity.

They sat silently after the last strains of the song faded away. I put my rebec aside.

After a moment, Avery smiled at us all. I could see the depth of his feelings for us, even me. "I'll go over what we know," Avery said to us.

I kept my mouth shut about you, Jillie. I knew I had to, just then.

"Diera is being forced into marriage," Avery said. "She's to be married tomorrow. We've nearly waited too late. We needed her in that castle, and she did good work for us there. No one has carried the burden as well as she has. She has fought hard, in only the ways she can, to avenge her father and bring her young brother to the throne. Now we need to get her out."

"Do we know yet what man she's to marry?" Wat asked.

"Here's what we've known about the three possibilities." Eris, who had been quiet so far, spoke up now. "Three vying for her hand. We've talked about this before, a decision Audemar has taken a long time to make. Whoever possesses Diera will be high in Audemar's good graces. Audemar will choose the man he trusts most."

I thought of Diera, the fragile and beautiful high-born lady, someone's possession. Then I thought of her as I had seen her last, striding purposefully down the corridors of the castle to see me to safety.

"And the three?" Avery nodded to Eris, breaking into my thoughts. "Let's go over what we know."

He listened carefully as Eris went over the first two possibilities, all the reasons Audemar might pick this man over that, and all the reasons she thought he'd pick neither. "It's a near certainty Audemar will go for the third man, someone in his own household," she concluded.

*Three, three, the rivals,* I whispered to myself.

"Audemar has assigned this man to the earl and the castle to keep an eye on things, especially on Diera," Eris went on. "The man is obscure, gently born but not a nobleman. Ordinarily Audemar would never have elevated a man like that to become part of the royal family. But Caedon is one of the Eight, and while he was probably the least important of them all when Audemar first seized the throne, Caedon has steadily moved closer to the top of Audemar's hierarchy, especially in these last seasons. It seems. . ." Eris hesitated. "It seems he has something Audemar wants. It's a trade. Audemar will give him Diera. And in return, Caedon will give Audemar his prisoners. He has been keeping them close all this time, waiting until the moment was right to reveal he had them. Now it is."

"Caedon." I felt cold, as if a poisonous snake had crawled up my leg. I remembered Diera's words. *That man thinks he'll marry me.*

Avery looked at Eris with narrowed eyes. "Eris, you haven't mentioned this before. Do you mean what I think you mean?"

Eris nodded. "Look, I'm not certain. But I think he has Domgall and Ryce."

"The princes," Wat said quietly in my ear. I felt him tense beside me.

"I tried to make sure," said Eris. "It didn't go well." She gave Conal a small smile. Conal just looked down at his feet. "The bargain appears to be, Caedon hands over the princes to Audemar, and Audemar hands over their sister to Caedon. Once Caedon has Diera and the status and power and lands that come with her, he'll do anything Audemar wants him to do, including killing Diera if Audemar asks him to."

"And you think Audemar might actually do that? After protecting Diera all these years?" Avery asked her.

"As long as he saw Diera as some pliable simpleton of a girl, someone he could use, no, he wouldn't have done such a thing," said Eris. "But now he sees she's not. She's been nothing but a problem to him these past fortnights. . ."

Avery turned to me with a wry smile. "Including somehow losing a young minstrel."

Eris nodded. "A pet with the other daughters." She gave me an annoyed look. "They were all crying and acting like ninnies when he disappeared, that boy. They all blamed Diera for her carelessness. I wonder who the careless one really was in that moment."

Wat's head snapped up. He and Eris stared at each other. Wat's eyes were pleading, Eris's hostile. Avery raised a cautionary hand.

"But here's the thing." Eris leaned toward Avery, ignoring Wat. "As we know, this man, Caedon, had actually been carrying out an investigation of the troublesome boy when Diera somehow lost him. The boy had come under suspicion. When he disappeared while in Diera's care, that put Diera under suspicion too. It would have been better for all of us if we had just left him there," she said, deliberately not looking at either me or Wat. "Who knows what that boy may have said or done while he was in that castle."

"Boy? What boy are they talking about?" Conal was asking Lorel.

"Not a boy," Lorel told him. "Our Mirin."

"Oh. Oh, yes, of course," said Conal.

"Caedon," Avery was saying, brushing past Eris's insinuations about me. "He's a dangerous man. I've known him since my youth. Nothing will stop him when it involves his own advancement. If he has the princes and can gain an advantage by turning them over to Audemar, he'll do it." He stopped, considering. "If," he emphasized. "We don't know whether Eris is right about that, and we have no time to investigate her suspicions. We'll need to set that aside for now, hard as it is." Avery's eyes looked haunted. He went on. "If Audemar gives Diera to Caedon and tells him to kill her, he'll carry out that order without a qualm. Audemar needs someone to do his dirty work, so none of the small gentry will think of him as a bloodthirsty tyrant. Some of them love him, remember. He's gone around doling out favors to them. They think he's a great king. He won't want to remind them he's the kind of man who kills off his own family members."

"Caedon suspects Diera of being in league with us," said Eris. She seemed to have dropped her half-voiced misgivings about me to turn to other targets. My cheeks were burning with shame and fury, though. "And if Caedon does, then Audemar does," Eris said. "It looks like they may be planning to resurrect those old suspicions about Diera, that she was somehow involved with her father's assassination. They can revive the rumors, lose the sympathy of the people for Diera. Then, she just disappears. And no one will care."

"By now, few will remember she was still a young girl at the time of the assassination," Avery said, nodding slowly. "So you think that for all these reasons, Audemar will pick Caedon."

"I think he will, and I think that means he has as good as chosen Diera's executioner. I've thought so for some time."

Now I watched as Wat straightened up. He stared hard at Eris. She ignored his look. "Eris," said Wat, and his tone was dangerous. "How long have you had these suspicions? Diera. The princes. You've known these things. Why haven't I known about them? Why hasn't Avery?"

"But I haven't known," said Eris. Her jaw jutted out belligerently. "I've wondered. I haven't known. I don't act on mere speculation, put lives in danger for mere speculation." Unspoken was her accusation: *Like you have, Wat.*

Avery put out his hand, silencing Wat, who looked about to speak. Hot words, I was sure. "Thanks, Eris. Excellent work, as always," Avery said to her. "And you did it at great personal cost."

*And at great cost to Conal*, I thought. When Conal left to find Eris, he had put himself in terrible jeopardy. But of course I didn't voice this thought of mine.

Eris sat back on her heels and stared down at her hands. I thought how inscrutable she was. From looking at her, you couldn't tell whether she was basking in Avery's praise or indifferent to it. You couldn't tell whether Wat's challenging words were troubling to her or whether she was brushing them aside.

"Well, then," said Avery. "We know what we have to do. Let's concentrate on that. Get Diera out of there. Wat, explain again how we'll get to her. All of us need to make sure we understand the plan down to the last detail."

I watched Wat get a grip on himself. When he spoke, his voice was even, controlled, though I knew him well enough that I could tell he was seething. "Our insider has it figured out," Wat said. "As you know, he's the person who discovered the vulnerable spot in the sewers. The castle was built at the same time as Tam Fort." He turned to me. "Where Avery and Conal and Eris and I all lived, when I was a boy," he explained. He continued. "This castle has many similarities with Tam Fort, which should work to our advantage. Diera is supposed to be dressed for her wedding by her personal maid-servant. Our man has recruited this servant."

"We're sure of that?" Avery was asking.

"Nothing is certain. We're as sure as we can be about a thing like that. Of course, if he and I had known about Eris's suspicions, we might have been able to make better plans."

"There's great risk," Avery said, breaking in, giving Wat a look of warning.

Eris leaned forward again, tracing a finger in the ashes of the hearth, deliberately turning away from Wat. She spoke to the rest of us as if Wat weren't scowling at her. "But greater risk in allowing Diera to be transferred from the palace, where everyone knows her and many love her, into Caedon's hands," she said. "He's planning to take her away with him to his estate. Once she goes through those doors, we may never see her again. We may never even know what becomes of her."

She paused for a moment. "Here's the sign I find the most ominous of all. Audemar won't be there for the wedding. The wedding of his own niece. He has spent years building up the myth that he rescued Diera from danger after her father's assassination. It made many believe he didn't collude with the assassins. He has spent years cultivating the idea that his niece is very dear to him. He has no children of his own; he thinks of her more like a daughter than a niece; that kind of drivel. But now he's distancing himself. Why would he do that? He doesn't want any taint adhering to himself when Diera is found dead. Or when she simply disappears. We have to act."

Wat made an explosive sound and half-rose to his feet.

"Wat," said Eris, turning to him at last. Her voice was sharp. "There's a traitor operating here, and all of us know it. I kept my own counsel until I was sure of what I knew."

Avery looked from one to the other of them. "You've both done excellent work," he said to them. "Let's have no more wrangling over who should have told what to whom. We don't have time for that." He looked around at us all. I saw he was at the end of his patience with the two of them. "We're out of time. There's a time for discussion and a time to act. Now all our words have to be about the actions we're about to undertake. Nothing must get in the way of that."

We all sat looking at him, considering his admonition.

"No more dissension," he said again. His eyes glinted in the firelight. "Go on, Wat," he said.

"Our man has developed a good plan, because we knew this day was coming. Just not as soon as we thought," said Wat. He kept his eyes on Avery, turning half-away from Eris so he wasn't looking at her. "Our man says that when the marriage takes place, the maid-servant will stall anyone coming to the door of Diera's bedchamber while he walks Diera down the back passage to the place where the sewers open into the walls. It's the place the servants toss the contents of the chamber pots. It's little more than a slit allowing sewer matter to be poured down to the lowest levels of the castle and out into the moat—"

*I know that place*, I thought.

"—but there's a place where this passage widens," Wat continued. "That's the place this man found, the place he and I shimmied down to try to get to John. I can tell you from experience, it won't be pleasant for Diera, getting down that passageway."

I visualized the sewer slit where the servants had emptied the castle's chamber pots. It didn't seem possible for anyone to slither down it.

Wat glanced aside at me. He read my expression.

"You just have to know where to look," he said to me. "There's a place where the opening ends at some masonry, and it has crumbled there. No one has bothered to repair it. The opening's big enough for a person. Just barely. Then, as you wedge yourself into it and inch yourself down, it widens out. Getting down that opening actually works. I can tell you that," said Wat.

"You didn't make it work for Johnny," said Eris, past his shoulder.

"We were too late," Wat said, not turning around. I could see the effort he made to control himself at this fresh volley of hurtful words from her. The muscles of his cheek twitched and his whole body went rigid. But he pushed past her reproaches. "Our man has it all arranged." Wat sounded almost normal. "He has dark clothing for Diera to wear, a plan to hide her wedding things where they won't be found, everything."

"Why would the maid-servant agree to this?" asked Torrin. "Won't everyone suspect her? Won't this put her life in danger?"

"She's in love with our insider," said Wat.

"Poor girl," murmured Torrin. "The Children keep her."

"He has a plan to get her out safely too," Wat told her.

Torrin looked skeptical. "Whyever would she believe him?"

Avery made an impatient movement, a small irritated crack in his composure. "Go on, Wat."

"Well, then. Once Diera is outside the walls," said Wat, "there's a bad patch until our man can get her past the clearing around the castle into the rough country."

"So that's where we come in." Avery stood. His gaze included us all. "Wat has gotten word to our insider that the time has come. We'll be there waiting outside the walls. If necessary, we'll fight off anyone who comes out of the castle to take her. The extra horse was left for us in the barn?" He said this to Conal, who nodded. "Good. Con, you tether it at our spot for Diera. As soon as we have her, we meet back here at the farmhouse. We ride fast for the cottage. If any of us get separated from the group, though—" and he looked around at us all—"and I mean this—do not try to get back to the cottage. Make your way as best you can to the best hiding place you can find, but do not allow any trackers to trace you back to the cottage. Understood?"

We all nodded.

"If you're taken," he continued, then paused and passed a hand over his forehead. "We have to visit this possibility. If you're taken, do your best not to tell them anything. But listen to me on this. You won't be able to stop yourself. There's no shame in it. The methods of Audemar's men are brutal, Caedon is a master of these methods, and they work. I'm taking Diera to a safe spot after the cottage. I'm the only one of us who knows where this is. So you don't need to think you've betrayed Diera if, the Children forfend, you find yourself in such a situation." He started hunting around for his cloak and weapons. "As soon as I have her out of the cottage, I'm relying on the rest of you to scatter in as many directions as we have people. Scatter and hide yourselves. You know how. When enough time has passed, when it's safe, I'll find you. Don't try to find me. Is everyone clear on this?"

We all nodded.

"Any questions?"

I had a question. It was *When? When will I be able to go after my sister?* But I knew not to ask it.

"I have a question," said Wat.

"What is it?" Avery stopped what he was doing and waited. He had a gift for that. For focusing his attention entirely on you, making you know your words mattered to him. Later, I told myself, he'd listen to me. I'd make him listen.

"It's more of a concern than a question," Wat said, his voice hard.

"Tell us this concern," said Avery. He looked grim. I could see him resigning himself to saying the unsayable. The unthinkable.

"The princes."

Avery nodded slowly. "Yes," he said.

"Let's say we're successful with Diera," Wat said. "Let's say Eris is right about Caedon having the princes and using them to trade for Diera. In that case, Diera's marriage tomorrow means that Audemar already has the princes in his custody. Audemar isn't too bright, but even he wouldn't be a big enough fool to hand her over to Caedon without getting his own prize safely in his grasp. Here's the thing." Wat stopped and swallowed hard. "We have no idea where they are. Not only that, but we have no idea what Audemar will do with them once he gets them."

"We will be successful with Diera," said Avery, addressing Wat's first statement. "We will. But you're right. The time we'll have to find and rescue the princes will be short." He paused. Clearly he didn't want to follow the train of his own thought. "Here's the hard thing I'm thinking." He stopped. He took a few deep breaths. I saw he was getting himself in hand. Then he went on. It was clear to us all he was making himself say it. "As soon as Audemar gets the princes in his power, I'm thinking he'll probably kill them. He may already have. The only thing we do know is that one child of Artur's is in immediate danger, and that there's something we can do about it."

"Suppose the princes are in the earl's castle?" said Eris.

"They weren't," said Avery. "But you're right. By now they might be. If they are, our chances of trying to get them out now are small. Probably no chance at all," said Avery.

"If we'd known earlier what Eris was thinking—" Wat glowered at Eris.

"She did what she could," said Avery. "She couldn't know what she couldn't know. Enough of that."

I looked from Wat to Eris. They were both on dangerous ground with Avery, and they knew it.

Eris, who was rising to her feet, sat back down.

"Our man in there has found no way into that tower, the place where the other children were being kept," said Wat to Avery, after a moment. "The servant who keeps them appears to be on our side, which is the only way we got a glimpse of them. But he's one among many, and the safeguards around that tower are tight. Anyway, if Audemar does have the princes, we don't know that's where he would put them, and we didn't see them there."

"We can't know," Avery said, nodding agreement.

"We take Diera, he'll be angry. He'll be looking for revenge," said Eris, raising her voice until our attention was on her. "And if the princes are still alive and being kept in the castle? Once we take Diera, once we've shown we can circumvent the defenses and security measures of the castle, will we get another chance to go in? Ever? Even if we can figure out how? Unlikely. Maybe you're right, Wat. Maybe we should try to get in there and take them."

"You're saying this now?" said Wat. The blood had risen into his face.

Avery turned wearily aside from them both. "He may keep them alive," he said, as if trying to convince himself. "Why would he spitefully do away with the most valuable pawns of all, just because one has slipped through his grasp? That's one way of thinking about it. Another way of thinking about it—he won't regard them as pawns. He'll see them as the ultimate prize, the final step in securing his own place as king. And he'll—" Avery was close to the breaking point, and we could all see it. "But Wat. Eris," he said, turning back to them. "If you are thinking we should hold off our plans to rescue Diera, I say no. This is something we can do. Something we have to do. In the case of the princes, there are too many unknowns. We don't even know you're right, Eris, that Caedon has them. Or did."

"Why would you bring up a thing this foolish?" said Eris, turning to Wat, her eyes narrowed and angry. "You're just muddying the issue."

Wat looked stricken. I glanced over at Eris, then quickly away. If anyone was muddying the issue, she was. I looked back at Wat. No one else could get to Wat like that. Only Eris.

"How far can we trust this man of yours on the inside, anyhow?" Eris continued, talking past Avery to Wat. "We all know there's a traitor somewhere in the movement. We know this. I've said it before, and you're all acting as if it's nothing. This is huge. Are we sure your man on the inside isn't the traitor, Wat?" She practically spat this at him.

"Eris, no, he's not. You have my word on that," said Avery, before Wat could speak. I had kept watching her. Moments ago, she was practically accusing me of being the traitor. Now the unnamed insider. She seemed to be grasping at straws. She looked panicked somehow. I'd never seen her like this. *You're under immense pressure*, I thought, looking at her. But of course we all were.

By now, we had all gotten to our feet and were beginning to think about bedding down.

Eris's eyes glinted. She opened her mouth to ask a question, but Avery waved her off.

"Wat is right to bring it up," Avery told her. His mouth tightened. "We have to think everything through, consider every possibility. If we're doing anything to endanger those boys, even though it's the only thing we can do, even though we can't know whether we're endangering them or not, the one thing we cannot do is lie to ourselves about it. We have to face it." He turned to us all. "The one thing we cannot do, ever, is lie to ourselves and each other about what we're doing here. Why we're here."

"You know who our man in the castle is, and so does Wat," said Eris hotly. "But the rest of us don't know. Nine Spheres, you've probably told Conal. And I'm your sister, not some—" She clamped her mouth shut.

The rest of us stopped what we were doing and stared at her in stunned silence.

"I don't feel like a trusted member of this movement," she said at last. She must have known she'd gone too far, aiming an insult at Conal, even though she didn't actually voice it.

"Trust." Avery's voice was cold. It was clear he'd had enough. "Eris, you will trust me. You'll trust Wat and Conal. Otherwise, you're out."

Wat made to go to Eris, but Avery put a restraining hand on his shoulder.

Eris stalked to the window. She stood with her back to us.

I thought, *Suppose Eris is right? Suppose Rafe is the traitor?* Then I remembered the intense look between Diera and Rafe, the one I'd intercepted in the carriage as we made our getaway. *Diera and Rafe*, I thought. *They're in love.*

But from the sound of it, Rafe appeared to be a man capable of getting a maid-servant to love him and risk her life for him simply as a tactic. Capable of treating this maid-servant as a disposable pawn in his dangerous game. I thought of the men in the bathing shed again, the men Wat and I had treated as disposable pawns, and I shuddered.

I blinked. I realized Avery was considering me with a grave look in his eyes.

"This is hard, Mirin," he said to me. "What we're doing is hard." I heard a scornful laugh from Eris's direction. I saw Avery tense, but he didn't turn around. He kept his eyes on mine. "You haven't had anything to go on. You've just been asked to trust us. You've been an immense help to us, and yet you must be very troubled." He laid a hand on my shoulder. In a rush, I felt like one of them after all.

Avery looked around at all of us. "As impossible as this may be, let's put these matters from our minds tonight, and especially any disagreements about strategies and tactics. Especially any second-guessing. It's too late for that. We need to act. You're all valuable members of the movement." He nodded over at Eris. "Eris, your information and your keen mind are beyond valuable. I know how worried you are about treachery. We all are." She didn't turn around. "Wat, your actions have been beyond brave. You took huge risks on behalf of the Rising, and so did our insider." He put a hand on Wat's arm and kept it there. "Let's try to sleep. In the morning, we have work to do. Hard, dangerous work."

Avery dropped his hand then and finished collecting his things. As he mounted the hewn-out steps to the second story of the farmhouse, just a log propped from the first floor to a broad loft running a full halfway over the main floor, I watched him, the tense way he held himself. I could tell how deeply troubled he was. We all felt his unease.

The meeting was over, and so we did try to sleep. No one followed Avery to the second story, not even Conal. Everyone knew Avery needed to be alone. None of us was very successful at carrying out his orders to sleep. I wasn't able to, or if I did, I only dozed.

Late in the night, I roused to see Wat get to his feet and creep to the door, listening at it. He flung it open and stepped outside. I heard a low murmur of voices. When Wat came back in, I saw him head up the steps to the second story. In a few moments, he came back down with Avery. In the firelight, Avery looked shattered. Wat brought him a quill, ink, parchment, sealing wax. Avery spent a long time writing something down. From my place in the shadows, I watched while he re-read it, sealed it, pressed his ring into the seal, and handed it to Wat, who took it outside. I heard muffled hoofbeats, going away.

*What has happened?* I wondered. But I tried not to think about it. If I needed to know about it, I'd be told. I couldn't sleep the rest of the night, though. I lay gazing at Avery, his profile to the fire, a study in grief. When Wat came back in, he threw a cloak around Avery's shoulders and knelt. Avery placed a hand on Wat's head.

It was a private moment. I looked away. Then maybe I did sleep for a candle's measure or so, before dawn called us all to the hardest task we'd ever known.

# Chapter Seventeen

# Foul Betrayers

We were taut as bowstrings ready to let fly, that next morning. No one was talking. We had the rest of the porridge for our breakfast, cold. Then we mounted, our horses champing and stamping in the frosty air.

I huddled deep into my cloak, worrying. When I'd awakened, Wat was not there. I was starting to feel a bit panicked when Avery maneuvered his horse over to mine. "Mirin, Wat went on ahead to meet with Rafe and make sure of some last details. He came back just before dawn, but now he has ridden to our rendezvous spot to wait for us."

I felt a burst of relief. No one else had seemed to worry about Wat's absence that morning, so I had known I shouldn't worry either. Yet I had.

Avery lowered his voice. "I'm going to tell you something only Wat and I know."

A thrill of alarm ran through me as I saw Avery's expression. "Something has gone wrong."

Avery nodded. "Diera's maid-servant disappeared in the night. Someone may have taken her. She could be dead. Or someone may have warned her. Or it may be she saw something she didn't like."

At my expression, he smiled a little. "My niece and Rafe have become very close, or so she tells me. But whatever happened with this maid, she's gone now."

"Nine Spheres," I muttered.

"Someone is betraying us, but it doesn't matter," he said. "We have a new plan. It's nothing we plucked out of the air."

I interrupted Avery. "Eris thinks I'm not who I say I am. Maybe she thinks—"

Avery laid a gentle hand on my arm. He pulled me close to him. "Mirin, you're the beloved daughter of your father and mother. I know that. John knew that. John knew things, saw things no one else could know. I see you understand what I'm talking about. John, my brother. He and your father were my best friends. The three of us spent our boyhood together. We went to war together. I trusted them completely. I trust you completely."

I blinked back tears.

Avery continued as if I hadn't interrupted. "We knew we'd need to have a second plan if something went wrong, and now it has." He placed a steadying hand on my arm. "This plan involves you, Mirin. You have your rebec?" I nodded, my mouth dry. "We're not going to be able to get to Diera before she is moved out of the castle to be taken down to the little temple in the dell below it. That's where she's to be married." He looked at me intently, as if trying to gauge my resolve. "Our plan is simple. We're going to ride out of the trees as her procession comes by. We're going to fight past her guards. We're going to take her."

"This is—" I had a hard time catching my breath.

"Yes. This is very dangerous. Some of us will die."

The calm way he said this was steadying to me. "What will you have me do, my lord?"

He touched me briefly on the hair, which was now long enough for me to braid back off my face. "Brave, like your mother," he said. "Like your father. Listen. This new plan depends for its success on exact timing. Diera has got to know, to the instant, that we're coming for her. She knows the part she herself has to play. Wat and Rafe spent last night strategizing with her. She needs a sign. And we need a sign, too—the exact instant we need to act."

I understood at once. "My rebec," I said.

"And your voice," he confirmed. "I'll show you where, but I want you to mingle with the crowd and stand in a particular spot along the route her carriage will take her. As the carriage moves past you, sing out as loud as you can. Sing the third verse of Johnny the Traveler's song."

Under my breath, I hummed and sang, *I'll sing you three oh. What is your three. oh? Three, three, the rivals. . .*

"That's it. You can do this?"

Blackbird Rising ✹ 275

"Of course."

"When the fighting starts, get as far away as you can. No one will notice you in the tumult. You'll have your horse tethered in the trees. Go to it and ride."

"Where, my lord?"

"I'm not sure," Avery admitted.

"I'll ride. I'll figure it out."

"Don't let yourself be taken. I couldn't stand it." He laid an affectionate hand on my shoulder and then wheeled away to tell the others. I thought about the many times I had decided he, or Wat, or both of them might kill me. I thought about how it seemed all of them had suspected me of being an imposter and a liar, part of Caedon's plot against them. Maybe they still did, some of them. But Avery trusted me. And all along, every one of them, whether they trusted me or not, had been taking immense risks to protect me.

I had this gift I could give them in return. And I would. In my mind, I promised this to Johnny in the Land of the Dead. *I will.*

We were all silent as we rode toward the castle. The mood was somber. In the trees just below it, we dismounted and tethered our horses. I was slipping my rebec from its bag, checking it, when I spotted Wat and Eris together under the trees.

"What you said to me last night, in front of everyone," Eris was saying to Wat.

"Eris, I—"

"After everything," she said to him. "After that woman tried to—"

*What woman?* I wondered.

"I know, Eris, I just can't understand—"

"After everything! And I'm the one who saved your life, when she tried to—"

"Eris. We can't leave things like this between us. We're about to do the most dangerous thing we've ever done in our lives."

"You think I don't know that? What could happen?" Then she looked up and saw me watching.

I looked down quickly.

She drew Wat away with her. Their murmurs were inaudible then.

I was cautiously looking after them again, trying to figure out about the woman, when Avery gathered us to point out the route of the wedding procession. I forgot then about everything but his words and the role I'd have to play. "Wat will be on the far side of the road toward the river. When he sees our charge, he'll sweep in from that side," he told us. "Rafe will be driving Diera's carriage, so he'll maneuver it to our advantage."

Eris stood quiet and astounded.

"No point in hiding it now. You'll all see Rafe," said Avery. "And so will they, the people of the castle. His cover will be blown if it hasn't been already. The big unknown is Caedon. Rafe thinks Caedon will be below at the little temple, waiting for his bride. He marries her, he sticks her in a covered cart we know he owns, he rides off surrounded by armed guards, and she's never seen again. So we can't let her get within his reach. We're all agreed. The greatest point of vulnerability is the moment Diera's carriage comes over the drawbridge out of the castle and she waves to the people." Then he turned to me. "Mirin, see that road marker near the guard boxes?" He pointed through the trees.

I nodded. Wat and I had walked past it many times.

"Stand there. I don't want you too far down the route, where the crowds are thickest. Your voice might get drowned out by the cheering." To the others, he said, "Mirin's voice is our signal to charge into the crowd." Looking me over, he said, "I wish we had some festival clothes for you to wear. In your boys' things, you're going to stand out, maybe attract unwelcome attention so close to the guards."

"How much time do we have?" I asked him. I was worrying about that myself. The guards spotting some innocuous young woman in festive dress was one thing; the guards spotting some ragged girl in men's trousers, quite another.

"Until midday," he said. "Do you know the village at the end of the Hundred, just down the road here?"

I nodded yes.

"We have a safe house there." He dug in the pouch at his belt and drew out an amulet. It was a small blackbird, carved obsidian from the Fire Isle. "Take this to the house farthest in the village away from the beadle's hall. The house has a thatched roof and a blue door. Knock, and when the goodwife comes to the door, ask her what she'll give you for this amulet. She'll take you in and find you something to wear when she sees the amulet. Everyone is lining up to watch Diera. Our village friend will be the only one left. She has a damaged leg and no husband. She doesn't get out."

"The one whose husband Audemar's soldiers killed last year?" said Torrin, overhearing us.

Avery nodded. "Her son, too. And they nearly killed her. They left her for dead. Can you find the house, Mirin?"

"I'll do it, my lord," I said.

"Good," he said. "Get back here as soon as you can."

I slipped off my horse and was away then, weaving through the little ragged forest to circle around to the road further down from the castle. From there, I could get to the village without attracting much notice. Maybe none. Avery was right. Everyone was lining up. I'd expect all the surrounding villages to be empty. For us clodhopper villagers, entertainment as thrilling as this doesn't come along very often.

Once I got well below the castle, I worked my way over to the road. Keeping to the edges, I made my way against the throngs of people surging up it in the opposite direction. They were too excited to pay me much mind. Wat and I had been in that village to buy bread and ale. I knew my way. I cut through a band of forest toward the village. As I went along, I found myself humming. I needed to get the song exactly right. The timing had to be perfect.

I looked over my shoulder. I thought I'd heard a sound, and I stopped stock-still, terrified someone was following me. But then I relaxed. Only some blackbirds, fluttering around up in the trees above me. I went on. I had the strange sensation the blackbirds were tracking me somehow. But every time I looked around me to spot them, they were sitting on branches looking perfectly ordinary, or squawking at each other and fussing, as blackbirds will.

I shook myself. I didn't have time for spooky stuff. I had a job to do.

I unslung my rebec and tried a bar or two, deciding how loud I'd make the opening chord to get the attention of the crowd. If I did it just right, I'd get the moment of silence I needed to launch into the song. Avery and the rest had to be able to hear it from their hiding place in the woods. I tried another bar.

A blackbird descended to the path in front of me and started toward me. Its feathers looked ragged. I could see it was injured. One eye was cloudy white. I sidestepped. It came after me, closer.

"Shoo," I said to it. It cocked its head at me. I looked up, then, recognizing the landmarks telling me the village was just around the bend in the narrow track I was following. But the bird was still coming at me, almost stalking me. "Shoo," I said again.

The village was in sight now. I'd reached the low wall of bricks made of wattle and daub that surrounded the village. The path into the village itself took me under an arched gateway. I pushed the rusted iron gate aside. It made that scrawing sound I remembered well from when Wat and I had passed by here. As I entered down the village path, I saw with relief that the blackbird wasn't following. It stood in the middle of the path, just outside the gate, and made a mournful croaking. Over my shoulder I watched as it flapped into a nearby tree.

I didn't have time to wonder at its behavior. As Avery had known, the village was deserted, or certainly seemed so. Just as he had described it, the last house in the village lane had a blue door. I went up to it and knocked.

For a long time, there was only silence. I feared the woman wasn't there after all. But then I heard a thumping. A hard-faced woman opened the door. She was leaning on a stick. When she saw me, she tried to slam the door and shut me out, but I jammed my foot in the door and shoved back with all my strength.

"Mistress, mistress, there's nothing to fear. I just want to show you something, something nice to buy."

"I don't want any of your goods," she yelled through the crack in the door.

Desperate, I fished the blackbird amulet out of my belt pouch and held it up at eye level.

The door sprang open and I nearly fell inside. She grabbed me by an arm, pulled me within, and slammed the door shut behind us.

"Why are you here?" the woman said. "This is very dangerous, you coming here like this."

"I know, and I'm sorry, but Avery says—"

At his name, she made that sign, the one they all make. "The Child keep him," she said.

"Things have gotten difficult," I told her, staying to the minimum, for her safety and my own. "I need to be at the procession, but look at me."

She sized me up right away. "Come with me," she said. She made her painful way to a back corner of the stone longhouse and rummaged in a chest. She pulled out a yellow festival dress and swiveled around, using her stick for a brace, to hand it to me, and then she left me to put it on. She was bigger than I. I practically wallowed in the yellow cloth, but it would do.

"Avery says, please take this with his thanks," I whispered, as she led me back to the door and cracked it again, making sure no one saw as she ushered me out. I handed her a small bag of coin. It was heavy.

"No, I couldn't—" she began.

"Avery commands you to take it. You've done a dangerous thing. He wants you well rewarded."

"The Child go with you," she told me, snatching the bag and practically shoving me out of her house. I saw how afraid she was, and I understood that. So had Avery.

I tucked the yellow kirtle around me as best I could, made sure the rebec in its bag was strapped securely across my chest, and started up the path back to the main road.

As I reached the gateway out of the village, a figure stepped from the shadows. Eris. She stood blocking my path, and she had both knives out.

I looked at her in confusion.

"You," she said. "You're the traitor. Admit it."

"No," I said.

"Yes. Avery knows it, and so does Wat. Wat doesn't want to dirty his hands with you. Wat's little protégé. What did he know? I had a talk with him. Now he sees." Her voice dripped with venom. "They've sent you away so I can deal with you."

Now rage substituted itself for the fear I was feeling. "That's a lie. And you know it." My mind was racing. Why would she tell this lie? Why try to stop me from getting to my spot along the road?

"Go ahead, little girl. Leave. I won't stop you. I won't hurt you. Just get out of here. That way." Eris jerked her head in the direction of the road, where it wound back away from the castle.

I stared at her, puzzled. I knew only one thing for sure. If Eris stopped me, I wouldn't be at the procession to give the signal. Treachery had stopped the first plan, the not-so-dangerous plan. Now this second plan, the very dangerous plan, was about to be stopped as well, leaving everyone vulnerable.

*Why?* I thought again. I knew she hated me. I knew she wanted me gone. Was that enough to brand me a traitor?

She had her knives in hand, but she was offering me a way out. The choice was clear. Stay and be killed, and I knew I would be. Eris was good. Or get away down the road.

"You." My eyes narrowed. I suddenly knew. She wanted me gone by the easiest method possible. If she bullied me into leaving, that would be enough for her. If she had to kill me, she would. The only reason someone would do this is to make sure our plan failed.

"You're the traitor." It didn't take my second sense to figure this out. Just common sense. My voice sounded calm in my own ears, but my blood was pounding.

With a howl, she leaped at me.

Muscle memory takes over, at moments like this. All the acrobatics Wat ever taught me rushed into my limbs, by-passing any fear or astonishment that may have been playing itself out inside me.

The gateway in the village wall was braced by an iron bar stretching across the top of its arch. I vaulted for the bar, grabbing it with both hands, and kicked out at Eris with my feet. I clipped her on the shoulder. If I could knock her off balance, maybe I could get away from her.

It was an act of desperation. There was no way I could win in a face-to-face confrontation, and both of us knew it.

My swing took me over her, and I landed in a forward roll on the path beyond her. I knew the element of surprise would last me only so long. At the end of my roll, I sprang to my feet and nearly tripped over my dress. I sprinted off into the woods, cursing the billowing cheap yellow cloth as I ran.

Behind me I heard her yelling. Some swift object whiffed by the left side of my face. I knew it was one of her wicked throwing knives. I knew her uncanny accuracy would kick in with the next throw, as she regained her bearings.

A ravine loomed ahead of me, and I threw myself to the side and down it. But she was still coming at me. I could hear her just behind. Ahead of me darted a small flock of blackbirds, flushed from whatever they'd been doing by my mad tumble down the ravine.

The old blackbird, the injured bird with the cloudy eye, rose up before me in a swirl of feathers. I shook my head, hard. This could not be happening. I wiped the sweat from my eyes with my forearm and scrambled to my feet.

Eris screamed my name. Desperate, looking over my shoulder, I ran headlong into the trunk of a massive oak tree, standing by itself in a small clearing.

I lay at its roots, semi-stunned. It seemed to me the whole tree exploded with screaming and shrieking. It was as if the entire crown of the tree rose up in a vast cloud above me. Hundreds of daws, screaming out, spiraling up. And then, as if one organism, the entire clattering swerved and arrowed down upon Eris, hard on my heels. The clattering of daws mobbed her. Bracing myself against one of the cumbrous knees of the oak, I struggled to my feet and stood astonished.

The blackbirds dove at her, talons out. They drove at her with their beaks wide. She threw up her arms to fend them off, but she went down.

I didn't stop to see any more. I turned and ran. Through an uncanny silence, I bolted away from Eris and the shrieking black cloud that had engulfed her. My breath came in gasps. Gradually I slowed to a walk. Wherever Eris was now, whatever had happened to her, she wasn't following me. I was still breathing heavily, my hand held to the cramp in my side. When my racing pulse gradually began to slow and I could take heed of my surroundings, I realized I had run back toward the castle, my panicked course paralleling the road.

I leaned against a tree, trembling and trying to still the thudding of my heart. I brushed off the yellow dress. It was snagged with twigs and smeared with dirt, ripped and slovenly. I put it as much to rights as I could, and then I picked my way over to the road.

By all Nine Spheres. Eris was the traitor, and none of us knew.

Later I'd realize how carefully she had guided us to make this desperate move to save Diera, and then how carefully she had undermined our plans in order to make our rescue as dangerous as possible, expose us as much as possible. I was sure she must be the reason that the first plan had failed. She must have warned the maid, or lied to her about Rafe. Or had her killed. Or something.

I remembered how close behind Conal she'd come when Conal had collapsed, wounded, before the stone cottage, and I wondered what she would have done if she had gotten to him before that. I wondered who had wounded Conal in the first place. I knew about her skill with the knife. I wondered now about her skill with the bow.

And today, she was attempting to set all of us up for a very public, very dramatic execution. Diera included, maybe.

In the moment, though, I couldn't stop to think about any of that.

I needed to get to my spot.

Through throngs of celebrating festive peasants, I shouldered my way up the road, disheveled and wild. The guards didn't give me a second look. I was one of the many, as far as they were concerned. I waded to the marker in my too-large yellow dress, my rebec in hand. The guards paid none of us any mind. No one expected a brazen direct attack. Anyone thinking that would be crazy. And suicidal. Eris had seen to that.

Nothing was stirring yet. I blew out a breath and tried to still my heart, which felt like it was pounding out of my chest. My biggest fear had been that I'd get back to my spot too late. But I saw I had some time. I needed to warn Avery about Eris. How I would do that, I had no idea. To tell him a thing like that about his own sister. To tell Wat.

I stopped, conflicted, calling to mind Wat's anguished expression as he had reached out to Eris and been rebuffed. His expression earlier as she had reproached him. There were long-held connections among these people that I barely understood—love and torment and feelings of being let down. I was an outsider and probably always would be.

The betrayal had happened, and Eris was the traitor. But the new plan was set in motion. It was all we had. If I told Avery what I knew, it would only shake him. If I told Wat, I had the feeling I wouldn't be believed.

As it turned out, none of that mattered. It was too late to stand around wondering about the attack of the blackbirds that had saved my life. It was too late to warn Avery and Wat about Eris. It was too late to do anything but play my part in the plan, because at that moment, the guards snapped to.

There was a great stirring, and the drawbridge began its creaking descent, tilting down across the castle moat.

Nine Spheres. Eris's attack, successful or not, had almost made me miss my signal.

At least, I thought, by the time Eris gets back here, it will be too late for her, too. Even though by a hair's breadth, her scheme to spoil Avery's plan had come to nothing. I had to be content with that. Afterward, I'd figure out how to tell Avery—and, what I dreaded more, how I'd ever be able to tell Wat.

Then I had another thought. *By the time Eris gets back here?* If she gets back here. What had happened to her, when hundreds of birds brought her down?

I didn't have time to consider her fate, because now the trumpets and olifants blew their fanfares.

The great gates of the castle began their laborious swinging passage outward. I could glimpse the prancing team of horses inside as they began to move forward.

The instant slowed. Time itself seemed to stop.

Afterward, in memory, I have revisited the moments in the woods, earlier, when I made my hasty goodbyes to the members of the Rising and ran for the village to find a dress.

The ragtag little group standing tense and grim. But not Avery. I remember his laughter, the gleam in the bright blue of his eyes, his tawny hair tossed back. How he sat proud and straight on his horse, the son of a king, kingly himself. A good man ready, even eager, to take desperate action in his quest to right a great wrong.

A good man beset by betrayers, betrayers as close to him as his own blood. First Audemar. Now Eris. And Audemar's whole circle of conspirators. *Eight for the foul betrayers*, Johnny's song rang in my head as the horses drawing Diera's carriage moved forward across the moat. *Eight for the foul betrayers*.

That moment in the woods was the last time I saw Avery alive.

# Chapter Eighteen

# Three, Three, the Rivals

As the gates swung open, I readied myself. It was time to do the only thing I could do. *The Children help us in our task,* I whispered. The first hooves of the bridal carriage horses struck the roadway at the end of the drawbridge, and the carriage drew abreast of the road marker where I stood. A hush fell over the crowd. Everyone strained forward to see the bride.

I knew I had mere seconds before they began to cheer, drowning me out. I edged a bit further toward the roadway and struck a commanding tone on my rebec. Heads turned in my direction. My voice rang out from the depths of my power, rich and full.

*I'll sing you three, oh!* I sang.

*Three, three, the rivals. . .* I drew the syllables out. Delighted smiles began to spread across the faces of the people around me.

*Two, two, the long-lost boys, clothed all in green, oh.*

The carriage drew parallel to where I stood. Diera was sitting erect on the seat, her head high. She turned in my direction. Our eyes locked.

> *Blackbirds rising, blackbird's eye,*
> *Green grow the rushes, oh,*
> *One lone blackbird in the sky,*
> *Green grow the rushes, oh.*
> *One is one and all alone and evermore shall be so.*

The people started to cheer as Diera's carriage pulled past me.

I kept singing, but now they were indeed drowning me out. *I've done what I could,* I thought, lowering my rebec and stepping away from the edge of the crowd.

No one was paying me any mind, just as Avery had known. I drifted backward out of the mobs of excited onlookers. A frenzy of activity burst past me. Riders from the woods rushed the road, trampling over the screaming crowd. The soldiers marching behind the bridal carriage reared on their own horses, then charged after the carriage, which was picking up speed as Rafe whipped the carriage horses. I tried to make out what was happening. I could not. There were too many bodies between me and the heart of the melee.

A man dashed by and stumbled into me. I fell, tripping on my long, brilliant yellow skirts. I picked myself up, automatically feeling for my rebec, feeling if it were damaged. It seemed fine. I turned and ran for the shelter of the trees. Once there I cursed my silly clothing, picking it up in handfuls and using my knife to hack the cheap flimsy cloth off me until I stood in rags. Better, I thought. I found my horse and clambered on.

Into the woods sped two horses, three riders. Torrin and Lorel, their faces fierce with joy. "We have her! We have her!" Torrin shouted to me as they dashed past further into the thickets. I saw clinging to Torrin's back a figure dressed in flowing white. Diera. As they thundered past me I caught a glimpse of Diera's face, a pale mask of grief.

Once they had pounded off, a profound silence moved into the thicket where I sat my horse, straining to hear what might be going on at the roadway. I knew I should ride out of my place in the woods. A search party was sure to be coming in this direction, and I was a vivid yellow beacon among the green. But I couldn't. How could I leave without knowing what had become of Wat? Later I realized I wasn't thinking at all of Rafe, of Conal, even of Avery. Even of Eris. I was thinking of Wat.

A crashing in the underbrush terrified me into action. I kicked my horse forward. Startled, the horse sank back on his haunches, then surged ahead. Behind me the crashing got louder, someone just on my heels.

"Mirin! Stop!"

Thank the Lady. Wat.

I tried to rein my horse in, but the poor horse was more frightened than I. Wat rode us down, grabbed the reins from me, pulled us all to a walk. Then he slid off his horse and helped me from mine.

"Wat!" I sobbed. I clung to him, then held him out from me in dread. His tunic was soaked through with blood.

"It's nothing, I may have a scratch. It's probably not my blood," he said roughly. I looked up into his face and fell silent at what I saw there. His face was white, his eyes rimmed with shock.

"They're dead. They're— Conal. He shouldn't have been there. He was too weak from his wound. And Rafe. They pulled him down from the carriage and killed him right before Diera's eyes." He stopped, breathing heavily. I could tell he was forcing himself to say it. "Avery is dead. They cut him down. I couldn't stop them." He reached his hand out like a blind man, staggered. Then he shook himself. "Have you seen the others?"

"Torrin and Lorel. They've got Diera, Wat. They've got her."

"Eris—did she come this way?"

"Wat. I have to tell you something. Eris . . . she . . .

"Which way did Torrin and Lorel go?"

I pointed.

"I'm heading to the cottage then. That was Avery's plan. The four of us and Diera, we'll think of something there, and we'll get out. I don't know where Avery was planning to take her, but we'll figure out something."

"Where—"

"I don't want you knowing." He grabbed me and flung me back up onto my horse. He pulled the reins down, and my horse lowered its head. "I—" he began. "Eris needs to come with us. She didn't ride through here? I saw her at the roadside. She'd lost an eye. I don't know how badly she's hurt else." He suddenly looked scared. "She might be badly hurt."

"I have to tell you something."

"I can't wait for that. Tell me later," he said over his shoulder as he mounted his own horse. "I need to find her."

"I'm coming with you," I screamed at him as he moved away from me.

"No, you're not," he called back to me.

But the full force of what he had said to me hit me. Avery was dead. I was crying hard now.

He wheeled back to me. "Stop crying. Ride. Ride until your horse drops from under you. Understand?"

I nodded, but I couldn't stop crying.

"Nine Spheres, girl, ride!"

"Where?" I choked out.

"Follow the river." He maneuvered his horse near me and reached over to grip me to him. "Follow the river as far as it takes you. Keep following them. Rivers are friends of yours. Go all the way to the cliffs above the ocean. Find somewhere there, keep out of sight. Do you understand?"

"Eris. It's Eris. She's the traitor," I cried out to him.

In the confusion of our horses thrashing through the thicket, I could tell Wat hadn't heard me. "I'll find you," he called to me as he rode away from me. "Go. The Sea Child keep you."

"Wat, wait—"

But he wheeled around, and with the flat of his sword, he smacked my horse on the rump. My terrified horse sped headlong in one direction. Wat whipped his own horse away and pelted in the opposite direction, the way the others had ridden.

I the outsider clung to my horse's mane, sobbing into the wind. A dead tree lay across our path. My horse gathered himself up and we took it together, soaring over and into a small clearing in the covert. But although my horse performed beautifully, I was always only an indifferent rider. I was tossed into the air from his back and came down heavily, my breath knocked from my body.

For a moment or two, I lay dazed. When my head cleared, I was looking at a forest of legs about me.

"Step away. Step away and give this astoundingly yellow young woman some air," a voice above me commanded. The legs retreated. "Get her to her feet," said the voice, and thick arms hauled me upright by the armpits. "All of you, go now. I have her."

I shook my head to clear my vision. The two men holding me up stepped away from me, and I nearly fell. Sir Caedon stood three feet away from me. Behind him, sedately drawn up, was his closed cart, richly decorated with carvings, harnessed to a team of four black horses in impeccable form.

"What a sight you are, Mistress Mirin. Mistress Mirin Farmeadow." He drew out my name mockingly. "I see you and your friends have stolen my bride."

I turned and was sick in the weeds.

He stood silently until I had finished choking out my breakfast. I wiped my mouth with the back of my hand.

He pulled his sword out of its scabbard. With the blade, he flicked at the canary ruins of my kirtle. He leaned over and took my knife out of my hand. I don't remember drawing it, but I must have. It fell from my nerveless hand into his. He tucked it away into the belt at his waist.

"You've stolen my bride," he repeated, an amused smile quirking his lips. "And you know," he said to me, as if we were having a quiet conversation, "it really doesn't matter very much that you've stolen her. I thought the two of us wanted her. Me. Audemar. And here, all along, there was a third vying for her. You lot. Now your friends have her. But as for me—" He eyed me shrewdly as I stood swaying before him. "I got a good price. And I'll get the rest of what's owed me. Don't worry about that.

"You know what I'm talking about, don't you?" he continued. "Quite a nice price. The king's traitor brother is dead. I kicked his body to make sure. With this foot." He held it out for me to look. I closed my eyes, thinking I might be about to vomit again, but he kept talking. "Only one of them is left now, besides Diera. Only one left with any drop of royal blood, bastard though he is."

I realized with panic he meant Wat. With rising panic that he probably also meant the princes were dead.

"And she's just a woman, Diera. But I'll get her too. I'm sure of it. That boy, as well. You're going to help me do it."

"No," I said.

"Oh, yes," he told me. "Three of us want her. Only one of us can have her. I'll be that one. Your friends may have her now, but that won't last long. Audemar, I don't think he realized what a hard bargain I was going to drive. Or it may be—" Here Caedon stopped and whipped his sword through some high meadow barley at my feet, shearing off the heads. "—it may be Audemar didn't realize what he was giving away."

"But you didn't get Diera, did you?" It wouldn't matter that I'd make him angry with my taunting. I was as good as dead. If I provoked him into killing me now, quickly, all the better for me.

"Not yet. Actually, I got something better. Something to trade. Something that will get me both of them in one neat package. Diera. And the bastard."

This "something" of his. I had no idea what he meant. I wanted him to get on with it. *Kill me*, I said to him, in my thoughts.

"I have different plans. The bastard. He has to go. Diera? Fine-looking woman. Nice hips. Good for breeding children. I think I'll keep her."

"She hates you. She loves someone else," I spat at him.

Caedon laughed, his eyes knowing. "A dead man," he said. "But love, you know, has nothing to do with it." He paused and eyed me up and down. "They've all been using you, Mistress Mirin. Now it's my turn to use you. You're on my side now."

"No."

"I have something to trade with you. Something you want."

He made a gesture to a man standing at his cart behind him. The man opened a flap in its tapestry covering.

"Please. Mistress Mirin, step closer. Look inside and see what I've brought you."

On numb legs, I staggered past him. He reached out a hand and held my arm in a pincer grip.

Inside the covered cart was a young girl, held by a very large man. Her eyes were huge. She was seven or eight years old. "Mirin!" she screamed.

"Jillie."

Caedon nodded at the man beside the cart, and he closed the flap. "Just a little something Audemar threw in with some other things I traded him for. He knows what I like."

"Let me go to her," I pleaded with him.

"Certainly not," he said.

I could hear your muffled screaming from inside the cart. You must have thought you were the abandoned of the world, Jillie.

I heard. Children keep you, I heard. "Stop! Stop him! What is he doing to her?"

"Oh, I don't know. I'll ask him later and tell you."

"What do you want? What do you want me to do?"

"I think you know. I want my price."

"You'll just have us killed after," I told him. I sank to his feet in anguish.

He prodded me with a toe. "Oh? You think so? But your freedom, and your sister's, would be such an easy exchange to make for two such rich prizes. You two, nobodies and orphans. Diera and . . .what's the lad's name, now?" Caedon stopped to think. "Walter. That's it. I already got the other bastard two of them, those brothers. Adding Walter to my list, that would make it a set. I wouldn't care what happened to the two of you if I could have the two I want. Get up."

He didn't prod me now. He gave me a painful kick in the ribs, leaning over and following up with some sharp fast open-handed slaps to the head that left me reeling. He hauled me to my feet again.

He summoned one of his men over from the little group they had formed at the edge of the field where we stood. "Take her and follow me."

The man held me up by one arm. I dangled from his grip like your rag poppet, Jillie. I stood dazed in the sunlight of the field, watching Caedon open the flap, get into his ornate cart, and be driven away, then waiting an interminable, indeterminate time until a horseman arrived. The man holding me bound my hands and tossed me up behind the horseman. He tied me to the horseman's belt.

We jolted away down the road. I tried to look back at the high road before the castle, where soldiers were still clearing the crowds, but I could see little. After that, I concentrated on not falling off the horse and getting dragged to my death or trampled. It took all my strength and resolve. Hard to do in the state of despair and pain where I existed now.

Part of me thought maybe it would be better that way, to be trampled under the feet of the horses. Part of me, the part that hammered at me fiercely, *Don't die. Don't die*, that part of me clung to the horseman like a limpet.

As we pelted down the road, a blur of black whizzed past my face. And another. Now the rider had his hat off, beating around his head with it. I looked back over my shoulder. An arrow of blackbirds pursued us, and more were dropping from the sky to join in.

"Nine Spheres!" the horseman screamed. He spurred his horse, and we left the birds behind. But they were gaining on us.

A flame of hope ignited in me. I looked up at the sky just as we swept underneath the gates of Caedon's manor. Hands grasped at me and shoved me inside. The great doors clanged shut, my rescuers shut out. The flame dwindled away and died.

Not my worst problem, I know, but one thing added to my sense of utter abandonment: I had lost my rebec.

# Chapter Nineteen

# Four Star Children

My cell in Sir Caedon's manor house was cold and dark. It had no window, no way to scan the skies for miraculous intervention from birds or from anything else. I was just myself again, weak and battered. I spent my days in stupor and despair, with no idea what had become of you, Jillie, and no idea what had become of Wat, or of Diera, Torrin, and Lorel.

Eris was out there somewhere. I knew that much. But, if Wat was right, lacking an eye. I sent up a prayer of thanks to my winged avengers. Without them, I knew I'd be dead. Eris didn't miss twice.

With Avery dead and the princes probably dead, the fate of the rebellion rested now on Diera and Wat. There was, I knew, a network of resistors and supporters extending throughout the Sceptered Isle. But at the head, Diera and Wat were all there was. Diera was a woman. A grief-stricken woman who had watched her lover killed before her eyes. Would anyone pay her any mind? And Wat was young, no longer a boy, but not the seasoned warrior Avery was. Besides, he was only a bastard.

Yet, even if they had a chance, they didn't know Eris was undermining them and betraying them at every turn.

The thing that bothered me most, when I wasn't thinking about your fate, Jillie, and the big things like death, grief, torture, assassination, and treachery, was the loss of my rebec.

Some days I couldn't stand being without it. I had no idea where it was. Broken in pieces back at the field where I was taken? A trophy held by Caedon? A useless object tossed carelessly aside onto the estate's midden, buried under other trash? Given to some random soldier as a curiosity, or picked up by one and carried off? I didn't know.

Sometimes I tormented myself by going over all the possibilities and ranking them, the best possibility at the top, the worst at the bottom. At the top of my list was this: I imagined some soldier or guard reaching down into the weeds, picking my rebec up, brushing it off, and taking it home with him. I imagined he had a young daughter. I imagined her asking, "What is this, Daddy?" I imagined her learning to play it and loving it and taking care of it long after I had been hanged or decapitated or whatever fate Caedon had in mind for me once he saw I would never turn against Wat and Diera.

I remembered what Avery had told us all: *If you are taken, you'll talk. There's no shame in it. Their methods are brutal, and they work.* So I supposed they'd make me talk. But afterward, I'd be dead.

At other times, I would think about you, Jillie. It was a bitter irony to me, remembering my naïve plan of enlisting Avery's aid to find you. If he couldn't get the princes out of some fortified tower, how did I suppose he'd get you out? And now he was gone. Now here you were, and here I was, both of us Caedon's prisoners.

Suppose Caedon did as he said? Let us go? If I gave him information? Maybe only a few pieces of information. Those thoughts were torture to me, too.

The worst torture of all was imagining what might be happening to you. Were they doing things to you? What things?

As the days dragged on, I tried to keep myself from wasting. I practiced the simple acrobatics Wat had taught me. That helped some.

And I sang. Until they cut out my tongue, I had that left. I remembered what had happened to Johnny in Caedon's prison, and I shuddered. But still I sang. I sat on the floor of my cell and sang every song I knew. Since I missed the stars most of all, I'd sing the verse of Johnny the Traveler's song about the stars, the fourth verse, over and over again:

> *Four for the four star children,* I sang.
> *Three, three, the rivals.*
> *Two, two, the long-lost boys, clothed all in green, oh.*
> *One is one and all alone and evermore shall be so.*

The four star children, I thought. Now I understood who they were. The Child of Earth. The Child of Sea. The Child of Fire. The Child of Sky. I had a connection to them in ways I didn't understand. Through my music. Through the birds. The blackbird, harbinger of the Child of Earth, symbol of The Rising. *Blackbirds are your friends.* Johnny the Traveler had told me that.

I had a long time to wonder about why that should be, but after a while, it didn't seem to matter much, some strange curiosity that had saved me from Eris's knife only to leave me rotting in Caedon's cell.

I had a long time, too, to mourn the dead. Rafe, who had saved me, a person he didn't know and had barely even seen. Conal, who had dedicated his life to the rebellion because he had first dedicated it to Avery. And Avery himself. With Avery gone, was there any hope at all? *Two, two, the long-lost boys, clothed all in green, oh,* I sang softly to myself. Sang it to myself and to the stars. Who would save those boys now? They were probably already dead.

I remembered what Wat had said, the day of our history lesson out in the woods, about the evil men surrounding the false king Audemar. *We're fighting them, but we're losing.*

Then I thought of Diera. She bore the royal blood. *So what if she's a woman,* I thought. *She's the hope now, and she's alive.*

I don't know how long I was in Caedon's cell. I lost count of the days. Food and drink were shoved under a gap in the door by some faceless servant. Otherwise, it's as if I had been utterly forgotten.

But finally a woman opened the door of my cell. I tried talking to her. She only stared at me, stone-faced. I found out later she couldn't hear or speak. She hauled me to my feet and shoved me ahead of her to a little room where she cleaned me up a bit and pulled a rough, shapeless garment over my head. Then she led me down a series of corridors and knocked at a big brass-bound door.

A servant opened it and led me in. I stood blinking in the brightness of the light in the room I had entered. And it was only rushlight. I think my eyes had nearly forgotten how to see.

Caedon sat in an ornately carved chair before me. The room was resplendent with rush torches and firelight touching two wicked curved blades on the wall behind him, the type of blade I heard Caedon refer to later as *saif*.

Over the coming several seasons, we had many conversations, strange as it seems to recount this now. Caedon told me these blades had been presented to him, in honor of his skill, by diplomats from exotic places I'd never heard of, places in the Burnt Lands. There were weapon racks of fine blades on either side of the fire, too. During the year or more of my enforced stay at Caedon's manor, I learned he was considered the finest swordsman of his generation.

But during this first meeting, I didn't know that. I just knew that I was surrounded by a great deal of sharp steel, with a strong suspicion Caedon knew how to use it.

"Mistress Mirin," he said.

"Sir Caedon."

"You're not looking well, mistress."

I curtseyed.

He laughed. "I've had you stashed away until I could find some things out. Now I have. So now you can be of use to me, as we agreed."

"I didn't agree to anything."

Ignoring this, he went on, "Before I tell you what errand you'll do for me, I'll let you have one look at your sister. You can reassure yourself that she's safe." He signaled to the servant at the door.

She led me out again. Again, we walked through a maze of corridors and small rooms, then descended a steep flight of stairs to the cellar. Under an echoing low dank vaulted ceiling, we crossed under rough wooden upright beams that looked to extend the entire length of the building. At the far end, I could see a series of doors with barred, set-in windows. The woman led me to the last, most remote one and indicated the window.

I peered in. What I saw made me scream.

I saw you lying on a fusty pile of straw, chained to the wall by one ankle. I could see how thin you were, and how chafed and raw your ankle was. You couldn't hear me. The window, beyond its set of bars, was not covered with the usual cloudy fish bladder. It was paned with that glass I'd heard about. They say this glass is in the windows of the better temples to the Lady Goddess, and in all different wondrous colors. This particular window was clear, though. I could look right in. But it was thick. When I screamed, you raised your head briefly. You seemed to hear something. Then you lay back down. I made frantic gestures at the window. The servant pulled me back. I hit at her, but she struck me. I was weak; I went down. Then she hauled me up by an arm and she forced me away. We made the long trek back to Sir Caedon's room with its rich tapestries and warming ring of hearthstones.

He rose as I was led back in to him.

"You're a monster!" I shouted at him.

"Oh, that's a bit extreme, I think, Mistress Mirin."

"You're killing her."

"It's true I don't expect your sister to last long. But you can improve her situation. If you please me, she can be given better food. That festering sore on her ankle can be looked to. Her straw can be changed."

"I want her out of there."

"You're getting a bit ahead of yourself, mistress. Her lot will get better as you earn it for her."

"How can you do that to a child and call yourself a man?"

"I call myself successful, and I do what I need to do to achieve my success. That's a model you should emulate, mistress."

The fight went out of me. He had you, Jillie, and I knew you were dying. "What do you want me to do?" I asked dully.

"Your first task is an easy one, Mistress Mirin. I've located your friends. I'll have you taken to observe them. You see, you won't have to tell me where they are. I already know. All you have to do is discuss what you see, when you are returned to me."

I had little choice. I agreed. I had the desperate thought I might be able to warn them somehow, when I got there.

"And you'll change Jillie's conditions, as you promised?" I said to him.

"On completion of your task, certainly," he said to me, and gave me a little bow.

"How will I know?"

"I'll have you taken to see for yourself how she is," he told me. "As you saw today. And now, mistress, as you are bound to serve me, I'll see that sealed." He motioned to a man standing just inside the door. He marched me outside, where the smith was waiting with his glowing iron. I tried to pull away, when I saw. But of course that was useless.

Back in my cell, I lay staring up into the darkness and nursing my wrist, where it burned with a ferocious pain. If I had had my liberty, I could have found herbs to make a salve for it. I know what I would have made instead. A witching charm to use against Caedon. I wouldn't care what I'd have to give up in exchange.

I lay there wondering whether I should pray to the Lady Goddess. *Lady Goddess save me when no help is near.* If I was spending my time imagining how I could use dark forces to attack my enemies, I expected she wasn't about to listen to any prayer of mine.

I sang softly to myself instead.

> *Four for the four star children,*
> *Three, three, the rivals.*
> *Two, two, the long-lost boys, clothed all in green, oh.*
> *One is one and all alone and evermore shall be so.*
> *Blackbirds rising, blackbird's eye.*
> *One lone blackbird in the sky.*
> *Green grow the rushes, oh.*
> *One is one and all alone and evermore shall be so.*

# Chapter Twenty

# Found

They gagged me with some rough cloth tied about my face and led me to a little ridge above a house at the end of a long, winding, obscure lane, those men belonging to Caedon. They forced me down in the underbrush of a small grove of trees.

It was night. "I don't know what witchery you practiced, mistress, with your friends the birds, but I'm not sending you out in daylight," Caedon had told me. A smile of amusement quirked up the corner of his mouth. "In this realm, you know the punishment for witchcraft is stoning, do you not? I've never seen one of those, a stoning," he said. "It might be an interesting sight."

But now, "Watch," one of my guards whispered hoarsely in my ear. His breath was foul.

The door of the house below us was flung open. A warm golden light poured out. Outlined against it stood Wat. I yearned to kick away from the two guards holding me and run toward him. If that got me a spear in the back, I didn't care. A vision of you rose up before me, Jillie. That made me stay in a crouch and watch.

Eris came out to ask Wat something. I couldn't hear what they were saying, but I knew who they were. *And it must be true*, I thought, *what my birds did to you*. I stared at her hard. Even from this distance, I saw she wore a bandage across her right eye, across the whole right side of her face, and her right arm dangled awkwardly from her shoulder. Her days as an expert with the knife were over.

But I also knew what it meant, that Eris was with them. The others still didn't know about her treachery. I saw Wat embrace her, and then they went back into the house. In a while, Lorel came out with Torrin. Torrin gave Lorel a quick kiss and went back in, but Lorel circled to the back of the house. I knew what she was doing. She was heading to the stable to see about the horses. Later, she returned to the house and closed the door behind her. All was quiet. My legs were aching and cramping from crouching so long. I shifted my weight to ease them. When I did that, one of the guards put his hands about my neck and squeezed, shutting off my air.

*I'm going to die here*, I thought. The other guard held my limbs so I couldn't thrash around.

"Will you be silent, mistress?" whispered the guard with the stranglehold on me. I nodded frantically. He eased up. The gag stifled my gasping.

They both went completely quiet. The door of the house was swinging open again. Into the starlight stepped Diera. She reached her arms above her head as if she might pluck one of the stars down out of the sky, a picture of grief and yearning.

I looked from guard to guard. They were practically salivating.

"Diera?" came a voice from inside. Wat's.

She slumped against the doorframe, then turned and went back in.

The guards and I waited an eternity longer, at least a full candle-measure. The house went dark. After a while, my captors eased me back up the hill, flung me on my mount, and rode me over the winding route we had come from the inn of a nearby town. They ungagged me before we got to the inn yard and allowed me to walk around until some of my stiffness was gone.

In the inn, they took me up to the room they'd engaged for me, thrust me in, and barred the door. I lay down on the bed, trying to stifle my sobs. At least my hands were free now. I chafed them, trying to get the feeling back into them.

But then I had the odd sensation of being watched.

I sat straight up in bed. A figure disengaged from concealment behind the door and leapt to the bed, clamping a hand over my mouth so I couldn't cry out.

But I was clinging to him and burrowing my head into his chest.

"You said you'd find me, Wat," I told him, when I could speak again. My whole body was trembling with joy.

"Shut up," said Wat. He was holding me down on the bed, and he had a knife.

"They're making me—"

"I don't want to hear your excuses," he whispered. His eyes blazed in the dim light from the window.

"But Jillie—"

"I'm telling you again. Shut up," he said.

I stared at the knife, then into Wat's eyes. The world went flat and dangerous. My mouth felt filled with wool. "You're here to kill me," I said. I looked at the knife again. That other moment flashed through my mind, the moment when he'd cut off my hair. He'd come at me with a knife then, too. But not to do this. "You want to kill me," I said again. It's as if I were someone else, saying this.

"Erin was right about you from the beginning. We all should have heeded her," he said, his voice tense and low. Then his face twisted in anguish. "Why? Why would you betray us?"

"I didn't." I had to force the words out. "Eris is the traitor. I tried to tell you, but you didn't listen."

"Eris is no traitor. She was severely injured, fighting to save Diera. She's my sister. Avery's sister. Diera's. She wouldn't betray her own blood."

*But you, outsider. You'd betray us.* Looking into Wat's eyes, I could see him thinking that, just as if he'd spoken the words. My pulse thudded in my ears. No point in explaining the blackbird attack on Eris. Who'd believe a wild story like that?

All in a rush, I realized some important things. How much I trusted Wat. How maybe I loved him. Yet this is what he thought about me.

In that moment, I gave up. I didn't want to live. I don't give up easily. I'd learned that much about myself. But that's what I did, just then. I gave up. It was too much. Caedon forcing me to betray the ones I had come to love, holding over my head the one I had loved most from the moment she was born.

Now this.

It felt as though someone had cut the strings of my life from me, and I had fallen at Wat's feet like a broken puppet from the mountebanks' shows.

"Think what you like, then," I said. "Just kill me. Do it quickly." I turned my face away. "I don't want to see you, when you do it." *I don't want that to be my last sight in this world.*

"Mirin—"

I hit at his hands then, some final burst of the will to live.

He wrestled me around face-down on the bed, one fist twined in my hair, the other hand holding the knife to my neck. But still he didn't act, just pressed me down into the furs of the bed so I could hardly breathe. I wrenched my head around in a panic and gulped in air. Still he didn't act.

That's when the anger rose in me, a red rage. "Stop stalling. You came here to kill me. So kill me," I told him, between gasps for breath. "It's nothing Caedon isn't planning to do to me, sooner or later. At least this way, he'll be cheated out of anything he can try to get out of me." Over my shoulder, I managed to look at him. I realized I needed to talk past my anger. "Promise me one thing."

"What is it?" Wat's voice was thick.

"Try to get Jillie out of there. They've got her. Caedon has her in one of his cells."

He nodded. Then he raised the knife.

We lay like that for a long moment. I stopped struggling.

"Wat," I said at last, into the bed coverings. "You're not a cruel man. Get on with it."

"They made you do this. Because of Jillie." Above me, his voice sounded strangled. He eased back and I managed to sit up and move around to look at him.

"Caedon is trying to make me turn on you," I told Wat, forcing myself to be calm. "He's saying I have to choose, you or Jillie, but the gods know Jillie and I are not going to get out of this alive. So go ahead. Do it." I nodded at the knife he held still upraised in his hand. He hesitated. "Before Caedon took me, I had no idea he had Jillie, if that's what you're asking."

"Why did you do it, then?"

"Do what?" I looked at him in confusion, trying to make out his expression.

"When you were in the castle and Caedon unmasked you, you made a bargain with him."

"No."

"You must have."

"No. He did nothing to me, except the thing I told you about." I didn't want to say the words. In Caedon's power, I felt dirtied by him all over again, even though he hadn't touched me. Not yet.

"Or maybe Erin was right," Wat was saying. "Caedon placed you with us from the beginning. Coached you on what to say to us."

"No," I said, shocked and bewildered.

"Then how did you manage it? I really would like to know that." His voice had turned scathing.

"Manage what?"

"Reveal our plans to Caedon. If we could have gotten Diera out the way we'd planned, Avery would still be alive. They'd all be alive."

"Ask Eris that. Don't ask me." A dull, despairing anger had risen in me again. "Did you know she tried to stop the new plan, too? When I went to the village to find a dress? She was there, Wat. She tried to kill me."

"And you escaped her." In the dim light, I could see Wat's mouth had turned up in a cynical smile, but his hand, the one holding the knife, relaxed and dropped to his side.

"Did she tell you what happened to her eye?" Now hope sprang up in me. Maybe he could understand. Maybe still. I put out my hand to him.

But his gaze went cold. "Eris saved my life," he said to me. "That last partner I had, the one before you? She set me up. Caedon was about to kill me. But Eris warned me. She's no traitor."

I thought about the words I'd overheard in the woods, Eris claiming she had warned Wat of treachery. I didn't believe it. "Why do you think I'm not screaming right now, Wat?" I ignored what he'd just said about Eris and kept going. I knew I was sounding desperate. I knew he would think I was just trying to manipulate him. My lips felt numb. "Why aren't I trying to get the guards in here? And tell me this. At the procession, when I left for that village, did Eris leave too?"

I found myself talking fast now, but part of me wanted to stop. Just let Wat end it. No matter what, I was a dead woman. Caedon would never let me live.

I felt a sharp metallic taste in my mouth. But I went on. "Maybe Eris gave all of you some story about how she wanted to scout the parade route. She must have told you something like that."

I'd had a long time to think about it, in Caedon's cell. How she'd betrayed us. How she was trying to finish the job. How she nearly did, and how enormously even that failed effort had cost us. Had maybe cost us everything. It burned, when I thought how she had essentially succeeded. Her work had murdered Avery and the others. So now I kept talking. "And what happened, that day when Conal was nearly killed? Tell me that."

Wat sat up on the bed and took his hands off me. But he raised the dagger high.

I lay back down, facing him this time. I threw my arms out to either side, burning with anger. *Take me*, I said to him in my mind. *End it.* I found I really did want to see, when he did it. I wanted to look into his eyes. I wanted to know, and I wanted him to know.

His breath came out of him in a sob, and he sheathed his dagger. Then he stared hard at something. He pulled me off the bed and dragged me to the window. He held my wrist up to the shaft of light coming in from the innyard below. With his finger, he traced Caedon's mark of bondage. "Dark Ones take you," he muttered, his tone savage. "And Dark Ones take Caedon."

Shoving me roughly back to the bed, he sprang to the window, threw the shutters wide, and leapt into the night

I rushed to the window and leaned out. Far below me, he slipped into the shadows and was gone. I was beginning to think I might do the same when the guards burst into the room.

*You said you'd find me*, Wat, I thought as they bound me to the bed. *And you did.* The next morning, they took me back to Caedon in a closed wagon. I couldn't part the flaps to see if my blackbird army was near. But by then, I didn't care.

# Chapter Twenty-one

# Man-Dog Rough Gray

Back in the hands of Sir Caedon, I tried to thrust Wat out of my mind. That turned out to be impossible. The people of the Rising were my friends. My family, even. That's what they'd become to me. And Wat had become something more.

They all thought I was the betrayer. Eris had fooled them all. She was the insider. I was just some little girl they'd found. My parents' daughter. Maybe not even that. Maybe some imposter. Caedon is clever enough to have managed something like that, the Lady knows.

Because of me, they thought, Avery is dead. Because of me, Conal and Rafe are dead. Because of me, the Rising is done for.

And now Wat thought he'd caught me spying on them for Caedon.

Avery knew the truth, but Avery couldn't speak for me now. Child knows Johnny couldn't speak for me. They could only watch bleakly from beyond the border of the Land of the Dead.

As for Eris. Eris was their blood.

*Audemar is your blood,* I pointed out to them all in an imaginary tribunal my mind insisted on convening night after night. *What about his betrayal?*

Rage and grief vied with me to see which torment was the stronger. My torment compounded when the guards hauled me before Caedon and I found out he wasn't going to let me see you, Jillie.

Not bothering to hide my fury, I raged at Caedon. "You promised," I said.

"I promised to make her situation better when you completed your task. Now you have. Now I'll look to her."

"In the meantime, she could be worse. Much worse."

"You'll have to wait until she's in better shape before I'll let you see her." He gave me a slow smile.

His words terrified me. He talked right past my fright. "It's time, mistress, for you to uphold your part of our bargain. How many rebels did you see at the house?" he asked.

"Four."

"Name them."

"Wat. Diera. Torrin. Lorel."

"Wat? Who is this—oh, yes, I see. Walter."

*Walter,* I thought. *That's Wat's real name.*

"No fifth?"

I realized then he thought I'd name Eris.

"No."

"Careful, mistress. I told you not to lie to me. If you lie to me, what will happen?"

"You'll do terrible things to Jillie." My hands were trembling now.

"Again, then. Who else."

He stood up and went to his weapons rack, selecting a sword, sighting down its blade, giving it a few practice swishes. Then another. He was waiting for my answer.

"I suppose you want me to say that I saw a woman named Eris," I said tonelessly.

Caedon re-seated the sword. He turned his reptilian stare on me. "Why didn't you name her, then?"

"You already knew who was there. Why do you care whether I left her out?"

"Careful," Caedon warned me again. "You're testing my patience. Answer my question."

"As you know perfectly well, Eris is not a rebel. You asked me to name the rebels, and I named them."

"Eris is not a rebel?" His eyebrows arched.

"Why play these games with me, Sir Caedon. Eris is your creature. You know that, and so do I."

Then I added, "Your maimed half-blinded creature."

Caedon backhanded me so hard I fell off the bench where he'd seated me and onto the floor. I couldn't help it. I began to laugh. He backhanded me again. After that, I was silent.

"In a few days, as agreed, I'll allow you to see your sister," he said after a moment. "At that time, you'll get your new assignment." His smile didn't reach his eyes. He hauled me to my feet.

"You may be as insolent as you like, mistress. You'll not anger me, but I'll see you punished every time. Or have the enjoyable task of punishing you myself. You might want to think on that."

He guided me out of the room with a hand on my back. The pressure of it there, his nearness, made my flesh crawl. But he only delivered me into the custody of my keeper and shut his door.

Back in my cell, nursing my bruised face, I wondered what he'd been after with his strange assignment. I decided he wanted to know how much I knew about Eris. He'd found that out. I wondered whether he thought Wat knew, too. I was sure he didn't know about Wat's little visit to me in the inn. The guards had heard the shutters crash open. They thought I was trying to escape. They didn't know someone else had been in the room with me.

All I had in my cell at Caedon's estate was time to think. So I thought quite a lot about the matter of Eris's treason. If Wat still trusted Eris, as it seemed he did, then Caedon was probably still using her to get information. She was one way Caedon hoped to bring Wat down and grab Diera for himself. She was one tool. And I was another.

But now that he knew I knew about Eris, too, Caedon might be wondering whether the others knew about her. In that case, I realized with a chill, Caedon might put even more reliance on me as the means to Wat's and Diera's betrayal.

Meanwhile, Caedon was keeping up his side of our bargain, if a pact with the Dark Ones can truly be called a bargain. He was treating you better, Jillie. Between trying to keep you alive and trying not to betray Wat and Diera, I felt like I was walking the sharp edge of one of Caedon's most formidable swords.

In my darkest moments, I wondered why I tried at all. Wat still thought I was a traitor. And Caedon was just toying with us, me and you, Jillie. He'd surely not let either of us out of his prison alive. In those dark moments, when I wasn't thinking of you and your peril but only of myself, I wished I could have provoked Wat into killing me in that inn room. Instead, I'd foolishly tried to explain. I hated myself then.

When I wasn't trying to second-guess Caedon, I was even more miserable. It's because I ached to think about Wat, and how his feelings about me had changed. It stung to think he had so easily fallen in with Eris's accusations about me. It stung that he thought I was the traitor. I began to hate him.

Step by step, Caedon led me into ever more treacherous behavior. More betrayals, first only small ones, then bigger ones. I told Caedon about my music, and how I used it as a signal. That was the first betrayal. But always, I held something back. I told him a different song was our signal, not the blackbird song.

Then I told him the whereabouts of the stone cottage. That seemed safe to do. I was positive the Rising had abandoned it. They'd have had to. But I still felt like a traitor as I described it to Caedon and outlined on his map how to get there. It was a place I'd felt safe, even trusted. Even loved.

Facing myself in the dark, I forced myself to admit it. *Not loved.* Appreciated, maybe. *Not trusted.*

"You see?" Caedon told me, after I had drawn him the map of the cottage. "This is not so bad, what you're doing."

"Yes," I said. I felt myself stiffening. "It is."

"You're thin as a reed, mistress," said Caedon, getting up from his chair and running a finger down my cheek. He laughed when I looked daggers at him. "Try not to be so tense. It's not good for your health. I need you healthy. You may not want to do my bidding, and that matters not at all to me. But you're doing it. I like that. I like to see obedience in my bondservants. It means I don't have to punish them. In return for your good service, I'm rewarding you, am I not?"

And he was. Although I was never allowed to see you face-to-face, Jillie, and I doubt you ever knew I was there, I could see that your condition was gradually improving. After the last big betrayal, you looked almost happy. You had been moved to a new cell, a small barred room on a sunny courtyard.

During these trips around Caedon's manor, I became aware of other children there. Caedon had a whole roster of young hostages in his charge. That's why the princes had been here. This is where Audemar kept many of the children he had taken. But when Audemar received the princes into his own hands in exchange for Diera, the princes were doomed. Wat had told me they would be, and he'd told Avery. Now I could see it for myself.

I had been in Caedon's custody for a season or so. I too had been moved to a better room. I had a window now, a small one, really only a crevice, and set high on the wall, but it let in a ray of sunlight when the time of day was right, and by then, that meant almost everything to me. I waited all day for that beam of light, and on cloudy days, I mourned. I even had a bed. I'd had a bath. My conditions, like yours, Jillie, were gradually improving.

Late one afternoon, my keeper arrived to escort me to the room where, before, I'd bathed some of the filth off me. This time the water in the big wooden tub was hot, and she let me stay in it a long time. She even gave me soap. I was astounded, but I hurried to make the most of the opportunity.

When I emerged from the bath, she sat me on a joint stool and brushed the snarls out of my long hair. Then she handed me rich clothing to put on.

I did it. I thought of trying to question her, at least through gestures, but as I knew by now, nothing would come of such an effort.

After I had finished dressing, she led me to Caedon's study and left me there. He stood up from behind his writing desk and looked me up and down. "You're better this way, mistress," he said. "I'm pleased. Now come with me. We'll dine with some people I need to see."

He moved from behind his desk and offered me his arm.

Confused, I took it, and he walked us both down to the great hall of his manor. My knees were rubbery, and my head swam, but I made it down the corridor. In the high arched doorway to the great hall, we stopped.

He gestured into the room. "Those are my guests," he said. "Say as little as possible to them. Do you understand?"

I nodded.

He seated me beside him. I knew that was so he could keep an eye on me. Then he greeted his guests, speaking graciously. He somehow turned himself into a cultivated host, although his wolfish eyes gleamed with the same yellow gaze as before.

The servants began bringing in all manner of delicious food and drink. I couldn't help it. I had to keep myself from gobbling down as much as I could hold.

The man on my left kept glancing over at me. Later in the evening, I felt his hand brush my thigh. I edged away from him toward Caedon, amazed at myself for actually thinking of Caedon as my protector.

This man said little to me, though, and I said little back. As the conversation flowed around me, I began to see who these people were. They were mostly men, although a lady or two was seated up and down the board. These were Audemar's people.

Caedon behaved deferentially toward them. That was the first surprise.

The second was how he took my hand from time to time and held it affectionately. I realized we were putting on a sort of show for these guests of his.

As the dinner ended, we rose from the table. Caedon wound his arm about my waist and walked me over to one of the most imposing-looking of the guests, a man dressed in an elaborate fur cloak. He had been seated at Caedon's right hand at table. I knew that meant he was very important.

"My lord," said Caedon, with a small bow.

"Sir Caedon," said the man.

They began talking about the state of the realm. I listened hard, trying to store away as much information as I could. My head whirled with the potency of the evening's wine, although

Caedon had allowed me only a swallow or two. With an effort, I concentrated on what they were saying.

The rebels were routed. The two of them were agreed on that. Sir Caedon was on the trail of the rest of the rebels. The other man was glad to hear it, but Caedon should know Audemar was perhaps getting impatient. Audemar wanted his niece back. Caedon needed to find her.

Toward the end of this conversation, Caedon did an astonishing thing. He bent over and kissed me on the neck. I started back.

He gave the other man a rueful look. "She's a bit nervous. She's new. I'm breaking her in," he told the man.

I felt a scarlet blush begin to rise into my cheeks.

"But very charming indeed," said the other man, scrutinizing me from the top of my head to the low, revealing curve of my gown's neck. "You are the lucky one, Sir Caedon." They were exchanging discriminating judgments about me as if I were some object, or some fine animal—a horse, a hawk, maybe.

Thank the Lady the evening was over then. Caedon escorted me back to his study. He sat me down before the fire, and then he sat beside me. He took my wrist in his hand. When by instinct I shrank away from him, he slapped me hard on the cheek.

"You did well tonight, but think who you are, mistress." He held up my wrist. "There's my mark. I'm your owner."

"Those people tonight thought I was your concubine."

"Yes, they did. I want them to think that. I want the world to think that."

"I'm not."

"You're anything I say you are," he told me.

Fear gripped me then. I knew he could do whatever he wanted to me.

"I may make you my concubine," he said.

"No."

"Indeed yes. But not right away. Maybe not at all. The man sitting next to you. He was taken by you. He may want you for his own purposes. He and I are talking about it."

"But you said you'd let me go, and Jillie, if I gave you what you want," I cried out.

"There are many things I want," he said. "The man who was seated beside you at my board is high in our good king's graces."

What was I willing to do, Jillie, to make sure you were safe? That was the dark thought running through my mind.

"I think we understand each other," Caedon said. "But if I'm to use you in this way, my little bondswoman, I need to teach you a few things. You were raised in some wretched village, I believe. You're not a lady."

I stayed silent. He must know who my parents were, I thought. He's taunting me. Or maybe he doesn't know whether I know. After all, I didn't know, not until recently.

"You'll accompany me to to the board many times, as you did tonight," he continued, "until I'm sure you know how to comport yourself around the court, and courtly people. In the meantime, I think we'll need to do something about your profound ignorance." He stood up and looked around him at the books lining the room. He took one down.

Then he re-seated himself beside me and opened it. "Here's an easy one to start with," he said. In the open book he showed me, I saw a woodcut of a fearsome creature, half man, half beast.

Of course I recognized right away who he was. Man-dog Rough-Gray.

"Let's just look through some of my books, and I will explain some of these things to you, things any child gently brought up would know."

I snatched the book from his hands and held it. I nearly cried. It reminded me so much of home and our mother. I could almost feel her beside me. I looked down at the page.

*"Now when Man-dog Rough-Gray rode out with his army to fight the king,"* I began to read.

Caedon stood up so fast the book tumbled out of my lap. He reached down to get it. "You can read," he said. He looked at me, dumbfounded.

"Yes, I can read," I told him.

"Can you read the language of the Old Ones?" he asked me.

"No, that I cannot. Only the boys who go to the Lady Goddess's school in the market town learn that kind of reading," I admitted. "And only one or two in our village were allowed to go to it."

"I could teach you," he said, almost to himself. "What an instrument you'd prove to be."

"Teach me, my lord," I said to him. I was thinking fast. Anything to avoid becoming someone's concubine, Caedon's or that man's, the one who had touched my thigh.

"How did you learn to read?" he asked me.

"My mother taught me."

"Then it's true, what they say about your parents," said Caedon.

My heart sank. The less he knew about my parents, the better.

Now Caedon strode to the door and opened it. My keeper stood outside. He motioned to her that it was time for her to lead me back to my room. She came into the room and put her hand on my shoulder to begin walking me out of the study.

But Caedon held out his hand to stop her closing the door. He drew me back inside.

"You'll prove very useful to me, mistress," he said. "I'm going to move you to a better room, give you better clothing. Your education begins tomorrow."

He seized me by the throat and kissed me. I was startled. No one had ever kissed me before. My life had been weapons, fighting, danger, not kissing. Caedon's mouth on me was like a hungry man's devouring his food.

Repulsed, I tried to squirm away from him, and he slapped me for the second time that night. He thrust his hands down the neck of my kirtle and squeezed my nipples hard. I screamed, and he slapped me yet again. My keeper stood by impassively.

"There. Go with your woman," he said, standing back from me now. At my expression, he laughed. "You don't like me, mistress."

My head was ringing from his blows. "I despise you," I said.

"All the better."

*This is a sport, for him,* I thought numbly.

A serving man had come to the door now, to see what was going on. "Bring me one of the others," Caedon directed him. Then he made a dismissive motion toward my keeper, and she led me away.

I spent many days in Caedon's study after that. I learned to read the language of the Old Ones. Caedon was actually a patient teacher. He actually loved his books and loved reading them.

Together, we read through a book of marvels by one of the Old Ones.

The book contained many stories. A man who sowed dragon's teeth in the soil and grew an entire army from those fierce seeds. A story about the Sun, and how he fell in love. How the Spring was made to go to the world beneath, and how she came back out, but only for half a year, creating Winter. How a great city in the Lyre Lands fell because of the folly of a prideful man.

My favorite, though, was the story of a blackbird who had once been a girl. Cruel men pursued her, until a goddess changed her into a bird so she could escape.

I wished I were that bird.

There was another story I loved, too. It was a story about a man who charmed the birds with his music. He played a lyre, not a rebec, but he learned the language of the birds, and then he knew all that they did. This story stirred a memory I thought I had buried deep inside. It was the memory of the last conversation Johnny and I had had. *Blackbirds are your friends.*

I remembered thinking how unlikely that seemed. I was a Child of Sea, if my father's stories of the Children were to be believed, not a Child of Earth. *How do you know?* I'd asked Johnny, skeptically.

*I told them about you,* he'd said. Like the man in the story, Johnny was a man who talked to birds.

Thank the Children, Caedon didn't put his hands, or his mouth, on me again, during all this time, but I realized some in his manor weren't so lucky. I supposed he was keeping me intact for this friend of Audemar's he had clearly decided to sell me or trade me to.

From that point on, I no longer believed he'd ever free me. But I hadn't lost hope he might free you, Jillie.

Strangely, his insistence that I commit small betrayals of the Rising slowed and then stopped altogether. I worried what that might mean. If he had caught and killed Wat, if he had caught Diera, I knew I would have heard about it, especially now that I was around people who talked and strategized incessantly about their power and how to keep it. That was some comfort. I kept my ears open at the many occasions Caedon made me attend with him, dreading what I might learn but desperate to learn all I could.

Clearly, though, something in Caedon's situation had changed. As I listened to the important men talk at his board, I started to realize most of them had completely discounted the threat of the Rising. As far as they were concerned, it was shattered and broken. Only the fate of Diera captured their attention, and that was because it was becoming an increasing source of tension between Audemar and Caedon.

Now that I knew Caedon better than I'd ever wanted to, I harbored the deep conviction that although Audemar expected him to do it—even Avery and the others expected him to—Caedon had no intention of killing Diera. Instead, he was going to force her into the role of wife and mother to his children. He was going to breed royal children. His real goal was the throne itself.

For that reason, he needed Wat dead. In fact, as I began to realize, ultimately he needed Audemar dead.

Caedon was playing the most dangerous game of all.

When I understood that, many puzzling matters fell into place. I'd never understood why, when he knew where Wat,

Diera, and the others were hiding, Caedon hadn't simply come down on them with all his men and taken them.

I realized now that Caedon was moving cautiously. He knew where the rebels of the Rising were. He knew he could take his prize. But he was Audemar's man, and he didn't want Audemar to know and grab Caedon's prize back for himself.

It seemed Audemar had traded Diera to Caedon in marriage in order to get the princes. He got the prize he wanted. But then, because of the Rising, Caedon lost his own prize in that trade. He lost Diera.

As Audemar clearly thought, that was Caedon's look-out. Audemar wanted Diera back. His bargain with Caedon was off. Both of them wanted her back.

Caedon's intention toward Diera was only one of his motives. As for me, he was grooming me. He was taking my measure. For what? I wanted to know and I feared to know, at the same time.

His words kept coming back to me, from that first morning he'd taken me. *They have been using you. Now I'll use you.*

I had been in Caedon's custody for a full year when he decided I needed to learn how to ride a horse, how to dance, how to do fine needlework.

"You'll be useless to me if others see what a country clod you are," he told me.

One event happened then that filled me with joy. It was an emotion I so rarely felt any more that it took me a moment before I recognized it. He called me to him one day. "Mistress, I have a gift for you," he told me. I looked at him warily. "This," he said. From behind him, he took a parcel off a small table and handed it to me, watching me carefully as I cut the strings and pulled the flaps of cloth apart.

I didn't have to act my joy. It was my rebec.

"You see? I am your friend as well as your master," he said. "Playing and singing are your best gift. Now you'll use them in my service."

I played and sang to myself in my cell. Caedon never asked to hear my music. He brought in people to give me lessons in the other skills, though. The needlework was the worst. From the time Old Cwen had tried to teach me embroidery so long ago, I was terrible at it. Besides, it bored me silly. But some old lady in Caedon's employ was set to teach me, and she went at it doggedly.

Dancing. That was easy. When the dancing master taught me the steps to some court dance, I just thought about the acrobatics Wat had showed me and built from there. The dancing master gave Caedon glowing reports about me. That gave me a strange kind of pride.

But horses. I wanted to learn. I did. Still, I was awkward around them. After my fourth or fifth lesson, though, the riding master and I made a circuit of Caedon's entire property, which was vast.

The air was fresh. The trees towered over me, whispering their messages down at me as I rode beneath them. I thought about my childhood in the woods and realized I needed to take these lessons seriously. This was a way to escape the close confinement of my life. From the marsh beyond the wall enclosing Caedon's domain, the blackbirds were singing.

During the next lesson, the riding master watched while I cantered back and forth across a fresh meadow at the edge of Caedon's lands. I rode alongside the border wall, my hair flying free behind me, and I forgot all about Caedon and the wickedness he'd done; forgot all about Wat thinking I was some traitor.

Out of nowhere a flock of birds swooped low over the wall and arrowed directly toward me. My horse shied, and I went down. The blackbirds screamed above me, whirling around me.

I lay on my back looking up at the sky and the wheeling birds. My champions. Harbingers, not birds of death. They were calling me. They were telling me something.

I was aware of the riding master's anxious face, looking down at me; I was aware of his shouting for help. But these things appeared to be coming to me from a vast distance.

The birds and their calls. *This is the wall*, they were telling me. *Beyond it, freedom.*

Shortly afterward, some of Caedon's servants were helping me up and taking me back to the manor house. I was bruised and muzzy-headed.

Caedon had me moved to a bedroom beside his. "I'll be able to watch over you, there," he said.

The thought filled me with dread.

So far, he hadn't handed me over to that other man. In fact, I hadn't seen that man again. I began worrying about Caedon's intentions toward me now.

Later during the day of my accident, he let himself into my room and sat on the edge of my bed, holding my hand. I wanted to pull it away from his, but I didn't dare. He saw that, and he was enjoying it. "My timorous dove," he said.

I had vomited, when they first brought me inside. Now I wanted to vomit again.

"The riding master tells me you're progressing well. That's good," he told me. "This fall is an unfortunate set-back, but you'll be ahorse again in no time." He looked down at his shoes, then back up at me, his eyes malicious. "And your young sister is doing well. Flourishing, in fact."

"Will you let her go, as you promised?" Nervously, I realized I hadn't seen you in a fortnight, maybe two, Jillie.

"You've done nothing for me lately, mistress. Why should I do that? She's an asset to me now, as you are. I'll keep the two of you."

I turned my face away. It was useless to upbraid him for going back on his bargain. I already knew he was a dishonorable man. I already knew how futile it was to bargain with a man like Caedon.

"You could do something, though," he went on. "Something important. You may have guessed, I don't actually need your help to take Diera. I'm about to. It will be easy."

"It won't be so easy," I practically spat at him. "Audemar doesn't want that now. He wants Diera back."

"Holy Lady. You've been listening, mistress. You've been learning. I thought you might. His Royal Highness and I are. . ." he paused delicately. ". . . at odds right now. And not just about Diera, although she's a part of it."

I suddenly recalled, as my riding master and I made the circuit around Caedon's lands, spotting a large group of men in a field. They appeared to be drilling with pikes.

*Who's the rebel now?* I thought grimly.

"As you may know," said Caedon, continuing to hold my hand and continuing to talk, "in the Eastern Baronies, my own country, Diera has powerful cousins."

I nodded. I knew that was true. Avery had gone into exile there, and his uncle had helped him get back secretly into the Sceptered Isle.

"In fact," Caedon said, watching me closely, "my would-be bride has gone there for refuge, she and that bastard boy. Walter. Not across the Narrows. Just over the border to Lunds-fort. The bastard has family there, it appears."

I felt a rush of relief. They were alive, and they were safe. Out of the realm. Out of Caedon's reach, and Audemar's too.

"I see that's something you didn't know," said Caedon. "I'm glad of it. I've been making sure to keep you ignorant of it, but you're a clever girl, too clever for your own good."

His fingers tightened hard on mine.

I gave a little cry of pain.

"So you and I," he said, "are going to take a journey to Lunds-fort ourselves. I've maneuvered to make myself King Audemar's ambassador to the Baronies. I'll bring my cultivated and charming concubine with me. At every moment, you'll be by my side. You'll play your rebec and sing. You'll dance. Ride to hounds. Show off all your graces. Everyone will see how affectionately I treat you. They'll think I'm besotted with you, mistress."

The urge to vomit was almost overwhelming now, but I lay as still as I could. I closed my eyes until the feeling passed.

"While we're there, you'll arrange a meeting with this Walter fellow. You'll tell him you have information about me to give to him and to Diera, for their ears only. At the last moment, they'll learn I've forced you back across the border, so they'll have to meet you there."

Without opening my eyes, I said, "They think I'm a traitor. Your plan won't work."

"They may think it now. By the time we get to Lunds-fort, they won't think so any longer. Why, they'll be desolate, because they'll see how wrong they were about you. They'll see how their distrust allowed me to ruin you. They'll feel terrible pangs of guilt. The poor things."

"How in the Nine Spheres will you accomplish that?" I began. Then my eyes opened wide. Eris, I realized bleakly. He was setting her up. *He's used her. Now he'll sacrifice her, and the others will know her for what she really is.* I couldn't say I felt sorry for her, but I knew her fate prefigured my own.

"You'll have what you want," I said. "Diera. Royal children."

Caedon smiled at me, his eyes enigmatic. He patted my hand and tucked it under the furs. "A clever girl," he said. Then he left me.

How would he force me to do this thing, I wondered, when he wasn't planning to release you, Jillie? He had nothing to hold over my head.

Except. Except that Wat hated me now. Diera despised me for a betrayer, the person who set Avery up for death. That's what they thought.

When they learned differently, they'd be sorry for what they'd believed of me. But things would never be right among us again.

And so I found myself doing what I'd never imagined I'd do.

I found a building, burning resentment deep inside, and I blew on the coals.

I could admit something to myself, now that I was older. I loved Wat. I hated Wat. I built a shield around my heart, and then I built it higher.

I didn't belong to the Rising. Wat had made that abundantly clear.

I belonged to Caedon. As he never tired of telling me.

# Chapter Twenty-two

# Journey

J ust as he had said, Caedon made preparations to go to Lunds-fort, the city on that slender fingernail of land adjacent to our own realm but belonging to the Eastern Baronies. Caedon had indeed gotten himself appointed ambassador to the Baronies. From what I heard around me at table, Audemar was relieved that Caedon's attention was diverted to Lunds-fort. Then again, Audemar had to know Diera was in Lunds-fort. His spies must have told him that. So I knew matters were more complicated than the table chatter implied.

Our preparations lasted for several fortnights. During that time, I allowed myself a small glimmer of hope. Caedon couldn't watch me night and day at Lunds-fort. Maybe I'd be able to get away from him there. I didn't know what I'd do then, but I'd figure it out.

Always before, the thought of you held me back from taking any kind of drastic action, Jillie. But Caedon had no intention of releasing you. He'd told me that himself. So now his hold on me was weakened. I began to imagine different ways to escape him.

Finally it was the day before our departure. Caedon summoned me to his study that morning. "You haven't seen your sister in a long time," he said to me. "I'll take you to her now."

As he led me down through the warren of rooms toward the place they were keeping you, I knew he was planning a last reminder. *Do do my bidding, or something bad will happen to your sister.* My keeper plodded after us silently.

*But if I'm free,* I thought to myself, *I might be able to arrange your rescue, Jillie. Now, it seems no matter what I do for Caedon, he won't let either of us go.*

We went into a small room. A window, barred and covered with the thick glass, allowed us to look into the neighboring room, where you were being kept. You looked nourished. You were thin, but not overly so. You looked good. At this time, you must have been nine or ten years old.

"What do you think, mistress? Am I keeping her well?"

"As well as a prisoner can be kept, I suppose."

"I'm glad we agree about that," said Caedon. He looked around him. A small desk was shoved to one side. He sat down at it and pulled out a quill and a piece of parchment. He scratched something on it and folded it. "There, now," he said to me.

I looked back at him, puzzled.

"I've just signed an order for your sister's execution," he said. "It will take place forty days from now." A full moon and a sen'night or so longer.

I cried out, but he moved to me and clamped a hand over my mouth. Then he forced my head upward. Dangling from the rafters was a noose. He nodded to my keeper, and she opened the door. A man came in.

"This man carries out such small tasks for me. How are you keeping, Wulf?"

"I thank'ee Lord Caedon, very well," said the man, who had a friendly, open face.

"Wulf, step to the window and look in."

Wulf did this, while I cowered in horror against Caedon.

"Do you see that girl?"

"Yessir, I see'ee," Wulf replied.

"I've given an order she shall be hanged. From that beam." Caedon nodded to the noose above us. Wulf looked up at it. "Do you see any difficulties?"

"Nossir, not a one. Although it may be—" he took another look through the window, "—she being so little, she may be too light. I can put weights on her legs, lord, or my assistant and I can jerk down on her legs. That'll be all it will take," he said.

I closed my eyes. I thought I might faint.

"No, don't bother with that. Leave her hanging."

"Aye, my lord. The rope'll do its work after a bit," said the man.

"You can go now, Wulf," said Caedon, and the man went out of the room again. "You see now, mistress?"

I whirled out of his grip and beat on him with my fists. Between them, Caedon and my keeper soon controlled me.

"Striking your master," said Caedon. "There will be punishment for that." He made some signs to my keeper.

Twisting my hands behind me, the woman forced me back the way we'd come but stopped at a door that led into a small courtyard. She shouldered it open and pushed me out in front of her.

Caedon followed her out as I ran to the farthest corner in a vain attempt at seeing if there was any way to scale the high wall.

Behind Caedon came the man named Wulf.

"Pardon, good man," Caedon was saying over his shoulder. "I still have need of your services. See that woman?' he nodded at me.

"Yessir," said Wulf.

"She needs to be beaten. But not marked. No bones broken. Do you understand?"

Wulf gave Caedon a low bow. My keeper came at me, trying to corner me. I ran at her and kicked her. But by that time, Wulf had called in two other men, and they wrestled me to the ground. They dragged me to a bench and tied me to it. The keeper bundled a cloak over me. I fought for air, and then Wulf and his men beat me. I supposed they used clubs or rods of some type. I couldn't see them, muffled and panicked by the folds of the big cloak. At first I screamed and tried to avoid the blows, but finally I lay moaning as they finished their work. It's hard to talk about now. In the moment, it seemed agonizing and endless. Now, looking back on it, I feel the experience as if it were a bad dream.

They pulled the cloak off me. Caedon came over and looked down at me. "Bruised all over, I warrant, but no blood, no scars, and—" he felt my limbs. I was too stunned and weak to try to push him away. "—and no bones broken. Good work, men." They made their bows and went away out of the courtyard. Only Caedon and the keeper remained standing over me.

Caedon looked down at me with a benign smile. "A pity, mistress. We'll have to delay our trip to the Baronies until you are more presentable. More fit to travel. By the time we head out, the date for your sister's execution will only be thirty-four or thirty-five days away, not forty. I wonder if we'll be back in time to watch it. Or perhaps to stop it. You do understand that if you please me in Lunds-fort, I'll tear the order up when I get back, don't you. I've given it to Wulf. If we're not back by that date, well, then, I suppose he'll just have to carry out my orders. He's a most obedient servant. That's the kind of servant I like, mistress."

I lay glassy-eyed in a heap as he left the courtyard. My keeper hauled me up and walked me the rest of the way to my room, and locked me in. I stayed hurting in that room for days.

Each day, Caedon would come in and have the keeper take off my clothes so he could examine my bruises. Each day, he'd touch me all over as I tried to put myself in a faraway place where I could imagine this wasn't really happening to me. Every day, he'd shake his head sadly. "You look as if someone beat you to a pulp, mistress. It will never do to have my concubine on display in Lunds-fort, with bruises like that. We'll have to give it another day."

I made small notches on my rebec as each day went by. Finally, on the thirty-third day, Caedon pronounced me fit for travel.

The next day, the morning of the thirty-second, we departed. Caedon's decorated and gilded cart waited outside the main doors of the manor. The baggage wagons were piled high. Out-riders surrounded the party, armed and formidable.

Caedon ushered me out of the manor and to the cart. He'd had a sumptuous traveling cloak made for me, and one of the baggage wagons carried an entire chest of the new clothes I'd wear at the Baronies' fortified tower in the city of Lunds-fort.

As we emerged, a raucous cawing and jeering of blackbirds burst from the manor's ramparts. I hadn't thought of the birds since my accident on horseback. Now suddenly into mind sprang the blackbirds' message, sending me reeling. *Outside the walls. Freedom.* Caedon supported me against him. "Sick, mistress? Shall we go back in for one more day of rest?" He took my hand solicitously.

In terror, I shook my head.

"Then get in the cart," he said. He shoved me hard between the shoulder blades toward it. One of the guards steadied me as I fell against him, and helped me inside. I winced at his touch. He closed the brocaded flaps.

After a time, Caedon climbed in after me, and we began our slow progress east. As the cart and its entourage wound through the hills and valleys, I couldn't help remembering the jolting box bed of the wagon Wat and I had taken down many of these same roads. And I couldn't help thinking about the message of the blackbirds. Had I imagined it? I'd had a blow to the head. But deep inside me, I was sure what I'd heard had been no imagining.

I lay against the cushions and furs of the cart, nursing my bruised body, and thought about these matters. Most of all, I thought about the mere thirty-two days I had left to do Caedon's bidding and get back in time to save you, Jillie. Caedon had de-creed a savage death for you. I wondered if you knew, and if it tortured you to think about. Since you were too light for the noose, I knew you wouldn't die right away. And Caedon knew I knew. He knew I realized you would dangle there slowly suffo-cating to death. To prevent this act of savagery, I would be required to commit the ultimate betrayal.

If I'd had a knife, I would have stabbed Caedon to the heart. If I'd had my charm . . . I thought longingly of it, there hidden away in Old Cwen's loft.

After a while, Caedon began to stir restlessly beside me. I was amazed. He and I were sharing the same human feeling, cooped up in this small jolting space and desperate to get out of it. I for-got sometimes that Caedon was even human. I thought sometimes maybe he was a demon, or maybe, when I felt his vul-pine eyes on me, a more polished, more richly dressed version of the man-dog in the book about Man-Dog Rough-Gray. He made an impatient exclamation and thrust his head out between the flaps of the cart. "My horse," I heard him call out to someone.

He turned to me. "I'll be back soon, my dearest love," he told me.

"You are one of the Dark Ones," I said to him. I had decided that no, after all, he wasn't really human.

"For shame, Mistress Mirin, believing in fairy stories," he told me. "Don't tell me you worship the simpering Lady Goddess or, even worse, the Children. An apt name. They're gods for chil-dren." He leapt from the cart. I was glad not to have to share the stifling space with him. But he was back in the cart almost as soon as he'd left it.

He bent over me with a strap. Without a word, he bound my left wrist to a strut holding up the roof of the cart. I lay back in the furs and watched him while he did it.

"There now. Don't think you'll slip away, mistress," he said.

I smiled at him, a bitter smile, I knew.

When he was gone again, I lifted the flap on my side of the cart and breathed in the spring air. He was right. As soon as I had realized we were well away from his manor, as soon as I had realized how easy it would be to slide out of the cart and make into the underbrush at the roadside, I'd have tried it.

Our progress was down a road by a river. I wondered whether it was the Dourdin, or perhaps the Dourkam.

I breathed in sharply. The Dourdin. Because there, ahead of us, lay the stone bridge of the Old Ones that I remembered from our flight, Wat's and mine, away from our pursuers so long ago. I remembered how we'd outwitted our pursuers by going through the holloway. Here's where we came out. I remembered stopping by the bridge to drink the cool, clear water that rushed under it. I remembered our camp by the riverside, and Wat coming at me with his knife. *I'm not going to kill you, silly goose*, he'd said. *I'm just going to cut off your hair.* My eyes pricked with tears. Now he did want to kill me. *Why hadn't he*, I thought. *He should have.*

The cart in which I was riding moved onto the bridge. Our whole train snaked over the bridge to the east side of the river and then progressed ever eastward.

Lulled by the rocking of the cart, I slept for maybe a candle's measure. When I next eased the flaps of the cart aside and craned my neck to look up into the cloudless sky, I saw a swirl of blackbirds following us in our slow progress down the road. I dropped the flap again and felt beside me for the beautifully embroidered bag that held my rebec. Although I found it a bit awkward with the confining strap on my wrist, I angled around in the nest of furs until I was in a position to play my instrument.

For many full courses of the moon, I had sung only light, innocuous songs. Now I sang the one song that meant something to me. It had been too heartbreaking to sing, lately. I sang the eighth verse of Johnny's song, and as I sang it, I remembered him.

> *I'll sing you eight, oh.*
> *Green grow the rushes, oh.*
> *What is your eight, oh?*
> *Eight for the foul betrayers.*
> *Eight for the foul betrayers.*
> *One is one and all alone, and ever more shall be so.*
>
> *Blackbirds rising, blackbird's eye,*
> *Green grow the rushes, oh,*
> *One lone blackbird in the sky,*
> *Green grow the rushes, oh.*
> *One is one and all alone and evermore shall be so.*

I sang and played softly. I was playing only for myself. Then, in honor of Johnny, I sang the sixth verse.

> *I'll sing you six, oh.*
> *Green grow the rushes, oh.*
> *What is your six, oh?*
> *Six for the six proud walkers.*

*Six for the six proud walkers...*

I lay in a reverie rocked by the cart, remembering the day Johnny the Traveler came to stay with us. He wore a brooch just like our father's, just like Wat's.

In memory, I saw our father rushing from our small house down the lane to greet Johnny. The two men clapped each other on the shoulder. Then they fell on each other and stood that way for a long time. I swear I saw tears in our father's eyes when they returned arm-in-arm to our house, where our mother waited smiling in the doorway to greet Johnny. Our father never cried.

You and I were excited, Jillie. Remember how we both jumped up and down like the children we were, not so very long ago?

"And these are Dru's and Elsebet's beautiful girls," Johnny said to us, bending down to us both to give us each a hug.

Johnny played and sang that very night. I sat by him at the hearth, enthralled. As the days of his visit rolled by, he taught me to play. "You have your mother's voice," he told me. He allowed me to examine his rebec, examine the weasel carved on the tailpiece.

"The weasel is an animal of Earth," I remember him telling me. "It is a wily beast, and faithful to its friends. It hides. It is strategic. But in the end, it is a fierce fighter."

I remember marveling when I saw he had a brooch just like our father's.

"See, the six bars. Those are the six proud walkers." Then he played and sang the verse about them.

"Why are they proud? Why do they walk?"

"They are proud because they are companions in a great enterprise," Johnny told me. "They walk together to show their solidarity. They'll never be parted from each other, not by death, not by anything."

I thought this was a grand story. I made him tell it to me over and over. Toward the end of the visit, I asked him, "You and my father are two of the six, the proud walkers. Where are the others?"

"They're around," he told me easily. "Someday you may meet them."

Now I pushed aside the flap of the cart to look up at the sky again, and I grieved. Then I shook myself. My carefully-built protective wall had fallen in ruins around me. I needed to build it back, or thinking about Johnny, thinking about Avery, thinking about Wat especially would torture me until I lay bleeding at their feet. I sank back against the cushions, listless, letting my rebec fall to the side.

We were on the road for many days. Most nights we stopped at great manors belonging to Caedon's supporters. One or two nights, I slept in the wagon. I have no idea where Caedon slept during all this time. I was just glad he didn't sleep beside me.

Late on the twenty-fifth day, the footing under the mules drawing our cart changed. From rutted roadway, the cart moved onto smoothly polished stones. The wheels whirred along it. I heard shouts ahead. Everything came to a halt.

Caedon climbed back into the cart beside me. "The border," he said.

We spent the night at an inn on the border. There was only one bed in our room. Rigidly alert, I lay as far away as I could get from Caedon, but I didn't need to worry. He never touched me. In the morning, he rose and I heard him outside our room conferring with some people. Men's voices. Their voices were strange. They weren't even speaking our language. Caedon was conversing with them. I realized they were speaking Caedon's own language.

We got back into the cart. *Twenty-four days*, I whispered to myself. We rolled across a bridge built by the Old Ones. Caedon began telling me tales of the land we had passed into. He recounted these tales in a bright and friendly voice, just as if I weren't lying beside him with mingled despair and murder in my heart. At this very bridge, he told me, the Old Ones fought a battle against a warrior queen—a marvelous story that could have come out of one of Caedon's books.

We stopped at a dock, and Caedon handed me out. I was glad to stretch my legs after all day in the cart. Marshes swept away from me toward a massive wall, built by the Old Ones, too, as I later found out. On the other side in the distance lay the Narrows. Great cogs and knarrs nuzzled into the dock stretching out into the waters. I could see their masts and sails from where we stood, and smell the sharp tang of the sea air.

Caedon's retainers brought us two fine horses, and he and I mounted them. Caedon reached over and kept a firm grip on my reins. I glanced at him with scorn. How did he think I'd be able to get away from him here, as I sat my horse clothed gorgeously, my cloak and finely embroidered kirtle flowing over my horse's caparison, and surrounded by his men. He must have realized that, too, because soon he gave the reins back to me.

We rode together at the head of our procession across the bridge and through the mammoth western swing-gate in the Old One's walls to enter the bustling city of Lunds-fort.

# Chapter Twenty-three

# The Trap

W e spent a sen'night and more in the great wooden tower that dominated Lunds-fort. Each day, I cut a small notch in my rebec. *Twenty-one days. Eighteen days. Sixteen days. . . .*

We had many rooms of that tower to ourselves. Caedon was an important man. Everyone treated us that way. While we were there, Caedon began teaching me the language of the Baronies, his own native tongue. From our lessons in reading the books of the Old Ones, I'd learned I had a facility with language. I picked up the language of the Baronies fast, especially since it was a lot like the language of the Old Ones. Our own language resembled it not at all.

Every night, we retired to our bedchamber. I'd climb into our big bed covered with furs. Caedon would make a show before his servingmen of getting into bed with me, giving me a hard look to warn me not to shrink away from him. But as soon as they were gone, he'd throw the furs aside and move to a place by the fire. Some nights, he'd leave the room altogether. When he'd return close to dawn, it was clear he'd visited some brothel.

I had no idea why he avoided taking me, his property, but I didn't care. I was just grateful he apparently didn't want anything to do with me in that way.

I knew he thought I was pleasing to look on, maybe even beautiful. A strange thought. That's how he presented me at court, as if I were beautiful. And that's how he had me dress and behave. He sent servingwomen in to me to dress me in the rich clothing he had brought with him in his big chest.

Once he got exasperated with me. "You don't even know, foolish girl," he said to me. He sat me down and handed me a little bronze mirror. I looked into its wavy depths. My eyes are gray, Jillie, wide, startled-looking in the mirror, and fringed with long, black lashes. The apples of my cheeks are pink, my skin smooth, my forehead high. My lips curve in a pleasing way, or so he tells me. He stood behind me and ran his hands through my long brown hair. My hair is not fair, not like the hair of the fabled women of the stories and the minstrels' songs, but Caedon told me it was thick and lustrous. Then he stood me up and put his hands around my slender waist, ran them over my breasts and flanks. Am I beautiful, Jillie? You don't know either.

Every day I'd go out on his arm into the great hall of the fortress, or to other public places, where he showed me off to the officials and nobles of the Baronies. I let my old acting mode take over in those moments.

But he never touched me, not beyond the public display of a chaste kiss or proprietary hand or arm on my body. Or that time when he made me look at myself in the mirror.

It gradually became clearer to me that Caedon was a man with certain unusual tastes and ideas regarding the bodies of others. I didn't know what they were, and I didn't want to know. I just felt a profound relief that I didn't seem to be a focus for them.

I lived in a state of suspended dread. I could tell from some things he did and some things he said that he was preparing his trap for Diera and Wat. Whatever I thought of them, whatever they now thought of me, I didn't want to be the means Caedon used to lure them into his trap.

Even worse, the date for your execution was looming, Jillie.

Every day, we did something impossibly exotic, at least to me. We danced. We went to banquets. We went to plays, which I watched with narrowed eyes, noting every move and intonation with professional interest, even though all the actors were men. Most days, I played and sang for the other noble guests. When I did so, I noticed Caedon moved away to a window embrasure or found a sudden errand to do. Yet he appeared to be proud of the rapt attention my music drew to the two of us.

Caedon had brought a number of his swords with us on our journey. These bristled in a stand in our quarters. He displayed his skill with them at more than one demonstration of swordplay where I was seated with the nobles and gentles who had come to see and admire his abilities.

He did have the skill he was vaunted to have. I had to give him that. No one could prevail against him. All of his opponents yielded to his lithe, wolfish speed and grace. I sat through all of these matches staring straight ahead with a small smile plastered on my face.

Later, as I moved through the rooms of the tower, I overheard bits of talk following me. "Proud." "Haughty." And once, which wrung a joyless laugh out of me, "Lucky."

The evening of the tenth day, as we stood alone before the hearth-ring in our quarters, Caedon called me to him in a state of barely suppressed excitement. We were alone. We'd just come in from a day of hawking. I didn't know falconry, but I rode along beside Caedon and watched.

"Hawking. There's a skill you lack," he told me. "We'll have to remedy that."

I could barely pay attention to what he was telling me. The nearer your execution loomed, the more my rising panic threatened to suffocate me. Sometimes I found it hard to breathe, and this was one of those times.

"Pay attention," he said to me, irritated.

I tried to get myself together. I raised my eyes to his, trying to act submissive and obedient.

Caedon's manner turned brisk. "Now, then. In spite of certain deficiencies of yours, we're working well together. I doubt anyone has noticed the small neglected finishing touches in your education. It may be, if you continue to prove of use to me, I'll work on that. I'm very pleased with you."

He smiled at me now. "Don't look so sullen," he said. His nearness was oppressive. He had taken to wearing some sort of orris root powder that was all the rage in Lunds-fort, and he was making me wear essences of lavender and roses. We both smelled great. Too bad that delightful bouquet masked rot and despair.

"In the end, you'll be glad you were bound in service to victory and not defeat," he told me, smoothing my hair off my forehead as I tried to suppress my look of scorn and my desire to cringe away from his touch. "You will, Mirin," he said softly. "I'll teach you."

He prowled around the room until his restlessness made me want to scream. My nerves were already badly jangled, and he wasn't helping.

"These people," he mused, as if to himself. I forced my attention to what he was saying, and realized with dread that he meant the ragtag remnants of the Rising. "They all travel together. Where one is, you'll always find the others. I'm relying on that," he told me. "It's time for us to undertake the task I've trained you to do."

I stood silent. After I had served my purpose, would he kill me, or have someone else do it? I didn't believe him when he implied I'd continue to be useful to him. I was useful in only one regard—a means of entrapping Wat.

I wondered whether I would even be allowed to go back with him to his manor and forestall your fate, Jillie. And if so, when? The time was growing short.

Of course, he could simply be lying to me. There might be no execution order. The whole execution threat could be a simple ploy to ensure my cooperation. But I couldn't take that chance. He was perfectly capable of having such an order carried out.

He cared not a whit for you. He cared not a whit for me. He had no honor, so he cared not a whit for any promises he made.

Caedon resumed his restless roaming. Now he came back to my side and took my arm, guiding me over to a table at the side of the room. "Listen to me, mistress. I'm about to give you my final assignment, so pay close attention. Your task is very simple," he said. "You and I will go to a particular spot I've chosen. I'll be nearby, although you won't see me. You'll do what you do best, play and sing."

I shook my head a bit to clear it. What was he talking about? Then I realized. He was setting me up. I'd be bait. Bait for Wat. And the others, too. Caedon was right. They kept together, always, and especially now, when they were so few. If I could lure Wat out of hiding, Caedon would get Wat, and he'd get Diera.

Caedon was examining me narrowly. "I see you understand how my plan will work, mistress. I think you're familiar with the role of singing messenger. Sing for me now."

I moved to get my rebec, but he put out a hand and stopped me. "No," he said, and his voice was hoarse. "That's not necessary, not right now." Some uncertainty in his manner made me turn to him and stare. A look came into his eyes, a look that was hard to read. Fear? Surely not.

"But this Wat fellow needs an invitation. We'll set up a small situation beforehand. Quill and parchment are here at this table. Write what I dictate." His voice had grown steely.

I moved to the chair he indicated. He pushed me down into it and nodded toward a quill on the table. I took up the quill.

"Does the bastard read?" he asked.

"Yes," I murmured. They all did, those brothers. I tilted my head to look up at him. "Artur, they say, had scholarship to rival your own, my lord. Before the lot of you killed him."

Caedon grunted. "Careful, mistress," he said. His eyes had turned strange. I thought he'd be enraged. His expression mystified me. He didn't slap me, as I thought he might. I wasn't sure what I was seeing there, in his face. It couldn't possibly be regret. Could it?

I turned to the parchment he'd set before me.

"Write this," he said, standing over me, his hands on my shoulders. His breath on my neck sent a chill up my spine, and I shrank from him as the fragrance of orris and lavender enveloped me.

"*Beloved Wat,*" Caedon dictated.

I wrote that down.

"*You may have distrusted me before, but everything I've done, I've done for you. You know that now. I've told Caedon nothing of any importance. I'm not suspected. Jillie is going to be released, and I believe Caedon to be telling me this truthfully.*"

My hand was beginning to tremble.

"Write, mistress," said Caedon in a low, menacing voice. His strange mood was gone. When I sat there paralyzed with fear, he made an impatient exclamation. Suddenly he was holding a knife to my throat.

He went on. "*In spite of his promises, I'm not sure Caedon plans to release me.*"

Caedon sighed. "Stop stalling. Write that down, mistress." He laid the blade of the knife against my cheek.

I wrote it down.

"*I'm here in Lunds-fort, as you probably know. I've found out how to get away from Caedon.*"

I wrote that.

"*Meet me outside the city, at the tavern just across the western bridge toward the tidal inlet's docks. You'll know it by the brewer's bush over the door. It's the only one. Write, mistress.*"

He pricked the knife just under my chin where my jawbone met the hollow of my neck. One of those lanes for the red blood was there, the kind that would spurt in a deadly fountain if you gave it an out. He could kill me in an instant. Part of me wanted him to.

"*I'll be sitting inside the tavern. I'll play you our signal on my rebec. I don't want to commit it to writing in case this letter falls into the wrong hands. You know the signal. Your Mirin.*"

I was writing Wat's death warrant. Maybe Diera's. The death warrant of the Rising.

Despite my resentment at them all, I had to act. Something. Anything. I made my hand tremble—hardly an act—and dropped the quill.

"Get that, mistress." Caedon's voice held exasperation and something more dangerous than exasperation.

I leaned down to pick it up. "It's under there—" I said.

"Get it."

I got off the chair and crawled under the table after it, but as I did so, I rolled into Caedon's stand of swords, knocked it over, and reached for one of the blades, trying to remember anything Conal may have taught me that could work.

It was a desperate act. Caedon kicked the sword away with his foot, hauled me up by an arm, shoved me roughly back in the chair.

"I'm looking forward to the things I'll do to you, mistress, when all of this is over." His voice was a savage whisper. "Write." This time he didn't bother with his knife. He held his arm across the back of my neck, crushing it down. He thrust the quill back in my hand. "Write."

My handwriting was a scrawl.

"Good. That's bad quillwork, mistress. I'm thinking this Wat fellow will see you're very frightened indeed." He took the page from me, read it over, sanded and folded it. "Yes. Good work. You're about to engage in your final act of treachery for me, mistress." He gave me a cold smile. He forced my head up until we were eye to eye. "But this act will be the real one, not the sham you used to imagine you were perpetrating on me."

"You're going to kill me after this," I told Caedon.

"You will have to hope I do not," he told me. "I may. But who knows? Once I train you in my ways, my. . .particular tastes, maybe you'll prove of use to me. You've changed since the days of your boyhood, mistress." Then he added, "We'll go in the morning. We'll move across the border. Now you'll write one more letter." He handed me another piece of parchment, and the quill again.

I took it.

"Write this. No salutation. Just write, *They've taken me west. We're stopping for the night at the hill where Reda's people once lived. I think you know it. Find me there, if you love me.*"

"Wat doesn't love me," I told Caedon, handing him the parchment with a shaking hand. "He hates me."

"I believe you're mistaken, mistress," said Caedon. His eyes glittered. "And when you're there, on that hill, then you'll sing your song."

"What song?" I said, desperate to buy time.

He looked at me from under hooded lids. "You know what song."

He took the two letters and called for a servant. He handed the servant one and kept the other, the little piece of parchment I'd written second.

The next morning, he, I, and a few retainers rode out of the city together.

*Day nine*, I thought. I was dressed much more simply than before. I had my rebec slung over my shoulder. I thought of dropping it along the way, letting it be crushed by the horses' hooves, but it wouldn't matter if I did. Caedon would just force me to sing without accompaniment.

The retainers rode close around us. I saw it would be impossible for me to make a break and try to get away. We stopped at the tavern at the tidal inlet where the great cogs and knarrs came to port, but only long enough for Caedon to take the small parchment with him into the inn. Through the door, I saw him pay someone.

He came back out and swung up onto his horse. "And now we set the bait," he told me, with a tight smile at my distress.

We rode hard all day. At night we pulled up to a farmhouse below some rolling hills.

"Tomorrow, we go up there," Caedon told me, nodding toward the highest of the hills as he handed me down off my horse. A woman came out of the farmhouse and led me inside. She drew me a mug of ale and handed me a loaf. Then one of Caedon's retainers took me to a small room in the back, windowless, and shut the door.

I ran to the door and tried it, just in case. Of course it was barred. As I pressed my ear to the door, I heard Caedon say to someone just outside, "That is indeed good news, my man. Here's gold for you." And then to someone else. "Everything's in order. They're following. Once they cross the border. . ."

Caedon must have moved further away from the door then, because his words became an indistinguishable murmur. I sank down to the floor in despair.

I was in a trap I couldn't get out of, and you, Jillie, you were in a trap. Traps of Caedon's devising. Traps he enjoyed springing. As for Wat and Diera, I was the trap he was setting up for them.

Then I had a strange thought. I recalled how Caedon had paced all through the night before.

Caedon, too, was in a trap, a dark trap of his own making.

What would it be like, to live in the skin of that savage animal? What wound had he sustained, to make him that way?

I pushed these thoughts away from me. Some animals were so damaged the only thing you could do for them was kill them. Kill them, or they would kill you.

# Chapter Twenty-four

# Underneath the Stars

D awn broke—*Day Eight*—and Caedon opened the door to the room where he'd put me for safe-keeping. He prodded me awake with the toe of his boot.

"Time for the best performance of your life, mistress," he said. He hauled me up by the arm. The woman of the household where he'd brought me watched me narrowly as I visited the jakes and washed with water from her well. As I walked to the back of her dooryard I saw Caedon's men standing around the perimeter.

A sick thudding began in the pit of my stomach. When the goodwife offered me food, I pushed it away.

"Suit yourself, mistress," said Caedon, and one of his men led me out to my horse and helped me mount. Caedon said a few words to his men, and then the two of us rode up a path that wound from the farm where we'd stayed the night toward the crest of the nearest hill. Near the top, we dismounted.

My hands were trembling as Caedon prodded me up the hill at the point of his sword until we reached a level place at the very top, a bald outcropping giving us a view of the entire landscape. We stood in silence as the sun rose higher in the sky. Caedon stepped to the place where the hillside dropped off to a deep valley. I looked, too.

For a stunned moment, I was reminded of the story in Caedon's book, the one about the man who sowed the dragon teeth. In the tale, the dragon teeth start to sprout. First tips of iron appear in the furrows, just as, in spring, the green blade rises from the buried grain. In the story, these tips of iron reveal themselves as spear tips. Finally, an entire army springs up in the field.

As I looked out over the nearest hill, something similar seemed to be happening. A vast army marched toward us. First we saw the tips of their pikes, the sun glinting off the steel points. Then the conical shapes of their helmets. Then they ranged in their hundreds before us up the hill and over it. Still, they kept coming.

Caedon smiled, shading his eyes and gazing out over the scene. "Ours," he said to me.

I realized something. This betrayal of mine wasn't the only thing Caedon had planned, just over the border from Lunds-fort. He had something else in mind, a much bigger betrayal.

"I'll show you another interesting sight, mistress," he told me, taking me by the arm and leading me to the other side of the hilltop. "Look. Across to the next ridge. Look carefully."

I squinted into the distance. Another army was ranged there. I could just barely make it out, but I could see a dark mass that took up entire hillsides. It was huge.

"Audemar's men," I guessed. "They'll crush you. Audemar must have thousands of men in his army."

Caedon showed his teeth in a grin. "Will they? Does he? I have more men, and I have the element of surprise. Watch and see, mistress. Before this day is over, you'll be glad you're with me. As for your friends—they're a gnat-bite only."

We were standing at the fulcrum of two vast armies. We had arrived at the moment before a momentous battle. Caedon had been busy. Far below us, I could see more men swarming up the road from Lunds-fort and massing around the farmhouse we'd just left.

"Things will get very hot right here at this spot. And fast. But first things first," Caedon said. "Time to deal with that annoyance. That gnat-bite. Begin playing. And sing as if your sister's life depends on it. Because it does."

He pushed me to the center of the open space, stepped back, and nodded to me. *He must know something*, I thought. *He must know Wat is within earshot.* At first I thought my mouth would be too dry to sing, but Caedon lunged forward then and nicked my shoulder with the point of his sword.

I began to play. I opened my mouth, and I began to sing.

*I'll sing you one, oh.*

My song rang out over the hillside.

*What is your one, oh?*
*One is one and all alone and evermore shall be so.*
*I'll sing you two, oh. . .*

There was a tree at the side of the path, just beside me, a large tree in a tangle of underbrush. I saw Caedon tense and move quietly to the tree. And ease behind it. I couldn't hear any oncoming footsteps, but Wat could be as silent as a cat when he needed to be. I didn't think he'd just stride up to me. No matter how much he thought he'd failed me, no matter what emotions he felt about that, no matter how much he believed my letter, I had the feeling Wat would still be cautious. And I also had the strong feeling he was very near. Call it my second sense, if you like.

Thinking back on that time, I am amazed I wasn't paralyzed with indecision. If I didn't fulfill his wishes, Caedon would kill me. It would have mattered little to me if not for you, Jillie. Don't think I'm all that heroic. I was sure he'd kill me anyway after I'd carried out his orders. Or maybe worse than kill me. I knew he was capable of that.

As for Wat. Wat had been ready to kill me himself that night at the inn. Wat had thought I was the worst kind of traitor, responsible for the death of almost all he held dear. Wat had left me in Caedon's hands when he could have gotten me out. Why in the Nine Spheres would I care what happened to Wat?

Unbidden, a vision of Avery sitting his horse like a king on the morning of his death rose before my eyes. Unbidden, a vision of Johnny looking down at me the last morning I saw him, seeing things about me that I couldn't yet see for myself.

A swirl of black dots against the blue sky resolved itself into a phalanx of birds. Blackbirds came screaming down at me from the zenith of the heavens.

I filled my lungs with air and sang it out, not the third verse in Johnny's song that came next, but a verse completely out of order.

> I'll sing you eight, oh.
> What is your eight, oh?
> Eight for the foul betrayers! Eight for the foul betrayers!

It was the verse that would give Wat the few seconds' warning he needed. I sang it in a vicious fury.

With a howl of rage, Caedon sprang from his hiding place, slashing backhand at me with his sword as he did. All that training Wat had given me kicked in now. I tucked myself into a forward roll and knocked him off his feet, cursing my awkward skirts as I did so.

There was a blur of movement beside me, Wat pulling me to my feet. "Go now," he shouted at me.

"No," I said between gritted teeth.

Wat tackled Caedon low as he tried to rise, shoving him onto his back into a bank of butcher's broom.

Wat rolled forward into a crouch, a knife in either hand.

"Go!" Wat screamed at me. "Horse at the bottom of the hill. Get out of here."

The men circled each other, Caedon scratched and bleeding, Wat pale and intent. Then they joined. I was frozen to the spot.

"Get her out of here!" Wat's voice was panicked. Someone grabbed me and hustled me down the hill. Torrin.

"No," I said. "No."

"You heard Wat. He's your master, isn't he?" It was Torrin.

"He's no master of mine," I raged at her.

She ignored me. "Do as he says, girl." She shoved me over the rough terrain, grabbing me by the arm and dragging me when I went down. At the bottom of the hill, she threw us both on mounts. Our horses took off furiously down the road and past the farmhouse, where men were assembling. Their startled shouts followed us as we veered off into the forest and kept going until we reached a river. We rode until our exhausted horses stopped dead, both almost simultaneously, drooping, their poor heads down, dripping with froth.

I slid off mine. "I'm sorry, my friend," I whispered into his silky soft ear. "I'm sorry for treating you in this cruel way. You don't deserve it." I lay weeping against his neck.

"Lorel will never forgive me," Torrin said, looking at her own horse. "Here's where we split up. I have to get back to Diera. She rode off down the river's other fork." She shook me roughly. "Go."

"Don't order me around. I don't belong to you any more."

Torrin stood taken aback. "You warned Wat. And you wrote him a letter that said—"

"Caedon made me write that letter. I hate Wat," I burst out. "I didn't do it for Wat or Diera. I did it for Avery. I did it for Johnny."

Torrin gave me a long, level look.

I looked around, suddenly terrified. "Wat—" I cried out. "I have to go back up there."

Torrin talked past all my words. She talked to my heart instead. "Listen. You gave Wat the time he needed to get the advantage. You did well. Wat can take care of himself. You know that."

"What if Caedon kills him?"

"I'm going to tell you something." She reached out and grabbed me hard by the neck of my kirtle. "We're wasting time. I'm going to tell you anyhow. You know where Wat learned his skills?" She forced me around to look at her.

"Conal." I was breathing in short, sharp bursts, the hysteria rising in me.

"Yes, Conal taught him some formal things about sword-play. He taught me and Lorel too. No, I mean Wat's real skills."

I had been trying to twist out of her hands. I stopped now and thought about Wat and the two men in the bathing shed, and I recoiled. "No," I said, gasping for breath. I felt as though all the breath had left my body. "I don't."

"Your father taught him."

"My father?" I stopped struggling, astounded. My father, the gentlest man I knew. What Torrin was saying meant that my father had been an accomplished assassin. A killer.

"Look, Mirin, I want you to think about something." Torrin's voice was urgent. "Your father was the best we had. Why do you think he would have let some common soldiers cut him down, that day outside your cabin?"

I looked at her dumbly.

"I can think of only one reason," she said. She let me go, and I staggered back. "He got slowed down. He was protecting your mother and your sister. That's how. So now your job is not to go back up there. Your job is to get as far away from there as possible." She moved toward her horse.

Something came to me. A thought out of nowhere. "Who was Wat's partner, before me?" I asked her.

She was rearranging her horse's saddle. She looked back over her shoulder and gave me a strange look. "Johnny," she said.

"No. The one after Johnny. The woman."

"It doesn't matter."

"What happened to her?"

"It doesn't matter. We need to get going, Mirin." Then she stopped. "That woman. She was feeding information about us to Caedon," she said.

"And we knew that how?"

She was silent.

"Eris told you, right?" I persisted. "Did you kill her, that woman? Did Wat kill her?"

Torrin's eyes widened. "No. No, he didn't. He—"

"He did," I insisted.

"No. He couldn't. After what happened with Johnny, he went through a bad time. He couldn't do it."

"So. Who did?" I was rushing ahead to ask this question, because I was too frightened to learn the answer, but I also had to know.

Torrin looked at me with eyes of pity. "It doesn't matter." She took up the reins of both horses. "I have to get Diera away from here. You'll have to walk."

"Children keep that woman," I said. The dead woman's beautiful embroidered kirtle rose up in memory. Wat and I had ripped it up and burned it. No vestiges of her remained on this earth.

As Torrin began to mount, I called after her, "Caedon wants Diera. He wants to become king."

Sitting her horse, Torrin looked off into the distance, back toward where Wat and Caedon were trying to kill each other. "Yes, that's why Caedon's army is waiting for his order to attack Audemar's army. Get out of here, Mirin. If you go back up there, you'll just put everyone in danger. The worst of it is, Wat will do anything to keep you safe." At my look, she reached down and shook me by the shoulder. "Anything. It was true before. He went off to that inn to kill you, and when he got there, he couldn't do it. Now it's a point of honor, do you hear?"

"He believed Eris. Not me. As you all believed Eris. About many things." My voice was bitter.

"She may have fooled us for a while, but in this matter, others weren't so blind. You're wrong about Diera. She saw what Eris was trying to do to you. She'd never been that close to Eris, as Wat was. Eris couldn't fool Diera."

"Diera barely knows me. She's only seen me that one time." But then I thought of the way our eyes met at the procession.

"Diera saw," Torrin insisted. "And then Wat saw. That was a terrible moment the likes of which I never hope to live through again. Now get out of here. And the Child go with you." Torrin took up the reins of the other horse and moved off into the woods. Over her shoulder, she called back to me, "Eris is dead." Then she melted into the woods with the horses, and was gone.

Now the day had begun to wane toward afternoon. I had no snare, no cloak, nothing but the clothes on my back and, amazingly, my rebec. By rights it should have been smashed or ripped from my shoulder, but I had it.

That's when I discovered Caedon's slash at me had left a deep gash in my upper left arm. I hunted around the forest floor, moving aimlessly at first, but I found enough mosses and made a pack of it. I held it to my arm to stop the bleeding some. When I was able to, I'd look for some herbs and dress the wound. It didn't seem that dangerous.

And if it were? I didn't care. I'd lost Wat. I'd lost more than Wat. I'd lost faith. I knew who had killed Wat's partner. But I shied away from that knowledge, because I couldn't bear to face it. The damage Eris had done could never be undone, and it tainted us all.

I knew in my bones the Rising had lost. If Caedon killed Wat, the last of the Six would be gone. I'd probably lost you, too, Jillie. Eight days, and I didn't know where I was or how to get back to Caedon's manor. If I did, I wouldn't know how to get you out. And I was on foot.

I worked my way out of the forest. The river was shallow there. I waded across, holding my rebec high. In the distance, I heard shouting and the clash of arms, but those men were occupied with matters of war. They'd hardly come after some strange girl darting past them down the road. They had a battle to fight.

I dried myself on a rock at the river's edge, shivering in the cooling air of twilight. As it grew darker, I began to move along the country lanes, at first aimlessly, then with more direction, scrutinizing the landscape, studying its curves to decide where a stream might run, a stream that might feed into a river. If I kept following these waterways, I told myself, I'd reach the sea.

When night fell, I slept against a tumbledown wall that looked to be the boundary of some abandoned farmstead. I was chilled, but I did sleep. During the night, I woke to see the entire sky spangled with stars shining their cold light down upon me.

I thought of the fourth verse of Johnny's song, and marveled again that I hadn't seen in it what I saw now. *Four for the four star children*, I sang. *Three, three, the rivals. Two, two, the long-lost boys, clothed all in green, oh. One is one and all alone and evermore shall be so.*

I remember thinking, when I first heard this star child verse as Johnny sang it, *oh, that is pretty.* But now I understood what it was trying to tell me.

*Blackbirds rising, blackbird's eye*, I sang. *One lone blackbird in the sky. One is one and all alone. . .*

Beneath the stars of the night sky, I wept. I wept for them all, even Wat. Especially Wat. He'd lost his brothers. He had lost his little brother Aedan. He had lost his older brother John, who had saved him from death. He'd lost my father, who had taught him everything he knew. He'd lost his sister Eris in the bitterest possible way. She'd betrayed him, and then she'd paid the price. He had lost Avery, his leader. His brother. But somehow, impossibly, Wat had saved Diera.

Audemar was just as much Wat's brother as Avery, and Audemar remained. I had a premonition that Audemar, for all his slippery, treacherous ways, was no match for Caedon.

Dawn was touching the eastern sky with rose. I trembled to think that by now, the fight between Caedon and Wat was already long over. One of them surely lay dead.

Wat had always seemed so much older than I. My master. But Wat was barely out of boyhood, and he made terrible mistakes.

*We all*, I said to myself, *make terrible mistakes, and underneath the stars, we all keep making them.*

Wat going up against Caedon and all his skill? It hit me then, the reason why Wat had screamed at Torrin to get me out of there. Maybe it was true, what she said, that I'd slow him down. But there was another thing. He didn't want me to watch Caedon kill him, the way he had had to watch as those he loved were killed.

I howled like an animal. I turned and started running back the way I had come. But I slowed. And stopped. Whatever had happened, it was over. There was nothing I could do about it now.

And I needed to get to you, Jillie. *Seven days.*

I began to walk.

# Chapter Twenty-five

# Finding the Way

As I made my way across country, I had little to go on. When Caedon took me, after the Rising had rescued Diera from her enforced wedding, I remembered the ride behind the horseman to Caedon's estate. It seemed endless, but it must not have been. I was half out of my wits from a blow to the head and from panic and grief, but it could not have been far.

And I also remembered my much more recent trip from Caedon's estate to Lunds-fort, especially how we had crossed the Dourdin over the stone bridge of the Old Ones. To get there, we'd progressed downward out of the hills. Caedon's manor would be up in those hills somewhere, not as high up as the earl's castle, but fairly close.

I had a pretty vague mental map to follow. It was all I had, though, so I set out. I knew very well how to get to the earl's castle, once I'd found my way to the main roads. Wat and I had traveled those roads behind the patient Millicent. When I was sure I was close to the castle, I decided I would cut over to the Dourkam and backtrack down it toward the Dourdin. Caedon's lands lay around there.

On the morning after I'd started my journey (*six days*), I stopped following the rivers. I'd come to a main road, and I recognized it as one of the ways to the castle. I didn't need to go all the way up the Dourkam into the high country. I just needed to make my way to the place where the Dourdin branched off near Withiel. When the road began following along the banks of a fairly large river, I suspected I must have reached the Dourdin. I just had to hope I hadn't passed the place where the Dourkam forked up into the hilly country. The fork in the rivers was my signpost, telling me how to get to you.

I was worried about stopping to ask someone. I looked wild. My kirtle was torn and dirty, my headcloth long gone, and my hair full of snarls and twigs. But I couldn't risk missing the fork.

Beyond me a little way up the river bank, I spotted a low thatched longhouse. It stood at the edge of a little village. As I neared the place, I saw a farmwife in a white headcloth. She was hoeing in the family vegetable patch.

"Goodwife," I called to her from a safe distance.

She looked up, startled. When she caught sight of me, she rushed at me, shooing with her apron.

I jumped back away from her.

"No beggars!" she screamed at me.

"I just want to know, Goodwife, is this the Dourdin River?"

She stopped at my civil tones. "Yes," she said, eyeing me uncertainly.

"Is the fork of the Dourkam upriver or down?" I asked, gesturing.

She pointed.

I nodded my thanks and headed off. Thank the Children, I hadn't missed the fork.

"Danger abroad," she called after me, maybe deciding I was a refugee and not a beggar. "The war makes the roads dangerous."

I kept going. I came to the fork late that afternoon. I was glad of it, but I realized I could spend days and days crisscrossing the countryside before I happened on Caedon's lands. And I didn't have days and days. I had six. By now, more like five.

I sat down on the bank of the Dourkam, discouraged, and slipped my shoes off. They were in tatters. I put my feet into the river to cool them, and when I went on, I left the broken shoes in the weeds by the riverside.

By twilight, though, I'd found the road to the earl's castle. I bedded down against a stone wall with some brush to guard me from suspicious eyes, and I tried to sleep. I'd had nothing to eat for near on two days now, and I worried I'd get too weak to go on. I had no traps or fishing line. No gutting knife. My feet were torn and bleeding.

But then over the top of the wall, I spied a light. Across the fields came the distant sound of music. I knew it was risky, but I limped toward the light and the sounds. As I neared them, I saw I'd come to a roadside tavern. The inn was ablaze with rushlights, and the torrent of talk and snatches of singing that poured out the tavern's windows let me know there were thirsty patrons within.

I edged up to the tavern steps and sat down on them, timidly. The tavern keeper might run me off, I knew. Or drunken louts might assault me. And I was dressed in fine clothing. That would seem suspicious. Still, my clothes were torn and muddy. No one would notice they'd once been the garments of a rich woman. I had to take the chance.

I unslung my rebec and began to play and sing, at first softly. Soon I had a small crowd gathered around me.

But the tavern owner came out then, and he was angry. "What do you think you're doing, mistress, a beggar woman on my doorstep?" he roared.

"Let her play," one man called out from the people surrounding me.

"Please, sir," I said, looking up at him. "I'll play and sing for my supper, if you'll let me."

"Let her play," someone else called.

So then the tavern-keeper relented. He allowed me to sit at his fire and play and sing, and he handed me a mug of ale and a small loaf of brown bread, too. After the last of his customers had staggered away into the night, he gave me a grudging smile. "You helped me out tonight, mistress," he said. "You're welcome back tomorrow, if you will."

"I'm a traveler, sir, and separated from my party during these times of war," I told him. "I'll have to move on."

"You can sleep in the cattle shed," he said. I slept there wrapped in my cloak, and he even gave me a bit of breakfast in exchange for my aid in drawing water and helping with the animals the next morning.

"My goodwife died in childbed last year," he told me. "I've no one to help me, not with the war on. You sure you won't stay?"

"I can't," I said. A panicky feeling was rising in me. *Five days.* "I need to get on toward Sir Caedon's manor."

"Dark Ones take him," the man said automatically and then caught himself. He looked at me with fear growing in his eyes.

"Dark Ones take him indeed," I told him. "I'm looking for my sister. I fear he has her." *What do I have to lose?* I asked myself. This man might be an ally.

"You're not the first, mistress. But I wouldn't go over there. The war's come to these parts. The king's men marched through a few days back. That's where they've probably gone."

"I have to," I said.

He nodded. I could see he understood.

"Do you know the way?"

He hesitated. Then he drew me a rough map on the back of his shovel with a lump of chalk. And he even went to the chest in his sleeping place to bring me some clothing of his dead wife's, and a pair of shoes. I took them gratefully.

I'd made certain to do one thing to keep myself safe while I bathed my feet in the river. From my tattered shoes, I had ripped off a bit of leather, and I'd made myself a kind of wristlet. I tore a strip of cloth off my already torn cloak and used it to tie the leather securely around my left wrist. For good measure, I made sure to keep the left sleeve of my kirtle drawn down over it. The last thing I needed was for someone to spot Caedon's brand on my wrist. Even though this man seemed like one of the many who loathed and despised Caedon as much as I did, I couldn't risk him seeing that brand and either realizing a chance to make a lot of gold by betraying me or, just as bad, thinking I might be one of Caedon's spies and attacking me. So as I questioned this tavern owner, I made sure my brand was hidden.

I was successful. In his stable, I changed into the fresh clothing, and then I made ready to resume my journey.

"The good Lady Goddess keep you, mistress," the tavern owner said as he saw me off. "I fear you'll need Her help." He gave me another loaf and a leathern bottle of milk from his cow and waved me down the road.

I could get to you in time, Jillie. According to the tavern keeper, I was less than a day's walk away. I could do it. I set out. As the leagues went by, I could see the signs of devastation that war had wreaked upon the land. Farmhouses standing empty. One whole village burnt to the ground. I began picking my way down the edge of the road instead of the easy middle. I might need to hide myself if soldiers came. It was as though I walked through a ghost landscape, though. I met no one. I heard nothing. Hardly a bird sang.

And then I rounded a bend to see, off the road to my left, the corner of a long wall. Caedon's wall. I knew it. My heart rose. I strode along it, eating my loaf as I walked, and drinking from the bottle. The ground along the wall was desolate and, as I could see as I came to a rise in the land, the ground on the other side as well.

But as I neared the manor, and my heart began beating hard, I realized I had no plan for getting you out, Jillie. None. I'd get there in time, but for what? To sit outside the gates while that man Wulf killed you?

But I pressed on.

If it meant giving myself up to Caedon at the gates, I'd do it.

As you see, without giving it a thought, I assumed Caedon had been the survivor in his fight with Wat. I assumed Wat was many days dead.

Once I'd gotten closer still to the manor, I began to run. Something had happened here. There was a scorched smell in the air. When I got a glimpse of the roofline, I saw a glow. Fire.

Abruptly, I rounded the last corner to find myself on Caedon's very doorstep. But I did not cringe back. I stood and stared. Caedon's manor was a ruin. The roof still smoldered. The door was broken down, blackened, and burnt. I shoved my way in. The light inside was dim. I ran through the crumbling halls, screaming out your name, Jillie. Only silence echoed back to me.

Eventually, I found my way to Caedon's study. The books were tumbled down, and most were burnt. I reached for one, then another. And another. I picked up *Man-Dog Rough-Gray* and shoved it into the bag with my rebec. Its pages were curled and scorched, the leather cover half burnt off.

Now, slowly, I traced my steps through the many rooms to the place they'd kept you. I knew what I would see. All the doors stood open, even yours. No one was there. In the room next to yours, the rope still hung from the rafters. I stifled a scream of horror and began to run through the manor.

By the time I got out of the house, coughing from the smoke and ash, I knew you were gone. I could hope someone friendly had come to take you. I could hope you were safe. But I didn't know. And I realized I might never know.

As I shoved my way out of the burned-up gates of Caedon's manor, I heard shrieking from the battlements, as if the demented ghosts of its inhabitants had risen up. But there were no ghosts. Only the blackbirds. They rose in a black cloud over the battlements and began circling.

I turned my back on them. They were friends of mine, Johnny said. Much good they'd done me.

Wat had told me, *Go to the sea.* I had no reason now to do it. I did it anyway. I began walking west.

# Chapter Twenty-six

# The Work of a Woman

I hadn't even gotten to the river before I saw all around me the signs of a great battle. Brush, even trees slashed and trampled. Then the bodies. First one, then small groups of twos and threes. I heard voices ahead and moved off the road. Men in the roadway were pitching bodies into a big wagon. Out in the field beyond, other men were prodding at bodies, looking for items to take. A weapon. An armlet. A torque wrested from a dead man's neck. The bodies were so sodden with blood and mud that I couldn't make out, from where I hid, whether these were Caedon's dead or Audemar's.

I made a wide circle around these men through the woods on my side of the road, careful to use my hunter's skills to make no noise. When at last I came back onto the roadway, I heaved a breath. I felt as if I'd been holding it all that while.

That's when I saw the horse. One horse, its reins trailing. With a sickening thud in the pit of my stomach, I realized I knew that horse. It was Torrin's horse. Another horse lay belly-up at the margin of the roadway. Tossed alongside, two more bodies.

I moved up to them quietly and crouched down. Lorel's eyes stared sightlessly at the sky. Torrin's body was thrown over Lorel's, as if protecting her. I gently touched both women at the pulse points of their necks, but I knew they were dead. Their clothing was stiff with blood, the reek of blood and death overpowering. *Hide,* an urgent voice was telling me, but I couldn't move.

Around me, the blackbirds settled into the trees. Harbingers of the Child of Earth? I thought. No. Old Cwen was right. Harbingers of death.

Yet I lowered my head in prayer. Or respect. I wasn't sure which. When I did, I saw something glittering in the weeds. I reached out for it. An enameled brooch. A blackbird in the green rushes. *Diera owns this,* read the words around the circle of it.

Diera had been here. I jumped to my feet and scanned the woods beyond the bodies. No one was there.

I hazarded a shout. "Diera!"

There was no answer. I knew the chances were good she'd been taken. And the chances were good that, should I keep on shouting, I'd be taken, too. I bent down to try to close Lorel's eyes, but they wouldn't close. I stood for a long time, just staring down at them, my two friends. Finally I smoothed out their clothing a bit, picked the brooch up from where it lay in the grass, thrust it into the pouch at my girdle, and made my way over to Torrin's horse, quietly grazing by the roadside. I wanted to keep vigil by the bodies of my friends, but I didn't dare. I stroked Torrin's horse gently. Then I swung up into the saddle and took the reins. I steered him to the edge of the road and took him at a walk westward, always listening for hoofbeats or shouts behind me. But the road was empty. As the horse and I rode west, a cloud of blackbirds rose up behind me, fluttered ahead, and settled in the trees. As I drew abreast of them, they did it again. They kept pace with me all the way down that road to the Dourkam River.

I followed the Dourkam back down to the fork, and then the Dourdin. I followed it the short way to Withiel, the town situated near the fork of the rivers where Wat and I had had one of our first big successes, back even before my boy days. I didn't dare try to sell Torrin's horse there. That would have drawn too much attention to me. And anyone seeing me on him would probably assume I stole him and send for the beadle. As I rode into the outskirts of the town, I dismounted in a meadow bursting with cowslip and cranesbill. "You should have enough to eat here, my friend," I whispered to him, rubbing his velvety nose. Then I walked away from him, hoping someone would soon find him and care for him. I kept myself from looking back.

I stayed around Withiel for close to the span of a moon's turning, earning my keep by playing in taverns. The war hadn't come to Withiel yet, but everyone there was on edge. More and more of the populace began moving out into the country. The palisade gates stood open now. All the guards had been recruited into one or the other of the two warring armies.

Inside the town, the tavern business was slow.

Even so, my singing and playing earned me enough small coppers to clean myself up and feed myself. At least I picked up news there. Some said the forces of Audemar were prevailing. These people pointed to Caedon's burnt-out manor as proof. I didn't mention I'd seen it with my own eyes. Others said the forces of Caedon were prevailing. Whatever news these people exchanged with each other, no one mentioned the Rising. The Rising scarcely existed. It was as if it had never existed.

After I felt I knew the tavern regulars, I risked asking the question that burned on my tongue—whether anyone knew the fate of the Princess Diera. My inquiry was mostly met with blank looks.

"Oh, you mean Artur's daughter? Isn't she long dead?" someone said.

"Oh, her," someone else said. "Wasn't she somehow involved in her own father's assassination?" These words filled me with fury, but I couldn't let that show.

Finally someone said to me, "I heard she's been taken." But when I asked where, and by whom, the man just shook his head.

No use asking about you, Jillie. Orphans of the war roamed the countryside. You could be anywhere. *If you're alive*, I said to myself.

I did learn that the rival armies were camped just downriver, on either side of the Dourdin not a league apart from each other.

One of them, I thought, must be holding Diera. The glittering prize both were fighting over. Caedon wanted to breed with her. Audemar wanted to kill her or maybe use her as a pawn in some other game of his. After my year and more in Caedon's hands, I wasn't sure which fate would be worse. Yet Diera must be alive. And if she were, there was hope.

Everyone in Withiel knew the peace in that town would be a brief respite only. Once one of the armies prevailed, that army would sweep into town and possess it. The mood in Withiel was tense. It became filled with refugees, because the land upriver was scorched and barren, while the land downriver was a boiling hive of armed and dangerous men.

I fell into a routine. In the early evening, I played and sang at one of the taverns of the town to earn my bread and board. During the day, I wandered the fields and meadows outside the town and along the banks of the Dourdin, trying to decide on a plan.

I had to face one bald certainty.

It fell to me to get Diera out. If I didn't, who would?

As I wandered the fields, the blackbirds gathered. *You. You're the one*, they shrieked at me. Is this the hard thing Johnny had seen about me so long ago, I wondered.

Yet it seemed foolish to imagine I could accomplish such a feat. All my friends had died to ensure Diera's safety, most of them highly skilled in the arts of war. None had succeeded. Surely Wat was dead. I shied away from the thought, but it had to be true.

I asked myself why in the Nine Spheres I'd take on such a task. But then Johnny's words would come back to me. I knew somehow I had been charged with this task, all those years ago as I sat at his knee and learned to play my rebec. It's what had made my mother cry out in her dreams, that winter. It's the weighty thing Johnny and I had left between us, the day he walked away. I knew now what his deep sadness meant. He knew he was to die, he knew I'd be robbed of my childhood, and he knew too the monumental task I'd face. Getting Diera out so she could claim her throne.

Johnny knew something no one else knew. Doing this thing to honor and exalt a woman would be the work of a woman. It was my work. I'd have to try.

When I went out to the meadows and the river, I took my rebec with me, and I played and sang Johnny's song. One thing I'd never understood. If the blackbirds were my friends, why did they come and go the way they did? Why show up sometimes and defend me, but other times seemingly taunt me, even attack me? I puzzled over that.

As I played and sang, I began to notice something about them. My music drew them. One or two would be randomly flying from tree to tree. Then there'd be six or seven. Then a flock. An entire tree, as full as the tree that had burst into frenzied activity as Eris came after me.

Without the rebec and my voice, too, sometimes they'd come, sometimes not. With the rebec, especially if I were singing, they always came.

I began deliberately to conjure them to me.

I'd lie back into a soft bed of celandine and bluebell to play and sing, watching the blackbirds making lazy circles above me, watching them take to the surrounding trees until the branches groaned under their weight.

There was one other thing I did to prepare for my task, out there in the meadows and along the river bank. I looked for certain plants. Between my stints at the tavern, I found time to compound the plants into potions. I always made sure to leave a salve or tonic with the innkeeper or the alewife. But I made potions of my own, too. Are you thinking now of my wicked charm? No, that's not what I was making.

Later in the day, I'd head back to town. I had set myself another piece of work as well. I drew myself a rough map on a piece of cast-off parchment. I divided the town up into sectors and visited each one in turn, going from group to group of refugees to inquire about you, Jillie. I got nowhere. I didn't forget you, though, no matter how hopeless the task of finding you seemed.

For you, though, the world must have felt very different. You didn't know I was looking for you. How could you know? You must have thought no one cared.

But my urgent need had become the task set before me by the blackbirds. I felt guilty, turning from the task of finding you to the task of finding Diera. But I knew I must. From one evening to the next, the talk of war intensified. I knew I couldn't wait much longer, or my chance would be gone forever. I was at a decision point. Accept what had been assigned me, or reject this deep thing lodged inside me, and lose it. Lose myself.

Yet I hesitated. It's as if I had turned into two selves, one questioning and attacking the other.

*This is my task*, I told myself.

*Why is it my task?* I asked myself. *Is it my task to aid a dynasty by saving its last member? Why is that important at all?* I asked myself. Why should I, an orphan and a nobody, care which member of the nobility becomes monarch of this land? Let those lusting after power look out for that power themselves. I have a lost sister to find.

After a day or two of asking myself these questions, getting nowhere, I started asking my questions of someone else. No, not the Children. Not the Lady. I started asking Johnny. As if he could hear me, four years dead. *You were their blood*, I told him. *You were their friend. Is that enough to risk everything, other people's lives, even kill the innocent, to bring a queen to power? A queen is just a woman like any other*, I told him. *A king is just a man.*

I got an answer, of sorts. *To bear witness.*

*Does this mean justice?* I screamed inside myself. Is it justice my whole family died for some idea? Is it justice Avery died? You died? If Wat is dead, is it justice he died, all for this idea?

*Justice is a kind of balance.* The answer came to me through the blaze of the sun, the heat of the earth, the sky, the rain. *The Children are balance. But beyond and above balance, the stars.*

Well. Don't ask me what that meant. It had to do.

Chapter Twenty-seven

# Lead Me

There came a day I wrapped Diera's blackbird brooch in a fold of cloth and tucked it into the pouch at my girdle. The pouch was already full of small leathern bags of potions. I put the rest of my few belongings, the damaged copy of *Man-Dog Rough-Gray*, an extra cloak, in a bundle underneath the straw of the loft where the innkeeper of the night before had let me sleep. I shouldered my rebec, and I walked out of town toward the banks of the Dourdin. There I played my song.

> *I'll sing you four, oh.*
> *What is your four, oh?*
> *Four for the four star Children.*
> *Green grow the rushes, oh.*
>
> *I'll sing you five, oh.*
> *What is your five, oh?*
> *Five for the symbols at your door.*
> *Green grow the rushes, oh.*
>
> *Blackbirds rising,*
> *Blackbird's eye.*
> *One lone blackbird in the sky,*
> *One is one and all alone,*
> *And evermore shall be so.*

The birds began to gather. I played through all the verses of Johnny's song. *It's time*, I said to the birds. *Lead me.* I started walking. As they had after I left Caedon's manor, they flapped and fluttered ahead of me, settled, waited for me to catch up, and flapped and swerved ahead another furlong or so.

We went downriver together, the birds and I. After several leagues of walking, I stopped. They had congregated in the trees on the western bank. I stood on the eastern bank. When I went forward, they stayed. So I returned and stared across the river at them.

I left them. I needed to find a way across. I knew I could swim across, but I needed my rebec intact. I kept walking downriver. About a league from the spot where the blackbirds had stopped, I came to a stone bridge of the Old Ones over the river.

*I recognize this bridge*, I thought.

From where I stood on the eastern bank of the Dourdin, I examined it closely. I could cross here, I thought, but I also thought of how exposed I would be. I wasn't quite sure where the armies were, but I knew they were close. If they spotted me, their archers could bring me down. I crouched in the reeds at the eastern foot of the bridge to consider what to do. But I didn't wait long.

A lone blackbird descended out of the trees around me. It was the ragged old hobbling blackbird with the blinded eye, the one who had appeared before Eris's attack. He opened his beak to scream. I saw he was their leader. Rising out of the trees, an arrow of blackbirds flying in close formation rushed over me, and back again, spiraling up, swooping low over the bridge. I followed them over. I walked across the bridge with a straight back, and then I began to run. If this happened to be the place I met my death, so be it.

As I darted across, I realized something important. This bridge of the Old Ones. It was where Wat and I had crossed, that day we fled from our pursuers. The day I became a boy. It was where Caedon and I had crossed the Dourdin on our way to Lunds-fort.

Once across to the west bank, I made my way up-river back to the spot where the trees were full of blackbirds. And now they led me further west, across fields and broken country. As quickly as they had assembled, they peeled away, and I was alone again. I felt as if I were the only living thing crawling across the face of the earth.

Ahead of me over a little rise, I saw a smudge of smoke. I heard the army before I saw it, a vast murmuring of thousands of men. And I smelled it, the wood smoke, the scent of meat roasting on spits.

With no cover to speak of, I found a crumbling stone wall and crouched down beside it, waiting for dark. When it came full dark, I made my way toward the noises of the camp. Great fires stood among the tents of the men.

I had learned to move noiselessly very early in my life, as I hunted for meat to supplement my family's meager diet. From Torrin and Lorel, I'd learned many techniques of stealth. I employed these skills now. That dawn, I had brought dark clothing, tunic and trousers, to change into once I'd gotten away from the town, and now I made sure to rub my face with the dirt of the field so I did not stand out in the firelight.

The camp was quiet when I got there. Most of the men were asleep, but not all. Those who were awake were huddled around the fires, and their eyes were fire-bedazzled. I found it easy to get into the camp without anyone spotting me. I moved from a large pile of packing cases at the edge of the camp to a huddle of gear wagons further in. If anyone spotted me by the gear wagons, they'd probably think me one of the half-grown boys all armies use to mind the gear. From each hiding place, I stopped to study the movement of the men around me. I noticed the progress of the watch around the camp and only moved when they were on the opposite side from where I hid.

I studied the tents, too. Many were small. These, I surmised, were the tents of the soldiers. At one end of the camp, though, there stood a large tent much more ornately decorated than the others. A guard stood outside. I told myself this must be the tent of the commanding officer.

I still didn't know who this commander might be. Both Audemar and Caedon might have commissioned trusted men to lead their armies. They themselves might be taking their ease in the next towns down the river, which, I had heard, had fallen into enemy hands. Audemar's town stood on the east side of the Dourdin, and Caedon's stood on the west. That was the reason I was thinking, hunkered down in a camp on the west side of the river, that the birds had led me to Caedon's camp.

I could imagine Audemar sitting pampered and easeful in his town's best house, waited on by servants. But everything I knew of Caedon told me Caedon would be leading his own army. By then I was sure that although Audemar may have ordered the murder of my parents, Caedon had carried it out. I tried asking him once. He hadn't answered.

I'd had a long time to think about vengeance. My heart quickened when I thought that vengeance might come tonight.

Yet I stopped myself. I was here for another reason entirely. I was here to get Diera out of Caedon's hands, if that's who had her. I was here to serve justice, and that just might not be the same thing as vengeance.

Why, though, I asked myself, would Diera be in a military camp? Why not back at Caedon's town, closely guarded?

You may be asking yourself that very thing.

You'll find my answer unsatisfying. There was only one reason I thought Diera was in that tent. It's because the birds had led me there.

There had come a point where I threw aside all reason. There had come a point where my second sense took over. The birds and the music were its agents. I followed their lead.

I worked my way over to the largest of the tents. I was close enough now to see shadowy shapes moving around inside it. Two guards stood outside, I now saw. A second man had emerged from the tent, and now the two of them stood at attention outside it.

I waited.

The light inside the tent went out.

I waited.

Between me and the guards stood a firkin. Every so often, one of the guards would go to that firkin and dip up a mug of something. Ale, probably. And drink it.

I maneuvered myself ever closer to the firkin until I was directly behind it, hidden in the shadow where the cloth of the tent had been pulled taut to a peg driven into the ground. I eased one of the leathern bottles out of the pouch at my girdle. I waited until the guards were distracted by some noise at the other side of the tent, and then I slipped close enough to the firkin to pour my potion in. I stepped back into the shadows and crouched behind a barrel, waiting.

It didn't take long for both men to dip up mugs of ale, and after that, not long at all before they were both slumped over snoring at their post. Making sure I wasn't seen by any of the others, the few still crisscrossing from fire to fire, I eased past the unconscious guards at the flap of the big tent. And here I took a great risk. I stepped into the tent.

I stood against the inside at the entrance flap, not daring to breathe. Before me I saw two beds of furs. In one, Caedon. I could tell. I knew him well enough by then, how he slept. In the other, a slight covered figure. I listened. Both seemed to be asleep. I moved quietly around the perimeter of the tent to crouch at the side of the slight figure, on the other side of it from Caedon, as far away as I could get from him. My heart thudded in my throat.

If this sleeping figure woke and exclaimed in fear, Caedon would be awake in an instant.

And what if this figure were not Diera after all?

But it was. As I crouched there, I saw in the dim firelight seeping under the tent that she was in fact awake. She opened her eyes and stared into mine. She said nothing. I placed a finger to my lips and she flickered her eyelids to let me know she understood. I backed to the edge of the tent and took out my knife, which I had made sure to sharpen at my tavern's whetstone. I slit the fabric of the tent and eased myself out, motioning to Diera.

She was a marvel. She rolled over as if stretching in sleep, and waited to make sure Caedon had not moved. She rolled off the low platform of furs and waited again.

We both froze. There was a movement from the other bed. Caedon had stirred.

I had to make a snap decision. We could wait to see if he'd lapse back into sleep, or I could get Diera out of there as fast as possible. I crouched frozen with fear just outside the tent.

I remembered then. Caedon was a light sleeper. He hardly slept at all.

He made an exclamation in the dark. He called out for the guards. He was sensing something amiss.

Diera tumbled out through the slit in the tent. We stood up and ran for it.

Behind us, we heard Caedon shouting. *At least the guards aren't going to respond*, I thought to myself desperately. But someone else soon would. Thank the Children we were at the far end of the camp. A few shadowy shapes crossed the firelight, some heading in our direction, others heading to Caedon's tent.

We reached the edge of the camp. This was the moment of greatest vulnerability; we had to sprint across the open space to get to the woods alongside the river. Then we had to get down-river to the bridge. We both began running hard, but I was fit for it, from many fortnights of rough living, while Diera was out of breath almost immediately. I pulled her along after me. Behind us across the field, I could hear the entire camp astir, and now light too blazed up behind us as torches were lit.

We made it to the woods alongside the river. I pointed in the starlight. "The bridge," I gasped. We kept running. I could hope the confusion behind us meant we'd have a good start on our pursuers, but it would be only a matter of moments before mounted men came after us.

At the bridge I didn't pause to worry that the moon had risen. I kept Diera running beside me. She stumbled and went down, but I yanked her back up. Half-limping, half-running, we made it across the bridge, but as we did, I heard the hooves of horses behind us.

Diera turned a look of despair on me.

"This way, lady," I said and managed a quick smile. I pulled her into the weeds on the east side of the bridge. I pushed her ahead of me. I knew where I was, and I suddenly knew where I was going. A dense bank of thorn rose before us, and rank tall weeds. I dove through them, pulling Diera after me.

She shrieked as we tumbled down; she must have thought we'd fallen into a hole.

I knew better.

It was the entrance to the holloway.

"Quiet now, my lady," I whispered to her. I led her to one side, where an earthen niche carved by the ages out of the towering embankment offered a sort of hiding place. It wouldn't be enough, if our pursuers knew of the holloway. But I doubted they did.

We crouched in the dark against the clay and roots of the alcove in the bank. I nearly laughed. Outside our hidden passageway, we heard crashing and shouting and cursing. It went on for an interminable period, maybe a full candle's measure.

Diera and I were scratched and bleeding from the thorns, but I didn't care. If Caedon's men didn't know exactly what to look for, they'd never find us.

Eventually, the sounds of the men faded. They were searching up and down the river bank in the dark, although they did have moonlight now to aid them.

"We may have to stay here all tomorrow," I whispered to Diera. "Are you cold, lady?" I took off my cloak and draped it about her. She was only in her nightdress.

"Torrin?" said Diera, putting her hand out and touching my arm in the dark.

"No, lady," I whispered. "I'm not Torrin." She had no idea who I was. I was glad. I wanted to keep it that way.

"Who, then?"

"Just one of the Rising," I told her.

It must have been close to dawn when I decided it was safe enough to make my way to the holloway's entrance and listen for any of Caedon's men. When I didn't hear anything, I touched Diera on the arm and helped her out onto the edge of the road.

"Let's get to Withiel," I told her quietly, and led her back up the eastern side of the river. We were careful, but we saw no one. Thinking about it later, I decided Caedon must have decided Audemar had sent spies to capture Diera away from him. He must have concentrated his efforts in that direction. So she and I were traveling in the opposite direction of any searchers, and that stood us in good stead. As the palisades of Withiel loomed now, I put out a hand to stop her. Dawn was graying in the east. "Let me tell you my plan, lady," I said.

She was to mingle with the refugees. I'd spend the next days finding safe conduct for her to the south and west. As I'd learned by cautious inquiry in the taverns of Withiel, some did know of Diera and the Rising, and these people whispered among themselves of towns loyal to her at the very end of the point of land reaching out into the southernmost outlet of the Narrows, the place where the Narrows merges into the Great Sea that stretches endlessly away toward the setting sun. Diera would be safe there in those loyal towns, at least for a while. And then she could join the people who loved her.

She had no idea who I was. She'd seen me once, when I was fourteen and a boy, so even though we could make out each other's faces now in the cold dawn light, she didn't recognize me.

I curtseyed to her now, and I handed her the blackbird brooch in token of my good faith. But then, she already trusted me. I'd gotten her out.

She stood in the pale early morning running a finger around and around the rim of the brooch. I started to speak, to urge her to hurry, but then she whispered, almost to herself, "A man named Rafe gave me this." She stood still for another moment, then raised the brooch to her lips and kissed it. She gave me a tremulous half-smile, and then she turned and began walking. I walked beside her, a catch in my throat.

As we came through the unguarded gates of Withiel, I found it a simple thing to conceal my rebec in its bag from her. If she had seen that, she might have known. But she couldn't know what was in the bag on my shoulder, and I didn't tell her.

Getting her brooch back made her anxious, though. She kept taking it out of the small pouch at her belt and fingering it, then putting it away again. I thought I knew why. The last she'd seen of it, she'd been with Torrin and Lorel. I debated whether to tell her about their fates. I decided I had to. She must have been wrested away from them. She might already know.

"Lady, I must tell you a terrible thing."

In the dim light of dawn, she looked at me, her eyes huge in her pale face with its cloud of dark hair.

"Torrin and Lorel—"

"Yes," she said. "I thought they must be. They're dead, aren't they?"

I nodded yes.

Her eyes filled with tears, but she brushed them proudly away. "They were brave women," she said.

"The Children keep them," I responded simply.

I took her behind one of the town granaries. "Stay here, my lady. I need to get you something to wear. You can't go walking around Withiel in your nightdress," I whispered. She tried to smile. Soon I returned with some patched clothing from the inn-keeper's wife at my tavern. "Wear these, lady," I said, handing them to her. I kept watch while she changed into them, and we stuffed her ripped and bloody nightclothes behind the granary.

Then I led her to one of the houses where the refugees had crowded in. I left her outside. She knew to keep her identity secret.

"I'll come to you soon, my lady," I told her. "As soon as I can arrange passage."

"Here," she said, taking off her golden armlet and pressing it into my hands. "This may help."

I nodded. Then I made my way back across the town to the stable behind the tavern, the place I often slept. I hurried, because I was dressed in trousers, and that would arouse suspicion if anyone saw. I had given Diera the old kirtle the alewife had allowed me, but I'd kept a tattered thing of my own. Once I got back to the stable, I pulled it over my head, and grabbed up the ale-wife's cast-off patched dun-colored cloak.

I lay back in the straw, exhausted. I'd try to sleep. *All in all*, I thought, *a good night's work.*

Then again, I wasn't that satisfied. I'd been so close to Caedon. Close enough to slit his throat. But I couldn't risk it. I had had a job to do, a job maybe I was born to do, and I'd done it.

On the roof of the stable, a few random blackbirds picked their way down the thatch, dowsing for insects. From where I lay in the straw I could see them just outside, past the timbers that held up the stable roof. I watched them for a while. They didn't pay me any mind at all. If one fixed a glittering eye on me, it was only before moving indifferently away. So I turned over on my side in the hayloft and fell into a dreamless sleep.

# Chapter Twenty-eight

# Shield Wall

Outside the house where Diera was staying, I sat on the step looking at her gold armlet. In the light of day, I realized I couldn't just sell the thing. People would take one look at me and think I'd stolen it. I needed to talk things through with Diera. And I needed to keep checking to make sure she was safe. The house where she stayed was packed with refugees, but some of them might be spies, and some of them might be thieves, and some of them might be worse. It was impossible to tell.

The man who owned the house was getting rich off the misery of others, which made me wary around him. A man like that might not be too particular whom he betrayed. He took the coin of desperate people and arranged safe passage for them. Then those people left his house. Whether they ever arrived at their destinations once he had their gold, though—that, I didn't know, and I suspected he didn't, either, nor cared very much.

So in the cold light of morning, I realized my task with Diera was not over yet.

This man, an oily fellow named Hap, came out onto the step and stared down at me. He knew who I was. I had visited his house before, to inquire about Jillie.

"Mistress, we have some new visitors here. Do you want to see, in case one might know of your sister?" he asked me.

"I know one of your new ones, Master Hap," I said. "She's my mistress. We were separated on the road." Now I risked something. I pulled up my sleeve and gave him a quick look at my brand, but I pulled the sleeve down again to make sure he didn't study it and recognize it as Caedon's. "I'm her bondswoman. It's the lady who came in last night."

"Ah," said Hap. "Yes. The lady. I told myself, this one is different."

"I need to go to her. She's had to make do with some terrible clothing I found along the way. She'll be angry and wanting something better."

"Go in, then," he said, stepping aside.

I ducked under the lintel and went into the stone longhouse. In the dim light, I spotted Diera at the other end, on a bench beside the fire. I made my way through the sections of the longhouse to the place where she sat.

"Mistress, I've been looking for clothing all morning," I told her, crouching down beside her. I gave her a meaning look. "Don't beat me, mistress. I haven't found anything suitable yet."

Diera nodded now. Right away she saw what I was up to. Remembering the ruse of her fainting fits long ago in the castle, I realized Avery and the others had taught her well. "Did you sell the armlet I gave you?" she asked me, making her voice sound severe. Others around the fire were noticing us and listening.

"I'm afraid, mistress. I'm afraid people will think I've stolen it from you."

Master Hap had come up to the fire now, and I could tell he was very interested in this exchange.

"Master Hap knows me, mistress," I said, looking up at him. "I've been here in this town for a while. You know me, Master Hap, don't you?"

"Indeed yes," he said. "And this is your lady?"

Diera rose to her feet and assumed a haughty air. "Lady Nelda, kinswoman to the earl's lady," she told him.

"Ah, my lady," said Master Hap, bowing low. "I understand the castle still stands."

"Yes, thank the Lady Goddess, it's well-nigh impregnable, but my party was attacked as we fled to it for safety. So now—" Diera spread her hands out. "As you see."

"How may I serve your ladyship?"

"I have a few articles I can sell, so I'll be able to get out of these rags," said Diera. "I'd like to arrange passage to a safer place. I doubt if I can reach the castle in safety. Someplace west, I think."

"Very wise, your ladyship."

Diera's manner was completely convincing—not hard at all. She was indeed a highborn lady, the highest born in the land.

"Where is that armlet I gave you, girl?" Diera said to me. "Don't give me some story about how you lost it." Her voice was heavy with sarcasm.

"Never, your ladyship. Here it is, your ladyship," I said, taking it out of my belt pouch.

"What do you think, Master—Hap, is it?" said Diera. "Where can my bondswoman trade this for suitable clothing?"

"I'll be happy to arrange that for your ladyship," said Master Hap. He and Diera exchanged a look. Diera knew, and Master Hap knew she knew, that he'd bring her back rich clothing in exchange for the armlet, and keep a nice commission out for himself.

"That would be greatly appreciated, Master Hap," said Diera.

"Your ladyship, may I suggest a better room in another house I own?" said Master Hap.

"That, too, would be greatly appreciated," Diera said, looking around her at her fellow refugees with a snobbish air.

One of them actually deferentially pulled at his forelock when her gaze rested on him, although she was dressed in little better than rags.

"Follow me," Master Hap told me. "I'll show you the house where your lady can find more suitable accommodation, and I'll get the clothing for you to take back to her."

I bowed low to Diera, and she nodded graciously to me.

So I arranged everything. I got my things from the tavern's stable, thanked the innkeeper and the alewife, and gathered up the clothing Master Hap found for me to give Diera. Together we went to escort Diera to a better house in a better part of town.

As soon as we were alone, she sank down with a sigh onto the bed in the room of that house. "Thank the Children for you," she said. "What is your name?"

"Lynet," I said, thinking fast.

"I was glad of the shelter last night, make no mistake, Lynet, but I think that place had vermin."

"This is much cleaner," I said, helping her change into the better clothing Master Hap and I had found for her. "And presenting yourself as a lady will help keep you safer, I think, than if you pretend you're an ordinary refugee."

"I believe you're right," said Diera. She was looking at my wrist, where the edge of the brand was just showing beneath my sleeve. I pulled the sleeve up and showed her my arm.

She gave a sharp intake of breath.

"Yes," I said. "Caedon's. So you see I understand the danger you were in, my lady."

"How did you know where to find me? How did you know what to do?"

"That's a long story, your highness," I said. "Better for both of us if you don't know it just yet. But lady—" I stopped, unsure of how to proceed. I had to know. "What news of your kinsman? Walter, your uncle."

Diera shook her head. "I don't know," she said, her voice low. "Maybe dead. Caedon told me he was dead."

I had to turn aside to keep from crying out. She told me nothing I hadn't already suspected. But the truth, told in this bald way, caught at my heart.

"I see you knew Wat," Diera said.

I nodded, dashing tears from my eyes.

"Torrin and Lorel. Wat. Avery. Conal. All of them." Diera's voice was halting. "Rafe," she said quietly. After a moment she continued. "I watched Rafe die." I was coming to understand about her and Rafe, why he was the one partnered with her in the castle. But an instant later, her mask dropped into place again, the serene look of a woman born to reign.

"I hear Eris too is dead," I said, keeping my voice even.

Diera's eyes turned cold. "Yes. She's dead," she said, and didn't elaborate. I didn't push it.

"But you're alive, your highness," I said. "That means hope." I knelt to her.

I could see she was touched. She made me rise.

"And," I continued, "We need to keep it so. We need to get you south."

"We," said Diera. "How many are left?"

"I don't know, your ladyship," I said. "None of us knows very much, beyond our own immediate circle." Then again, because I couldn't help myself, I said, "So is it certain your uncle is dead?"

"Wat? Caedon said so. You seem to know Caedon as well as I do. He's capable of lying, when it suits his purpose. It's possible Wat is still alive. It's possible Caedon simply wanted to fill me with despair, as he always does. He succeeded, whatever the truth about my uncle turns out to be." Her voice sank to a whisper. I was on fire to ask her how Caedon was doing, whether he showed any signs of some wound. Could it be possible he came damaged out of his encounter with Wat, whatever he might have done to Wat in return? I realized I'd better not ask her such things.

"Wat and I were very close," said Diera. "He was more like a brother to me than an uncle. We were nearly of an age."

I nodded, not trusting myself to speak. "And Prince Avery," I said at last. "He is gone out of the world, leaving it a lesser place."

Diera smiled at me and clasped my hand warmly.

"Well, now, your highness, I need to start working on your passage south," I told her. I bowed low to her again and left her in the room.

I knew I didn't trust Hap, but he was the best I had. So I worked with him to find a convoy heading west. Exchanging some of Diera's rings for passage, Hap arranged for us to join one.

"We leave in the morning," I told Diera as soon as I had made this arrangement through Hap. "I don't know how much we can trust Master Hap, so we'll have to be on our guard."

"And you'll go with me?" said Diera.

"Indeed yes, your highness. I'm your bondswoman, after all," I told her with a smile. "But we won't be helpless. With some of your gold, I bought this." I lifted the skirt of my kirtle high enough for her to see the sharp, well-balanced knife strapped to the outside of my right calf, much better than the one I'd taken from the tavern. "I know how to use it. Torrin and Lorel taught me."

After we had breakfasted the next morning, we headed out into the innyard, where two ill-looking fellows waited with broken-down nags of horses for us to ride. A small party of five or six were heading in the same direction with us. Three of us were women.

The first days of our trip down the roads to the west were uneventful, except for one anxious time our guides led us into the woods to avoid Audemar's encampment. We were headed for a town on the sea-cliffs, where Diera knew she could connect with members of the Rising who would then lead her the rest of the way south.

By the third day, the land began to flatten out from craggy hills to the rolling green meadows of the Riverlands. I felt a tug of nostalgia. We were nearing the market town close to my village.

The third day, we all bedded down for the night around a fire that eventually burned low and went out. Diera and I huddled close together in our cloaks for warmth. I woke to faint starlight and a dim moon obscured by rain clouds to realize something was wrong. Raising my head cautiously, I saw our two guides, clubs in their hands, moving stealthily toward the place where the men of our group, and the other woman, lay sleeping. I realized they'd kill these men first, and then once the strongest members of the group could no longer protect us women, they'd come after us. Part of me wished they'd attack me. I'd show them what a weak woman I was. I fingered the knife strapped to my leg.

But I needed to be prudent. I wasn't crazy. I nudged Diera awake. I nodded to the shadowy forms on the other side of the glowing embers of the fire. She rolled over to look, too. I nodded at her again, and she nodded back.

With a shout, our two guides attacked those men, and the men screamed in agony. Under cover of the noise, I motioned to Diera, we grabbed up our small bundles of belongings, and we eased off into the underbrush.

"Follow me," I whispered. Too bad we had to leave the horses behind, poor stone-bruised animals as they were, but they were hobbled on the other side of our small camp, and there would be no easy way to reach them. The attack back at the camp was, thank the Children, taking a longer time than our rascals of guides had expected it would. Diera and I were able to get well away from the camp and off the roadway into the broken country. When I thought we must be far enough, we found a thicket to hide in until dawn.

At first light, I slipped away to snare a rabbit. After scouting around us, I saw we were safe and could build a fire, so we did, and then we breakfasted.

"You're very resourceful, Lynet," said Diera.

"I've had to learn to be, my lady," I said.

"And you're not anyone named Lynet, are you?" She eyed me shrewdly.

I gave a guilty start.

She laughed and pointed out my rebec, which had come half out of its bag. "You're that boy, aren't you."

"Yes, my lady. I admit it."

"But why would you lie to me?"

"Lady, you think me a traitor," I said.

"I think no such thing. Eris is the traitor. Was, I should say."

"I couldn't be sure you thought so," I said, blushing.

"How could you be a traitor? You rescued me from Caedon. You're risking your life to get me to safety. Mirin, isn't it?"

"Yes, my lady."

"That's settled, then. No more masquerades, if you please."

"Forgive me, your highness."

"You call me that, but I'm not your queen."

"Oh, yes, you are. You haven't been crowned, but you will be. Everyone in the Rising is working for that."

"A woman can't be monarch. That's the law."

"The law is wrong, your highness," I told her.

Deidra was silent for a moment. She looked over at me, started to say something. Stopped. Started again. "Mirin," she said. "I understand something now. Something that puzzled me. Why you asked after Wat."

I busied myself putting my rebec away and didn't answer.

"You know," she said slowly, "When he discovered Eris, what she was, and realized—"

"No point in revisiting old hurts, lady," I said, trying to keep my voice even. Trying to wall off the pain. "Eris succeeded in her plan to damage all of us in as many ways as she could. At least she didn't succeed with you."

So we left it at that.

By that time, I had kicked dirt over our fire and scattered the embers. We were back on the road. "I think this is safe, my lady," I told her. "But we must be ready to get off the road at the first strange noise. We'll travel easier on the roadway, as long as it's safe to walk it."

No sooner had I said that than we heard a faraway clanging.

"Those are battle sounds, lady," I told her. "Goddess take it. We need to get off the road."

I guided her into the underbrush. We made our way across country until we came to the brow of a hill with a steep dropoff. The noise of battle seemed to come from directly beneath us. I motioned to her and we inched forward to look down.

Spread before us was a vast field. Our road meandered through the center of it, Dark Ones be cursed. Two armies were drawn up, one on either side of the level place.

"We're going to have to go through that," Diera said, clenching and unclenching her hands.

I stood surveying the scene. "Looks like it. Or retrace our steps east and south to go by way of Ponset-Ford. That will take us days out of our way down dangerous roads. Caedon holds that territory."

I lay at full length, watching the armies below us and gnawing my lip as I thought through our options, mentally cataloging all the roads Wat and I used to take as we played the towns around there. There was no way past unless we thought we could stroll through the middle of Caedon's and Audemar's massed armies.

From our hillside vantage point we saw, on one side of the level, men ranged in four columns. The men in front had thrown up their shields into an overlapping wall. Pointing to the shield-wall, Diera breathed in sharply. "See there? Audemar's insignia."

Audemar's army was backed up to the Dourdin. I stood up into a crouch, screening my eyes with my hand. I lay back down on the bank beside Diera. "I'm no military strategist, lady, but if I were Caedon, I'd feel glad that Audemar's back is to the river."

She nodded, looking where I pointed. "He has nowhere to go, if Caedon drives him back," she said. "He's a foolish man, or his general is."

*This is as good as an education*, I thought to myself, gazing out over the field of battle. "Caedon can circle around his left flank and force him to the river," I said. I remembered the endless diagrams Avery and Conal and Torrin would linger over, where Avery drew them in the ashes of the hearth at the stone cottage, and they—and Wat and Eris, too—would discuss, for many candle measures at a time, the advantages of this military situation over some different one. Avery would rub out the diagram with his toe, and draw them another one. He'd quiz Wat over and over, using these diagrams, while Eris would usually prowl restlessly away. I'd crouch in the corner and try to follow along. Of us all, only Lorel had no interest in the diagrams. When the rest of them started talking over the various scenarios, she'd just move outside and look to the horses.

"But lady, while battle tactics might suggest Caedon should try to encircle Audemar's army, he doesn't know this ground. I do. The ground over there beyond Audemar's far flank is marshy." When Wat and I had come by here, we'd always have to steer Millicent away from the area so she wouldn't sink into the sodden ground. "If Caedon tries to outflank Audemar there, his soldiers will sink into the bog."

Diera looked over at me. "How in the Nine Spheres did you learn these things, Mirin?"

"Avery taught me."

She smiled at me and clasped my hand in hers. "What you said just now. It's exactly what he would have said."

*He taught you, too*, I thought.

Then I realized how I'd spoken. "His Highness Prince Avery," I amended.

"You don't need to be formal with me, Mirin. Yes, Prince Avery. But also, our beloved teacher."

We smiled at each other again, though pain underlay that smile we shared. *All of those brothers were my teachers*, I thought. *Avery. Johnny. And Wat was my teacher, too. All gone now.*

"But look," Diera said, pointing. "Audemar has the higher ground. There's the advantage he has." We both swiveled then to gaze down the long expanse toward Caedon's side. Caedon's army, too, had formed up its shieldwall. Diera and I both sucked in our breath. A squadron of horsemen on Caedon's side came riding up to the front lines. "See that?" she told me. "They have lances. That's something they do over in the Baronies. Not here, usually. The ground's too broken for that kind of cavalry charge. But see what a long smooth expanse Caedon can use between these armies. He has room for his horsemen to ride Audemar's shieldwall down and break it."

Audemar's men, with a mighty bellowing, started rushing forward.

"They know it, lady. Look at them, they know it! They're trying to lessen Caedon's advantage." We could see how Audemar's army relied on infantrymen and bowmen. Very few mounted troops. But they were closing the distance so Caedon's advantage with his mounted troops would be lost.

Caedon saw his danger, or his general did, and unleashed his horsemen. The two armies met with a clash in the middle. The mounted men with the lances formed up into a mighty hammer pounding at Audemar's center and breaking the shieldwall, driving through Audemar's forces, driving them back toward the river with a roaring and a clamor. Behind the mounted men, Caedon's bowmen ran forward in a disciplined charge. They knelt short of the line of battle. They aimed their bows high, pulled them back, let fly a dense buzzing cloud of arrows arching up and over Audemar's shieldwall to rain down on the men behind it. They were firing uphill, and so many of their arrows fell short.

Even with this disadvantage, they and the mounted men with their kite shields and couched lances began opening gaps in Audemar's shieldwall. Through these gaps poured Caedon's infantry, slashing and thrusting with pikes, javelins, wicked two-edged longswords. Even from our distance we heard the groans and screams of dying men and horses. Audemar's lines stubbornly held, but then men began to break and run back, regroup, turn to fight again.

"They're being pressed back to the river, lady," I said. A whole column of Caedon's men were wheeling around to get at Audemar's flank. As they came up behind Audemar's men, I saw how they floundered on the boggy ground and began going down.

"There," I said. "Audemar is using the marsh to protect himself."

"It protects him, but it doesn't give him much room to maneuver," Diera observed. "Caedon is going to crush Audemar against the river and the marsh. Caedon is going to win."

"You have the right of it, lady," I said. I appreciated then how much Audemar's early successes had depended on Caedon. Now, as Caedon's opponent, he was crippled.

I looked out over the battlefield, thinking our problem through. "We need to get out of here," I said. It might be several candle measures but it might be sooner before Caedon sent armed men up this hill to scout Audemar's other flank. Our perch wouldn't be safe for long.

Diera and I needed to head west. But the heaviest fighting was to the west and to the bridge over the Dourdin there. It would be insanity to go there.

I came to a hard conclusion. We'd have to go around, head east through hostile territory on a long circling track to the south.

"Let's make our way down this hill to the edge of the battle-field," I told Diera. "The whole thrust of the battle is toward the river. If we head in the opposite direction, maybe we'll be able to move around the fighting." I pointed out underbrush and clumps of trees that could serve us for cover.

But I didn't like this second option. I didn't like it at all. The part of Audemar's army that had moved to the river was doomed. I agreed with Diera there. But many of them would soon see that safety lay east, just as we had. They'd try to break through and retreat in that direction. I didn't like our chances, heading through Caedon's territory to the east, surrounded by desperate bands of Audemar's retreating men.

I couldn't see any other way. I motioned to Diera and we angled our way east down the hill, making sure we kept to the trees and low brush. I knew how to move silently. Diera, although she tried her best, hadn't had that training. I hoped we weren't making enough noise to attract the attention of any nearby soldiers.

But the soldiers were busy, too busy to notice a few strange outliers crossing the field. I led Diera down a shallow ravine that looked as though it slanted down the battlefield east and out of the heavy fighting. As we crouched there sheltered by brush, I surveyed the landscape before us to see where we should move next.

Diera gasped and pointed. A knot of warriors engaged in ferocious hand-to-hand fighting, though comfortably far away from us, had begun edging closer to the spot where we hid. Some bore the insignia of Caedon on their shields; some bore Audemar's. They were clad neck to knees in chainmail hauberks. They hacked at each other with swords, maces, and vicious axes. From where we crouched, we could hear their grunts and the landing of blows. We could hear the clash of their shields.

"Dark Ones take him. There's Caedon himself," said Diera, her eyes wide. "See that helmet, the golden one? Caedon had it made especially for himself. It was in his tent the night you got me out. See, there's a wolf on the crest. Caedon's sigil." She stared at the fighters. "I'll warrant my uncle is not over there fighting," she whispered. "He's probably back at the river, keeping himself safe."

I was puzzled for a moment. Then I realized the uncle Diera meant was Audemar.

As we later found out, Audemar had already left the field. He was already fleeing south with a good remnant of his army, leaving the rest of his men to be slaughtered by Caedon's.

As we sheltered in the ravine, the fighting intensified and moved even closer to where we'd taken cover. I shook my head, then, dismayed. "We'll never get past those men," I said. What irony, to escape Caedon at his camp and then to risk capture on the battlefield by the very man. We couldn't let that happen. We'd have to go back up the hill and hide there, maybe until the battle was over. But doing so would be almost as dangerous.

Then I nearly laughed out loud. I knew. We'd go west after all, and I suddenly saw how we'd do it.

"Lady, I have a plan. We're getting closer to the coast. Some of the people around here are fisherfolk. They're the Sea Child's. They're not afraid of the water."

She looked at me, puzzled.

"Just follow my lead," I told her. I smiled to myself. I'd heard those words before. They'd just never come out of my own mouth. I motioned to Diera to follow me, and she did.

We made our cautious way back up the hill. "Now we backtrack a bit," I told her. We picked our way down the hill to the west and north, staying off the road. Thankfully, the fields around us were deserted. I led us on a long perpendicular course across to the place where the fields sloped down to the river's edge. When we got to the banks of the Dourdin, the battle came to us as a muted roar from far downriver of where we stood.

I crouched in the reeds. Diera crouched with me. I looked over at her and she looked back at me. Her eyes were trusting. *Lady Goddess*, I swore to myself. *She thinks I know what I'm doing.* But then I took heart. By now, I knew this river well. My blackbirds had led me down it. Not this far, to be sure, but we were getting close to territory I had known since childhood.

The air was mild. A light breeze riffled the waters. "You're not afraid of the water, are you, my lady?" I asked her softly.

"I'm the Earth Child's," she said, looking across the river. I could see she was apprehensive.

"Don't worry," I told her. "We won't swim it. But as we came through this morning, I saw signs of a village upriver from here, and I think there must be fisherfolk who ply their trade there. They may be able to help us." Staying on the banks and away from the road, we made our way the several leagues' walk to the river hamlet. It was just growing dark as we approached.

Our supplies were running low by then. "We'll see if we can buy something to eat here," I told Diera.

"Maybe there's an inn," she said. She looked around hopefully in the dusk.

"I doubt it, lady. See how small and poor this village is."

"Are the people dangerous here?" said Diera.

I laughed. I had grown up with such people. "No, lady, although we probably shouldn't show how much coin we are carrying. There are ill-doers in villages just as there are in cities."

As we stood talking it over, a woman came out of the door of the nearest house and stared at us.

"Well met, Goodwife," I called to her. "We are travelers hoping for a bed and a bite to eat."

She disappeared back inside the house. In a moment, a man came to the door, and then he approached us, carrying a rush-light. He looked us up and down suspiciously.

"We're travelers separated from our party," I said to him. "Downriver, it's dangerous."

"Aye," he said. Something about us, probably the good cloth of our traveling cloaks, settled his mind. He pulled his forelock.

"We have coin for a bite of supper and a bed, if you have those to spare," I said.

For a long moment, he thought about it.

Diera pulled out her purse.

"Aye, come in, then, gentles," he said to us. And we followed him into the smoky confines of his tiny house.

Diera handed him some coins, and he motioned to his wife. She came out from the corner where she was hovering and gave us a curtsey. Then, silently, she dipped up bowls of gruel for us, and gave us a spoon to share. From behind her, two small children clung to her apron and peeked around at us.

Diera smiled at them.

The gruel, I saw, was a kind of chowder with savory bits of fish in it. I had guessed right about this village. I recognized the fish from my own days of fishing in the Riverlands.

"We only have the one bed shelf," said the man, when we handed his wife our bowls and the spoon.

"We don't mind," I told him. "Last night we slept on the ground."

So that night we spent wrapped in our cloaks on the crowded bed shelf with the entire family. But it was warm. In the night, I heard the patter of rain on the thatch, and I was glad we were at least dry, too.

In the morning, I woke early. While the goodwife showed Diera where to wash, I sat by the hearthstones and quizzed her man.

"We need to get down river," I told him.

"There's fighting, mistress."

"Yes, we were on the road and realized how dangerous it was. That's when we cut over to the river."

"Many's the one of them afraid of the water," he said with a chuckle. "Ye're safer here, mistress."

I made the sign of the Sea Child.

After a startled moment, he nodded at me. "Aye, mistress," he said softly. "Ye're not afraid. I see that now."

"I'm thinking," I said carefully, "that if we could get a boat, we could slip past those fighting men, slip past them on the river. I'm thinking that in a place like this, there are boats and fisherfolk." I looked over at the nets and a big oar propped against his far wall.

He laughed then. His eyes lit up, delighted. "Aye, so there are," he said. "But it's dangerous, mistress, and few there'd be who'd want to risk their boats. No boats, no fish," he said. "No fishing, no eating."

I moved our conversation away from danger and toward the best ways to catch river bream and dace. By the time Diera came to the fire, the man—who told me his name was Hob—and his wife Marjery were my fast friends, and they were trying to think how to help us. But the two of them agreed. It was just too dangerous. I was thinking Diera and I would have to give up and go the many leagues around the battlefield south before we could move west again. We'd have to make a much wider circle, because we'd just seen how difficult and dangerous it would be to cut across even a corner of the area close to the fighting.

Then a broad-shouldered young man came to the door, which now stood open to the morning sunlight. He peered in.

"These the gentles?" he said to the man, nodding his head at us.

"Aye, Sut, and ye might have a civil tongue in your head toward 'im," said Hob.

The young man named Sut pulled his forelock and looked abashed. "I hear ye want a boat. I hear ye want to go downriver." I didn't stop to ask myself how Sut knew this. From my days as a villager I knew. Somehow, news like this spread. It just did.

"That's a dangerous thing, Sut," Hob said.

"Daegal and I, we're naught afeered," he said. "We'll take ye, gentles."

Hob and Marjery looked at each other and began to laugh.

"Nothing like the young," Marjery said, wiping the tears of laughter from her eyes. Her apple cheeks and broad forehead shone. "You may go with these two, my ladies. They know the river better than any."

Sut and his friend Daegal went off to prepare, while Diera and I sat by the fire to stay warm. The day had dawned chill.

Marjery said little as she bustled about doing the work of her home, but smiled at us, almost as shyly as her small daughters. As the time drew near for our departure, though, she plucked me hesitantly by the sleeve.

"I'm afeered for ye, mistress," she said, almost whispered. I had to lean close to her to catch her words.

"It's dangerous out there on the roads," I said, nodding my agreement.

"Lady-likers say—" she began, then clapped a hand over her mouth.

I made the sign of the Sea Child then and Diera, who had overheard us, made the sign of the Earth Child.

Encouraged, she began again. "Them that's Lady-likers say it's sinful for a woman to dress as a man. But your ladyships might want to—" she was too bashful and worried about offending us to continue.

I saw right away what she was trying to tell us. "Oh, goodwife, you are right!" I exclaimed. "We'd be safer in men's things."

"Aye, my lady," she said, and her eyes sparkled. "The two of ye being so slender, folks would think ye lads, especially if ye keep the hoods of the cloaks up. My brother left some of his things, before he ran off to join the soldiers." A shadow crossed her face.

"You must be worried about him," I said, putting a hand on her arm. "And goodwife, I serve this lady." Here I nodded at Diera. "You don't need to call me lady, not me."

Marjery had already whirled away from us, bustling back with trousers and tunics.

We rushed to change into them. Outside, we could hear Hob talking to Daegal and Sut. It was time for us to go.

"Please, goodwife," said Diera, handing our kirtles over to Marjery. "Take these, with our thanks."

She looked at them dubiously. "Oh, lady, these are too rich for a poor woman to wear."

"But goodwife," I said. "Look at this well-made cloth. The weaver who made this knew her trade. With your needle, you can turn these to good service, and see? You can unstitch the embroidered bands and remove them. You'll have two fine ribbons for Fair Day."

She dimpled up then and took them with a curtsey.

When we stepped outside in our men's things, the two stout lads put their hands to their mouths in astonishment. Then they grinned.

"That's a grand notion, your ladyships, and the two of ye make fine lads," the one named Sut said to us. Daegal was too shy to say much of anything. He just blushed and looked at his shoes.

We said our goodbyes to Hob and Marjery and the two little girls. Diera pressed more coins into Hob's hard hand, although he was reluctant to take them.

"The Children keep you both," he said to us, making the sign of the Sea Child over us.

As we followed Sut and Daegal to the river, Diera looked over at me with frank curiosity. "Why would you tell the goodwife you're not a lady when you are? Do we have to continue our mistress-bondswoman charade?"

"You know," I said slowly, thinking about her words. "I spent most of my life in a village as small and poor as this one, and I thought of myself as one of the villagers like these."

"Yet you read. And you don't speak the way they do."

"I suppose if I'd thought about it, I might have realized there was something different about my family," I said. "But I never even noticed. Or didn't wonder about it."

We had no time to speak of my strange upbringing further, because we had reached the banks of the Dourdin.

Sut and Daegal led us down to their boat, drawn up into the reeds at the riverside. I leaped in and Sut helped Diera step over the gunnels.

I took her hand. It was cold and trembling.

"These fellows know what they're doing," I whispered to her, and she nodded quickly, pulling her cloak about her and perching uncertainly on the rough wooden seat in the middle of the boat. Sut and Daegal poled off into the water, and the current swept us downriver. With their paddles, they kept us steady in the main channel.

But I knew we were taking a risk.

As we neared the battlefield, the clamor and clanging of weapons grew louder. Sut and Daegal put their heads together, conferring in soft voices, and then steered the boat for the overhanging west bank. One of them looked out for roots and other hazards, while the other kept us traveling downriver as close to the west bank as we could get.

As we reached the bridge over the Dourdin and looked across the river to the east bank where the worst of the fighting had taken place the day before, I could tell how much quieter everything was now. I saw bobbing downriver a multitude of silvery humped shapes, as if vast shoals of mackerel ebbed and nudged against the bank. They were bodies, armed men drowned in their mail in the river.

I glanced over at Daegal and Sut. Their shoulders were tense. They steered us among the bodies, which grew thicker all around us.

Diera suppressed a horrified exclamation.

The nightmare face of a man surfaced suddenly beside our boat, his mouth wide and desperate. He gasped and called out something in a strangled voice, and lunged for us, grabbing the near gunnel. Our boat rode dangerously low in the water as his weight threatened to overset us. Sut raised his paddle and brought it smashing down on the man's gauntleted hand. He released his grip with a gargling roar. Daegal poled him off us while Sut, with his paddle, made the boat shoot downstream in a welter and spray of water. Diera shrieked.

I sat rigid in the boat, holding onto both gunnels. Behind us, the man sank down underneath our wake. He didn't come up.

Sut and Daegal steered us into the quieter waters where the river flowed past a downstream bridge. No bridge of the Old Ones, just a rickety timbered construction across the Dourdin. As we swept underneath, our heads barely cleared the underside of the bridge deck. The battlefield and its grisly load of corpses lay behind us. Diera was trembling.

"They're being dragged down by their armor," I called to Sut, nodding back toward the shoals of corpses.

"Aye, mistress," he said. "And most of them can't swim. They fear the water. We're clear now, my lady." He addressed this to Diera. He gave her a kindly look. He saw how frightened and distressed she was. When she made the sign of the Earth Child, he and Daegal looked at each other over her head and smiled.

Not too many leagues later, they paddled us into a little cove. Sut jumped out and pulled the boat up onto the small gravelly beach there. Daegal helped me and Diera out onto the west bank of the river.

"Our thanks to you both," I told them. "You've saved us leagues of walking down dangerous roads."

Diera reached into her purse and pressed coins into their hands. They beamed at us both.

"Brave lads," she told them.

They laughed. "We do this every day, my lady," said Daegal.

"Not in conditions like these," I said.

"Nay, you're right there, mistress," he replied.

"Be careful on your way back," I told them. They pulled their forelocks and stood smiling at us as we walked away from them.

Diera drew a shuddering breath. "You of the Sea Child may be fine with our watery passage, but I for one am glad to be on dry land," she said. "How gracious these people are. How hospitable," she said as we picked our way back to the road west.

"Your people, my lady," I said. "They'd be amazed to learn they've been helping their queen."

"If that's what I am," said Diera.

"You are," I insisted.

"If that's so, then I promise you this, Lady Mirin—" She smiled and shook her head as I started to protest. "I promise you this," she repeated. "If it is the will of the Children that I reign, I promise to do everything in my power to carry out my grandfather's wishes. I promise to honor the Children in everything I undertake. I promise always to think of the welfare of these people, just as they have been thinking of my welfare, a stranger and a traveler totally unknown to them."

How can I tell you what an honor it was to hear her say this, Jillie? I hoped then that one day you'd come to know her.

Later, as we walked the roadway under tranquil skies, Diera said, "I, like you, Mirin, am a reader, the legacy I received from my father the crown prince. He was mostly too busy to bother with me, but he taught me to read, and the language of the Old Ones, too."

"I read it also, a little," I said.

"How astonishing, Mirin."

I smiled at her, and I knew my smile was grim. "Caedon taught me."

"That's very strange. Do you know, he taught me too? Father was caught up in his own studies. He set Caedon to me as a teacher." After a while, she said, "No one should have left me alone with a man like Caedon. Or any young girl."

I looked over at her in shock. She kept walking, her face averted from mine.

We trudged on in silence. Then she said, "Did you know Caedon and my uncle tried to imply I had something to do with my father's assassination?"

"I've heard as much, my lady, but have never believed such a thing. I know too much about Caedon and his ways."

I reached out to her to give her a reassuring hand, but somehow instead we found ourselves standing on the road, weeping into each other's arms.

After a while we both wiped our eyes and could smile at each other. "So strange, thinking how closely entwined the good things I learned have been with the bad," she said. "Caedon damaged me in many ways, terrible ways, but he helped me read one of the Old Ones' books once, a treatise on a different way to rule. It was about a commonwealth, a society where all work together toward the good. That's the kind of kingdom I wish we had." She laughed. "Ironic, isn't it? To learn something good from someone like Caedon. But think about it. Just think about a kingdom like that." Her laughter rang out joyous over the green hedges where we walked. "That! That would be something, Mirin."

My spirits lifted. Underlying our talk along the way, there lay a deep sadness. We had both gone through harrowing experiences, some of them at the hands of the same man. We were both in love with the dead, and both our hearts were broken. I was glad to hear Diera's laughter.

As we walked westward, I realized something important. I had shielded my heart from this task of mine. I had doubted it. I'd accepted it at last, but I had never let my guard down. *Some help those in power on one side, some help those on the other*, I'd thought to myself. But now I saw. Now my shield wall had fallen.

To Johnny in the Land of the Dead, I sent my silent thanks. *You were right, Johnny*, I told him. *Whatever happens now, this task of mine, helping this courageous queen, is just and true.*

Ours were not the only dead. We heard later ten thousand men died during those two days of the Battle of the Dourdin. We heard that many of Audemar's men had drowned in the river, weighted down by their mail, terrified of the water.

Audemar himself escaped, but in the western part of the realm, he was never to pose much of a threat to Caedon again. Fairly soon after, the west was Caedon's.

# Chapter Twenty-nine

# Yours

By the time Diera and I parted ways, we'd become close. I admired her courage and grace. They reminded me of Avery's. She didn't look like Avery, or like Johnny and Wat. She was dark, while they were fair. "I take my coloring from my father," she told me once. I'd never known Artur the crown prince. But I knew Diera had the same spirit as her uncles.

What she must have suffered at the hands of Caedon filled me with fury and horror. I didn't know how deep her suffering reached. *Deep*, I thought to myself. To be able to help her—that was a way, I thought, to serve all who find ourselves in the power of an animal like Caedon.

On a mild, windy day, we stood together above the sea cliffs, waiting for the contact Diera had on the coast to meet us and take Diera south. I looked out in wonder across the vastness of the Great Sea. Something there called to me.

"I'm the Sea Child's," I told Diera. "But this is the first sight I've ever had of the sea."

She looked at me closely. "Of course you're the Sea Child's," she said. "Your eyes should have told me that. But I know your story. Drustan, my uncle Avery's friend, was your father, and he comes from these cliffs."

We both stiffened then. A man was walking across the meadow above the cliffs toward us, leading two horses. I had made a slit in the seam of my trouser leg so I could draw my knife more easily. Now I had it out, just in case. But the man stopped a good distance away and hailed us. He gave Diera a sign she recognized. So then we relaxed, and he came across the meadow to us.

If he was amazed to see his queen dressed as a lad, he betrayed no sign of it. He knelt to her.

As Diera mounted the horse he'd brought her, she looked down at me. She reached to clasp my hand. I knelt then too.

"The Children go with you, your highness," I told her, looking up into her face.

"Won't you come with me, Mirin? I fear for you, leaving you here," she said.

"I need to stay here, your highness," I told her. "There's someone I need to wait for, here." I didn't tell her the someone was Wat. She'd think I was crazy. I felt half-crazy myself, waiting for a dead man, and not only that, a man who'd tried to kill me. A man who'd thought the worst of me. In spite of what Diera had told me of Wat's regret, I couldn't get past it, and besides, he was surely dead. So only the Children knew what I thought I was doing there.

"I'm headed to the southern towns," she told me. "Come there and find me, as soon as you finish this task."

I promised I would.

I watched as she rode away from me, and then, alone again, I thought about what I needed to do. *Get to the sea*, Wat had told me. Here I was.

The hard thing walling my heart away had fallen. I'd performed the task I owed to others. Now I owed some time to myself, to think about what I was and what I wanted, walking alone underneath the spheres, no magic, no insistent birds, just myself and the music I played.

*To bear witness*, Johnny had called it.

I'd wait here. I'd wait a year. That's the time I'd allot to my vigil or whatever nonsensical act I thought I was undertaking here. After I'd paid this respect to the dead, and maybe in a way to my lost childhood, I'd go south. I'd find Diera then, and I'd do whatever she needed me to do.

Luckily, the realm had moved into summer, so the weather was mild. For a few days, I lingered at the sea. I went to the cliffs where the land dropped off, the very edge of the mainland of the Sceptered Isle. I stood on the high sea cliffs overlooking a gray expanse so vast the eye didn't believe it. But in another sense, maybe my second sense, I felt I had come home. I didn't want to leave. I knew I couldn't stay there. I couldn't find anything to eat, any way to keep myself. I'd have to go back inland.

Wandering the lanes and countryside, I slept under the hedgerows as the other beggars and vagabonds did. Now that I'd accomplished my task and had seen Diera to safety, I felt a flattened and muted kind of sorrow. I had seen my task through to the end, the important task of leading a queen out of danger into safety. But personally, I felt failure. I had failed Wat. I'd failed you, Jillie. And Wat had failed me.

When I looked into the bleak future, I knew only that I'd have to make some kind of life for myself, what kind I had no idea. I knew I had to stay out of the notice of the authorities, at least for the year I'd promised myself. Living under Audemar's auspices was risky. Living under Caedon's even more. And I had no idea which of them controlled this part of the realm although, after the outcome of the battle, I suspected it was Caedon. Eventually, I found out from chance encounters and overheard conversations that I was right.

But war was still being waged throughout the west. Whenever I talked to anyone on the road, it was clear to me that control of any particular locale could change hands practically overnight, as one advancing or retreating army took possession of the lands they traveled through. You could go to sleep with Audemar as your king, and wake up the next morning with Caedon.

I spent my time as a vagabond in the broken lands bordering the sea. I didn't care where I went or what happened to me. As for you, I was so far away from where you and I had been imprisoned that I knew I'd never find you. Don't hate me, Jillie. I gave up.

I suppose some deep-seated instinct for survival kept me eating. I had found I could make a little coin by singing and playing along the roadway or on the corner of a village street. Sometimes the authorities ran me off. But sometimes they allowed me to stay and sing. This is the way I kept from starving. The only way I could stay clean was wait for a midday warm enough to wash myself in a stream. I was never far from a stream or river. I kept to the water always. I wasn't sure I believed in the Sea Child, but I did feel I was connected somehow to water. I had felt it all my life.

When I was too tired to go on, or too discouraged, I took to rubbing my thumb over the carving of the blackbird on my rebec. That comforted me somehow.

Now that my task was done, the blackbirds paid me no mind. To them, I was just another person crawling far beneath them on the surface of the earth. To me, they were just flocks of birds flying randomly around overhead.

Sometimes I camped in one of the many abandoned cottages that dotted the landscape. War and poverty had driven the owners off. But the penalty for squatters was severe—loss of a hand. So at first I didn't risk it.

I'm sure you wonder how I, a young woman alone on the roads, kept myself from danger, especially the danger of evil men. I hadn't spent my time idly around my rebel group. Conal wasn't the only one of them I'd learned from. As I'd told Diera, Torrin and Lorel had taught me to defend myself with a knife. I had learned to handle myself. Now, in one of the abandoned shacks, I found a whetstone. One of the only valuable objects I owned was the knife strapped to my calf. I made sure that knife was as sharp as it needed to be.

I had fashioned a snare by now, too, and a fishing line, so I could use the knife for skinning and gutting, and for cutting myself twigs to skewer the meat whenever I could find a fire. If no one would lend me the use of a fire, or start one for me, I sold the fish and rabbits on some village lane and bought myself bread and cheese. Someday, I promised myself I'd find the coin to get a flint like Wat's. Then I'd be dependent on no one.

But the knife had other uses. With just the basic training Torrin had given me at the stone cottage, I could defend myself with it when I needed to. A few times I had. Once I left a man bleeding, and I didn't look back. I still don't know if I left him dead or alive.

Surprise was one of my best allies. None of these evil-doers expected a starved young woman like me would be able to fend them off. So far, I always had. *If only Torrin had been able to teach me more*, I thought. I remembered her, and Lorel, with a deep sorrow. They'd been kind to me. Beyond kind.

Bad men were one danger, cold and exposure another. As the year wheeled around to harvest-tide and approached winter, necessity turned me into a squatter in spite of the dangers. The village closest to the sea cliffs had experienced plague in addition to war, and fairly recently, too, so I passed many vacant dwellings.

The countryside was dotted with them, abandoned one-room cabins dug down into the earth, like our parents', little more than shacks. The people who used to live in them had died off, or they'd been starved out. They were peasants who had owned one pig, maybe a cow, a few chickens. Almost always, a small garden plot gone to seed stood just outside the cabin door. The peasants didn't own their land but rented it from some distant landowner who extracted rents from them that kept them permanently just this side of beggary. When the peasants had to buy seed to plant new crops, when they had to buy goods they couldn't get elsewhere, they either had to make the all-day trek to a market town or else buy from the landowner's own factors at exorbitant prices. When things got really bad, they had to sell themselves and their children into bondage just to eat, or die.

I knew because our parents had been among these people. Or I thought they had. Strange to realize they hadn't been born to such a life. It was all you and I knew, Jillie, as children.

As I walked the roads, I thought about claiming one of these shacks for my own. I didn't want to lose a hand, the Lady knows. But winter was coming, and I didn't know how I'd manage. In the end, that's what I did. I chose one as far off the best-traveled roads as I could find, and I kept a sharp eye out for the beadle's men. I wintered there without incident. The nights were long; the wind off the sea howled about the eaves and through the cracks and broken places in the thatch and the walls of wattle and daub, but at least I had some shelter. During the day, I tried to keep busy with trapping and with practicing my rebec. At night, I tried to keep from freezing to death.

Eventually, I found my way to one of the bigger market towns along the coast, and my life settled into a more stable routine. My rebec was the means of my livelihood, but for safety's sake, I'd long since learned to make myself sound and act ordinary. No more dramatic crowd-pleasing Silvertongue flourishes. I was just a quiet musician the tavern keepers could rely on to entertain the customers and not cause any trouble.

But when I was alone in the countryside and was pretty sure I'd encounter no one for leagues around, I unleashed my voice, letting it soar, singing my grief and troubles to the sea from the top of the cliffs.

One day I was hurrying from one tavern to another, hoping to arrive in time at the second one to beg a bite from the kitchen wench before my set. A big man wrapped in a cloak against the brisk wind that day was walking in the other direction. He bumped into me, knocking me almost to the cobblestones, but he caught me by the arm and pulled me up, pulled me close to him.

"Mirin Far-meadow?" he said into my ear.

"I'm not the woman, you're mistaken, sir," I practically squeaked in fright.

He said nothing, just thrust a small cloth bundle into my hands and went off, fast, down the street and turned down an alley, lost to my sight.

I was shaken. I stared at the bundle in my hands. Should I open it? What kind of danger would it present?

The man could be a friend. This could be the message I had been waiting for during the seasons since I'd left Diera. Not likely. But it really could be a message from Diera to come south.

Or the bundle could be a way to entrap me. If I opened it, the beadle's men might descend on me and arrest me.

I hurried to the tavern where I was about to sing and fingered the little bundle. It was lumpy, tied with string. Finally I summoned up the courage to snap the string. The cloth petaled open to reveal an object that made me put my hand to my mouth. Made me cry. I ducked my head into the tavern. "I won't be able to sing today. I am sorry. I'm sick," I told the ostler, and hurried away.

When I wanted privacy, I headed out of town on a certain little-trod path where I had found the shrubbery thick on both sides of the road. I could duck under the overhanging foliage and find myself inside a green alcove. I did this now. Then I pulled the edges of the cloth aside and stared my fill.

What I held, Jillie, was a brooch like our father's. Like Wat's and Johnny's, Avery's, Conal's, and Rafe's. The brooch of the Six Proud Walkers. I remembered now how our mother used to beg our father to leave his at home, or to scuff it up with mud so it wouldn't stand out. It was too rich for a poor man to wear, she'd tell him. The brooch might attract too much attention. He'd crust it over with mud, but he refused to stop wearing it.

I put the brooch up to my lips and kissed the cold metal. The brooch was pierced with the pin designed to hold it to the cloak. The pin with a blackbird carved into the knob at the end.

Funny the things a child will accept as a given, while to any adult, they shout out their message to all. I think wearing that brooch was the one act where our father refused to be discreet. I'm wondering if the brooch might have been what gave him away. Someone must have denounced our family, probably Eris, once Johnny had come back with news of us. Then Audemar had sent Caedon after us. I realized with a chill that Eris must have betrayed Johnny, too.

I remembered how, after Johnny had left our house on that long-ago day in early spring, I'd questioned our father about the Six. He usually brushed questions like this aside, but this time, he sat me down and told me more. His brown eyes were serious.

I remember how Johnny, our father, and our mother had had to discuss whether Johnny should teach me. At the time, it seemed simply that our mother thought it wasn't my place to learn. Now I knew she was terrified I'd get drawn into the Rising. She was right.

But Johnny and our father seemed to agree that although danger awaited me, it was somehow my fate to learn what Johnny knew. And at last our mother had given in. I think now she must have realized it was a force she wouldn't be able to fight.

So when I asked our father about the Six, he told me more, Jillie, even though I didn't understand at the time what he was telling me. "Three of us were the best friends any could have. Johnny. Me. And one more, Johnny's half-brother." Now I know Johnny's half-brother was Avery. "We did everything together. Later, three more joined our group. One was a man who served Johnny's brother. The two of them were never apart. This man served and taught us all, but he was just as much our brother." I know this fourth man must have been Conal. "There was a fifth, a crazy fellow, a bit younger than we were. A rogue if ever there was one, but we loved him." Rafe.

"Who was the last, Father?"

"Funny you should ask that. Johnny's next-youngest brother. When the five of us got together to hunt and carouse, as boys will, Johnny's littlest brother hadn't even been born. But this middle brother was just old enough to tag along. We thought of him as kind of a pest, the way you think of Jillie."

I remember looking down as my father said this, feeling guilty at all the times my friends and I had run off, leaving you to sit down in the dirt, forgotten and forlorn. I hope you'll forgive me for that, Jillie.

"But one day," continued our father, "that boy showed he was the bravest of all of us. A terrible thing happened to his family, to their mother and their little brother, his and Johnny's. Their youngest brother was just a child, maybe six years old. Jillie's age. Bad people came to kill them. This middle brother was there when the killers came. He fought until he couldn't fight any longer, but they were too many and too strong. Someone got word to Johnny. He arrived just in time to save his brother's life, although his mother and little brother were already dead. Johnny got his younger brother away. That was the day Johnny's young brother grew up. Shortly after, we saw this boy for the man he was becoming. That's when we became six."

*Wat*, I thought to myself.

Under the green branches, I grieved bitterly. I lay there limply, feeling as a lie and a betrayal the warmth of spring, the hope of the buds on the tender sprouts around me.

I remembered Johnny in our back garden, squinting into the sunlight and playing for us. His eyes were crinkled, laughing, and brilliant blue, a blue like Wat's. A blue like Avery's. Johnny was a tall man, taller than Wat, and broader in the shoulder than my father. But not burly. Lean and rangy. A ragged scar ran from one corner of his eye on the left side of his face all the way down to the corner of his mouth.

I remember tracing it with my finger.

"Mirin!" our mother cried out, shocked at my rudeness. I knew what she'd say to me later, how I was too old to do an impolite thing like that, old enough to know better, and then some.

"Don't scold her, Elsebet. This is my scar," he told me. "An honorable wound. A battle scar." He winked at me.

He had another scar on the inside of his left wrist, a burn deep into the flesh. A brand. I knew not to ask about that one. Even though I was young, I knew this mark meant someone had wished him ill. Someone powerful had taken Johnny and had done this to him. Now I knew exactly how.

When he wasn't playing and singing to us, or wolfing down great helpings of our mother's good cooking, Johnny walked with our father to the edge of the meadow. There they'd stand, deep in talk. Once, I followed. Our father sent me back. Our father usually indulged me in everything, so I was angry. As I marched away from them, I tried to hear what they were talking about.

"—getting past it now? How about the wound? Has it healed? It's a lot to ask of a boy that young, after what he—"

I couldn't hear any more. *What boy? What wound?* I wondered. I'm thinking now they were speaking of Wat. The dreadful ordeal he endured, watching strong men drag his mother and small brother out of their house and put them to the sword before his eyes. The way he kicked and bit to prevent it. The way he almost died himself, except that Johnny had gotten there in time and had fought their way out of the deathtrap to safety. Later I found out that was how Johnny had gotten his scar. It's how Wat had gotten his own scar zigzagging angrily down his arm.

During my year on the edge of the sea, I'd had a long time to think over these memories. They've been, I think, the key to everything that happened afterward.

Now I ran my finger across each of the gold bars on the brooch. I knew who all six were. Six proud walkers, all there together.

A hope started to grow inside me. A hope that somehow Wat was alive and had found me. But fear beside it. A fear that our enemies were using the brooch to bring me into the open, and take me. Underneath, a different fear. I feared my feelings for Wat. Did I love him, or did I hate him? I didn't know which it was.

I spent a few days out in the countryside, afraid to go into the town. It was an open town. Here on the sea cliffs, towns didn't fortify themselves with the palisades of the inland towns. The cliffs themselves were these people's protection. I felt lucky I didn't have to show a parchment to come and go. But the beadles' men and their spies were everywhere. Bounties for information about low-level criminals were high enough to tempt families so poor they might not make it through the next hard winter. Even squatters and vagabonds could be taken and jailed.

It was a suspicious society. No one knew from one day to the next whether some disgruntled neighbor would call down the authorities upon them and their families. And the beadles punished first and didn't wait around to investigate or ask difficult questions. The beadles got very fine bounties, from Audemar or from Caedon as the case might be, for every punishment they carried out. Bounties and advancement.

If Ranulf the Good had made it his mission to right wrongs like these, I decided, he must have been a fine king. Yet if Artur, his heir, had promised to continue his father's reforms, I saw why some people might try to keep him from doing it. There were people who benefited from the old corrupt ways. There always were. If a tyrant like Audemar came to the throne, by fair means or foul, and if that tyrant promised to continue the corruption, people who fed on corruption would back Audemar. I could see why principled men and women would rise up and resist instead. Audemar's betrayals were very foul indeed.

But the foulest of all was Caedon.

So the little bundle with the brooch both thrilled and terrified me. After a few days of hiding, though, I told myself I had to move on. Get down the coast to a safer town where I wasn't known. Or choose differently, dangerously. Choose to go into town, hoping I wasn't being set up for some ill fate.

I had to risk it. I walked into town. I went to the tavern to tell the owner I was back and ready to work. He gave me a strange look but sent me into the kitchen house behind the tavern for something to eat.

I began to relax.

Things would be fine. I'd ask around discreetly for the stranger who had dropped the bundle into my hands and try to find out more about him.

I stepped out of the kitchen house and straight into the arms of the beadle's men, who seized me, tied my hands with a rope, and marched me away. I felt numb. Not even desperate. It was over. I almost felt relief. Over my shoulder I saw the tavern owner looking after me with satisfaction.

The men shoved me into the beadle's room at the stone hall where the town conducts all its business. I stood there, ignored, until finally the beadle got around to my case. He came over to me and looked me up and down.

"Mirin Far-meadow," he stated.

I thought of denying it. "Yes," I said.

"This is the girl," he told his men. "Take her to one of the cells."

"Sir. Sir. Please hear me."

He looked down his nose at me as if I might be one of the vermin that had crawled in from the offal in the street.

"Make it fast."

"What are the charges against me? I've done nothing wrong." I was hoping he'd say, "Squatting," or "Vagrancy." That would be a relative relief, just a lost hand. But I was expecting him to say, "Enemy of the state. Take her to the gallows."

Instead, he said something very strange. I had to shake my head a bit to clear it. "Don't get uppity with me, mistress. We know what you are." He looked down at his writ, then back up at me. "Runaway apprentice. The law will come down hard on you."

The men grabbed me under the armpits and marched me to a cell. The door clanged open. They threw me inside. The door clanged shut. Alone in the windowless dark, I fingered the golden brooch in my belt pouch. The beadle's men would soon search me and take it away from me, maybe charge me with theft, too. Stealing something that valuable was a hanging offense.

And I thought with despair of Caedon and his brand. Someone must have spotted it. I checked to make sure the left sleeve of my kirtle was pulled well down over it.

But the beadle had said *apprentice*, not *bondservant*.

"What in the Nine Spheres?" I thought.

The next moment I put my hands to my head in disbelief.

"Just hand her over, if you will," said a voice. A big, booming voice. A Kenning the Juggler kind of voice. "No need to beat her. I'll beat her myself."

"As you wish, young master." That was the voice of the beadle, unctuous now. The cell door clanged open again.

"Mirin. Mirin. Mirin. What a disappointing apprentice you have made. I'm going to have to beat you. You know that, don't you?"

A resplendent young man stood before me, befurred and be-ringed and beribboned. He wore a fancy cap. It was Wat. I stared at him, astounded. I managed to choke out a submissive "Yes, master."

"Just follow my lead," he muttered to me, hustling me out of the cell.

And now I had to bite my lips so a startled laugh wouldn't force its way past them.

I wasn't laughing, though, when he marched me through the beadle's hall and into a covered cart outside it. He wasn't laughing either. He put his head out and spoke to the man on the wagon seat.

"Let's get out of here before they realize I paid the clerk off to change the arrest writ," he told the man. The man on the wagon seat threw Wat an incredulous panicked look and we jolted away. As soon as the town was behind us, Wat stripped off the fur cloak, the cap, and the gewgaws that bedecked him and threw them with an exclamation of disgust to the other side of the cart.

He didn't say much. He asked if I were hurt. I shook my head no. I felt in my belt pouch for the brooch of the six proud walkers and handed it to him. He took it. He told me we'd be spending a day moving down the roads south along the coast. To the far south on the coastal peninsula were a few towns that were declared for Diera. They would probably fall to Caedon's next assault, but at the moment, they were havens for the remnants of the Rising. When we got there, we'd be safe, he told me. I looked down at my hands. I just nodded.

I stole a quick look at him. He looked different now, wearing his hair long like a lord's. But he was the same Wat. A ghost come back from the dead. A man I loved. A man who'd thought the worst of me and left me in Caedon's hands. A man I hated.

For the entire rest of the morning, the two of us said nothing at all. Once we were out on the desolate roads, Wat pushed aside the cart's tapestried side hangings. He stared out one side of the cart, and I stared out the other. The fresh breeze blew past. I tried not to think at all, just gaze up into the blue of the sky and the overhanging green branches.

Finally, he motioned the driver to stop the cart. He handed me out. "Stay here for a bit," he said to the driver. "We're going to walk into the next village and find something to eat."

"Is that wise?" said the driver, looking around uneasily.

"We'll be fine," said Wat. "I don't think we were followed. They're stupider than I thought, or maybe that clerk is smarter."

He took me by the elbow and steered me down a shady path leading from the road back past some neat fields. In the distance, the longhouses of a small village lay around the townland, a forgotten island of peace in a realm at war.

We walked for awhile along a low stone wall, picking our way carefully over the ruts. Halfway to the village fields, he cleared his throat. "There's the village," he said. He sounded as if he'd never talked before, as if he didn't know how to do it. I moved on ahead of him.

But then with no warning he reached out and put a hand on my arm. I looked back at him. His eyes burned into mine. He took me by both hands and pushed me to sit on the wall. He stood before me, staring at his shoes. Suddenly, he was down, kneeling at my feet. He pulled the knife from the scabbard at his belt and offered it up to me, handle first, keeping his head down.

"Mirin," he said, his voice low and tense. "My lady. Kill me. Do what you want with me. I won't stop you."

"Kill you?" I said, bolting to my feet and smacking the knife out of his hand to the ground with a clatter. "I don't kill my friends. Some do, I hear." I heard my voice fill with scorn and rage.

"I deserve this," he murmured. He didn't rise.

"Get up. You look ridiculous down there," I told him.

He stayed kneeling.

"Really. Nine Spheres. Get up."

He didn't. "You can go to that village if you want," he said, his head still down. He reached into the pouch at his belt and drew out a small bag. I saw it was heavy with coin. "You can use this to get away. Or you can get back in the cart with me. When we get to the southern towns, you can book passage to the Baronies. There's enough gold here for that, and then some. You'll be safe there. You'll have enough gold to start a life there. I'd recommend that. I doubt things will stay quiet around here for much longer."

He looked up at me now. His face was pale and drawn, his eyes anguished. He was shockingly thin. A lock of his hair fell down in his face, shadowing it. He was a stranger to me. I turned away from him.

But he reached for my hand, opened my palm, and closed it over the leather bag of coin.

I let the bag fall with a solid thunk at my feet. "I don't want your gold."

"Mirin. At least let me do this. I have no excuse. None. At least let me make some kind of amends."

I covered my face with my hands. To my shame, I burst into tears and sank back down on the wall.

In an instant he was by my side on the wall, pulling me to him, kissing the top of my head, soothing me, patting me. "Tell me you forgive me. Please forgive me. By the Children, I swear I was in the wrong." Then he muttered, "I'll never forgive myself. Never." Then he looked down with horror at his own hands. "What am I doing, touching you, after—after what I did."

"You nearly died because of what I did," I said to him. "At least I have to think you did. Caedon, they say. . ."

He finished the sentence. ". . .is the finest swordsman of his generation." Then he looked into my face. "Caedon made you do it. I know what he is. I know how he operates. He—he used Jillie, and he—" Wat fell silent. Then he burst out, "You told me that, at the inn. And I left you there."

We sat together for a long time. After a while, I took his hand and held it close. "Wat, I think I hate you. And I think I love you. Both."

"You're mine," he said fiercely.

Then he gasped and turned away from me. "That's wrong. You'll hate me til I die. I say the wrong things. I do the wrong things. The truth of it is—" He faced me. "I'm yours. Do whatever you will with me, Mirin Far-meadow. I'm nothing much. A bastard who couldn't even protect his own brothers." His voice went lower and lower. He was practically whispering now. "I couldn't protect you. What's worse, I didn't protect you. Wait, don't say anything."

He looked over at me as if knowing I was about to protest that I didn't need any protector. "John made me promise. That last harvest-tide, the season before they took him, he came to us, to the stone cottage, and told us all he had learned about Drustan. Your father. Where he was living. How he had carefully made a life for you and your mother and sister, away from any harm. We sent John to Dru to warn him. We knew he—all of you—were in danger. Someone had found out where you were living and had passed the information along to Caedon. It was Eris, but we didn't know that, we just knew all of you were in terrible danger. We sent John to look for you and try to warn you.

"But when John got there, he saw what's inside you, Mirin. He came to us, to let us know. He took me aside and made me swear an oath to protect you. You in particular. I think he knew he wouldn't be around to do it himself."

"No wonder you hated me. What a bother I was to you, having to look after some skinny little girl."

"I never hated you. Nine Spheres, Mirin, the voice you have. John was right about you. And he saw other things in you. I don't even know what he saw. I just—after John, I'd had a partner, and then things. . ." He paused for a long time.

My heart broke for us both.

"...things took a bad turn. After that, I told the others I didn't want a partner. I'd work by myself. But when we found you, I knew what I had to do. What John saw in you was right and true. We all saw it, that day at Old Cwen's house, when we met you."

I was thinking hard. "My father did it, didn't he. It was my father who killed that woman. The woman who was your partner after Johnny."

Wat looked away from me and didn't answer. When he resumed talking, he acted as though I hadn't asked that question. "I didn't understand why it should fall to me, to take you on as a partner. But later, I was glad it did. And then." He sat looking down for a long time. "Then I failed you. I believed Eris, not you. I failed."

"I've given up everything I believed in to save my sister, and now I've lost her," I said. "I had these ideas about my parents, that they were simple people, victims of some mindless evil act, and I've lost that, too." We sat together on the wall for a long time. Finally, I let out a breath I felt I had been holding for a year. A weight lifted off me. "Do you understand how strange it is, that we two are still alive?" I asked Wat.

We clung to each other, and we both cried.

After that, we were easy with each other. We laughed. We explained. We cried some more.

As we sat there together on the warm stones of the wall, Wat closed both my hands in his right hand and with his left brushed the hair back off my face. He studied me as if he were trying to memorize me. He ran a finger down the side of my face. "Do you know how beautiful you are, Mirin Far-meadow?" That's when he leaned down to me and kissed me.

We kissed.

The only kiss I'd ever experienced was Caedon's filthy mouth on mine. I decided not to call that a kiss at all.

Wat kissed me some more. It was like the soft meeting of everything that was warm in me with everything that was warm in him. He kissed my hands. Then he kissed my right wrist. I tried to pull the other away.

He took my left wrist and turned it over, so he could see Caedon's brand.

"I swear this to you, Mirin Far-meadow," he said at last. "I failed you once, but I won't again. Caedon is going to pay with his life for doing this to you."

"Caedon thinks I belong to him. Legally, I do. This will prove it to any court of law in the realm. Of course, I actually belong to you. You're my master, and I'm your bondservant."

Wat was shaking his head no. "That's a lie," he said.

"That's what all of you told me."

"We lied to you."

"Don't tell me. You did it to protect me," I said drily. "And I was just a young girl, so I believed you."

"We did lie. We thought—" He sagged beside me. "We were wrong to let you think that."

I felt a hot fury rise in me. How naïve I had been.

"Let's go," he was saying. "We need to get to the southern towns by nightfall. Or—" He stopped and looked at my expression, a worried crease between his eyes. "Or here. You could stay here. Or I could find you a ship—"

"Wat, stop it," I told him, giving up my anger in a great rush, and whether that was a victory or a defeat, I don't know. Both, probably. "Let's get past this," I said. "Let's agree. We're together, and no one is going to part us again. We'll talk about everything. We'll say everything to each other over and over and over until both of us understand. But we start here. This place. Us. Together."

I had never seen the boy Wat may have once been. Now I did. He lit up all over. His smile reached his eyes. Every terrible thing dropped away from him. And I think the same thing must have been happening to me.

After a bad time apart, we had resumed our journey.

We got back in the cart, and we made our way south. We lay back in the furs together as the cart rocked us gently, and we held each other like tired children.

# Chapter Thirty

# Nine Spheres

"C ome out!" Wat was banging on the door.

"No!" I shouted back. I was in an enormous tub. The water was hot. Every so often, I'd plunge myself under to come up sputtering, happy, and clean.

"We're going to be late."

"I don't care."

"Don't make me beat you."

"Just try it."

Reluctantly I hauled myself out of the water. I stepped to the roaring, snapping fire, good in the light chill of a spring morning. A linen kirtle of sea-mist lavender with silken bands of green lay splendidly across the big bed of the inn's best room. I sighed to think of the rustle of that cloth against my skin.

The door opened.

I squealed and grabbed up the biggest of the towels. "What are you doing in here. You can't look!"

"Soon I can," said Wat, giving me a grin.

"Not yet," I told him. "Get out of here."

He shut the door behind him as he stepped back out into the hallway. "Hurry it up," he called through the door.

We were staying at an inn on the coast, far to the south, in a rebel town. The people of the town would have to fight, maybe in a matter of a fortnight or so, but for now, the place was a safe haven.

Today was a festival day, the coronation day of the Sceptered Isles' rightful monarch, Queen Diera the First. What can I tell you about the events that led to this day? Some were glorious, others agonizing to think about. The discovery of the graves where the two young princes lay. The deepening grief over the loss of many friends: Avery and Rafe, killed outright at the rescue of Diera. Conal, who died very soon after, of wounds sustained while he stood over Avery, trying to protect the one he loved most in life. Grief over those who had died before. Johnny. My mother and father. Artur. Little Aedan, only six years old when he was cut down with his mother outside the house where Wat and Johnny had grown up. Torrin and Lorel.

There were more complicated kinds of griefs. Even grief for Eris. Just as I thought he might have, Caedon had killed her. He killed her with his own hands. What were her thoughts then?

None knew. None ever would. She died a lonely and sordid death.

And I felt another complicated kind of grief, for you, Jillie, found and then lost again.

There was an even deeper grief I had no name to give. Lost innocence, maybe.

But many were heroes there, that day, to see Diera crowned. People who had given everything they had to bring Diera to her throne. The best of it was my reunion with Old Cwen.

Diera's was a bittersweet victory. The town was loyal to Diera, but it was surrounded by towns loyal to Audemar, and it was menaced by Caedon's approaching army. As soon as she was crowned, Diera would board a cog in the harbor below and set sail across the Narrows for lands of her kinsmen in the Eastern Baronies. They had welcomed Avery earlier. Now it was Diera's turn to seek their refuge. One of the barons over there, it was said, had sued to make her his bride. Diera refused him. "I'll never marry," she said. I thought I maybe knew why.

We all felt it was important, before she went, for Diera to be crowned on the soil of our own realm, and this was a request she embraced.

The ceremony was simple. Diera came before a priestess of the Children, who placed her hand on Diera's head and blessed her in the name of the Child of Earth, Diera's own patron, and in the name of the Child of Sea, the patron of the town, and in the names of the Children of Sky and Fire.

As nearest in blood to Diera, Wat was given the honor of bringing the crown to the priestess to be placed on Diera's head. It was a simple circlet of gold. A goldsmith of the town had made it by melting down two of the six proud walkers' brooches, Avery's and Conal's. Wat kept his own brooch. Two of the brooches had never been seen again when our father and Johnny died, and Rafe's brooch, too, had been lost. Audemar's men had taken our father's or maybe. . . my heart faltered when I thought of that terrible day and the dark leader on the rise of land in our meadow. . . maybe Caedon. It was a certainty Caedon had taken Johnny's. Rafe's might have been left behind in the castle. None knew.

Wat had sent for Avery's and Conal's from the secret niche where they were hidden in our stone cottage. Now the priestess blessed the crown and placed it on Diera's brow, settling it down as a fillet over her veil. We prayed.

I had my own part in the ceremony. I played and sang the seventh verse of Johnny's song. *I'll sing you seven, oh. What is your seven, oh? Seven for the seven stars of the heavens.* These stars you can see any clear night: the Seven Sisters, some call them. Four fell to land, the Children. Three fell to some hidden place of the earth, no one knows where. They've never been found. But we see the traces of all seven humming their eternal song above us in the night. Someday, our priestesses tell us, we may find the others.

You see I know much more about these things now.

When the coronation was over, we all crowded into the town's banqueting hall. We ate a magnificent feast prepared for us by the town's best cooks, who paraded in procession with dish after dish. Afterward, as was the custom, there were the granting of honors and boons and the giving of gifts.

As the first honor she granted, Diera called Wat to come before her. Wat knelt. Diera stepped down from her dais and moved to Wat's side. She looked to the captain of her guard. He handed her a long, beautifully inlaid sword. Turning to us all, she said, "For his service to throne and family, for his courage and honor, I proclaim this man a Companion of the Realm." Raising the sword, she tapped Wat lightly on each shoulder. "Rise, Sir Walter the Steadfast, Queen's Companion."

Wat stood, and we all cheered. Wat, as a bastard, hadn't had a surname. Now he didn't need one.

"Take this sword," said Diera, handing it to him. "Use it well in our service."

"My queen, I will," said Wat. We all cheered again.

I was called next. "Lady Mirin of the High Sea Cliffs," Diera announced me to all. "I proclaim this woman a Companion of the Realm, and I bestow on her this weapon." It was a beautifully long and vicious dagger, chased with gold, a blackbird of gold on one side of the hilt, a fisher bird, sign of the Sea Child, on the other. I knelt. She tapped me lightly on each shoulder with the dagger. "Rise, Lady Mirin the Defender, Queen's Companion."

After a few other like honors, Diera went to a special ornately carved chair for the granting of boons. Sweeping her long veil aside, she sat.

Wat was the first in line. "I beg a boon of Your Highness," Wat said. I had to stifle a giggle. He was using his big Kenning the Juggler voice.

"What is your request, Sir Walter?"

"The hand of this woman, Lady Mirin of the High Sea Cliffs, to be wedded to me as my wife." We had worked this out beforehand with Diera, so it was not a surprise. Still, I was amazed at how hard my heart began to beat.

"Step forward, Lady Mirin of the High Sea Cliffs." That is our surname, Jillie, our father's actual name being Drustan, Earl of the High Sea Cliffs. I don't know if you even know that. "Do you consent to this man's request for your hand in marriage?" Diera was saying to me. "It's not his place to demand it. It's not my place to grant it." Diera leaned toward me and we locked eyes. "It is yours to grant or deny as you so desire."

"I grant Sir Walter's request, Your Highness," I said.

"And you here witnessing, do you all agree?" said Diera, rising.

"We do," chorused the assembled guests.

"Priestesses of Sea Child and Earth Child, step forward." As the priestesses made their way over to us, Diera leaned in to me and said, just under everyone's hearing but mine and Wat's, "Nine Spheres, girl, are you old enough to be married?"

"I'm eighteen," I said, indignant. Diera and Wat exchanged grins over my head. I didn't have time to get angry with them, because there were the priestesses, and Wat and I had to swear our vows before them.

Another cheer rose from the crowd as Wat took me into his arms and kissed me. On the lips! Yes, he really did. In front of everyone. "No one would take you for a boy now," he murmured in my ear.

"I might have to beat you for that," I murmured in his.

"This is great," he whispered to me as we re-seated ourselves at the banquet table. "You're an heiress. You're the daughter of an earl. I'm rich!"

I kicked him under the table.

There were many other such honors and gifts and favors to be asked for and granted. Wat and I sat leaning together on the bench, our fingers entwined.

One of Diera's officials stepped up to her now and handed her a piece of parchment. She glanced at it, then at us.

"What's this?" Wat whispered to me.

"Hush. I don't know," I said to him.

"Assembled guests, I have something to read to you. This has just come to me by special courier, dated a year ago and sworn before a notary in the north. It was thought lost, but it was only hidden away for safety until it could be sent to me." Diera stood and read in a clear voice.

*I, Avery, Prince of the Sceptered Isle, take the authority of the kingdom upon me in the aftermath of the foul murder of our rightful king Artur. Today I have learned of the deaths of Princes Domgall and Ryce, Artur's sons and heirs. As their deaths are now confirmed, and as the next in line has proved a betrayer and usurper, this day the succession comes to me. I proclaim myself rightful king. Considering that I have no direct heirs, I decree that in the event of my death, the law disavowing a woman monarch shall be void. It is only right that Diera, the oldest child of Artur, our murdered king, succeed me as lawful queen and monarch of this land.*

Wat leaned over to me and said quietly, "Diera needs no one's permission to become queen."

I raised an eyebrow. "I seem to remember a person telling me no woman could ever rule the realm."

"That person was wrong. As in many other things." His eyes had turned serious. "But I'm glad Avery wrote it all out. Now there'll be no question her reign is legal." Then he looked down and squeezed my hand hard. "You know he found out about the princes' deaths the morning before we went in to get Diera. He had just enough time to write this decree. He was king for maybe half a day. I think he knew that would be the way of it."

"Shh, she's reading more," I said. Thinking back to the night and morning before those terrible events, though, I finally understood what I had witnessed. Wat kneeling before Avery in the firelight. The courier hastening away with Avery's letter.

Diera was continuing to read.

*In addition, I bequeath my worldly goods to my beloved half-brother Walter. My lands in the north, my castles, my horses, my arms, and all my chattel go to him at my death. Furthermore, retroactively, it is my wish that I adopt Walter as my son. This adoption will take place outside the line of succession.*

Diera looked over at us. "There's a lot more. The lawyers will go over it all with you tomorrow," she said to Wat.

Wat nodded. His hands were trembling. I took them firmly in mine. "You're an heir. The rightful son of the rightful king. I'm rich!" I whispered to him. It helped a little, I think. He could give me a smile. More cheering.

Of course we both knew that all our newly-acquired lands and chattel and what-not had already been confiscated by Audemar or Caedon, or both, depending on place and season. In actuality, we were as poor as we ever were. "Maybe we can find Millicent and go back out on the road," I whispered. That did get him laughing.

Our laughter was cut short as one of Diera's stewards brought forward a long, ragged line of war orphans. Those of us at the banquet table felt our hearts breaking. These were only a few of the many children left to roam the countryside, starving and dying.

I looked down the line of hollow-eyed, hollow-cheeked children, winding all the way through the banquet hall and out the door into the street. The stewards and some of the other servants began moving down the line, handing each a piece of bread and a cup of milk. After a moment, Diera leaped to her feet. Brushing the tears from her cheeks, she stepped to one steward's side and took the basket of bread from him. She began handing the thick pieces of bread, smeared with butter, to each child, laying her hands on their heads, blessing each in the name of the Children.

As I scanned the line, I felt my heart stop. One of the children, a young girl, leggy as a colt, maybe around ten years old, moved haltingly toward Diera. Her eyes were enormous. She was thin and dirty. Her arms and legs were scratched and scabbed.

Jillie, it was you.

I can't remember how I got to my feet, how I got around the table, but I found myself kneeling beside you, gathering you into my arms, feeling the sharp thin bones of your body sagging against me. I heard myself saying, over and over again, "Jillie. Jillie. Jillie." Wat was by my side then, and Diera. We could see how terrified you were. You shrank away from us. Your eyes were blank.

"Jillie, you will get better. I promise this," I whispered in your ear.

Do you remember this moment, Jillie? In a way, I hope your answer is no. I hope in the mercy of the Children it has been erased from your mind.

The rest of the banquet was a blur to me. I was seeing to you, finding you a safe place to sleep in the inn beside me, finding you food and clothing.

And so joy and sorrow intermingled at that banquet. I worked to make you feel safe. I wondered if you ever would, when I looked at you during those days after finding you. You never talked much after we found you. I didn't know what you'd seen, what you'd known, and I still don't. It gave me nightmares to think of, and it still does.

Oh, life after that was hard. I won't deny it. Wat and I had to flee to the outermost edges of the realm. Diera went into exile to the Eastern Baronies with her court, and she persuaded me to let her take you with her. Wat and I knew we would be living rough for many seasons, maybe years. In the end, we undertook a dangerous sea voyage. Giving you into Diera's keeping was the best thing we could do for you, or so it seemed at the time. Still, it was hard. It was hard to part with you, after finding you at last. Did we all do the right thing? Only you can tell me that, Jillie, and now that you are gone again into the chaos of war, you aren't able to. Maybe I'll never know.

But treachery was abroad. After the departure into exile of the royal party, Wat and I were hiding out above a cove where some rough and maybe untrustworthy men were going to sneak us aboard ship for the rocky isles to the west.

"It will be fine," Wat told me. He was trying to reassure me about the sea captain, a scurvy-looking fellow with a long scar beside his nose.

I gave Wat a skeptical smile.

"No, really. The man was our family retainer. My mother trusted him completely."

*And you see how well that worked out for you*, I said to myself. We were both moody and unsettled.

"Do you remember the eighth verse of Johnny's song?" I asked Wat, after a while.

He nodded briefly. I hummed it to myself under my breath. *I'll sing you eight, oh. What is your eight, oh? Eight for the foul betrayers...*

Oh, I don't want to think about that, those seven men—and one woman—who stole the realm from its rightful ruler. Although Audemar had betrayed his own blood, I was beginning to think the worst betrayer of all was Caedon.

Wat was nearly killed in his fight with Caedon on that hill overlooking the rival armies. One day soon after he found me again, Wat told me what happened. We were sitting on the sea cliffs overlooking the waves. "That's your ancestral manor, up there," Wat told me, pointing. "John told me once he remembered seeing you there as a small child."

"You sound old and wise, my master." I poked him. We lay back in the heather, enjoying the warmth. "I don't remember being there," I said, looking over in the direction he had pointed. "Just some hazy flashes of memory."

Wat had taken off his tunic to lie in the sun.

With my finger, I traced the scar down his torso, relic of the shocking wound from his battle with Caedon on the hill overlooking the two armies. I reached around and traced his other scar, the one on his arm, the one he got from Caedon's assassins as a boy when he tried to defend his mother and little brother. Then I leaned down and kissed him. We both settled back together into each other's arms. The sun shone down on us. "I wish I hadn't left you on that hill. It killed me to leave."

"It would have killed me if you had stayed," Wat said, after a moment. "I would have been trying to protect you. I would have died. That's just a fact."

"Why didn't you die. This should have killed you," I said, tracing the line of his scar again. "Caedon did his best to kill you."

"Caedon can try. Nine Spheres, girl. . .

I finished the thought for him. "You're hard to kill."

That's when he told me the whole story, just as I am about to tell it to you.

As Wat and Caedon rolled and grappled, Caedon lunged for his sword. Wat kicked the sword out of Caedon's hand again and down the hill away from him. "I thought I had him then," said Wat.

"All that juggling," I said.

"Yes indeed," said Wat, with satisfaction. "But he was good, was Caedon."

"You know he is supposed to be. . ."

". . . the finest swordsman of his generation," Wat finished for me.

"No, he really is," I told Wat. "He has a lot of swords. Diplomats from the Burnt Lands bring him big curved pointy ones to hang on his wall. I saw him fight in Lunds-fort. Nobody could beat him."

"Still no match for Kenning the Juggler."

"Kenning the Juggler lost," I pointed out.

"Only because Caedon cheated. His men came sneaking up from behind and cut me down."

I wanted to keep joking, but I couldn't. I shook my head. "Wat. Why aren't you dead?"

"The Children stood by me," he said.

"Or luck," I told him.

He smiled at me and drew me in for a kiss. "Or luck," he said. "Nine Spheres, you should have been there. There was a blast on a horn. I'm lying there waiting for Caedon to finish me off, and they all just start running."

"What was it?"

"The strangest thing. It was Audemar."

"So you're telling me the civil war between Audemar and Caedon began over your nearly dead body?"

"Pretty much," said Wat.

"No," I said. "You're lucky, but that lucky?"

"Not as much luck to it as you think. Lorel and Torrin were in the bushes, waiting for a chance to move in while Caedon and I were fighting. Audemar's appearance was the distraction they needed. Caedon and his men went to the brow of the hill to see what the commotion was about. They weren't worried about me. I was lying there bleeding to death.

"But as soon as their backs were turned, Lorel and Torrin pounced on me, got me on horseback, got me out of there. Caedon's men chased us for leagues. So they told me. I was out of it by then. So, luck. Yes. It was lucky they escaped, and me with them."

"And lucky that you didn't bleed to death in the process," I said.

"Yes, that too. But not the kind of crazy luck you're thinking. They were excellent horsewomen, those two, and well trained in the skills they needed to evade Caedon's men."

I looked over at him skeptically and shook my head. A man bleeding to death, someone throws him on the back of a horse unconscious, and jounces him for many leagues over rough land before he gets help? Unlikely, I thought.

But then. There he was, right there beside me, lying in the sun with a smile on his face, his hair the color of ripe barley sticking up in spikes all over the place from where it had come loose from the thong he used to bind it back now, bits of grass in it, his eyes the blue of the azure sky serene above us.

I had to kiss him again then.

Still, the dark thoughts insisted on coming back.

*Luck*, I thought. Torrin's and Lorel's luck finally ran out. Where was the justice in that? My own father killed an innocent woman. Bad luck that Eris fooled them all. Where was the justice?

"Pretty lucky that Audemar decided to attack just then," I said, trying to keep those thoughts away.

"Well," said Wat. "You know better than I. Caedon managed the whole thing. He just didn't foresee my survival."

I thought back to the moment Caedon had showed me the two armies, ready to join in battle. And I thought about the battle Diera and I had witnessed. "The civil war. What news of it now?"

"Some say Audemar is winning. Some say Caedon. Me, I don't know," said Wat. He pulled me over to him and we sat up and began getting our things together. We were needed back in the town, and you needed me, Jillie. As we stood and brushed ourselves off and I picked the spears of grass out of his hair and bound it back off his face, Wat pointed. "We're getting out of here. We're going that way." He was pointing west, across the Great Sea spreading out its foaming rollers under the cliffs beneath us.

"But I'm not giving up. Just biding my time. Diera has some powerful allies in the Baronies. We'll see what happens. As for Audemar. . ." His eyes darkened in that way they had. "When I find him, it will have been better for him had he never lived."

"Caedon may find him first."

"I have plans for him, too. Especially him. I need a rematch."

"I may get to him before you do, Wat. I have a score to settle with that man."

"You? You're just a little girl."

I punched him in the shoulder. Hard. When he winced, I bit my lip. "I wish I had been there to heal you, at least," I said as we walked together back down from the hill. "After your fight."

"I don't remember that part. I wasn't in my right wits during most of it. I had a terrible fever."

"How did you get through it?"

"I had the best healer of them all."

"I'm the best healer of them all."

"No, you're not. There's one better."

"There's only one better. No! You mean—"

"Torrin and Lorel got me to Old Cwen. I don't know how they did it. And now we can't ask them." He pulled me closer, and we stood quietly, I in the crook of his arm.

He didn't look at me, but he said, very low, "I couldn't have borne it, to have you there watching Caedon butcher me. And what would he have done to you, after? I would have had to die thinking how I wasn't able to spare you that horror. That's what was about to happen. It didn't—but it should have. The only good thing was Torrin getting you out of there. That's what we'd come to do. Get you out of there. We don't leave anyone behind, and I— I'd never leave you. You understand?" Then he swallowed hard. "But I did leave you in Caedon's power. That time."

I reached over and took his hand. I stroked it. "You wouldn't have left me there forever."

"But he could have—something could have—"

"I nearly got you killed," I told him.

"I nearly got myself killed, and you too. And Torrin and Lorel—if they hadn't been there, I'd be dead. But now they're dead. If things had happened differently, then—"

"You know, all these things that happened, they're a snarled skein of events. If you try to pluck one strand out of the skein, it all unravels," I said. I laughed at his expression. "You men know nothing of skeins. Trust me on this."

I was quiet for a moment. "If Eris hadn't done what she did. Dark Ones take it, if King Ranulf the Good hadn't put Eris in bondage. We could go on and on."

He nodded, but I saw he couldn't speak.

I leaned against him. I whispered, "If I could have gotten to Avery to warn him before Diera came out of the castle, Avery might still be alive, but Diera might be dead. Or—remember what Avery told us? If all of you had stopped trying to rescue Diera until you'd found out the whereabouts of the princes, Caedon would have taken Diera. If you could have gotten to Johnny sooner, Johnny might be alive, but if Johnny hadn't gotten to you in time, when you were just a boy, you'd be dead and you and I would never have met. If I had been wearing my regular clothes and not off hunting when my parents were killed, I would have been killed myself. If. If."

I gazed out over the cliffs. "The Children know, we don't control the pattern. Just a bit of it, and we go at it blind."

As we stood looking out over the cliffs, the wind came up, and a cry on the wind. From the neighboring field rose a flock of blackbirds. They rose as a single entity. They swooped as one over the field. And then they swerved over us, heading south.

There was peace in this place, right now. There wouldn't be peace for long. There was balance, right here, right now. There wouldn't be balance long. Real justice was in the overarching stars.

I realized something then, something I'd always discounted as luck. There are things underneath the Nine Spheres that can't be explained. Miraculous things. Maybe the most miraculous of all is love.

When I think about Wat and his long hard struggle back, my heart breaks. When I think how I wasn't there to see him through it, my heart breaks. When I think about the resentments Wat and I bore each other for too long, my heart breaks. When I think about all the misunderstandings, all the broken threads in the pattern, my heart breaks.

But mostly Wat makes me smile.

What makes me smile most is my wedding night. Wat and I had gone back to the inn after the marriage ceremony, and the naming of me and Wat as Queen's Companions, and the will, and the coronation, and the finding of you, Jillie. At last we were alone.

Wat closed the door and turned to me. I blushed scarlet.

"You're a goose, Mirin," said Wat.

"I'm not," I said.

"No, you're not," he said, his voice dropping to a whisper.

We stood on either side of the bed and stared across at each other.

"What if I don't know what to do?" I told him, worried.

"What if I don't?" he replied.

We figured it out.

How? I'm not going to tell you that!

Get out of here.

I'm shutting the door.

Oh, don't go yet, Jillie, little sister, wherever you may be. I'm going to sing you all of Johnny's song. You won't hear it, I suppose, but I'll sing it to you anyway. There's a last verse, the ninth, and it's the best of them all.

> *I'll sing you nine, oh.*
> *What is your nine, oh?*
> *Nine for the Nine Spheres over us.*

We are all nested, sphere upon sphere, in a marvelous machine of a universe, nine spheres made of crystal. And they revolve around, one inside the other. That's what the ninth verse is about.

The day after our wedding, Wat and I walked the cliffs again. I took out my rebec, and I sang the blackbird song with all my heart. I'll sing it one more time for you.

> *I'll sing you one, oh.*
> *Green grow the rushes, oh.*
> *What is your one, oh?*
> *One is one and all alone and ever more shall be so.*
> *Blackbirds rising, blackbird's eye.*
> *One lone blackbird in the sky.*
> *One is one and all alone and ever more shall be so.*
>
> *I'll sing you two, oh.*
> *Green grow the rushes, oh.*
> *What is your two, oh?*
> *Two, two, the long-lost boys, clothed all in green, oh.*
>
> *I'll sing you three, oh.*
> *Green grow the rushes, oh.*
> *What is your three, oh?*
> *Three, three, the rivals.*
>
> *I'll sing you four, oh.*
> *Green grow the rushes, oh.*
> *What is your four, oh?*
> *Four for the four star Children.*
>
> *I'll sing you five, oh.*

*Green grow the rushes, oh.*
*What is your five, oh?*
*Five for the symbols at your door.*

*I'll sing you six, oh.*
*Green grow the rushes, oh.*
*What is your six, oh?*
*Six for the six proud walkers.*

*I'll sing you seven, oh.*
*Green grow the rushes, oh.*
*What is your seven, oh?*
*Seven for the seven stars in the heavens.*

*I'll sing you eight, oh.*
*Green grow the rushes, oh.*
*What is your eight, oh?*

What is your eight, oh? I can't sing this verse. It troubles me so. The eight betrayers are still out there somewhere. I'm going to have to stop now.

But think about us all, Jillie, nested in the inmost sphere of the Nine. The way to the Nine is music. As the spheres revolve, they sing, and singing in their glory, move. Their singing is justice, higher than balance, higher than all. That day as I sang on the cliffs, the blackbirds rose. As blackbirds do, they swirled in a pattern over our heads, a pattern so complex no eye can discern it, spheres within spheres the music that they sing.

The Children shine on all of us.

Wherever you are, Jillie, may They shine on you.

I hope you have enjoyed *Blackbird Rising*, Book One of the Harbingers series. Please leave a review of my novel on amazon.com and other sites. I care about what my readers think! Please visit my author page on amazon.com, and my author web site, www.janemwiseman.com. Follow my blog about speculative fiction, www.fantastes.com, or follow me on Twitter, @jane_wiseman and on Pinterest, janemcw.

I also hope you will stick around for Book Two of the Harbingers series, *Halcyon*. I've added an excerpt at the end of this book. You can find the full novel soon on amazon.com. Have fun! Jane

*Jane Wiseman roves in a great triangle from southern Virginia to Albuquerque to Minneapolis, trying not to take the dreaded wrong turn at Albuquerque. She loves fantasy in all its forms, enjoys her family, reads all the time, tries to write the kind of stuff she'd like to read, and paints. The painting above is titled "Selfie." As you can see, even in painting she goes for the quirky over the realistic every time.*

### *A note of acknowledgment:*

Thanks first of all to my wonderful editor and daughter, Margaret Govoni. You steered me away from many mishaps and missteps. All the rest are mine alone.

Thanks for all the helpful suggestions I've gathered from a number of online Litreactor workshops, www.litreactor.com, and from the writing workshops at the Tinker Mountain Writers' Workshop and the (sadly now defunct) Taos Summer Writers' Conference. The instructors' comments and suggestions were of course incredibly helpful, but I have valued beyond measure the comments and suggestions of my fellow workshop attendees. Thanks to all of you! You may not have been able to save me from all my writing sins, but you saved me from many.

And thanks to all you Norrathians out there, especially a few special battle buddies of mine. You know who you are. You are my fantasy friends in the purest sense of all.

# NOTES ON BLACKBIRD RISING, from the author:

This novel is a work of fantasy, not historical fiction. Just the same, it is indebted to history. For visual depictions of some of the scenes and ideas in this novel, visit my Pinterest board, Medieval Life—10 th Century, janemcfw. For a play list of songs in the entire Harbingers series, including this book, see https://janemwiseman.com/a-harbingers-play-list/

THE TIME-PERIOD is roughly early medieval, in a realm vaguely resembling several of the Celtic, Anglo-Saxon, Viking, and Norman kingdoms and military groups vying for power in the 10th and early 11th century British Isles shortly before the Norman Conquest. The landscape vaguely resembles Cornwall, King Arthur territory, with hints of different ethnic groups and warring factions.

TWELVE REALMS:

> THE SCEPTERED ISLE stands in for the united Heptarchy (seven main kingdoms) of mainland Anglo-Saxon England, but also includes the northern part of the realm (Scotland), the Western Isle (Ireland) and the northern isles (islands off the coast of Scotland— Inner and Outer Hebrides, Orkney, and Shetland Islands). It does not include the area around Lunds-fort (London), however.
>
> THE EASTERN BARONIES stands in for a loose confederation of powerful feudal lords spreading across medieval France and parts of Germany. In my tale, the Eastern Baronies also own territory on the mainland of the Sceptered Isle—the land around Lunds-fort (London) and along the eastern edge of the mainland—in addition to their strongholds across the Narrows (the English Channel).

THE SOUTHERN PRIMACY stands in for medieval territories in Italy (as well as Portugal and Spain), the homeland to which the Old Ones (ancient Romans) pulled back as their empire dwindled.

THE LYRE LANDS stands in for the vestiges of ancient Greece and the lands rimming the Aegean in the medieval era, including that vast metropolis the Vikings knew as "the Great City," Constantinople (Istanbul).

THE REALM OF THE ASP stands in for the ancient Near and Middle East.

THE BURNT LANDS is a vague concept to people of the Sceptered Isle and similar northern realms. It stands in for North Africa and below, through Sub-Saharan Africa, but people in the northern realms know little of these lands.

THE ICE-REALM stands in for medieval Norway and, in a loose sense, the other parts of Scandinavia.

THE FIRE ISLE stands in for medieval Iceland.

THE MOUNTAIN FASTNESSES stands in for the Alpine regions of Europe.

THE TRADE ROAD FORTIFICATIONS stands in for the old Silk Road of the late ancient world through the Renaissance, stretching along the Eurasian steppes.

THE SILK LANDS stands in for China and southeast Asia.

THE FORGOTTEN KINGDOM stands in for the Indian subcontinent. No one in Mirin's world knows much about this place.

ALSO:

UNKNOWN LANDS (the Americas) across the Great Sea stretching to the west. Travelers have come back with tales of these lands but no one knows whether they really exist.

THE CONCEPT OF TWO COMPETING RELIGIOUS GROUPS , worshippers of the Lady Goddess vs. worshippers of an elemental universe controlled by earth, sea, fire, and sky, is fantasy but based on some actual bits of information about belief systems in post-Roman Britain and medieval beliefs in general, especially medieval ideas about the body and healing. (Present-day astrologers have their own settled ideas about these matters. I know nothing about their ideas and don't pretend to.) People in Mirin's world have a vague sense that there were even older gods than these, although they don't know much about them.

THE OVERALL CONCEPT OF THE UNIVERSE is Pythagorean: nine revolving crystalline spheres carry the heavenly bodies (sun, moon, stars, planets) around the earth at their center. As the spheres revolve, they sing—although only those pure enough can hear this music of the spheres. This idea from the ancient classical Near East and then Rome (mentioned by Cicero in *De Republica*, a book Diera has read—although the ideas she gets about commonwealths don't come into the West until much, much later on) was widespread in the medieval period, made its way into medieval Christianity, and became important in the Renaissance, especially through the so-called Dream of Scipio in the re-discovered 6th part of Cicero's book—obviously long before anyone knew anything about the way the actual physical universe works.

THE REBEC is a real medieval musical stringed instrument from around the 10th century. The rebec preceded later stringed instruments such as the lute, the gittern, and the citole. Unlike the lute, which is built of strips of wood, the bowl of the rebec was carved from a single piece of wood. It may be the precursor to the violin. When Mirin plays it, she inspires a kind of Justin Bieber-like adulation, and the music she plays is that type of get-down fiddling that has persisted through the centuries into present-day American Appalachia.

THE FOLK BALLAD *GREEN GROW THE RUSHES, OH*, really is very mysterious. Its actual imagery probably refers to esoteric Christian ideas, but I have repurposed it, shortened it, added the blackbird refrain to it, and generally played fast and loose with it. Because real ballads often work that way, I don't feel the need to apologize. (By the way, there's another folk ballad with the same name, or nearly, that you'll often hear in Celtic-themed concerts or on Celtic-themed albums. It's based on a Robert Burns poem. This is not that song.)

OTHER SONGS MIRIN SINGS ARE MADE UP THINGS , except *My Beloved Has Gone Away* (*My Lief is Faren In Londe*), an actual Middle English love song. The gallant but silly rooster Chaunticleer sings it to the hen Pertelote, in Chaucer's *Nun's Priest's Tale*.

THE BLACKBIRDS of my novel are fantasy birds—part-jackdaw, part-raven, part-carrion crow. The way my fantasy blackbird perches on marsh reeds is most reminiscent of the American red-winged blackbird. The way actual blackbirds fly together in complex patterns is a mystery science has yet to solve: http://www.audubon.org/magazine/march-april-2009/how-flock-birds-can-fly-and-move-together

SANITATION was terrible in the world of the 10th century, and it's terrible in Mirin's world. Yet there's some evidence against the popular notion that these people never bathed. There's evidence that many 10th century people enjoyed baths. Mirin enjoys them. Nevertheless, the towns and cities of the 10th century were running with raw sewage and teeming with rats, lice, fleas, and other vermin, which were responsible for many of the worst diseases of the era: typhus, typhoid fever, the Black Plague (bubonic plague), and others. It's pure fantasy that my characters aren't crawling with lice and fleas. Everyone was.

MAN-DOG ROUGH-GRAY is a character in an Old Welsh poem about King Arthur, *Ymddiddan Arthur a Glewlwyd Gafaelfawr* (The dialogue of Arthur and Glewlwyd Gafaelfawr). It goes by other names as well. The poem describes Arthur's exploits against a number of foes, including the dog-headed men (maybe werewolves) led by the fearsome Man-Dog Rough-Gray. The poem has been dated from the 10th century, although recent scholarly work dates it later, and it has antecedents in the much earlier Welsh Triads. I've stuck my own version of the story into Mirin's world.

HOLLOWAYS are a world-wide phenomenon, ancient trails worn into the landscape so deeply that they've become overgrown tunnels. A number exist in the British Isles, pre-dating the Roman occupation. For example: https://www.telegraph.co.uk/culture/3667487/A-lost-wilderness.html

THE BATTLE SCENE in this novel is a composite of actual battles fought in the mid-11th century between Anglo-Saxons and their Viking and Norman opponents, including the Battle of Hastings in 1066.

I MUST APOLOGIZE for my petty thefts from W. B. Yeats, A. E. Housman, the 1559 Anglican *Book of Common Prayer* (and 2 Samuel:23—Lord forgive me for those two), Geoffrey Chaucer, Homer, the Roman poet Ovid, William Carlos Williams (and Pieter Bruegel the Elder), J. M. C. Crum, William Shakespeare, the great classic British comedian "always leave them laughing" Tommy Cooper, Edmund Spenser, and John Milton—especially you, Mr. Milton. Cribbing one of your best lines, for shame! They're all no doubt rolling their eyes in Great Poets Heaven.

excerpt from

# Halcyon:
## Harbingers, Book II: Child of Sea

*Some say that Alcyone, grieving for her love lost to storms at sea, cried out to the gods. So touched were they by Alcyone's tears that they turned her into a bird, the kingfisher. When the kingfisher is flying, the seas are tranquil. Such days are known as halcyon days, and "halcyon" is another name for kingfisher.*

# From Chapter One:

*Come all you mothers, listen well to me!*
*Come to catch your elf child, elf child, elf child,*
*Chase your naughty elf child*
*underneath the sea.*

That's what I sang at the village fire in the big hall on the last night, the last good night we had. All us women were gathered around the hearth while our men exchanged farm tips with each other by the door. Everyone was laughing and joking. This song, especially, made the women laugh. It's an unsophisticated little ditty, nothing like the ones that must be popular at court. We were as far away from the courts of kings as we could get, Wat and I.

I thought at the time that my song had no dark undertones. Events proved me wrong.

I thought of our little village as a charmed place, sheltered from the dangerous things underneath the Spheres. That was wrong, too. Maybe some sort of warning should have risen from the hidden place inside me, summoned by my music. But that night, song failed me.

The gathering was one of the last purely happy times I spent with other peasants like me. I might not have been born a peasant, but I was reared as one, and now I found myself living that life once more, singing a simple song to simple people, glad to be among them, glad to feel safe and loved.

The song is a cautionary tale. It's about a woman who gave birth to an elf-child who ran away to live beneath the waves, and every verse is sillier than the last. What that mischievous child got up to! How her mother scolded!

I loved living in the little village. I should have known better.

Living there meant laughter, good neighbors, good food, singing only for pleasure, not in the service of some sinister plot—experiences I hadn't enjoyed lately, especially not in the last few difficult years.

Wat and I had lived in the village for only a few seasons now, but we were starting to feel like we belonged. Not like strangers come over the water. They should have been wary of us, those good people. They were not. They were kind and generous folks and had no notion of the darkness rising up beneath the calm surface of their lives, a dark tide of events as monstrous as the fabled sea creatures said to menace this coast.

No hint of any terrible thing marred our happy time. Just the pleasures of the evening, uncomplicated and hearty. With my rebec and my voice, I was made especially welcome. Then home in the dark to our own small cottage at the edge of the village we went, Wat and I, laughing and shivering and pulling our cloaks around us in the cold. Our eyes must have been bright with the ale we drank.

Once we reached our doorstep, everything changed. The hazy feelings of good food and drink vanished in an instant. I felt it through to the marrow of my bones, as if the temperature of the air had dropped beyond frosty and brisk to a dead cold. The feeling was an old too-familiar dread. My hidden place opened up to me, a window into the deep places inside. This happens to me. A darkness comes on me. I almost never get any warning. Or not much. Not enough.

I put out a sudden hand, grabbing Wat's cloak.

By now he knew what I meant when I did something like that. We knew each other well by now, Wat and I. He stopped and gave me a sharp look in the moonlight, his body going tense under my hand. I looked to the shadowy doorway, and Wat's eyes followed my gaze. He nodded almost imperceptibly.

I stepped ahead of him, seemingly casual. When the killer leaped from the shadows, I swiveled hard into him, my knife already in my hand. Before the man could act, Wat stepped behind him and had him in a lock about the neck. Wat was fast, his arm pressed down on the man's throat, throttling off any cry.

This stranger had thought he had surprise on his side. But no. We did. I finished him off with a brisk flurry of stabs up underneath his rib cage. He didn't have the chance for much of a struggle.

We stood over his corpse. Both of us were breathing hard. Wat bent to push aside the man's hood. He examined the man's oddly tranquil face in the moonlight, but we knew we'd see nothing unusual about him. We knew we'd find nothing in his clothing or about his person to tell us who he was or why he'd come. But of course we did know why he'd come.

I reached automatically to check my rebec, to make sure it hadn't been smashed. How I'd ever find another one in this remote, rough place— Thank the Children it was fine.

Wat got to his feet. "They've found us." His voice was soft.

shrike
publications

Made in the USA
San Bernardino, CA
26 February 2019